For Robin, Tiffany, Jill, and Andy, thank you for your support, comments, and time helping me put this together.

And to my wife, Christine, you have struggled with me through this entire process and given me the encouragement and strength I've needed to bring this to a successful conclusion.

First Edition: November 2023.

Library of Congress Cataloging-in-Publication Data
Keenan, Randy
The LooseThread/Randy Keenan – First Edition
ISBN: 979-8-9887929-0-1 (trade pbk.)
ISBN: 979-8-9887929-1-8 (audiobook download)
ISBN: 979-8-9887929-2-5 (e-book)

THE LOOSE THREAD

BY

Randy Keenan

PROLOGUE

Monday, January 12, 896 AD – Evening

Wisps of smoke from hundreds of chimneys mottled the evening horizon, partially masking the crescent moon overlooking Kyiv. Trees, bereft of greenery and draped in ice, lined the banks of the Dnieper River – a testament to the deadly chill strangling the town. It was still early yet, and most folks had only recently retired from the day's toil. Still, the fireplaces must be kept ablaze to stave off the spectre of death. Rooftops sagged, straining under the weight of the heavy snows of the past few days, and desolate streets mourned the sun's descent as the slush covering them crystallized into a new sheet of glistening ice.

Mykola and his son Pylyp, huddled under a bundle of wool blankets, sat in the front of the cart, cautiously making their way back home. The horse pecked its way across the frozen bridge, struggling to stay upright, while its breath poured out as hot steam into the frigid night air. Both men were exhausted from the trip, but winter was a cobbler's busiest time of year. Folks willing to endure shoes and galoshes with torn seams or holes while the clime is gentle abruptly change their priorities once freezing water or snow reaches those tender feet. However, supplies such as swine hair and leather had to be replenished often – an arduous trek through the deadly Ukrainian winter to suppliers several miles upriver. The day had stretched relentlessly, and their faces blistered from the biting wind. Thankfully, their journey was finally nearing its end.

Dull light reflected against the shop window as Mykola pulled the cart up to the stable. His family was still awake – at least some of them. "Get her bedded down, and be quick about it," Mykola barked as they unhitched the cart from the harness. Pylyp tended to the horse as Mykola stomped his boots outside the workshop's back door. The simple cobbler shop doubled as their home, with the family living upstairs and in the rear. The door creaked open, and a shivering Mykola entered, tossing the stiff, frozen blankets to the floor. "Hello!" he bellowed – loud enough to get the attention of any not completely asleep.

"Papa!" came a shout from above as tiny footsteps bounded down narrow stairs. Dimitri burst into the room, wrapping his arms around his father's legs. His brown hair was wild and unruly, and he wore a gray sleeping gown stretching to his knees. He had pleaded to go with Mykola this morning,

5

but Sveta wouldn't hear of it. Mykola looked down into the eyes of his younger son and noticed tear lines on his cheeks.

"What is this? You are weeping?" his father whispered disingenuously, for he knew the source of these tears. Abramov, his father, hadn't been well for weeks – vomiting routinely, unable to stand long enough to complete even simple stitches. They had tried everything they knew: rest, medicines for fever and pain, but nothing could break through.

The business, too, was suffering. Abramov was the master cobbler – he had been mending shoes most of his life. Unfortunately, while Mykola learned everything he knew about the business from Abramov, he didn't possess the trained hand and eye steeped from decades of experience. So, as work had piled up, Mykola had taken on the final stitching himself – knowing the quality would not be as perfect as Abramov could manage.

Sveta, his poor wife, had taken on the role of nurse in addition to wife, mother, and shopkeeper. Her days were longer and her temper shorter as she was pushed beyond her limits. She lumbered from the bedroom just as Pylyp stomped through the rear door. Mykola saw in her heavy eyes the toil and agony of a day wrought with customers, a feeble old man, and an energetic Dimitri. "How is he?" Mykola inquired.

"I have seen nothing like this. Father has not slept for days, and his fever is scorching. It is heating that entire room now, as ridiculous as that sounds. That strange twitching has returned – he has been at it since midday, and his breaths are so shallow and meek. He might not make it, Mykola."

"He will make it. My father is tougher than people give him credit. He once wrestled two wolves at the same time just to see if he could." Mykola feigned a grin and rubbed Dimitri's scruffy black hair.

"That is but a story. My own father boasted of pulling carts of firewood by himself when the horse was sick, but the palsy took him all the same. Father Yuri sent word that he will call on us tomorrow afternoon, but you should go to him now, Mykola. Tomorrow may be too late."

He gazed up the stairs. "Pylyp, get those wet clothes off and grab a clean blanket. I want all of you down here tonight." Mykola sighed and resigned himself as he slowly began climbing. As he ascended, he actually felt the air getting warmer. *Crazy woman – got me believing her tales, now,* he thought. Though Abramov's room had a small stove, the narrow hallway should have been frigid.

6

Upstairs were only two rooms, one for Abramov and one for the boys. The door to the left was open, and he could hear his father rustling inside. "Father?" Mykola stepped inside. The room was quite plain, with a bed, tiny dresser, and wood stove in one corner. Simple, green curtains covered the lone window, but snow piling up on the window ledge could still be seen between the curtain panes. The walls were bare but for an innocuous painting of a gray and white speckled duck that Abramov had owned since he was young.

The warmth pressed in on Mykola as he approached the bedside. He sat in the chair they had brought up and looked down at his father. His legs and arms were unnaturally darting quickly from side to side, knotting up the bed sheet. He laid his hand on Abramov's forehead. The poor man was sweltering, and his bedding and hair were soaked. The stink of sweat and sickness smothered the room. The fever had also taken its toll on his body. He now looked 70 but wasn't yet a month over 53. Abramov was thin from not having eaten a hearty meal in over a week and drinking very little water. "Do you hear me?" Mykola leaned in closer, quietly listening. There was no response aside from eyes moving behind thin eyelids.

Unexpectedly, a grin crept across Abramov's face. No longer sickly and desperate, he now looked cunning and sheepish. "Father? What is going on? You now seem to be almost smiling. Are you but pretending to sleep?"

In an unfamiliar voice, Abramov spoke. "He is gone and will not return soon." The voice sounded like his father's but as if he were underwater. Abramov continued twitching while his eyes darted faster and faster behind his eyelids. Beaded sweat poured down the old man's face. Suddenly, his expression changed dramatically again from that devious grin to one of extreme agony – as though experiencing a pain unlike any he had encountered before. Then, it shifted abruptly back to that same uncomfortable, sneaky look. He was breathing much faster now, though still uneasily shallow.

Mykola was stunned, speechless. His father had not spoken in days, and now, to have only said something like this perplexed Mykola's soul. "Father. Papa. What can be happening? You must be awake, for we are talking – you and I. And if you are awake, I would have you speak to me. Where does it hurt?" The only response was a dreadful silence. Tears welled up in Mykola's eyes as he tried to comprehend those bizarre words. He did his best to hold back the current – for his own sanity as much as his father's.

7

What could this mean? If my father is to leave this earth, why speak to me like this? What madness has you, father? Mykola stayed for hours until he began nodding off, despite his best efforts.

A deep rumbling under the bed jolted him awake. At first distant, the noise grew louder with each passing moment. Abramov was no longer twitching and seemed finally at rest for the time being. His expression had faded back into one of a sickly, older man – one exasperated from endless pain with no relief in sight. The rumbling grew louder. Mykola wiped his exhausted eyes and knelt beside the bed, searching for its source. Nothing looked unusual under the bed, but the noise seemed to be coming from beneath the floor. He laid down, placing his ear against the wooden slats, listening. Yes. He could hear something within the floor – a definite rumbling that had matured into a deep growl. Mykola crawled away hurriedly and stood in terror as the growl grew louder. There could be nothing under that floor growling so. Mykola had grown up here and knew the house's design. The shuddering growl, now having swelled to something that might come from a large bear, was coming from a tiny space just big enough for a rat.

Mykola's eyes swelled with tears as he watched his father lie on that fragile bed mere inches above that horrific roar. The floorboards started vibrating under Mykola's feet, as though whatever creature was making that noise would soon burst through. All of a sudden, the roaring ceased, and the room filled with chilling silence. The only noise was the rattling inside Abramov's chest as he struggled to breathe. The dam holding back Mykola's sobs finally burst, and streaks of salty tears crawled down his blistered cheeks. He could do nothing for his father now, but pray. This sickness was one medicine could not cure and rest would not alleviate. Desperation and hopelessness overwhelmed him, and he continued sobbing as he left and headed back downstairs.

Dimitri and Pylyp were asleep on the living room floor, and an emotionally drained Sveta was staring through him. Her dark curls lay lazily over her right eye as she slumped in her chair – sleeping with open eyes. She had been a rock through this whole affair – keeping both the family and the business running, but lately, she was showing signs of breaking down. He covered the children with another blanket and helped Sveta to their bedroom. On the way, he paused to hang their tiny "Closed. Please come back tomorrow" sign in the window.

*   *   *

Thursday, January 29, 896 AD – Late Afternoon

Weeks had passed since that night, and only silence remained. The shop equipment, the last, the weave, all stood still. The kitchen, the stove, the plates, spoons, and the knives all rested as comatose as a star snuggled against the backdrop of the darkest night. Mykola and Sveta made no sound like veiled shadows of a shadow. The children had been sent to Sveta's sister on the other side of the river days ago. Despite the demand, Mykola had taken no new business, and Sveta had gone from merely a poor, stretched soul to utterly morose – sentenced to watch her family separate and fall into decay and depression. Her dress was filthy, and the house needed cleaning, but it was all she could do to prepare the few scant meals keeping the three of them from starving. She had gradually become accustomed to the stench of their house and shop. Nothing mattered anymore, as each today stretched longer and was more draining than the yesterday before.

Abramov had wasted away to nothing. His frail frame shuddered with each exhale as he desperately clung to life – one painful breath at a time. Sveta was astounded that he was still with them. While Mykola had been the only one visiting him for a week and a half, he had updated Sveta. For only a handful of minutes each day could Abramov speak, and he had managed to utter but a few heartfelt lines in passing. Mykola had experienced no more of what happened that dark night, beyond the ever-present swelter filling Abramov's room and the hallway outside.

The deadly winter storm had finally passed, but its chill lingered. Mykola sat, half-heartedly stitching for an impatient customer, listening to the wind batter the shop windows. His work was suddenly interrupted when a gentle rapping broke the room's silence at the door.

"Sorry – please come back another time!" Sveta had learned the phrase well and blurted it out in rote as people occasionally tried to call.

"It's Father Yuri. We have come to see Mykola!" shouted a grim voice from outside.

Mykola and Sveta exchanged confused glances – they hadn't expected help before Abramov eventually passed. Father Yuri, their caring local Priest, had listened intently when Mykola explained everything his poor papa was going through. In the end, it had been Father Yuri who had suggested that perhaps Abramov was battling dark spirits. He had begged Mykola to limit his exposure to Abramov – that his presence only fueled the wicked flames. Finally, father Yuri had placed an arm around Mykola, urging him not to

9

abandon hope and that he would call for someone more experienced in these dark matters.

Sveta pulled the blanket from her exhausted legs and feet. Thin, faded slippers were the only thing shielding her feet from the bitter cold floor as she shuffled through the clutter. "Father, please," Sveta motioned inward as she opened the door for Father Yuri and his unknown companion – a giant of a man who had to duck somewhat to merely pass through the doorway. This stranger wore a threadbare black overcoat, buttoned from knees to neck, with a blue scarf wrapped around his shoulders.

"Hello. Sveta, Mykola, I would like to introduce you to Father Alec. Here Father, let me take your things." Yuri gathered the scarf and coat from Father Alec as he unbundled. Sveta and Mykola soon noticed that Alec was not only tall but also quite gaunt. Father Alec's tunic hung loosely over his wiry frame, making him seem a living scarecrow.

"It is a pleasure, Father." Mykola forced a weary smile as he greeted them. The three men shook hands as Sveta took their things, though Father Alec held on to the leather bag hanging loosely at his side from a leather strap across his chest.

"I am sorry for not giving you more notice, but I barely made it on time to the carriage myself," Father Yuri apologized. "Mykola, how is Abramov?"

Mykola peered into the eyes of Father Alec, as his mind struggled to form the words. Alec's eyes were amber, beset by heavy, brushy eyebrows. In those eyes, Mykola saw nothing – no love, no hate, no compassion, and no ambivalence. *Who was this strange man Yuri had summoned, and what motivated him to come so far?* At long last, Mykola's mind managed to provide his mouth a few words, "Feeble and ... veiled, Father."

"Veiled?"

"It is hard to describe: as though he is lying just under a thin, impenetrable curtain. I can see him, but when he opens his eyes, he does not recognize me."

Father Yuri opened his mouth to offer a few solemn words, but before he could begin, Sveta returned with three tankards. "Would any of you care for some mead?" she asked as she sat them down. Father Yuri closed his mouth, took one of the mugs, and followed with a shallow gulp. Father Alec refused politely, but Mykola joined Yuri. Only awkward glances were exchanged as Sveta hurriedly gathered up some of the clutter, trying to find seating. "Gentlemen, please come. Sit. You must be weary."

10

"My sweet child," Father Alec began in a deep, rolling voice, turning toward Sveta. "It is you who should rest, for you are more weary than we have words to describe." He glided over to Sveta, placing his hand on hers. He kissed the back of her hand as he gracefully guided her into the chair. "Your family suffers from pain generally unknown in this world, but *your* struggle is now at an end. Soon, we will ascend those stairs, and when we at last descend, this unfortunate business will be behind you — for better or worse. So, I beg you — sit, child. Rest."

Mykola was awestruck. This stranger, seeming so shallow and emotionless at first, spoke in poetry.

Father Alec turned toward Yuri and Mykola, "Mykola, my son, Yuri, my friend. . . Let us now attend poor Abramov and discover exactly what we are facing." The three men approached the stairs and began to climb. With each step, the air got thicker and warmer. By the time they reached the top, Yuri was already breathing heavily. Alec, noticing Yuri's condition, offered, "My friends, let us wait outside but a few moments. It would not do to enter while so exasperated." As they sat in the hall, Father Yuri and Mykola somberly stared at the floor while Father Alec began softly talking to himself — so softly, in fact, no one else could understand. Gradually, though, it became easier to breathe the warm air, and Father Alec rose. "Shall we now see what we have here?" He helped the others up and entered Abramov's room.

Abramov lay in a pool of sweat as his thin legs twitched back and forth. Few hairs remained on his head, and his face bore no expression. He was not alert. His hollow chest rattled terribly with each breath. The poor man had wasted away and wouldn't have the strength to fight much longer.

"Hello, Abramov," Father Alec began speaking gently as he reached out to hold the man's hand between his own. Abramov awoke instantly and squinted at Father Alec, not seeming to notice Yuri and his son behind. He smiled a frail, tiny smile as a tear began its slow march down his face. "Poor man, we are here to help you. Through the power of Christ, we are going to help you today. You have journeyed alone far too long. It is nigh time you found peace." As Alec finished, Abramov's legs began to twitch faster, and his breathing became more labored. He pulled his hand away as his arms also began twitching. Finally, Abramov turned from Father Alec and glared at the ceiling of his tiny room for a few moments — eventually closing his eyes wearily.

Mykola brought over a chair, should they need it, and walked to the far side of the bed. Yuri remained standing quietly behind Father Alec. Alec knelt

11

and began praying, "Lord Father, who art in Heaven, we ask for Your divine power to come into this room. Envelop this poor soul. This family has suffered much, but we know Your healing touch can give this man peace. Lord Father. . ." Alec repeated his solemn prayer again and again. Father Yuri was now praying along with Father Alec. Mykola remained silent – his eyes filled with tears that he would not allow to flow.

With each passing prayer, Abramov became more and more restless. Both legs and arms convulsed dramatically. Occasionally, his back would arc, or his head would jar quickly from side to side. His face contorted, revealing extreme agony. Abruptly, all movement stopped, along with his rattled breathing. He opened his eyes, glaring at Mykola, and screamed out, "You bastard child! Your father lies here dying, and you bring these to help?" Abramov's voice again sounded as though he were yelling underwater. Each vile syllable gurgled out as venom. As he finished, he lay back down and continued those violent tremors. Mykola finally surrendered to the mounting well of tears.

Alec had relentlessly continued prayer throughout the ordeal, but he lightly tugged the bottom of Yuri's tunic. Yuri understood. He stopped praying long enough to walk over and place his arm on Mykola's shoulders.

All three men were sweating now as their bodies endured the sweltering heat of that room. Finally, Abramov shattered the relative calm, screaming a piercing cry of anguish and raising his head. Afterward, he immediately collapsed. His twitching never stopped. Mykola looked at his father through the tears. He shuddered, noticing that haunting smirk creeping back across his father's face. Memories of that horrible night a few weeks ago flooded his mind despite all his efforts to forget. Then Mykola noticed something else – Abramov's arms. They now bore horrible bloody sores – new sores that weren't there when they entered. They were fresh and had just started to bleed. Above each elbow, an open wound had been carved – in the shape of a crescent moon with a hollow circle above. *How could that be?* Until that moment, Mykola had almost convinced himself that terrible night weeks ago had been exaggerated by the decrepit dark side of his mind's imagination. After all, he had gone directly from that freezing night air into Abramov's oven. But now, the terror from that night returned and bore its way into Mykola's soul. *Father Yuri is right – something wholly evil lives inside him!*

Father Alec continued, with his head lowered and eyes shut, praying for what seemed an eternity to Mykola, but the prayers had grown louder and more forceful following Abramov's outburst. Eventually, however, Alec ceased his prayer, opened his eyes, and gazed into those of Abramov. Alec offered no reaction to that malicious grin or the bloody sores on his arms. "Demon, who art thou? I would know your name." Abramov continued to twitch but said nothing. "By what name are you known, demon? I command you through the power of God almighty and Christ, his son, to answer my question! What is thy name?" Again, no answer, but Abromov's grin grew viler. "Demon, you have been commanded by the most High – give me your name!" Father Alec pulled a small wooden crucifix from his bag and held it toward Abramov. Abramov gazed blankly at the crucifix and began loudly gurgling. Father Alec repeated his command and moved closer to Abramov, holding the cross directly in his face. The convulsions magnified while the tiny bed squeaked and cracked as though it, too, was nearing its end.

Deadly silence enveloped the room as, abruptly, all convulsions and rattled breathing ceased. Abramov opened his mouth to speak, but nothing came out but foul, warmed breath. Father Alec, again, repeated his demand, "Demon – You have a name, and God Almighty himself commands you to provide it!" Father Alec was yelling now as he stepped forward and laid the crucifix on Abramov's chest. Abramov raised his head and opened his mouth again, but this time he spoke.

"We are called Furcalor. Leave us! This one is ours!" the demon spat at Father Alec. Abramov's head collapsed backward into his sweat-soaked pillow.

Father Alec reached out to retrieve his crucifix but jerked his hand back. The tiny wooden cross had scorched his palm. He quickly used his tunic as a mitten, removed the cross, lay it on the bedside, and motioned to Mykola and Father Yuri to leave the room. All three went across the hallway into the boys' room. There they sat, leaning against different walls for quite some time. No one spoke.

"We have made progress, gentlemen, though it may not seem so right now," Father Alec tried to cool the tension and reassure a broken Mykola. "This devil has succumbed to the will of God by surrendering its name. Your father is infested with a devil, Mykola – a parasite attached to a host. I have performed this practice before, but it is never easy for the family. I will not coat my tongue with honey and tell you this will be easy, my son. It will be far from easy. The only promise I will make is that the hour is approaching when this scourge will no longer infest your house. A demon, by uttering its name,

13

acknowledges the presence of a higher authority. Soon, that authority will command it to abandon its host entirely."

"What are those marks, those bloody sores, on his arms, Father?"

"Mykola, my son, do not concern yourself with marks from the dark ones. They are most certainly not fatal and will heal quickly enough once your father is free. We should speak no further of this right now. Yuri, come closer." Once they were near each other, Alec whispered, "My friend, Mykola is near the end of his suffering. When I signal, go to him. Escort him back here to rest. This demon is strong and will not surrender without sacrifice. I would not forfeit any part of poor Mykola, for he has sacrificed much already."

Father Alec walked to Mykola, placing his hand on his shoulder. "Let us once more go to your Father, my son. Let us confront this dark one united through Christ."

The room remained quite hot. Father Alec walked to the far side of the bed while Yuri and Mykola remained closer to the door. Abramov writhed in his bed, clearly in desperate agony. His mouth was open as if to scream out in terror, but no sound escaped those parched, thin lips. Mykola bent down, whispering, "Papa, I know you are inside somewhere, and I see you hurting. How can I help? I cannot bear to see you agonize this way!" Mykola's eyes swelled with tears again as his father moved his lips, struggling to speak.

Abramov slowly opened his eyes a mere sliver, peering into those of his son. Gently smiling, he whispered, "You have given me everything, my s . . ." Abruptly, Abramov began to grind his teeth, and he jerked upright violently. With that horrible smirk that had haunted Mykola for weeks, he turned to face his son.

"You have given nothing, bastard! We will own this one for many days still, and his suffering will be great." The deep, gurgled speech flew bitterly, and Mykola collapsed on both knees by Abramov's bed, sobbing as a child.

One glance from Father Alec was all Yuri needed. He hoisted Mykola up and left. Father Alec stepped to the foot of the bed, facing Abramov directly, and pulled out a tiny vial of water. He uncorked the top and sprinkled some onto Abramov, triggering even more violent convulsions. "God, through Christ, through the Holy Spirit, has blessed this water, devil. Feel it sting – it is but a bit of water, demon. Imagine how great your suffering will be compared to the full majesty of God."

Softly at first, Alec heard a growling from beneath the bed. Alec knew this was the same thing Mykola had experienced. Nevertheless, he ignored it

14

entirely, resuming his prayers. "Christ, my Father in Heaven, grant Abramov and me the strength to endure, Oh Lord. Expel this devil, for surely it is not here of your will. This family has endured such suffering and pain." This prayer Alec repeated three times – each one louder than the last as the growling intensified. By the time he finished his third recitation, Alec was screaming at the top of his voice. Abramov laughed maniacally as he plunged his fingernails into his cheeks and cried out as blood oozed from the wounds. The floorboards beneath Abramov's bed began to crackle and splinter as whatever lay underneath attempted to force its way into our world. It would surely claim Abramov's life for itself if it came through. Alec had only moments.

"By the Power of Christ, I compel thee demon, leave this soul! It will not be yours!" Again, "By the Power of Christ, I compel thee demon, leave this soul! It will not be yours!" Each time Alec screamed over the shredding of boards and thundering growl – another showering of the blessed water. The growling was monstrous, and Father Alec heard a distinct "POP!" as one of the floorboards buckled under the pressure, and a powerful force shoved Alec backward to the floor. The lone window shattered, casting shards of broken glass into the dark night air. The small stove and lantern were instantly snuffed out. The room was dark.

Seconds mattered. Father Alec righted himself, grabbing the crucifix once again. Holding it aloft with his left hand, he turned to the demon, pressing his right arm toward Abramov's face. "This arm is yours, demon; take it instead! Christ commands thee – accept this sacrifice!!" As Alec uttered the last syllable, he lost consciousness and collapsed in a crumpled pile.

A scant few feet away, Father Yuri had waited in the children's room with Mykola for some time. Since leaving Abramov's room, they had heard nothing more from Father Alec or what might be happening in there. Aside from the swelter, everything was serene and still. Yuri's mind wandered across the hall. *Why had Father Alec said nothing more to Abramov or the spirit inside him?* If he had said something, Yuri would certainly have heard it. These were but two tiny rooms separated by a narrow hall. Nevertheless, neither of them had heard a sound.

Finally, Yuri's curiosity got the best of him, and he returned to Abramov's room. The gruesome scene inside mortified him. The window had been blown outward, and the stove was cold. The lantern that had been hanging on the wall lay shattered on the floor. Father Alec lay unconscious near the bed, the few contents of his bag scattered about. However, the most gruesome and perplexing change was where Alec's strong, healthy right arm rested only an hour ago, now lay a limp, shriveled, brownish-colored limb, wretched skin sagging from each finger. Neither Yuri nor Mykola had heard the slightest sound amid this tremendous chaos. Yuri focused first on Father Alec. "Father! Can you hear me?"

Father Alec opened his eyes and softly began, "My brother, what happened – where is Abramov?"

Yuri had been so overcome with despair over Father Alec, he hadn't noticed Abramov. He grabbed Alec's good arm and helped him up, and the two priests looked into the bed of an exhausted, but peacefully sleeping, Abramov.

*   *   *

Wednesday, February 25, 896 AD – Mid-Morning

The Cardinal's desk, adorned with intricate woven designs, matched the chamber. The Vatican palace was a model of opulence, and the Cardinal's office was adorned to belong in such a place. Stained glass split the sunlight into brilliant blue, red, and yellow rays as they filled the room, landing on dark, exquisitely stained hardwood floors. The Cardinal was not currently in, which suited Friar Thomas just fine. He had been charged to pick up some things from the Cardinals' offices and distribute them as needed. On the corner of the desk lay a few items for Thomas: three letters to be posted for delivery, one chart meant for another Cardinal, and a piece of parchment, stamped in the corner with the Cardinal's seal. A prying Friar Thomas glanced at the parchment and scowled at the appalling nature of the hand that wrote what appeared to be a journal –an activity report from a Father Alec somewhere in the Ukraine. Thomas quickly gave up trying to make out the scrawl and simply read the Cardinal's instruction – "Storage." He gathered the parchment and other items and made his rounds. Later that day, he arrived at the door to the Vatican archives and delivered the parchment to a far less inquisitive young Friar Peter.

Without a second glance, Peter took it downstairs and tossed it atop a large pile of sundered documents in the dark underbelly of the Vatican, where it would spend eternity as a forgotten relic.

PART ONE

"I believe a lot of our lives are spent asleep, and what I've been trying to do is hold on to those moments when a little spark cuts through the fog and nudges you." – Rufus Wainright

Saturday, October 24, 1998 – Mid-Morning

Sarah sat patiently in the front seat, staring intently into the truck's fogged side window as the hills outside, mourning the imposition of their brown winter cloak, passed by quietly. The world seemed to stretch on forever from up here. In all directions, hills gave way to sprawling vistas and valleys as more hills lined up behind, repeating the process. Trees cropped up occasionally atop the rolling landscape in stark contrast to the silver clouds blanketing the morning sky. It was rather majestic, and it would be a simple matter to get lost in it all. Before long, the problems and stress from home would begin fading into memory.

Of course, most of this was lost on Sarah – although wonderful dogs, chows aren't as concerned about rolling majesty as one might hope. Nevertheless, she sat quietly gazing outside, occasionally smearing her nose sweat on the glass as she shuffled. The truck got along well, except for the damned windshield wipers. A light rain had been falling all morning, and while it wasn't enough to flood the roads or even make any good-sized puddles, it was just enough to coat the air with thick moisture that stuck to everything – especially the windshield of Sam's little Ford truck. The right wiper only made about half the swath it was meant to and delivered a persistent high-pitched squeal the whole time it ran. Sam had been forced to choose between constant annoyance or a violent accident – and he had chosen annoyance.

Sarah didn't seem to mind the wipers much, but she may have just been pretending. Sam always brought Sarah on his treasure hunts, and she did her part: breaking up the loneliness of the drive. She was a full-coated black chow and had been with Sam since she was a puppy. He had rescued her about six years ago and had not regretted his decision to keep her for even one day afterward. She had been difficult to train but finally picked up on the few things he needed. Of course, that didn't mean she knew how to keep her nose off the truck window, but that came with the territory.

Sam left home yesterday afternoon for this estate sale outside San Luis Obispo today. He was hoping to find some great antique furniture. After digging for information on the late Johnathon Halpert, Sam discovered that Mr. Halpert's family were English and had immigrated to the United States during the Great Depression. Samuel hoped, as with most wealthy European families, they had a good deal of their furniture brought over with them. Unfortunately, the best antiques were usually from overseas.

The late Mr. Halpert had passed away a few months ago in his home in the hills outside of San Luis Obispo, California. He had left only two survivors, neither of whom had any interest in their uncle's country estate or vineyards, and would be far happier with the estate sale proceeds than having to parcel through all of his old things. That formula was ripe for a person like Sam. If there were any old furniture in that house, it would be sold by an estate administrator rather than a fussy relative. Sam had found many great pieces this way, including the Victorian armoire and grandfather clock sitting in his home in Anaheim. Though not a furniture dealer by trade, he loved dabbling in it as a pastime – collecting, restoring, and selling great old furniture, all the while keeping some of the best pieces for himself, of course.

The little truck bounced along, a tiny crucifix swaying from the rearview mirror as they meandered through the hills. Sarah didn't even seem to have much trouble balancing on the front seat. It wouldn't be much further, at least not according to the instructions Sam had gotten yesterday. He had left the main road quite a while back and was starting to worry that he had taken a wrong turn when he finally came upon the grandiose entrance. The wrought iron gate was pulled open already with an "Estate Sale" sign attached. The rain began to let up as Sam made his way up the long drive. Massive oak trees with wide crowns full of thick leaves spanned each side of the drive, blocking much of the already sparse sunlight.

Sarah started fidgeting when she sensed the truck slowing as they finally cleared the trees – hoping she would be able to stretch her legs. Unfortunately, a few cars were already parked in the drive, all far more expensive than Sam's. "Look at this, girl," Sam whispered to Sarah. "We're not gonna fit in, are we?" Sarah turned and looked quizzically at him. He chuckled and parked the truck beside a crimson Audi.

Before his eyes stood a Spanish-style sprawling villa with three large arches creating the front entryway. It had a tan stucco exterior and stood three stories tall in places. Large picture windows covered most of the front, and vine-covered shutters adorned the sides of a few smaller ones. Sam got out, making sure to lower the windows for Sarah. "You gotta stay put, for now, girl," Sam muttered into the cab at Sarah. "I'll be back soon, though – I promise. Be good." He meandered past the few other cars up to the massive front doors. The left door stood open, displaying a "Come In – Sales Counter in back" sign. Still not seeing anyone, Sam wiped his feet on the tattered doormat and stepped inside.

The grand and eternal nature of the place immediately struck him. Dark paintings and solid, ancient furniture adorned it majestically. The house had an old-world feel – like physically stepping through the pages into a Jane Austen novel. Several older ladies in the grand foyer, looking over a painting, turned to see who had just arrived. Sam's presence was underwhelming: just over six feet tall, with a wiry build and short reddish brown hair. His rustic faded T-shirt and jeans couldn't compete with their opulence, complete with hats and designer handbags. Not knowing how else to respond, he simply stared back at them blankly through his awkwardly placed thin-framed glasses. Apparently, satisfied that he was of no consequence, they returned to their painting while Sam strolled through the room and down one of the main hallways.

Room after room had the sort of furniture befitting a palatial estate such as this, and all with a little white price tag attached: elaborate bedframes, rich tapestries, oak vanities, and enormous wall mirrors trimmed in gold – so large Sam felt like he was looking into another room on the other side. He began noticing that the prices accurately reflected the full retail price – not good news. At retail, there was no room for him to move a piece after restoration. Though a fond collector of antiques, Sam knew this had to be at least moderately successful, or he was only squandering money that should be invested in stocks – the same way his few friends seemed to be making a fortune. Sam's steps echoed throughout the wing as they struck solid hardwood floors and decorative inset tiles. While nosing about, he heard voices across the hall and decided to investigate.

Two women were in the room, one much younger than the other. The older woman frantically told the younger to rearrange some furniture in another part of the house. She wasted no time letting her know what she thought about her ability. The young lady, apparently named "Maggie," wore a red dress that hugged her legs just enough, and her wavy auburn hair perfectly captured the sunlight coming through the window. She had a rugged attractiveness, requiring no extra touches or makeup. The other lady, unlike Maggie, looked like the female equivalent of Ed McMahon. She strutted about

21

uncomfortably in a loose-fitting (thanks be to God) gray suit and black heels, peering unforgivingly at Maggie through thick, black-rimmed glasses. The two had started whispering when Sam entered, but occasionally a word or phrase could be picked up. Soon enough, Maggie hurriedly nodded a few times, blurted a curt, "Of course, Ms. Barbara," and shuttled away. Barbara then gazed at Sam, who had just turned away swiftly enough to appear merely a disinterested shopper.

Barbara, carrying a notepad, scattered pages sticking out of the edges, approached Sam. "Are you enjoying your visit to the estate this morning? We have danishes set out in the dining room if you like." Barbara offered in a polite, but disapproving tone. Sam figured he didn't exactly look like the sort of customer she had hoped to attract.

"No, thank you – quite full already. Love these pieces, though. How old is some of this stuff?" Sam feigned ignorance – offering her precisely what she likely expected from him. "Oh, we have pieces dating back to the Victorian era or earlier brought over when the Halpert family crossed the Atlantic. Not many estates carry precious pieces such as these; I can assure you – especially not out '*here.*'" She seemed to say that last word as though it brought her physical pain to work so far away from downtown L.A. or San Francisco. Sam couldn't yet tell whether her particular flavor of arrogance was of the palm tree or ocean-side cliff variety.

"You're not used to working in these parts?"

"Heh!" Barbara grunted at Sam, "Seldom in *my* line of work do you come across an estate with real history in their collection being so far away from '*normal*' life. It's difficult to find quality buyers willing to travel this far from civilization – especially the sort of buyers we need for an estate like this."

Arrogance flowed from her mouth like rain pouring from a rooftop gutter after a deluge. Feeling unwelcome, Sam replied meekly, "I see . . . well, good luck to you anyway," and quietly strolled away, smiling. For all her self-proclaimed proficiency, Barbara had betrayed her weak negotiating skills. In her effort to shame Sam away from the sale, she had revealed that she was disappointed in the turnout. That desperation might work in his favor if he were patient. Sam turned to follow the trail that Maggie's steps had echoed. With any luck, they would not only lead him to Maggie but also to those danishes.

Sam heard Barbara come out of the room behind him and exit through a side door. He kept walking, however, as he wasn't interested in what Barbara was doing. Her approach to this business was one he had encountered many times. Some view these pieces as a means to an end, like jewelry, worth only whatever they can be immediately sold for. They've forgotten that furniture is living, breathing merchandise with a story all its own, unlike jewelry or art.

An eighteenth-century sitting chair selling for one price at any high-end auction house could sometimes be recovered in silk and sold for fifty percent more. It could occasionally be refinished with a rustic walnut sheen and go for even higher. It could be combined with two other chairs from the same maker and style, creating a parlor set worth thousands more still. Furniture had been lived in – not just hung on someone's neck or a wall. Things that get lived in get worn, and that wear creates the opportunity for rebirth and re-imagination. That was where Samuel's passions lie – in re-imagining this furniture, particularly old, heavily used pieces from families such as the Halperts. Of course, the challenge lay in discerning which to restore and which to leave alone.

Eventually, he heard voices from the northern hall, a section he'd not yet explored. It sounded like a man and woman's voice throwing out numbers around. Sam followed the voices into a massive dining room. Across the room stood Maggie and some older gentleman hugging a cup of coffee, looking down at a desk. *Why was there always someone with a damn coffee?* As Sam entered, Maggie turned to face him. "There are danishes and juice on the table if you like, sir. I'll be over shortly but must step out for a moment." Sam nodded in agreement as she turned back to the gentleman and whispered, "I understand your concern, but my boss set these prices, and there's little I can do personally. I'll ask her to come speak with you." She excused herself and brushed past Sam on her way out.

After grabbing a warm apple danish, Sam sauntered over to see this desk causing such controversy. It was a simple, flat surface writing desk with a few scratches on the surface and scuffs on the legs. It was clearly a 1950s-era piece with little character or potential, but the price had been marked as $300. He knew now why the price was being challenged. That desk wouldn't fetch more than $50 in any second-hand store. Sam, losing interest in this whole estate, took another bite of danish and began milling around the dining room.

He noticed a curious-looking buffet against a side wall, smothered with all sorts of loose items. It was rather old and likely imported from Europe. The delicate mouldings and decorations reeked of Victorian England. The wood was dusty and in need of care. He couldn't locate a price for the piece at

23

first, the surface being covered with all manner of plates, knives, dinnerware, and other odds and ends. Finally, after some looking, he found a small tag on the edge of the buffet, but reflecting a handwritten $400! The tag looked older than the tags on everything else, and Sam guessed it might have been from some prior sale. He poked around further to convince himself it wasn't a stray accidentally placed there, but in the end, he realized the infamous Barbara had made a tragic mistake. This buffet would easily sell for much higher in a high-end auction house with no work whatsoever. He might multiply his investment ten or fifteen times over with a few touches.

The other gentleman remained against the wall, sipping on his coffee, staring blankly out the far window across the room. Apparently, he seemed uninterested in anything but that horribly overpriced desk and had no desire to browse. As the sound of footsteps from the back hallway grew louder, Sam swiftly left the buffet, took another bite of danish, and began eyeing some of the relatively cheap prints on the dining room walls. Maggie entered the doorway and made her way to the impatient shopper. Sam, finishing up the tiny danish, casually headed in that direction.

Maggie gingerly approached the other gentleman. "I'm sorry, sir, my boss went into town for a moment, and I can't possibly accept your offer without her approval. If you'd care to wait . . . "

The gentleman, becoming less gentlemanly, abruptly cut her off, "I'm not going to wait – I'm going to explode! You must know that desk's price is outrageous, but it's nice, and I want it! So I'm offering you $80, and that's more than fair."

Maggie began to stammer, and Sam sensed she was not used to these sorts of confrontations. Her light red hair rested uncomfortably on her shoulders as she stepped back from the angry customer. "I've only been on this job a few weeks, sir, and I . . . I'm sorry that I don't know enough about that piece to negotiate the price, but my boss..."

He interrupted again, his voice continuing to rise, " . . . is going to be upset when I leave without buying anything – especially when I call your office tomorrow and let them know how you refused to work with me," he stepped forward countering her retreat. The man was now towering over the poor girl.

What an ass!

By this time, Sam had made his way over to the couple. As he passed Maggie, he caught a hint of her perfume in the air. "What seems to be the trouble here, sir?" Sam tried to be as polite as possible. Maggie sighed with

24

relief at the sound of his voice.

"None of your damn business. Why don't you go wolf down another danish and wait your turn?"

"He wants to buy this desk for way less than marked, and my boss isn't here to work with him right now," Maggie blurted.

Sam pretended to look the desk over, "nice piece here, Ma'am," he lied tenderly. "I'll give you more than this guy's offering just to settle the matter. How about $120?"

The man turned to face Sam directly, "Are you kidding me? It's not worth half of that, but you're too ignorant to know anything about furniture. Don't they have books out here in the sticks?"

Sam, ignoring his attack, waited patiently for Maggie's answer.

"I just can't, without speaking to my boss. This is just awful – I am so sorry." Maggie looked up at the ceiling, apparently desperately wishing she were anywhere else.

"This must be a joke, but I have to play along. How about $180? That's almost three times what this thing's worth, but it would look great in my den. You can't turn *this* down, too!" The man briskly reached into his wallet and started pulling out $20s.

Maggie opened her mouth to speak, but Sam interjected quickly, "$220 – and I'll even buy something else, say . . . " Samuel looked around the room pretending to scan for something interesting, " ... that buffet over there – not sure what you're asking, but it looks cool."

Maggie and the other man looked at Sam incredulously. "Uh ... ok, I'll do it, sir." Maggie smiled and made for her receipt book. "Will that be cash or credit?" She moved swiftly, trying to escape the coming storm.

"Are you insane? What kind of bullshit is this? OK – you're in on it. So this is some sort of con to get me to keep raising my price? Well, I'm on to both of you. You can keep that damn desk." The angry gentleman stuffed the cash into his sport coat and shoved past Sam, storming toward the front door.

Maggie came back with her receipts, "Thank you, sir; that animal would have gotten me into serious trouble either way if it hadn't been for you. My name is Maggie. What's yours, and you never answered if this was cash or credit?"

"Credit, and my name's Samuel, thanks." Sam handed her his card.

Her delicate fingers slid the card through the imprinter, and Sam caught a glimpse of a shiny ring on her finger. He had no plans on pursuing

25

Maggie afterwards, but it was disheartening to find out she wasn't available – a story he heard often. Samuel couldn't be too disappointed, though, he did have a promising blind date back home tonight that Gerard had arranged – his wife's friend or something like that. Which reminded him – he couldn't stay up here all day. "Miss, if you'll help me clear it off, I'll get out of your way?"

Maggie smiled as she hurriedly helped Sam shuffle all the scattered odds and ends from the buffet surface. At one point, she paused unexpectedly while gazing down at Sam's arm.

Sam grinned, noticing her look of puzzlement. *She's seen my scar.* Sam had a long scar running down his right forearm, which never took anyone he dealt with long to notice. "Long time ago. Broken glass when I was a boy." As soon as the words escaped his lips, his grin melted into a forlorn scowl. There were memories there that were too painful to share.

Sam managed to get the desk and buffet loaded into the back of his truck without too much fuss. Though neither remarkably toned nor cut, Sam stayed fit working with the furniture and frequently volunteering with the kids at the local YMCA. As he pulled out of the drive, he looked over at an eager Sarah as she stared back, with her famous blank stares and tongue hanging out. "Well, looks like we got more work, huh, girl?" Samuel smiled as he drove past Barbara on the way out. Of course, once she discovered how little he had paid, she'd be furious, but he'd be long gone by then. Back home in Orange county – alone.

*   *   *

Saturday, October 24, 1998 – Late Evening

Sam's house was just ahead, and he could already see Sarah's charcoal face gazing intently out the front window – a constant vigil awaiting her moment to either ward off an intruder or make sure she didn't miss any leftovers, whichever came first. She started barking when his truck pulled up beside the house and stopped in front of the garage. Sam sighed as he parked the truck and turned off the ignition. As he climbed out, he grabbed a white bag in the front seat beside him. After all, he couldn't disappoint the one female actually a part of his life. The night air was calm and stifling. Bugs circled around the porch light outside the side door, frequently ramming into the globe. *For creatures that had supposedly survived through the age of dinosaurs, they keep running into the globe a lot. You'd think they would have figured out light bulbs some time ago.* His bug gazing was interrupted by the pattering of Sarah's paws on the laminate, rushing toward the door to

26

welcome him home and get a whiff of whatever he might be carrying. *I wonder what she'd think if I brought home a girl instead?* Not that he had brought anyone home since Gwen, but it would be better if he didn't think of Gwen tonight – lonely Saturday nights are best spent cuddling up to only one disaster at a time.

Tonight's disaster had been Stacy, his mysterious blind date Gerard had arranged. To be fair, it wasn't Gerard making any arrangements; it was Gerard's wife, Pam. Gerard had just gotten stuck calling him to clear it. For some reason, unknown to him, most women he knew were always trying to set him up. Even single girls tried to set him up. Blind dates were usually so awkward and cumbersome that he seldom agreed to them, but since Gerard was asking, he reluctantly said he would meet Stacy at Ramon's tonight. Sam's biggest fear on a blind date was the awkward silence as he strived to fill the conversation void. Unfortunately, this typically only made the conversation even more awkward as it became more strained and thin.

Sam entered the kitchen, and Sarah, eagerly awaiting his petting of her head, paced anxiously. Her eyes betrayed her excitement to see him, unlike Stacy's blasé stare when he approached her at the restaurant. With each step, as she realized he wasn't a waiter or someone going to a different table, her expression grew more and more disconnected and less and less engaged – like slowly drawing a heavy gray drape across a window where only a few heartbeats earlier fresh sunlight had been freely pouring through.

"What did you do tonight, girl?" He asked Sarah sincerely, as though her answer might be something totally remarkable. Instead, her response was to simply shuffle from standing at his right leg to standing at his left. After all, the leftovers dangled from Sam's left hand. "Nothing good, huh? Well, me neither, but I got to spend $80 on my worthlessness. At least yours was free." To Sarah's disappointment, Sam placed the food in the fridge and pulled out a brown beer bottle. He knelt down and rubbed her face. Sarah loved that and showed her gratitude by licking Sam's chin with her purple tongue. After a few moments, Sam rose and made his way into the living room.

Sam's house wasn't large, with a kitchen, dining room, living room, small study and bathroom downstairs, and a couple of bedrooms upstairs. Plain furniture adorned the living room – brown leather recliner, cream sofa, covered with a sheet to avoid the inevitable black dog hair waiting to cling to the suede, and a much more prominent than necessary television across from the sofa. Sam reached the recliner and plopped down, opening the beer

27

somewhere between stopping at the chair and his butt finding its way into the comfortable groove in the dark leather it had sculpted over the years. After turning the beer slowly in his hands, mindlessly studying the label (as if it would be any different than any of the others), he took a slow draught and sat the bottle on a stack of puzzle books nearby. Finally, Sam reached over and grabbed one of his best friends in the world – the remote control.

Sam re-experienced one of the universe's great mysteries when he noticed, after an hour of constant channel flipping between wrestling matches, infomercials, and news broadcasts, that nothing worth watching was on despite having over 200 channels of potential. Sarah could not have seemed more disinterested. She had collapsed in her rust-colored bed between Sam and the sofa, staring wistfully toward the kitchen. Sam's thoughts, unable to find anything to distract them, drifted back to his evening with Stacy.

Unlike most first dates, the big problem with Stacy had nothing to do with awkward gaps in conversation. Tonight, however, Sam experienced the ugly twin sister of the awkward silence – the conversation steamroller. Once she came to terms with her disappointment over his unassuming appearance, Stacy had launched into a conversation with herself that had no end. She had recently returned from a hiking trip in Costa Rica, and she plowed on through from the time Sam showed up until the time the food arrived, discussing zip lining across the canopy of the rain forest and playing with the monkeys there. Having never hiked or camped outside of the Sierras, Sam didn't have a rainforest story. He didn't have any good, "and then the monkey stole my beer," stories either. Though he tried to find a segue into her conversation, he felt like a toddler. Though he could see the cookie jar on the counter, no matter how he stretched, it always remained just out of reach. Stacy and her three cousins had trekked through the whole area for two weeks while staying with her uncle's friends. Sam's uncle had taken him and his cousins to the drive-thru Beer Barn one Saturday night when he was a kid and let them all share a beer, but somehow that story didn't seem like it would hold up.

Hoping to at least chat about their dinner also turned out to be a fantasy. His halibut was delicious, and he was getting ready to share his "my grandmother could fry up some really great fish" story, but Stacy had beat him to the punch with her "I had salmon like this when I went with my ex on a hang gliding trip" story. Sam had been relegated to eating his dinner quietly and nodding periodically as Stacy had rambled on. Stacy dominated the

28

conversation all the way through dessert. Only once, when the check arrived, did she pause to ask how he was doing and make her obligatory "I'm sorry – I feel like I did all the talking" speech. By then, Sam had already resigned himself to thanking Pam for arranging such a great evening.

Sam had seldom even been out of California. His work as a social worker offered no real opportunity to travel, and the few vacations he did manage were usually to an antique expo in San Francisco or San Diego. Outside of dealing with conversations like Stacy's, though, he was generally satisfied. His job allowed him to meet a lot of different people and help them get their lives together. He worked for family services in their Anaheim office. Each day was spent desperately trying to make a difference for the children whose names showed up in his case files. Every one of them was experiencing the worst moments of their life, and he fought to cut that time as short as possible. Sam had learned early on to focus on the children – on freeing them from their situation – rather than trying to punish the parents. He wanted the victories of his career to have meaning and not be overshadowed by a miserable justice system.

When he wasn't working or disappointing women, he lost himself in his furniture. Sam eventually converted the detached garage into his furniture workshop and storeroom. His love of antique furniture was the only part of his father's stranglehold on history that had rubbed off on Samuel. His father taught both U.S. and World History at high school and the local community college and always preached his ancient wisdom. However, instead of empowering Sam, his sermons bred a hatred for all things historic – except for the magic of transforming antiques.

As Sam's thoughts drifted away from Stacy, back to his furniture, he got the urge to take a closer, slower look at that buffet from the Halpert estate. Forgetting to take his beer and turn off his TV, he got up from the recliner and returned to the kitchen. None of this was lost on Sarah, who jumped up when she saw him. "What? You hungry already?" Sam asked Sarah, who stopped a few feet from the fridge to stare longingly in his direction. Sam chuckled as he grabbed the leftovers from the fridge and put a bowl together for Sarah. He carried Sarah's food bowl with him, Sarah following closely behind, out the door, and over to the workshop.

Sam's furniture workshop was divided into two parts: a storage area for finished pieces waiting to find a home and a workshop where current projects sat waiting for their chance to come alive again. He entered the

29

working area where the buffet and the desk had sat since he brought them home earlier. He sat Sarah's bowl down near a second rust-colored bed on the workshop floor. Sam started toward the buffet as she wolfed down her halibut and rice. Before reaching the buffet, however, he stopped short at that ridiculous writing desk. Although quaint, it wasn't even close to a quality antique. He had only purchased it to get the buffet at such a steal. Of course, that meant now he was stuck with this thing.

It had a flat writing surface with no superstructure or roll-top feature. It had some ornamentation but nowhere near enough to give it character. Sam would naturally clean and re-stain it, but that wouldn't help it do any better at auction. He hated just selling it in a classified or donating it to charity. Samuel never liked handing a piece over to someone without knowing they would take care of it. But what was to eventually be done with the desk remained a mystery. He squatted down and pulled the few desk drawers out to get a better look at the original color and see their condition and their railings. *This desk was lightly used,* Sam thought to himself as he looked the upper drawers over. Unfortunately, the bottom drawers were not as lucky, with damage to their tongue and groove corners. *Someone just treated it like storage with no intention of it being functional.* The damage wasn't terrible, though; Sam could easily repair it, although it meant pouring more energy into a piece he hadn't wanted.

Sam's legs began to tire, and his squat became a kneel. He reached over to pet Sarah, who had just finished eating and waddled over to show some gratitude. As he leaned over, petting her head, he noticed something white under the desk's surface. It was an envelope taped below, where no one would notice it. *What could this be?* Sam fetched his flashlight and a nearby X-acto knife. He carefully flipped the desk over and, being careful not to damage the wood, slowly plied the tape free. The tape was quite old, and all but a few tough spots came off fairly easily. After a few moments, he finally removed the envelope and peeked inside since it had no address or markings. He slid the knife under the flap and cautiously opened the envelope to avoid damaging anything that might be inside.

He found a small piece of faded yellowish-brown paper clipped to yet second, smaller envelope. This smaller envelope appeared to have been mailed to Mr. Halpert back in the 1950s and bore a postmark from Rome, Italy. The small paper attached to the envelope had but two sentences scrawled in handwriting along the top, *"Got a call from the Vatican today about this. I fear*

30

for Manuel, as I've not heard from him in years." Samuel wrinkled his brow. Mr. Halpert had been a successful professor of British literature at Cal. State in San Luis Obispo, and it wouldn't have been like someone of his stature to use those words loosely. *He was certainly scared enough to hide it under this desk, though.* Still skeptical, Samuel pulled the message from the second envelope, removed the single sheet folded inside, and began to read:

November 16, 1958

Dear Johnathon,

I hope this letter finds you and your family well. It has been a long time since my last correspondence, and I beg your forgiveness on that count. However, I am hopeful that the future sees us corresponding more instead of less, as has been the current trend.

I am excited, John, for I may have uncovered something truly magnificent! Unfortunately, my current post in Vatican City requires the utmost confidence, but I had to share my enthusiasm at least. John, as it turns out, Professor Gregor may have been right after all. I am not sure of anything yet, but you can imagine my chagrin after the hours spent trying to convince you the man was a looney-bird. I knew you would be excited, given your devotion to his theories.

I am gathering my work and preparing my presentation materials, and I hope to present my findings to the Cardinal soon. If approved, you will be the first with which I plan to share this historic news. I assure you the documentation is quite burdensome, has taken me a sufferably long time to assemble and decipher, and much work still remains. I am certain, however, that it will be shared with you and the entire world soon enough. It is thrilling, John, to be so close to definitively answering that eternal question we debated for so long after all these years!

Sadly, I must close for now so that I might continue my progress.

Farewell, my friend,

31

Sam couldn't resist rereading the letter from this mysterious Manuel character, more slowly this time. *What did Manuel think he had discovered, anyway? How important could it possibly have been, and why would someone from the Vatican bother calling on Mr. Halpert?* The answers existed in 1958 when that letter was written, but time had likely forgotten them. Any answers that might still remain certainly weren't going to be unearthed that night; Sam scoured every inch of the desk to assure himself there weren't any more cryptic messages attached anywhere. Finally, after re-reading the message a third and again for a fourth time, Samuel folded the paper and tucked it back inside the envelope. Sam had church tomorrow morning and didn't need to spend all night asking questions to a letter that would yield no answers. No longer concerned with the buffet, at least for now, he and Sarah staggered inside, calling it a night.

"The sciences, each straining in its own direction, have hitherto harmed us little; but some day the piecing together of dissociated knowledge will open up such terrifying vistas of reality, and of our frightful position therein, that we shall either go mad from the revelation or free from the deadly light into the peace and safety of a new dark age." – H.P. Lovecraft, The Call of Cthulhu

Saturday, September 27, 1958 – Evening

Pale light shined on Manuel's tiny desk, a feint flicker standing vigil against the vast darkness of the basement, casting fragile shadows on the cold, stone floor. The small extension cable powering his lamp was the only evidence that he was indeed in the twentieth century. No heat, air-conditioning, or electricity had been installed over the years – a testament to the neglect and isolation he found himself. His workstation was but a plain wooden table adorned with a handful of pens and the black desk lamp he had been given when he first began working for the Vatican. Countless sundered papers and sheets of parchment lay among file cabinets, boxes, and atop tables. Many even lay discarded in bulky, unorganized mounds on the stone floor – tossed aside over the centuries by clerks unconcerned with what happened to them. The papers stored in darkness for so long gave the basement a powerful, musty scent that had taken Manuel some time with which to grow accustomed. Nothing of interest had found its way down there – only the blackness, which had become his sole companion, an endless sea of forgotten documents, and, once in a rare while, the occasional mouse.

A graduate from Cambridge with a Master's of Languages, Manuel had dreamed of much more when he had eagerly accepted the post at the Vatican several years ago. The pay was great, and he had entertained visions of translating ancient documents teeming with history for the Vatican Archives – actually working with material that mattered and might lead to him being published for his endeavors. Despite those delusions of grandeur, the documents with which he found himself saddled, although old, held no historical value. Most were merely reports from Bishops, Archbishops, and Priests throughout the centuries writing back to the Vatican regarding their work. So, instead of ancient historical documents in the archives, he was stuck translating field notes and status updates piled in a dank, forgotten dungeon.

33

His days on the rowing team with his friends at college faded further and further away as each day of mindless tedium blended into the next.

Like most things that find themselves neglected, time seeks to destroy. Many older documents had already been lost to mildew and rot over the years. This deterioration had driven the Vatican to hire someone like Manuel. Though not a Catholic, he had graduated near the top of his class with an astounding grip of most languages having European or Middle Eastern roots. He was tasked with translating each document into both Latin and English and reproducing them in a uniform fashion so the text might be preserved and catalogued – although the original document may deteriorate over time.

Tonight he was struggling to translate one of the oldest documents he had yet come across– a status update from a Ukrainian priest written on heavy parchment toward the end of the ninth century. The priest, a Father Alec, apparently plagued with horrible penmanship, was reporting on events with which he had been involved recently. Other than its extreme age, it was utterly unexceptional and ordinary – at least it had been until Manuel came to a passage regarding the priest's handling of an exorcism.

Manuel rolled his eyes and whimpered a sigh as he continued translating. He held demons, exorcisms, and the notion that a person could be possessed with extreme skepticism – believing, like most, those stories were either the stuff of horror tales best spun around a campfire or tragic, misplaced claims made by folk ignorant of diseases such as Tourette syndrome, epilepsy or the like. His beliefs would come crumbling to the very ground by this recounting of an exorcism of a demon, apparently calling itself "Furkalor." *That name rings a bell. Do these Catholic priests all share the same horror stories?* He continued translating until, at once, his hand stopped writing, and he dropped his pen as his mind abruptly wrapped itself around why the name "Furkalor" sounded so familiar.

Manuel's breath poured forward with each exhale as he sat motionless in the cold, unwilling to work further, terrified of what he might read. As he stared blankly into the darkness, the hairs on his arm began standing on end as the basement felt far colder than it ever had. Manuel had seen the name Furkalor previously. He eventually stood up and hobbled to a box of his work neatly stacked near the stairs – each step slower, more deliberate than the one before. Finally, after a moment of rifling around, his hands trembling as he fumbled through translation after translation, he reluctantly found what he

34

was looking for – a translation from a Father Blanc in Paris several months ago. Father Blanc had reported the exorcism of a demon with the same name.

Manuel, with his hands still trembling, carried the translation back to his table, laid it beside the old parchment from the Ukraine, and, leaning over the documents with his hands resting on the table, began reading Father Blanc's report carefully to ensure he did not confuse any details: *"The demon, calling itself 'Furkalor,' caused Marie's [the victim's] voice to sound as though she were underwater . . . alarmed to notice the rather sudden appearance of a bleeding wound on her right arm above her elbow – in the odd shape of a crescent moon with an open circle above . . . throughout the ordeal she suffered from extreme fever and muscular spasms and her room seemed to swelter many degrees above the rest of the house."* His eyes turned red and swelled with tears as Manuel, confronting the evidence in front of him, forced himself to turn to this Father Alec's tale from the Ukraine: *". . . demon finally, upon much persistence revealed its name unto me, that of 'Furkalor,' had caused much damage to Abramov bringing him to the brink of death from incredible fever and pure exhaustion as his body trembled with severe convulsions. His son noticed a wound on his right arm in the shape of a crescent moon with a hollow circle hovering above. . . greater oddity in the vocal pitch of poor Abramov, as his voice echoed as would one in a pool of water. . . the room generated an intense heat –despite the extreme winter gripping Kyiv."* Minutes of desolate silence followed. Manuel rose and stepped backward as his knees buckled under him. He collapsed in a pile onto the stone floor of the basement.

Refusing the mounting tears the privilege of passage, he swallowed his weakness, turning it to anger, a skill the Vega family had always known well. His heart pounded violently, each beat echoing against the silence of the desolate dungeon. Manuel madly pulled at the hairs on his head, desperate for an outlet for the emotional intensity pulsating through him. Despite his protective rampart of anger, cynicism, and resentment, carefully constructed over his 26 years, visions of a life wasted in vane pursuits – women he had slept with; people he had cheated; lies told to professors, family, and friends; angry curses hurled at priests from his childhood. All the wickedness of a lifetime poured over his defenses, flooding his thoughts as he lay trembling on the floor, feverishly trying, in vain, to explain or justify what he had just read. The insurmountable problem was not that these two accounts were so similar, both demons having the same name, heaping such similar misery upon their victims, but that the reports had been written about eight centuries apart and on opposing sides of the continent. Those two exorcists could not have known each other, and no common source, nor cause, would serve them in concocting a fake scenario such as this – these accounts were genuine.

Everything Manuel had come to believe about spirituality was false. He was naked in a blizzard – his cloak of skepticism, self-gratification, and confidence stripped away with but a few pen strokes from ages long since forgotten. Manuel was not Catholic. In fact, he did not truly believe in a God or a devil, for that matter. That notion was as foreign to him as the concept of electricity would be to a water buffalo, but here, in black and white, stood undeniable evidence that there was, in fact, a very real demon out there, somewhere in the netherworld, named Furkalor, and even more critical, a force, professed by the Church to be God, had repelled it more than once. Demons, along with the God they feared, were real.

*　　　*　　　*

Wednesday, August 12, 1959 – Late Evening

Wall sconces masked the lighting along the stairwell walls, bathing them in but a slight sheen of pale yellowish light. Soft crimson carpet masked Manuel's footsteps on the long stairs leading to the Cardinal's chambers. He had been eagerly awaiting this opportunity for weeks – a time when his boss, Cardinal Hickman, would be in his chambers and unencumbered by guests. Over the past year, Manuel had focused his efforts in the basement on anything he could find detailing an exorcism or involving demonic possession. To his complete amazement, several demons had recurring entries – dozens, actually. The sordid details appeared and re-appeared consistently: similar flesh wounds, demonic names, accents, sounds, symptoms, even environmental effects like extreme heat or cold, sudden unexplained breezes in closed rooms with no open windows or doors, and even heavy condensation on windows and walls, were woven throughout these reports like a tapestry lining a dark, secret crevice of reality – the one most people spend a lifetime convincing themselves doesn't exist.

Facts easily disguise themselves as coincidence, but only once. The facts leaping from these historic pages appeared numerous times, leaving no doubt of their authenticity. Of course, the priests writing these reports could not have collaborated, given their separation in time and space. Nevertheless, the documents were genuine, and each had even been stamped by the Vatican before being "filed" in the basement below. These "patterned incidentals," as

36

Manuel had called them, were authentic and appeared repeatedly. The fear, doubt, and resentment Manuel had originally experienced had been supplanted by adrenaline-soaked excitement. He had uncovered, in the most unlikely of places, something far more climactic than anything stored in the Vatican Archives, or anywhere else for that matter, and he desperately needed to share his discovery with the rest of the world. Professor Gregor's theories had been right all along, despite Manuel's repeated arguments with him and others to the contrary, and he would help Gregor prove it.

Manuel, his arms full of ancient manuscripts and other papers, finally reached the top of the stairs and found Cardinal Hickman's living quarters. He managed to wrestle one knuckle free and rapped at the closed door. The door swung inward, revealing a balding, tall, thin man dressed in a blue T-shirt and sweat pants with bare feet jutting out the bottoms. Manuel paused, not accustomed to seeing a Cardinal out of uniform, finally managing a simple, "Good evening, Cardinal Hickman. Did I catch you at a bad time?"

"Manuel? Is that you hiding behind that unholy mound of papers?"

Manuel chuckled slightly, "Yes, sir. I have found something I think you need to see."

"If you've uncovered something in the 'rat's nest,'" as the clergy referred to the basement Manuel had been assigned, "I am quite certain I would rather not. But I will oblige since you have been so kind as to haul this little sample of the nest up to my home." The Cardinal showed Manuel inside and pulled up a chair for him. He then went to the kitchen, poured himself a fresh hot cup of coffee, and, without offering one to Manuel, returned to his divan and sat down. He pulled his eyes from the steam rising from the coffee to look Manuel in the face. "Well?"

"Yes, of course, sir." Manuel piled the documents gently on the wooden floor, careful not to damage any of the older specimens. "This is difficult to explain, but I have read several excerpts recounting tales of demonic exorcisms by Vatican Priests, and I have noticed, well, patterns."

Cardinal Hickman, holding his mug with both hands, took a slow sip. "Patterns?" he managed finally.

"Yes." Manuel started with the two accounts of Furkalor he originally uncovered and went on to explain the two other accounts of Furkalor he had found before moving on to other accounts of demons such as Malphas, Paimon, and Zepar, to name but a scant few. For almost an hour, he spelled out intricate details and repeated coincidental facts surrounding the accounts

37

of demons with the same names. He had prepared for this presentation for weeks now, over and over in his head, each time adding more detail and additional support. Manuel finally reached his conclusion – still gripping one of the ragged transcripts, and peered at Cardinal Hickman, awaiting his response. The anticipation was palpable, and he dared not even breathe.

The Cardinal had not been excited or engaged, asked no questions, and failed even to raise an eyebrow during Manuel's entire presentation. His response, having at last reached the end of his coffee, was to ask simply, ". . . and what now? Assuming these 'stories' you relish are real and not simple embellishments of desperate priests, what would you have us do?"

"That's the best part, sir; we need to release these documents to the world! Countless souls are refusing to believe in a God who seems so definitively to have abandoned them. Our world was shaken to its core in the second World War, and how many lives were destroyed? The world should know that these accounts, and the demons within, are real, and, even more importantly, there is a force out there strong enough to repel them."

The Cardinal sat his cup down and rose from the divan, looking down at Manuel, "I'll keep your words and discovery under advisement, my son. Continue your research. Everyone appreciates the tireless hours you are spending down there."

Catching the scent of defeat in the air, Manuel humbly gathered his things and left. On his way back, he kept reaching the same conclusion: *he doesn't believe me. He hears "demons," and his mind closes down, as my mind would have done just months ago. I have to find someone more open than Hickman. Someone willing to see this thing through for what it truly is – someone willing to deliver this tiny bit of light into the darkness of our Godless world.*

*   *   *

Monday, October 12, 1959

He carefully placed each document into the bag, particularly the older ones – they were so fragile already. Thunder clapped outside of his window as he continued packing. Occasionally adding in bits of clothing here and there to help secure the documents and to, well, give him some change of clothes. His time at the Vatican had ended, though no one yet knew of his decision. By the time he failed to show for breakfast, he would be far from Italy, with the Vatican behind him.

He sat on the edge of his bed glaring outside his sole window, rain beginning to pound upon it, as a memory rushed into his mind – one of the few he had of his parents. Rain was beating against the windows of the front room. His father, a simple tradesman shipbuilder at the docks, was putting on his coat, preparing to go out into the night with friends opposing the forces occupying Seville. War had recently come to Spain. Young Manuel and his twin sister, Marta, hugged their father, fearing the worst. Then, as the door closed, Marta had turned and asked their mother how their Papa had become so brave. She knelt and smiled at her two children before whispering, "Your father is far more than just brave, my darlings; he is courageous. Bravery is simply doing what your heart desires, ignoring all dangers or fears, but courage is when, instead of just doing what your heart wants, you do what your head tells you is right and charge ahead, knowing all the horrible things that might happen. Your Papa left tonight not because he wanted to fight but because he knows that it is right – for España and us." Their father never returned. He and Marta were afterward sent to live with their aunt and uncle in France, but he had never forgotten his mother's words.

Am I doing this for myself or the greater good? The memory challenged his motives, and it was a valid challenge, even he had to admit. He had dreamed of working on something historical to help him get published, and he had certainly found it. But d*oes the world need what I am giving them, or is it that I need what the documents might give me?* His beliefs about God had been irrevocably transformed based on these writings, but was the self-serving demon of his own still lurking inside him – seeking fortune and fame? *A brave person would present these documents to the world because his heart yearns to do so; a courageous person would do it because it needed to be done.* At long last, Manuel satisfied himself that his motives were pure. He remembered how he felt sobbing on that basement floor, his entire belief structure crashing down around him. He also remembered a warmth and a sense of purpose he had never known afterward. There was a force out there bigger than himself, and thousands, millions of others like him needed to be shown what he had seen and be given the opportunity to bask in that same warmth.

Despite numerous pleas to anyone taking the time to listen, Manuel had ultimately accepted that it would be up to him to reveal these findings to the world – firsthand. He had gathered several documents, including his translations, enough to serve as a representative sampling. Knowing that he wouldn't be able to tote the entire collection of historical papers with him, he had hidden the remaining accounts inside the walls of his chamber. He zipped up his bag, grabbed his umbrella, and stepped outside into the pouring rain.

"There comes a time in every rightly constructed boy's life when he has a raging desire to go somewhere and dig for hidden treasure." – Mark Twain, The Adventures of Tom Sawyer

Wednesday, January 27, 1999 – Early Evening

The package looked smaller from inside his truck, leaning against his front door. At first, it perplexed him, but then Sam remembered the "Friends." By that, he remembered pleading with the "American Friends of Cambridge" to share anything they had on a Professor Gregor that would have been teaching theology at Cambridge in the late 1940s. He had hoped for a phone call in a day or two, but his frustrations magnified when two days became two weeks, and still no word had come.

These last three months had been a whirlwind for Samuel. *Had it already been that long?* Time seemed to stand still for everything in Sam's world except for that cryptic letter he had uncovered under that old writing desk. He had gone to bed the night he originally found it, but couldn't sleep as he mentally kept going over the letter and the strange note. Nothing seemed to add up. *What could someone working in the Vatican have discovered that would have caused so much trouble and maybe even gotten him killed?* For several weeks, he had tried reaching the late Mr. Halpert's relatives to see if any of them had known of someone named Manuel, apparently a former friend of Mr. Halpert's. Those efforts were ultimately in vain.

The letter's context hinted that perhaps Manuel knew Mr. Halpert from school. Luckily, Cal. State had a short biography of Professor Halpert on its website. The late Mr. Halpert got his undergraduate from Cambridge University in England but did his Master's and Ph.D. work at Brown University here in the states. After getting nowhere speaking to the rather uncooperative folks at the alumni department in Cambridge, Sam learned by mere chance about an organization in America called the "American Friends of Cambridge" out of Chicago. When he had called them, the nice lady on the other end had promised to look up this "Professor Gregor" and see if anyone by that name was teaching at Cambridge during that time. When he had asked the same questions of Brown, they informed him that there had not been a Professor Gregor teaching at that school before their current Professor Gregor, who was only 39. He had heard nothing from the Friends of Cambridge since that phone

41

call and was getting quite discouraged until today when he spotted this simple package outside as he pulled into his driveway. It might hold answers to some of the questions that had consumed him for the three months since discovering that letter.

He got out of the truck, walked over, and picked up the package. It was, in fact, from Chicago! Ignoring Sarah inside barking her frustrations, Sam eagerly tore the box open. There were four items inside bundled in a pink rubber band: a short letter from Margie Stone; a paper written by a Professor Thomas Gregor entitled "The Proof' from 1923; a collection of articles written by other theology professors, both from Cambridge and elsewhere; and finally a tribute to the Professor in the "Varsity," the student newspaper, from November of 1959 upon his death. There were around 200 pages of material to sift through, and Sam wasted no time getting started. He rushed inside, and after a quick pet on Sarah's head followed by a hurried walk with her around the block, Sam headed straight to his desk in the workshop and began poring through the material.

Sam started with Margie's letter, but it contained little more than a short apology for taking so long and a listing of the package's contents. The only intriguing thing for Sam in that letter was a tiny personal note near the bottom from Margie. *"This Professor seems to have a sorted history — preaching controversial theories and encouraging heated religious debate in the classroom. Conflicts were common, and the Professor seems to have been asked to stop more than once. I'm not sure why you are looking into Professor Gregor, but I hope you'll not be dragged down the same path. Sincerely, Margie Stone."* Sam had already suspected this Professor had been controversial based on Manuel's letter, but he had no idea what Margie meant by *"same path"* in her note. This Professor Gregor began weighing on Sam's mind as he flipped to the tribute article in the "Varsity."

The article started kind and benign towards the late Professor. He had taught there for almost 40 years and was a legend among theology students. His most popular course was entitled "Comparative Theological Boundaries," a course apparently devoted to contrasting theology from several cultures — primarily Christian, Buddhist, Hindu, Islam, and Judaism. Sadly, he had taken his own life at the age of 67, but his funeral had been well attended. This history seemed horribly tragic to Sam, but he also noticed a second page attached to the article. As he flipped to it, he saw it contained an article

42

printed just weeks before the Professor's death. Toward the bottom of page 4 had been printed:

"Classroom debate gets serious – two students treated at the health center.

Last Thursday, a classroom debate got ugly in Professor Gregor's Comparative Theology class when Professor Gregor, as he typically does, encouraged and engaged his students in a candid debate regarding the existence of God. Holding to his now-infamous theories, Professor Gregor challenged the students to discuss why the vast majority of the world believes in an entity that cannot be verified. Chris Shelton, a sophomore, and two other students (requesting to remain anonymous) began shouting at one another until one threw a chair at Chris, igniting a bloody brawl. Both students treated last week are in good condition and should return to classes in a few more days. Professor Gregor was sanctioned and is required to attend a hearing regarding the incident, as this is not the first time his controversial theory has made tempers flare."

What was this theory that had created so much controversy? Is this the same theory Manuel and the late Mr. Halpert had debated? Sam sat aside the news clippings and picked up the academic article by Professor Gregor himself. Time seemed to melt away as Sam waded through page upon page of the article's narrative. This Professor assembled building blocks of what he deemed the "Ultimate Proof." The theory unfolding before Sam's eyes filled him with wonder and awe. *Could God truly be proven to exist?* Despite his father's disapproval, Sam had grown up in the church but had never encountered anything as eloquent as Gregor's "Proof." This Professor Gregor was attempting to *prove* that God truly existed. Page after eloquent page elaborated this theory, which was often far more intricate than Sam could follow – connecting ideas from various unrelated fields: Physics, Theology, Literature, History, Archeology, Philosophy, Government, Chemistry, and Biology. This Professor Gregor was a brilliant writer and theologian, or at least he had been when he published that paper in 1923. His commanding grasp of the dense material engrossed Samuel. At the paper's conclusion, however, the Professor had been forced to confess an inescapable gap in his theory: the lack of what he dubbed "objectively verifiable evidence" of a supernatural realm. This final building block, despite the Professor's best efforts, which included exploration of witchcraft, numerology, astrology, along with a host of

43

other pseudo-sciences, had not yielded one piece of credible evidence that was "objectively verifiable" – that is, able to be verified by an independent third party. This gap, claimed the Professor, was the ultimate flaw in his proof and that without such evidence, the existence of God could never be proven to the satisfaction of the modem scientific community.

Sunlight had faded by the time Sam finally finished the paper, and darkness had settled in for the night. Sam pulled himself away and went inside to get a drink. He made his way to the couch, toting the package's remaining contents. Article upon article echoed the scornful sentiment of seemingly every other academician to review Gregor's work. Gregor had been universally renounced by every other critical analyst and renounced harshly. Ironically, while holding such abhorrent distaste for Professor Gregor's theory, most made several remarks admiring both the exhaustive breadth of the research and his superior grasp of logic and reasoning. It appeared to Sam as though these academics were willing to follow the Professor on this path of enlightenment until they discovered where the road ultimately led. Professor Gregor's conclusion and ultimate belief that humanity stood but a hairsbreadth away from truly proving the existence of God drove the academic world away from his work. Sam thought it odd that academia, which screamed at the top of its lungs for mankind to always quest for knowledge with an open mind, had condemned the Professor's conclusion without fully examining the evidence for themselves. When challenged, academics forget that pure knowledge does not discriminate between the Muslim and the Jew, the Hindu and the Buddhist, nor between the Christian and the scientist.

Night continued its march and was finally approaching dawn when Sam finished. He was mentally and physically exhausted and couldn't believe he had done nothing all night but scour the information in that package. Sam lumbered upstairs and cleaned up, although the prospect of focusing on his case files seemed remote. That puzzling letter had consumed him for three months, and now, rather than answers, only new, more intricate questions sprouted to life.

*   *   *

Thursday, January 28, 1999 – Late Morning

Time dragged while Sam tried focusing on the Peterson file. Three times already, Sam had caught himself making simple mistakes. Not only was it difficult to stay focused, or even awake for that matter, but he also couldn't stop replaying everything he had just read. This Manuel/Professor Gregor

44

situation was getting to him, and he needed to put an end to it before being robbed of more than sleep. Sam knew what had to be done. He dropped his pen and went to see Rosa.

Rosa Cervantes, a proud immigrant from Guatemala, had ebony, shoulder-length hair resting atop a white blouse, at least two sizes too small. Rosa's specialty was finding people, and she was highly skilled. She had access to practically every database available and could usually find someone in minutes. Whether from credit card charges, employment records, bank accounts, or something else, Rosa always knew under which rock to look.

Sam shuffled in and closed the door. Rosa looked up at him. "You look sick, Sam. What's wrong with you?"

"I didn't sleep last night, that's all. I'll be better tomorrow. But, Rosa, I need to find someone. Can you locate someone in Europe?"

"Well, I have a handful of databases over there, nothing too elaborate. What sort of case you working on?"

"Nothing like that . . . it's just..." Sam got a little worried, knowing Rosa was not supposed to search people for purely personal reasons. "Well ... it's a missing person, I think. His name is Manuel. I only know he attended Cambridge University in the late 40s and early 50s ... Oh, and he worked for the Vatican for a while."

"The 50s? When was the last time anyone saw him?"

"He's been gone a long time. One of his good friends here in the States hasn't seen him since then."

Rosa smelled something strange, and it wasn't just her overpowering hazelnut coffee. "Sam, who is this guy, really? Why you need to find him so bad?"

"Okay, Okay ... I need to know where he is, Rosa, because I think he knows something about my father." Sam lied, hoping to gain some traction. "He knows – or knew – my father a long time ago, and I need to see if he's out there. I can't let my dad know I'm looking, though. It would ruin everything. His birthday's coming up, you know?"

"Alright, I'll help this once, but I don't think I'll turn up much. Just sit down and let me poke around a bit." Time stretched as Rosa nosed around the computer network until she eventually looked up with a shallow grin. "I am guessing it's this guy, Manuel Vega," she announced proudly, pointing at her monitor – Masters of Languages from Cambridge in 1952. I don't see anything about the Vatican, but the Vatican doesn't publish its employment data.

I'm guessing this is your guy, though. The only other Manuel attending Cambridge around that time is doing time in prison right now."

Sam stewed over the possibilities – his head swimming. *Could this Manuel Vega be the same guy who wrote that letter to Mr. Halpert? Did he truly uncover something at the Vatican? Finally,* Sam opened his mouth to speak, but Rosa beat him to the punch.

"I have this number, but it's probably not good anymore. The college filed his next of kin in case of an emergency. It's a Frenchman named Hendrick Wurzlet and his wife, Angelina. Of course, if those were his parents, they would be getting on in years by now, but with the different last names, who knows? She smiled as she scribbled the name and number onto a sticky note. "But remember, I never did any of this. Right?"

"Sure thing, Rosa, and thanks again, seriously." Sam quietly retreated back to his office. He already knew his next move. One phone call to Gerard would get him the French interpreter he needed. Sam grabbed his phone.

"Hello, Gerry?"

"Sam?"

"Yeah, it's me. How are things down at the shop?" Gerard ran a mechanic's shop (at least on the surface). Sam heard the stool creak at the shop as Gerard pressed his bulk onto it.

"You know, little of this – little of that. Got Jacky pulling a double since Frank didn't come in again. So, you know Jacky's pissed. I'm pissed. And, when Frank does show his face, he's gonna be pissed by the time I'm done. But, you didn't call to hear me bitch, did ya? What's up?"

"I need a favor. Doesn't Pam speak French?"

"She does some. Why? You looking to hit on a French honey? Le Cat got your tongue? Haw – haw." Gerard always thought more of his jokes than others did.

"Not quite. I need her to call someone for me. You think she's home?"

"Better be. The last time she went out during the day, she came home in a new Cadillac. Why don't you give her a call? Hopefully, she'll be in a good mood."

"She better! After that wonderful date a couple of months ago, she owes me a lot more than a lousy phone call – remember Stacy?"

"You got that right. Look, I need to get moving. See ya later, right?"

As the phone clicked off, Sam nervously dialed Gerard's home number. A male voice answered after a few rings, "Hello."

46

"Uh, hi. Is this Tim?" Sam hoped this was Gerard's older son instead of, well ... someone else.

"Yeah – who's this?"

"Oh, Tim, this is Sam, your Dad's friend. Is your mom around?

"Sure. Maawwuummm!" he bellowed.

"She'll be right on ... " Tim yelled out as he slammed the phone down loudly and went about wasting time in his own way.

Soon enough, a thick female voice, strained from years of inhaling Camels, came through the line, "Hello?"

"There she is. The maker of bad dates, herself."

"Bullshit – that one was your fault. Stacy is fun and gorgeous. She said you didn't even smile when she told you her cute story about the monkey running off with her beer. I don't see how you blew it with her."

"Blew it? " chuckled Sam. "Don't you normally have to say something in order to blow it? But, listen, I didn't call to argue about Stacy anyway. I've thought of a way for you to make it up to me. This is gonna seem a little weird, so listen carefully . . ." Sam laid everything out for her, from finding the envelope to getting Hendrick's number from Rosa. He needed her help calling him, but she had to know the whole story. Pam seemed eager to help, though concerned about Hendrick's age. Pam finally said she would do it later that day.

Hours passed as Sam eagerly waited. His work had faded into the background as he hadn't done anything truly productive all day. The excitement and worry intensified, and he didn't know how much more he could, or wanted, to take. Finally, after what seemed an eternity, the phone rang. Pam had gotten through! He hadn't been Manuel's father at all but rather his uncle. Manuel and his sister had been sent to live with them back in the 1930s. Unfortunately, he had also not heard from Manuel for over 40 years, and the police hadn't recovered anything. Then, Pam let loose with some good news. Manuel's sister, Marta, was still alive and living in Seville, in southern Spain. Hendrick had actually given Pam her phone number! Samuel had warned Pam not to mention anything about the letter to Hendrick since it might have made her sound crazier than she actually was – if that was possible. Regardless, she convinced him she meant well and needed to speak with her. Pam had even better news: Marta apparently spoke very good English. Sam thanked her repeatedly and hung up.

And now. There was Sam, holding in his hand the phone number of

47

the sister of the man he had been searching for these past three months – the man who claimed to have discovered something magnificent while working at the Vatican just before mysteriously vanishing from the face of the Earth.

An odd silence followed Sam's dialing Marta's number, and his hands began sweating as he awaited the connection. A few silent heartbeats passed before static filled the line. Eventually, that static yielded to a distant ringing. The line rang again and again. *Perhaps this was an old number. There are at least a thousand ways this could have gotten screwed up.* After a fourth ring, Sam was returning the receiver to its cradle when he heard a meek "Bueno?" from the other end of the line.

He jerked the phone back to his ear, "Hello? Is this Ms. Marta Vega of Seville, Spain?"

"Who is calling, por favor?" The voice sounded elegant but thin – as though from someone who had just finished her marathon and was now forced to sprint a few meters more.

"You don't know me, ma'am. My name is Samuel Johnston, and I live in California. "

"Mr. Johnston? I am Marta Vega, but I am confused, Sir. What could you possibly want with me? I don't know any Americans."

"That may be true, Ma'am, but your brother certainly did. You do have a brother? A Mr. Manuel Vega?" Silence was the only answer he got – a silence without end. Finally, Sam, taking solace that the phone had not been hung up, gingerly spoke into the silence. "Ms. Vega, I can assure you I mean no harm and certainly did not mean to upset you in any way. I'm going to let you go now, but if you would like to speak with me, please call me at 714-563-1249, and I will be happy to call you right back, so you don't get charged, or you can feel free to call me collect. I would be thrilled to speak with you for just a few minutes about your brother if that would be all right." He repeated his number, closed with a polite, "Good Day, Ma'am," and softly hung up.

Sam stared blankly at his phone and the same file he had been avoiding most of the day. He slowly ran his hands through his hair and sighed heavily. *How could it end like this? To get so close to . . . to what? What did I think would happen?* This whole struggle to uncover what Manuel had found seemed foolhardy at best and slightly mean at worst. He sighed another quiet sigh of resignation and reached to pick up his pen. Just as his hand found the pen, his phone rang, shattering the stillness of his office and scaring him out of his skin.

48

He picked up the receiver, "Hello?"

"I'm sorry, Sir. Is this Mr. Johnston?" came that same meek voice from only moments earlier.

"It is – let me call you right back, Ms. Vega, alright?"

"Fine. Adios."

Sam, surprised that she had called him back at all, stunned that she had called so soon, immediately dialed her back. "Hello, Ms. Vega. Are you alright?"

"Yes, I'm fine, thank you for asking. I should be over it by now, I suppose, but I always get overwhelmed when the subject of my brother comes up. Can you tell me, how do you know him?"

"I don't actually know your brother, Ms. Vega. I have heard of him, though. I uncovered a letter from 1958 written by your brother to a Mr. Johnathon Halpert, and it raised a lot of questions. Mr. Halpert passed away last October, and none of his surviving family knew anything about the letter or Manuel at all. I was hoping that, if I could locate Manuel, I could ask him a few questions about his work he mentioned in his letter."

"You have a letter, you say, written by my brother?"

"That's correct, Ma'am. I found it hidden under a desk I bought from Mr. Halpert's estate. Unfortunately, it is rather cryptic, but I believe it references something your brother discovered while working at the Vatican. A note was also attached to the letter mentioning that people from the Vatican had called Mr. Halpert asking about Manuel. I guess I was just hoping to shine some light on what might have happened to your brother or what his letter was referring to."

"This is amazing, son, truly and utterly amazing. After all these years – to find another piece of my brother's legacy. Who would have dreamed it possible? You see, I, too, received a letter from Manuel referencing something he had found at the Vatican, but he was frightened that someone would find him and take it away. Shortly after I got his letter, some men in dark brown suits showed up and searched my place, apparently looking for something and asking questions about my dear brother. Of course, I didn't mention the letter, but I've suspected all along those men were responsible for my brother's disappearance." Marta's voice became shaky as her composure deteriorated. She had crawled out on the thinnest branch of a mighty tree, but any minute, that branch would snap, and she would plummet into a wave of emotion accompanied by tears and wailing. These feelings had likely been hidden away

49

for decades, but the hope ignited from Sam's letter and possibly discovering more about what might have happened to Manuel seemed to raise this tragedy back to the surface.

"A second letter! You have a second letter? That is wonderful, Ms. Vega. Would you consider mailing me a copy? I would love to compare them."

"As would I, son. However, I am terrified about sending my letter through the mail, even if just a copy. Should it not reach you, my only link to Manuel would be available for anyone to see, and who knows what that might mean if my brother is even still alive? For that same reason, I dare not ask you; indeed, I would plead with you not to send me a copy of your letter."

Sam was surprised to hear Marta clinging to hope that Manuel was alive. He knew that, in all likelihood, Manuel was gone and would never be heard from again. The only fragments left in the world of Manuel Vega were a couple of letters mailed to two different continents over forty years ago.

"Well, certainly, that would be for the best, Ms. Vega. We have to be cautious about this sort of thing, right?" Out of compassion, Sam hid his sarcasm behind a mask of concern as best he could. *Surely, anyone hunting Manuel would have either caught him or given up searching at some point in the last forty years.* But still, he needed to be sensitive to her feelings. "I am sure a solution will present itself eventually, Ms. Vega. Can I call you again sometime?"

"Dear boy, please. I am desperate to find out what happened to my brother – of course, I would love for you to call me again. One last thing, Mr. Johnston, if there's any way you can manage it, I would be happy to show you my letter in person."

Sam was taken aback. *I can't follow this ghost's trail around the world. How far am I willing to go to answer a riddle that may have no answer, or even worse – an answer so inconsequential that the effort to uncover it looks ridiculous in retrospect?* "Well, Ma'am, I'll have to consider that," not knowing what else to say. "Thank you very much for everything, though. Good day."

"Adios, son. Do take care," was her only reply.

*   *   *

Saturday, May 15, 1999 – Mid-Morning

The gentle hum of the plane's engines whirred in the background as passengers crammed oversized baggage into tiny overhead bins. Sam had never flown further than Las Vegas, but now he was sitting on a plane bound

50

for Madrid. From there, he would catch a train south to Seville. He had hated waiting until May to leave, but it had taken longer than expected to get the money for the trip and, as the trip's true purpose would likely be a horrible dead end, he had wanted to go when Spain would be prime for sightseeing. He leaned back against his headrest, closed his eyes, and tried ignoring the growling argument between two flight attendants behind him.

Gerard had been the one that finally pushed him over the edge. He had gone to Gerard's house, and, as usual, a quick visit evolved into dinner, and he and Sarah wound up hanging around most of the evening. At some point during dinner, Pam brought up that call she made to Hendrick, but Sam had simply replied with, "I'm still working on it."

But Gerard, not being one to be brushed off quite so easily, pushed back. "Are you shitting me?" he grumbled. Gerard's hair-covered face wrinkled in disgust. In fact, his face was always covered with hair, but not exactly a beard. It always looked like he hadn't bothered shaving for several days. Sam figured a full beard couldn't gather the courage to grow in. "You have the safest damn life I've ever heard of. You never smoke, you only drink fucking light beer, and you don't even speed on the highway. You need this, pal! Get your ass on a plane and go find this jackass – whoever he is. Yeah, it's probably a road to nowhere, but at least the rest of us get one good story worth telling at your funeral." As he finished his pearls of wisdom, he pointed a thick finger at Sam accusingly.

"Nice, Gerry. I don't know. It's a lot of money, and you have no idea how ridiculous this whole thing sounds: a cryptic letter, a dead professor, and a missing Spaniard. Add an expensive flight and a pathetic Social worker, and you've got a real tragic comedy on your hands."

"Do whatever you want, buddy. But I'm telling you, this sounds like your one opportunity to get out there and at least fucking nibble on the tiniest piece of life."

That was pretty much how it had ended that night – with Sam questioning his sanity most of the way home. He couldn't sleep much that night thinking about the madness of going all the way to Seville to meet this woman and read her letter. He knew he could swing it, though, if he wanted. He had plenty of vacation time available. Pam could watch Sarah. He could sell off that nice buffet and get plenty of cash for the trip. Then, of course, he could use his vacation some other way, take care of his own damn dog and keep that beautiful buffet for himself, like he had planned. But in the end, nothing would

51

happen if he didn't go. His life would continue as it had in the past; he would never have his own "then the monkey stole my beer" story.

"O divine art of subtlety and secrecy! Through you, we learn to be invisible, through you inaudible, and hence we can hold the enemy's fate in our hands." – Sun Tzu, The Art of War

Tuesday, May 4, 1999 – Mid-Day

Thick silver clouds, outlined in the slightest shimmer, hovered lazily above somewhat less than majestic glass and steel pillars of downtown Athens. Herds of people bustled through the fairly congested streets, like herds of people typically do on any typical day in any typical city, unconcerned by, or simply unaware of, the thick clouds blanketing the sky above. The attention of the throng far below, however, remained singularly focused upon reaching their ultimate, likely trivial, destination. Amidst buying things for people they mostly didn't like, buying drinks they didn't really need, and running to and from jobs they generally didn't enjoy, the Athenians littering the streets essentially operated on auto-pilot – floating through this day as they'd floated through those before it, each one a small step closer to their last.

Although life usually seemed to simply run its pre-programmed course, occasionally, though quite rarely, someone disrupted the pattern. These people lived precariously – unaware of what the next moment might bring, potentially dragging them to their crushing end or lifting them to wealth and glory. Living on the edge of life's razor, they walked alongside the drones, making up the general public. They ate where everyone else ate, shopped where everyone else shopped, and rode in the same elevators as everyone else. They are utterly indistinguishable. Victoria was just such a person.

Victoria Sawyer was a smuggler and an expert on not being noticed. Her vigilance bled through her unassuming appearance. Though a bit taller than average, her golden tan provided some camouflage among the darker-skinned Mediterranean women. Cheap sunglasses and grungy tennis shoes blended with an otherwise touristy look – denim jeans and auburn hair hanging loosely around her shoulders, draping the edge of an aqua-colored top. Despite being in great shape with an athletic build, her clothes hung deliberately loose to discourage unwanted attention. Her special talent for remaining hidden while in plain sight would soon be essential.

Through the horde crowding the sidewalks, Victoria had somehow managed to keep a watchful eye on him. Not that it was a terrible challenge –

Jozef's ability to blend into a crowd was as adept as a water buffalo hiding in a throng of field mice. A nervous, sweaty glance over his thick shoulder or a quick, unprovoked sprint across an intersection highlighted his awkward, fumbling attempt at subterfuge. He was obviously new to this sort of thing, and Victoria pitied the poor guy. Unfortunately, there was no way out for Jozef, and there had been nothing she could have done on that score. In about three hours, give or take, he would most likely be lying dead, bleeding into a storm drain in one of those dark little crevices of the city decent people hurry past without daring to glance inside, fearing what horrors might be lurking. Still, she hadn't abandoned all hope. Perhaps he would only endure a severe beating, living the rest of his days trying to forget this one macabre episode when his life abruptly detoured from its own pre-arranged course.

Jozef, unknown to himself, was being followed by two men, far better at remaining hidden than himself, though Victoria had also kept track of them since they left the theater. Her job was the package, a wadded-up bundle covered in burlap roughly the size of a golf ball. Jozef had foolishly arranged for the pick-up in the Hollywood Showcase theater. That claustrophobic environment with so few patrons (it being mid-day during the week) had not afforded him the luxury of opportunity. There had been no way for her to organize a plan where he snuck away without any guests watching the whole scene unfold. However, through extreme creativity and adaptability, Victoria found a way to deliver some simple instructions for him to get the package to her without those uninvited guests having any hint when it happened. She had quickly orchestrated an elaborate game of cat and mouse for Jozef and his followers, ultimately allowing him to drop the package in a specific waste basket without drawing any attention to the fact. Jozef's path was rife with backtracks and distractions, primarily aggravating and confusing the two brutes trailing him.

While she had managed to get the package without being noticed, there had been no way to arrange such an escape for Jozef. Jozef had worked out the pick-up with Hector, her moderately deranged boss, and she had not been consulted in the matter. Though certainly bleaker for him, Jozef's future would soon inconvenience Victoria as well. At some point during Jozef's inevitable fate, most likely sooner rather than later, Jozef's lips would betray his arrangement with Hector regarding the package and its ultimate destination of Malta. This would certainly lead the uninvited guests to Hector's boat waiting at the docks, with ample time to arrange a convenient search by

54

local police (or worse). With Hector's boat no longer a reliable option, her trip to the tiny island of Malta in the Mediterranean would require an alternative arrangement. She didn't dare seek assistance from another private owner as Athens was their town, not hers. She had no way of knowing who was a friend of whom.

Luck, or pure misfortune, depending on perspective, seemed to be with Victoria, however. The *Majestic Princess,* a passenger cruise ship, was scheduled to leave port in mere hours from the moment Jozef stepped outside that theater. One phone call to Hector and one to a friend who knew a couple of helpful cab drivers, and Victoria had secured a ticket for an extravagant seven-day voyage. On the third day, the *Majestic Princess* would dock at the popular tourist port of Valletta on Malta. Getting the package off the ship in Valetta would require some elaborate planning, but she would have a few days on board to sort it out. Naturally, Hector had been less than pleased about the likely loss of his yacht and even less pleased about having to splurge for a pleasure cruise to get Victoria out of Athens safely, but he had agreed to use that ridiculous theater as the pick-up location, so Victoria's pity was in short supply.

* * *

Tuesday, May 4, 1999 – Late Afternoon

A quick trip to a department store and a couple of "borrowed" pieces of luggage later, Victoria was standing at the rear of a long line of families, retirees, newlyweds, and more than a few desperate singles. Although fortunate to land a spot on a ship that would eventually get her to Malta, Victoria abhorred using a traditional cruise ship riddled with potential landmines. Naturally, people were the first of such problems – thousands of them, any one of whom she may have had dealings with in the past and who could blow any chance of her remaining discreetly hidden. Communication was another challenge. On a private yacht, Victoria's only contact would be from people she worked with, but on a cruise, one call from a customs official and the entire security detail of the ship would be looking for her and that little package. Perhaps the greatest pitfall of the *Majestic Princess*, however, was speed, or definitive lack thereof. Over three days, this ship would meander across the sea, lazily reaching a destination Hector's boat could have reached overnight. Those three days would give anyone trying to stop her plenty of time to organize a way to intercept her just as she came within sight of her drop-off.

55

*　　*　　*

Thursday, May 6, 1999 – Early Evening

The *Princess* was an easy place to remain hidden, but almost impossible to spot someone paying a little too much attention. The passengers were equally diverse – from families on vacation to singles hoping each night's encounter would surpass the night before to couples celebrating honeymoons or anniversaries. In fact, it was one of these anniversary couples to which Victoria had been attached for meals. Traveling alone, there had been no way to secure a private dinner table, but she had bluffed the staff into believing that her mild case of deipnophobia (rather rare fear of dinner conversations) would be best managed sitting at a smaller table.

The Tuckers, like Victoria, were American, but in an effort to avoid questions, Victoria opted for her Spanish accent, facing as a researcher from Madrid returning home on this luxurious cruise in honor of her recent graduation. Ronald and Susan, as the Tuckers insisted Victoria refer to them, were a fairly harmless, though chatty, middle-aged couple in their late fifties. Victoria needed only nod and smile once in a short while, and the Tuckers took over, filling their meals with tales of their children, their recent sightseeing excursions, or their robust collection of printed mugs they'd scrounged up from every corner of the earth.

Victoria had (other than these unavoidable meals) remained tucked away in her cabin, working through her departure tomorrow morning when they reached Valletta. Time was running out, and although she had avoided as much attention as possible, she had not yet worked out how to get the jewels through tomorrow's heightened security. Jozef's captors would certainly have notified the authorities by now, likely posing as innocent victims of stolen property. So, while she sat across from the Tuckers, attempting to tackle her problem from a fresh perspective, their droning conversation turned to their exciting plans for visiting Malta.

"We always enjoy sightseeing in Europe – so much history. You don't realize it until you leave the U.S. Some of our oldest sites date back only two to three hundred years. Over here, there are ruins and cities dating back thousands of years. From ancient architecture like cathedrals and castles to prehistoric relics like Stonehenge. . ." Susan continued her tirade for quite some time, but Victoria had grown accustomed to this sort of rambling from the Tuckers. Unfortunately for Victoria, Susan decided to engage Victoria in this discussion a little more personally. "What are your plans tomorrow, dear?

56

Are you going on any of those excursions when we hit Malta? The tour director made it sound like there are many choices available." With that, both Ronald and Susan glared up at her in unison.

"I do not think so – rather pricey, those excursions," Victoria mumbled absent-mindedly, hoping that would resolve the issue. "Probably just take some sun on the beach."

"Such a waste for a great destination like this!" Ronald exclaimed while hacking away at his sirloin. "This island has some wonderful history, Vic." Ronald had deemed it appropriate to call Victoria "Vic" during their first dinner, and the practice had continued. Rather than raise a fuss and draw undue attention, Victoria had simply grinned politely and let it pass. Ronald continued, "Why don't you join us on the 'Greater Malta II' excursion – our treat, of course? Consider it a graduation present." Both Tuckers beamed at Victoria with an eerie smile, awaiting her eager acceptance.

Things were falling apart. Tomorrow morning, she had to smuggle a package of assorted jewels past a small army and couldn't possibly do that while trailing the Tuckers. At best, she wouldn't succeed, and the jewels would have to be flushed. At worst, she'd get herself and dear Ronald and Susan killed in the process. So she had to respond quickly; pausing would only be seen as an attempt to avoid their generosity, which would only spawn attention and unease.

Victoria leaned in and whispered, "I am afraid I have not been completely honest. This cruise is not entirely a graduation gift. My research at the University, which I'm not supposed to share with the public," as she mentioned this last bit, she quickly glanced around the dining room as if to ensure no one was eavesdropping, "has a great deal to do with a potential cure for melanoma. Certain ethnicities, like those of people in tropical environments such as Malta, are immune to many forms of skin cancer. My team has a theory that their immunity has more genetic factors than merely skin pigmentation. I am contacting some researchers tomorrow and will probably be tied up most of the day." Ronald and Susan soaked this up like Dorothy peeking behind the curtain in the Emerald City. "My father has no idea I am working on this trip and would be furious if he found out. So, I have tried my best to make my journey seem a pure vacation, but I am very much engaged tomorrow. Truly, I am sorry to have misled you, but please, do not breathe a word about me or my research to anyone. It would mean a great

57

deal." At that, Victoria looked at the Tuckers pleadingly, first at Susan, then at Ronald.

"My dear, I wouldn't think of breathing a word to anyone," whispered Susan while Ronald, his mouth stuffed with a larger-than-necessary bite of his dinner roll, nodded agreeably. "It's such a shame you'll be busy *all* day, though. There are some truly amazing sights on this little island. The blue grotto is this terrific sea cave that you can rent a boat and explore – really spectacular."

"Plus, the Mosta Dome cathedral," blurted Ronald, having managed to wolf down that dinner roll. "One of the largest domes in all of Europe. The place got bombed by Germans during World War II, and three bombs smashed into the dome while people huddled inside having church. Two bombs bounced off, but one pierced the dome, crashing onto the cathedral floor – and, miracle of miracles, not a soul was killed, and the bomb never detonated! Incredible hand of God stuff there, right?"

Victoria nodded politely while managing a tight smile. *Where was God's incredible hand when other bombs were tearing through nearby hospitals and orphanages?* "It sounds extraordinary, and I will try to see some of it if I can break free. I truly appreciate your concern for me – both of you." She picked up her wine glass, downing the last few swallows. She had done her best to placate them, and Ronald and Susan, convinced they had tried their best, returned to their more typical, less intrusive conversation, and the dinner ended without further incident.

*   *   *

Thursday, May 6, 1999 – Evening

The real problem is security. They're going to be watching carefully for someone trying to get those jewels past their checkpoint. Few things in my favor – they shouldn't know if I'm a male or female – never personally talked to Jozef. Also, throngs of people will be herding through there simultaneously. Should mean security will be in a hurry, not able to peer through every pocket anyone might have. Negatives, of course, only one security point and no way to get off this ship beforehand. Victoria had gone over it for the past few days and had not yet come up with a solution – at least not one with enough chance of success to convince her it was worth a shot. Since the *Majestic Princess* had not been her original plan, she had no contacts in the crew, her preferred method to sneak something off of a ship like this. Trying to warm up to a crew member in such a short time would likely only present an opportunity to blow

58

her cover and endure a less-than-desirable sexual experience. Losing the jewels only to inherit gonorrhea didn't seem like a quality trade at this point in her career.

On the way back to her cabin from dinner, she approached the main elevator as two young girls rushed in front of her, apparently arguing about something they felt was quite important. Victoria, struggling to unravel her dilemma, couldn't help but overhear.

"*You* told me to take it, Millie."

"No – I told you to *hide* it. Now, he's going to find it on you, and we'll both catch it."

"Where'd you think I was going to *hide* it? Under the pillow? You knew we had to take it from the room. Now, you're acting like this was all my idea. You always do this, you . . ."

The shorter of the girls stopped, suddenly noticing Victoria. Both girls' faces turned two shades of red while they scrambled to think of what to say. Victoria couldn't help but grin a little at their cute awkwardness before chiming in, "Don't worry. I'm not going to tell '*him*' – whoever '*him*' is. Now," she continued as she knelt on one knee, "what are your names, might I ask?"

"I'm Emily," answered the taller of the two, doing her best not to look directly at Victoria, "but everyone calls me 'Millie.' This is Angel, my little sister." Angel didn't utter a sound but stared with large brown eyes.

"Well, Millie and Angel, can you tell *me* what it is you took? I might be able to help you find a really good hiding place."

"It's our dad's whiskey flask," Millie replied. Angel kicked Mille in the foot when she spoke up but remained silent. "He doesn't need it."

"I see." There was clearly a lot more to this tale than Victoria wanted to pry out of them. *The scariest ghost stories are only shared in whispers and only among friends.* "Have you girls seen the water outside?"

Caught off-guard, Millie hesitated, obviously noticing how silly the question seemed, "Of course we have. Not much else for kids to do out here but look at the water – ALL the time." Angel, though still quiet, loosened her glare just the tiniest bit.

"Ahh . . .," Victoria replied, "That's the problem. I didn't ask if you've 'looked' at the water. I asked if you've 'seen' the water."

Both girls' faces became muddled. "What's the difference between 'seeing' and 'looking'?" asked Angel timidly, finally breaking her silence.

"Well, I can't just tell you the difference, but I could show you. Would you follow me to the railing just over there?" Victoria pointed outside the glass doors beyond the elevator bay. She then got up without waiting for an answer, walked outside, and crossed her arms atop the ship's railings. Only a few moments passed in silence until she heard the pitter of tiny flip-flops shuffling behind her. Both girls walked to her right side and stared out at the water. Victoria smiled.

"You know you have five senses, right? You can hear, smell, touch, taste, and see. To really 'see' anything, you have to turn off the other four senses. Do either of you have anything in your mouth?" The girls shook their heads in unison. "Good, it should be easy not to worry about tasting anything. Touch won't be too hard, either. Step closer, where all you can see is the water outside, and put your arms down at your side. Be careful not to touch your clothes."

Both girls obeyed slowly, willing to follow along so far.

"The next two are a little bit trickier." Victoria continued hypnotically, "You have to concentrate. Let's start by closing our eyes. Now you can't see. I need you to turn everything off: no sounds other than my voice and no smells, even the salty air. Don't say anything or do anything – just concentrate on my voice. When I tell you to, I want you to open your eyes and really 'see' the water. I won't talk to you, but you must also turn off all the other sounds. Focus 100 percent of your attention on the water. Ok, give it a try – turn off your ears, nose, tongue, and fingers and open your eyes for one whole minute."

Victoria turned her head slightly to watch Angel and Emily gazing intently at the waves swallowing their vision. Neither girl did anything except focus on the Mediterranean Sea as it passed quietly by. The girls seemed not to notice a lady reading a magazine passing just behind them. After a minute, as promised, Victoria broke the moment by placing one hand on each girl's shoulder. "Well, what did you see? Anything?"

Emily turned to look at Victoria, "I saw the water turn from green to white as it climbed each wave, and I saw a fish swimming beside us, but if we're racing, we're winning because he doesn't swim as fast we do."

"Great. That's really good. Angel, how about you?"

"I saw the gold of the sun resting on the water way out there, but not so much on the water by our ship, and. . ." Angel hesitated, apparently not wanting to finish.

60

"Was there anything else, Angel?" prodded Victoria gently, kneeling beside them again.

"I, I think I saw tears . . . but there aren't any tears out there. Was I imagining them?"

"Maybe," Victoria replied, "but maybe it was more than imagination. Sometimes, when you're focusing very hard, you can see your memories. Maybe the water made you think of wet tears flowing down, and you saw those tears when you focused. Did you cry today, Angel?"

"No. Millie cried yesterday, though."

"Angel!" whispered Emily to her sister, alarmed at her opening her big yap. Angel stopped abruptly, looking up at her big sister. Emily's eyes met Angel's and started to swell.

Victoria just looked into Angel's face, not changing her expression or saying another word. At first, the silence echoed along the deck of the ship. Then, after a few moments, Angel turned back to Victoria, "Daddy hit Millie yesterday. He didn't mean to, though. He just does that sometimes when he drinks, and we were giggling out loud when we should have been sleeping, so we kinda deserved it this time. I guess." Angel turned, glaring back out at the horizon, slowly sinking into darkness over the glossy face of the sea. "Yesterday, it was just the one slap, but sometimes it's worse. One time, he even pushed me down the stairs. He was really sorry about that, though. Bought me a new bicycle when I got back home." Her voice seemed to trail off, but she continued gazing into the horizon as it darkened.

Victoria, stifling a powerful swell of hatred and long-forgotten tears from her past, maintained eyes of compassion and looked into those of Emily. No words were spoken, but the silence spoke tomes. After a few seconds, Victoria reached out, placing one hand on her shoulder and the other against Angel's back – still not making a sound. Angel's lips quivered as their eyes met. Victoria removed her hand from Angel's back and opened it in front of her. Angel slowly reached into her jacket pocket and pulled out a pewter flask, placing it into Victoria's palm. A lone tear trekked its way down Victoria's face as she looked at both girls. "It's not your fault, girls. I know you won't believe me, not for many years, but I promise you – it's not your fault. I can't stay here with you right now. You both need to be strong for each other. Remember, you *never, ever* deserve to be hit." Victoria removed her hand from Emily's shoulder and gave each girl a quick hug. At that, she turned away, forcing any

61

remaining tears into submission, knowing that Emily and Angel's fate, not entirely unlike her own, was beyond her control.

*   *   *

Friday, May 7, 1999 – Dawn

The morning sun crept above the horizon, marching forward, signaling a new day. The port city of Valetta still slumbered under its last few minutes of darkness. The *Majestic Princess* had pulled to port overnight while Victoria sat in her room, walking through the scenario in her head over and over again. For most of what remained of the morning, she had been leaning on the balcony watching as waves crashed upon the beach, her cabin, with all its lights off, at her back.

Today's chain of events would unfold, and she had concocted as good a plan as she was likely to come up with – a series of events, each triggering the next, like dominoes standing on end, waiting for just the tiniest nudge to begin the process. There was a chance, though not a strong one, that she could escape the *Princess* with the bundle of jewels and her identity unknown, but it required luck. A good smuggler takes care of contingencies as well as contingencies for those contingencies, leaving nothing to blind chance. Victoria was a good smuggler, far better than good, actually, but Hector had boxed her in on this job. *Hector knew better than to choose that theater.* She grit her teeth, reminding herself to revisit that issue the next time she is in Venice.

However, Victoria had no options left but to let her plan unfold and hope she prevailed without ditching the cargo or, even worse, getting herself caught. People in her line of work don't simply get a written warning in their file when they make a mistake. She grabbed the burlap-covered bundle from the safe and placed it into her bag. Along with her papers and cash, Victoria had carefully made the bag seem touristy, with sunblock (taking care to have used some previously to avoid the bottle seeming new), gum (a few pieces removed from the pack), couple of magazines (with some pages dog-eared), hairbrush (all blonde and red hairs removed), disposable underwater camera, a wadded-up towel on the bottom, and that pewter flask conveniently on top. She opened her cabin door, glancing back over her shoulder, ensuring everything looked like she intended to return. Satisfied, she took a deep breath and stepped into the hallway. The first domino had fallen. With luck, the remaining six would fall in their turn.

62

Victoria headed upstairs for the cattle call, otherwise known as the open breakfast buffet. The gangplank would soon open for visitors to disembark, but she didn't dare be the first person in line. In fact, she had to time her exit perfectly to ensure the security checkpoint would be at its most crowded, and the breakfast buffet was the perfect gauge for that sort of thing. Most families visit the breakfast line for half an hour before realizing their pants won't stretch any further. At that moment, overstuffed tourists would return to their cabins to gather their things for their exciting day in Malta. That process takes most folks ten to twenty minutes. So, once the breakfast line bulged at its seams, the security detail would get extremely busy in roughly half an hour. Victoria needed only to wait and watch the crowd from a back corner of the deck while keeping her head quietly buried in a magazine.

At first, it ran quite slowly; only a few cattle came to graze at once – early risers. Then, the mob began to form. The smell of eggs and bacon wafted through the air as the lines mounted. Soon, the crew struggled Zeeble2@2making omelets fast enough, and the poor guys filling the juice dispensers began breaking a sweat. Her time had come. She put away her magazine, ensured no one was giving her any unwanted attention, and made her way to the breakfast line herself. She ordered a ham and egg sandwich between two big pieces of toast and had it wrapped to go. She headed downstairs after a quick pit stop in the ladies' room. The second domino had just fallen.

Victoria made her way to the queue. She smiled as she turned the corner into the long hallway, seeing it packed with folks desperate to soak up all of Malta they had paid for. Similar to the technique she had shared with Emily and Angel, though far more evolved and practiced, she cycled her senses. She first closed her eyes and listened. Several hundred voices talking simultaneously faded to a dull drone she could easily tune out, not unlike static. However, other more distinct voices caught her attention. They were distant but grew louder as the mass crept forward. *Security patrols.* Two such voices sounded repetitive and uninspired. *Frontmen, used to asking the same questions to a thousand people each day.* Those frontmen weren't alone this morning. Other voices, too far away to make out the words, had joined them. She knew enough – they were barking orders. *Most likely directing staff to rifle through bags and other suspicious items. Something else in their voice, they were nervous – on edge. That was hopeful. With luck, those security chiefs at the gate aren't professionals or familiar with people like me. They didn't sound*

63

like this detail was just another routine search. Nervous people make mistakes. Allowing her ears to downshift into neutral, she focused on scent. Nothing there seemed distinctive – little more than the sweat of hundreds of people crowded together in an unforgiving hallway. Taste and touch were equally ungratifying.

Finally, Victoria opened her eyes. The scene couldn't easily have been more chaotic. Families struggled to corral small children whose patience had been spent; elderly folks leaned on and were supported by the few handrails; couples of all ages stood, straining forward, growing ever more frustrated as they discerned how much longer they'd be held up and compared this unforeseen delay against their other arrangements. Victoria focused specifically on the security checkpoint. She only saw six officers, which was encouraging – she had suspected as many as ten. Two of those six would not be an issue as they were clearly ship personnel. The others set upon them to resolve some "problem." Everyone had their bags and pockets checked after passing through a metal detector. *Metal detector is standard issue for airports and cruise liners like this. They can't identify jewels. Even better, the guy running the metal detector would not be an issue. Only leaves three guards as any real concern – the two checking bags and that big guy there.* One member of the security force, clearly the senior officer of the detail, kept moving from side to side, overseeing his operation. Victoria's eyes honed in on his hands. He was not holding a photo. *They don't know what I look like,* Victoria mused. Her luck had held up, and she only needed one final push. She couldn't resist a grin as the line moved forward a few feet as more and more folks poured into the hallway behind her – far quicker than security could process. In her head, she heard the crash of the third domino slamming down.

As she progressed, Victoria's eyes pulled back to the crowd ahead of her and noticed two little blonde heads about forty feet ahead sporting matching blue bows – Emily and Angel. Beside them stood a male, roughly six feet tall, with eyes masked behind thick sunglasses. *Hallway's not that bright, actually – probably nursing a hangover.* A wry grin crept across her face as she caught a glimmer of inspiration. She quickly spun around to face a group of three young men behind her, pretending they were above standing in line with common passengers. Their fairly dull discussion about last night's finer points ended abruptly when they noticed her turning. "Excuse me," Victoria began with her best thick Spanish accent, "would you be kind enough to hold my place for me? There is someone up there I need to speak with." Disarmed by

64

her directness, the boys only managed a nod before she dropped a "Gracias, gentlemen" and strode forward.

Kneeling beside them and setting her bag at their feet, she uttered, before either girl or their father could manage a word, "Hello girls, I see you are going on a trip? Going to the beach, maybe? I love the beach, but it can be scary when you're alone, no? Would you mind if I tagged along with your family, sir, just for a little while?" She asked, looking innocently into the mirrored sunglasses hiding his likely bloodshot eyes. Neither Emily nor Angel uttered a sound. When their father opened his lips to reject her rather awkward request, Victoria stood to face him more directly, with the blank stare of a naïve girl alone in a strange land. She held his gaze as he spat his rejection as lucidly as he could manage in his state. Victoria feigned disappointment and mild surprise as she knelt by her bag and pulled out her camera. "Would you mind taking a quick picture of me with your lovely companions?" He muttered a "fine" and took the camera. As Victoria attempted to stand, she "accidentally" dropped her bag, spilling its contents on the floor. As Emily and Angel's father sighed under his breath, he reluctantly knelt down to assist, setting his own beach bag down in the process. In the ensuing chaos, Victoria adeptly slipped the pewter flask inside his bag without him seeing. Once she was organized again with her camera back, she nodded a curt "thank you" and returned to her place in the queue. If her luck held, she had just positioned dominoes four and five to gracefully fall in unison. Domino six would be out of her hands.

The line continued plodding forward ever so slowly, much to the exasperation of the ship's passengers. Eventually, Emily, Angel, and their father approached the security checkpoint. Victoria stood back in her place, gazing at nothing in particular, watching the scene unfold from the corner of her eye. The father placed his bag on the conveyor and stood back while the girls went through the metal detector. As he passed through the detector, she noticed the man operating the scanner motion for the security chief. They had noticed the flask in his bag, right on cue. Once he had been patted down sufficiently, their father was motioned to the scanner. Victoria shuffled along, doing her best not to let on like she was giving this scene any attention. She knew that flask would ignite all sorts of suspicions. *No one takes alcohol off of a cruise ship – the over-priced booze on board can be purchased for less than half at the shops and bars in town.* Also, it was highly against policy to bring alcohol back onto a ship, especially in an open container like a flask.

One of the guards now held the flask and was pressing the matter with Emily & Angel's father. He was waving his hands in response, though unsure what to say. *It is his flask, after all.* Victoria had also been careful not to leave any fingerprints except for any he, Angel, or Emily might have placed. She had paid meticulous attention to where & how she had touched the flask all along. As Emily & Angel were escorted away while their father feverishly tried to explain the flask, things were coming to a head. Finally, the inevitable, the oversized head of security unscrewed the flask and examined its contents. The line continued forward. Victoria casually took her breakfast sandwich from her bag and took a small bite from one corner, keeping the wax paper wrapped around the sandwich's bottom half. She kept pace with the line but needed to start looking interested in the situation ahead. *Everyone else will be watching this right now.*

The man's voice was booming as he stared incredulously at the contents of his flask. *A scrap of burlap and three unpolished emeralds.* He was screaming that he knew nothing about those jewels – undoubtedly doing wonders for both his obvious hangover and credibility. He continued screaming as he was escorted into a holding room beyond the perimeter. *Depending on who gets called in to "ask the questions," he may leave this ship alive, but he wouldn't be leaving with those little girls. The sixth domino had landed right where it needed to – in the small of domino number seven's back.*

Soon after the father of Emily & Angel had been escorted out of sight, Victoria reached the security checkpoint herself. She placed her bag on the conveyor and started through security. She went to take another bite from the sandwich in her hand and chuckled that she was still holding it. She got an embarrassing grimace on her face and handed the sandwich to the gate guard to hold until she could finish security, flashing him a slightly flirty smile. She made her way past security and through the checkpoint. She grabbed her bag and thanked the guard as he returned her sandwich. She casually walked around the corner, behind security, and down the gangway.

Above her, gulls fluttered aimlessly across the mid-morning sky as the smell of the salt air filled her nostrils, and the echo of the final domino hitting the floor filled her mind. Victoria had arrived in Malta. She re-wrapped her sandwich, careful not to lose any of the forty-one remaining jewels safely tucked inside.

66

"Let us then suppose the mind to be, as we say, white paper void of all characters, without any ideas. How comes it to be furnished? Whence comes it by that vast store which the busy and boundless fancy of man has painted on it with an almost endless variety? Whence has it all the materials of reason and knowledge? To this I answer, in one word, from experience." – John Locke, An Essay Concerning Human Understanding

Friday, May 14, 1999 – Mid-Morning

Lukas sat upright in the wooden chair, its wafer-thin padding skinned in aged crimson velvet, trying his best to focus on the lecture, but it was proving especially difficult this morning. Although the lecture hall could hold several hundred people, the program's 25 recruits were packed, front and center, in tight formation. The chamber had but four tiny windows that couldn't open, and air conditioning was a luxury seldom afforded recruits. Sunlight bathing Vatican City streaked through the two eastern windows in the back, contrasting starkly against the dank chamber, before finally resting on the worn golden carpet. This month had not been easy, but he was closing in on the program's final week that would, he hoped, find him officially sworn in as one of the newest members of the Swiss Guard.

They had arrived by train from Zurich just over four weeks ago, and the training and orientation program ensued in earnest. Almost half of their time had been spent on the field and practice grounds – learning to function while wearing the brightly colored Renaissance style uniform, complete with shoulder coverings, breastplate, morion helmet with its bright ostrich feather on top, and expert training in the use of the medieval halberd used while on ceremonial duty. In addition to field training, the recruits endured a strenuous regimen of classroom instruction. Courses included language training in both English and Italian, Papal history and customs, and Vatican procedures. Today, they were chained to a guest lecturer, some Papal attaché, discussing the more technical aspects of Vatican security. This gentleman wore a gray suit, had thinning, tightly trimmed gray hair, and peered into the crowd through wire-rimmed glasses. He spoke in a uniform tone with minimal emotion or inflection.

He droned on, ". . . know your job is to protect the personal body of the Pope and the Papal palace. There are several other agencies working equally hard for the same end. Principal among these is the Corpo di Vigilanza, our local police force. They are all Italians and are tasked with arresting criminals, handling border control and traffic issues, and conducting criminal investigations. Should you catch someone violating Vatican law or practice, you turn them over to the Corp for questioning and . . ." The lecture continued for well over another hour, also covering the roles of the fire brigade and even the Italian Army. Lukas had taken decent notes but was ready for the droning to finally end. He preferred working in the May heat in full uniform, easily an extra sixty pounds, to these passive lectures.

The Swiss Guard's proud heritage has continued for almost 600 years in its current role as "Defenders of the Church's freedom." It was this tradition, and the quite healthy pension, that had attracted young Lukas to the Guard while attending the Swiss military academy. Lukas had been raised a proud Catholic and clung to a devout allegiance to the Pope and everything the Vatican represented. He had short brown hair, and his uniform was always clean and pressed. At 6'4", he was taller than most recruits and, though not quite 22 years old, he approached his training and education with an earnest sense of duty. That devotion and stern demeanor separated him from most other recruits. He rarely drank and didn't particularly enjoy the post-workout cigarette like the others.

The lecture drew to a close, but their guest speaker ended on a different note than he had expected. "Although there is a veritable patchwork quilt of agencies and units designed to help maintain security and safety here in Vatican City, we are all too few in number to cling to such a closed-minded idea that any function is 'not in our job description.' To that end, my good recruits, cooperation, and teamwork are vital. I believe, now, that Major Schmidt has prepared an exercise regarding such cooperation. Good day to all of you, and may God guide you during your post here." With that, he hurriedly folded his papers, stepped away from the podium, and turned and briskly shuffled away without so much as a nod to the Major.

The Major, seemingly unconcerned by his guest's abrupt departure, approached the podium. Major Schmidt was a portly man, unusual for a member of the Swiss Guard, but still in decent shape, donning the same standard non-ceremonial blue uniform as the recruits. He was a man of action and purpose, and all recruits knew that the less they said to the Major, the better off they were likely to be. He adjusted the microphone and began, his thick German dialect pouring from the podium.

"This morning, we wish to expose you to a short exercise involving interviewing a potential criminal suspect. While tasks such as this are typically and routinely performed by the Corp and not by the ranks of the Swiss Guard, the skills employed are worthwhile for any Guard serviceman to comprehend and take to heart. Pay close attention. In particular, watch the suspect's body language and how he responds in addition to what he says. Based on your impressions of this interview, you will be asked to identify if you think the suspect is guilty of auto theft and should be brought in for a full criminal interrogation or if they are likely innocent of the offense."

The video ran for about 15 minutes and was fairly benign: no dramatic outbursts or physical assaults — only a straightforward question-and-answer session regarding this suspect's actions and whereabouts. Only two people were in the session, the suspect and the interviewer, sitting on opposite sides of a small table. Something about the video seemed odd, but Lukas couldn't bring the problem into focus in his mind's eye. Once the video had been completed, the Major again addressed the recruits, "Please quickly write your assessment of the subject and identify your prediction regarding guilt or innocence and a short description of how you reached your conclusion." After a short pause, the Major spoke up again. "Now, I would like to engage you in some dialogue regarding what you have seen and your impressions. Gut, let us start with you there." The Major was pointing to a burly recruit on the back row.

Quickly, he responded, "I think he was guilty. He claimed innocence too frequently, and it seemed unnatural."

"So, you assume unnatural behavior is an indicator of dishonesty? What brings you to this conclusion?"

"Innocent people would not overreact to such a simple interview."

The Major responded, "This is important, recruits. It does no good focusing on your definition of 'normal.' Instead, focus on 'normal' behavior for your particular suspect. To establish 'normal' for your subject, try asking a series of non-threatening, day-to-day sort of questions and observe how he or she 'normally' answers. Remember, people being interviewed by someone threatening like a police officer or, even more extraordinary, a Papal Guard in full uniform, will naturally feel significant stress, even if completely innocent or being honest."

"Let us try again." The Major looked up and scoured the group, finally focusing on a wiry fellow from Interlaken. "You, Mr. Hausen. What was your impression?"

Mr. Hausen had been scribbling something furiously and put it away quickly before answering. "Well, I said he . . . he seemed guilty. It took him a long time to answer questions."

"Interesting. You assume truthful answers come more quickly?"

Mr. Hausen responded, "Yes, honest answers should not require such lengthy pauses."

"I will have to forgive your pause, then, after I first called on you? " The Major chuckled dryly before continuing, "However, your assumption is accurate. Several studies have shown that truthful answers do generally come quicker. Truthful answers, on average, are returned in roughly 0.5 seconds, versus deceitful answers, which usually take 1.5 seconds. However, it is important to remember not to make a hasty judgment based on only one observed trait. What if the suspect was distracted, like yourself, Mr. Hausen? Or perhaps the suspect is dim-witted, always pausing before answering. As we just mentioned, a brief round of non-accusatory questions at the outset can be of great value."

Without so much as a pause, Major Schmidt immediately landed on his third target, Mr. Guillone from Lucerne sitting eagerly in the front. "Guillone, sir, what did you make of our subject?" Lukas never cared much for Guillone as he came off as brazen, with an overabundance of false confidence. It hadn't helped his case with Lukas, either, that he came from a wealthy family and made sure the group never forgot.

Guillone spoke up quickly, obviously trying to avoid a long pause before his answer, "I, too, believe the subject to be guilty."

Major Schmidt frowned and snapped a harsh rebuke, "While I appreciate such a quick response, I do not, however, appreciate an incomplete one. Our objective is clearly to examine what led you to your conclusion. So, why only give me your conclusion, forcing me to press further?"

Guillone meekly replied, "I beg your pardon, Major. I drew my conclusion from the suspect's body language. He never looked the interviewer in the eyes. In my experience, eye contact is usually a good indicator of truthfulness."

The Major's countenance lightened a little. "Very good, Mr. Guillone. You have identified another indicator of interpreting a suspect's responses. Honest answers are usually given by looking directly at the questioner. There are some points of caution, however. Often, subjects attempting to deceive a questioner will glare into their eyes as an intentional effort to convince him of their honesty."

"Even more disturbing," he continued, "it is possible that an angry suspect would stare into the eyes of his questioner, not to convince them of their honesty, but as a challenge to determine superiority, not unlike a child's staring contest. This behavior is easily countered by allowing the suspect to 'win' their challenge. Their misbegotten sense of dominance may yield a false sense of pride, allowing the suspect to drop their guard. On the other hand, it could lead them into contradictions or getting sloppy with intricate details."

I would like to take one more before we break for mid-day. Let us see, yes, you there, Mr. Dietrich." The Major was pointing directly at Lukas.

Lukas smiled and politely replied, "Major, sir. I believe the suspect did not steal the car." About halfway through the Major's speech regarding eye contact, Lukas focused on what disturbed him about the video. "I came to this conclusion because I do not believe this video is an authentic interview by the Corp. The previous comments about long delays and poor eye contact are not isolated to the suspect. The interviewing officer, too, fails to make eye contact and waits unnaturally long before responding. It bothered me when I first saw the video, and though I did not know why at the time, I now recognize this behavior. This is how bad actors behave when they have a poor command of their script and do not know how to improvise. Their mind is busy thinking ahead to their next line instead of genuinely reacting to their co-star."

The Major couldn't help himself and let out an unprecedented belly full of hearty laughter before composing himself enough to respond, "Well, Mr. Dietrich, we have used this video for six years, and you are the first to discover it is not authentic. You have caught us on that one. Many interviews and interrogations are inconsistent and make poor teaching material, but the Corp put together this one for our use. Congratulations, Mr. Dietrich – exemplary attention to detail."

Major Schmidt turned his attention toward the rest of the group, who were still laughing at how Lukas had shredded the training video. "As you leave, you will notice thick binders containing important information regarding interviewing suspects. We will cover the material on your exit exam next

71

Tuesday morning. After lunch, Major Hoerring expects you in the yard in full uniform. Good day."

*   *   *

Friday, May 14, 1999 – Early Afternoon

Vatican City is an intricate place – full of buildings, plazas, gardens, and secrets. Some secrets were held by Church leaders, and some were known only to the Pope himself. The city itself even kept a few secrets of its own. One such secret was a tiny alcove nestled between the rear of the café and the side of the Vatican Archives. The alcove was secret not because no one knew of its existence but because few knew how special it truly was. The alcove formed a narrow walkway between the two buildings whose arrangement, coupled with the overhang from some apartments higher up, bestowed on this particular alcove a genuine blessing: it was only kissed by direct sunlight for ninety minutes just before dusk. The remainder of the time, it basked in shade. So, the sweltering heat baking the Vatican had little effect, leaving the tiny alcove significantly cooler than the rest of the city.

Lukas had stumbled upon this marvel early on in his training. During their first twelve-hour run at ceremonial duties, the overbearing heat and weight of the medieval armor had certainly taken its toll. Afterward, Lukas had strayed from the group just a bit and, through pure happenstance, strolled through the alcove on his way back to the barracks. The alcove had been remarkably cool, and Lukas had opted not to share this information with the others. Throughout the remaining four weeks of training, it had become his secret place to occasionally escape the midday heat. It had some greenery, but few flowers, an uncomfortable bench along one wall, and no real view whatsoever, but the temperature and solitude made the tiny alcove one of Lukas' favorite places amidst all the grandeur of Vatican City – a sanctuary from people, the sweltering heat, and the stress of the program.

After lunch, almost forty-five minutes before he was expected in the training grounds, Lukas had the perfect opportunity to visit the alcove and relax before donning his breastplate and helmet again for the exhausting ceremonial drills. He lazily strolled behind the café, but to his surprise, the alcove was not isolated as he had expected. Today, someone was already sitting on the tiny bench tucked against the archive wall. As suddenly as Lukas' surprise over his unwelcome companion began to wane, a new surprise struck him – this uninvited guest was none other than the guest lecturer from earlier.

He sat quietly sifting through papers pinched by a large binder clip along the top.

Lukas approached him for no reason other than to deny this guy the alcove's solitude – just as he had been denied. Lukas leaned against the café wall, doing his best not to glare at the man directly. Naturally, however, despite his best efforts, all he could do was look at the guy, and in fact, the longer he looked, the more he realized he wasn't that old nor frail, with an average, perhaps even slightly athletic build. He was certainly older than Lukas, but he probably wasn't likely yet fifty, sitting there quietly in his somewhat oversized gray suit, complete with jacket and tie and shiny black shoes placed firmly on the pavement. Wire-framed glasses rested atop his forehead as he pored through the material, maintaining complete focus – as though Lukas were not even there.

After a minute or so, he smiled thinly and looked up from his papers directly at Lukas. Lukas had just deemed this encounter a touch too creepy to maintain his façade when the man opened his mouth slightly, let out a shallow sigh, and began softly speaking. "Lukas Dietrich. Age 21 – from Zurich, Switzerland." His German accent was thick, but he spoke in English. Although his diction was excellent, his dialogue remained naturally fluid, with each syllable deliberately pronounced. He looked back at his papers while introducing Lukas as though Lukas needed to be introduced to himself. "Your primary and military school scores were outstanding, as are your evaluations here – so far. Outstanding perseverance in field training and endurance ratings are – how do they say 'off the chart'?"

Who was this guy, and how does he have so much information on me? Lukas felt more curious than threatened but offered no response.

The guest continued without pause, providing more intimate details, "You blend in with your squad but do not truly feel like you belong. You worry that you are not viewed as an equal but rather a nuisance to be simply tolerated. You eagerly await your swearing-in ceremony – less because of personal satisfaction but more so to finally feel like a necessary part of something – something far greater than yourself. Being a member of the Guard feels like your one shot to be actively involved in doing God's work. . ."

Lukas, finally reaching his threshold, interrupted, "Excuse me? Have I done something wrong or inappropriate? Who are you, and how did you get so much 'information' on me?" Lukas stepped forward, no longer leaning against the wall. This encounter had become too awkward. He turned as to leave before it became any more "personal."

Holding an apologetic hand forward, the gentleman flipped the pages back down and sat them on his lap. There was but a slight pause before his hushed tone resumed, though now far more conversational, "I apologize. Let us begin with a few basics, shall we? You are to be in the yard for training in forty-two minutes from now? So, allowing time for walking and dressing, you must depart here in eight minutes, more or less. Will you indulge me for these eight minutes, and then you will likely never see me again – unless of your own choosing?"

Lukas merely nodded in response. Quiet indulgence seemed far more appropriate and respectful than abandonment.

"Excellent. My name is Alfons, and I work for the Pope – not entirely unlike a member of the Guard, but then again, vastly different in so many ways. You are a good Catholic and have been your whole life, based on your file, at any rate." Alfons leaned forward as though this next bit was too secretive even for the isolated alcove. "I am presenting you a choice, which will require either an assertive step based almost entirely on faith or a dogged continuation on your current path toward a likely distinguished career in the Swiss Guard. But before that pivotal moment of decision falls upon you, let us use three of our remaining seven minutes to divulge a few scant morsels of information."

Still speaking softly and leaning forward, Alfons continued, "You may have heard my introduction this morning as a security attaché for the Pope. That is my official title, but it fails to adequately describe my job. While most details regarding my job must remain confidential – at least for now – allow me to provide the following: The Swiss Guard protects the physical *body* of the Pope, while I, and the few others like me, protect the *office* of the Pope. The Pope, in addition to being human, is also a religious and political office, requiring resources far beyond Cardinals and Bishops to ensure its success. I am a man of God, which, while providing comfort in knowing my efforts help perfect God's will on Earth, also gives me the clarity and sanctity to question, on rare occasions, my directives, even if from the Pope himself – in the extreme case. The Pope's humanity cannot be the rotten apple spoiling the whole barrel."

"I have been at my post for well over 25 years and have performed well, not well enough for me personally, but the Church seems to think highly

74

of my accomplishments. I work both inside and outside the Vatican as the need arises. God is my employer, Mr. Dietrich, and he is hiring today.

There is nothing in here about cinema, Mr. Dietrich. Do you like movies?"

Lukas was too awestruck at this ordeal to answer straight away. The whole thing was intriguing but suspiciously cloak and dagger. Before he knew it, however, he had already answered, "Yes, I do."

"Did you see that new film released recently, 'The Matrix'?"

"I did. Great film.

"Indeed. There is a moment in that film where a character is given a choice; he can either return to life as he knows it or remain with his new friends, exploring this new world of which he is only vaguely aware. Well, I'm not proposing a new world, Mr. Dietrich, only a new perspective on the one you already know, but the same fundamental choice is now at your doorstep."

This guy is certifiable, or worse. He is probably going to ask me for money now. Lukas mentally dismissed this conversation as one of those random, unfortunate wastes of time everyone endures at times – but he continued listening.

"I have used six of our total eight minutes already, so I will conclude. You will leave here in two minutes, go to the training grounds, and complete your fieldwork for the day. I would appreciate your candor regarding our meeting, but you would feel uncomfortable sharing something like this with your squad, at any rate. After your exercises tonight, you will do one of two things: either complete this day as you completed the day before it – diligently studying or desperately trying to have a few minutes alone to mull over your thoughts; or you will pack your belongings, hand in a completed form 874 as would anyone forfeiting their position in the Guard, and make your way back here. I will be here until 9:45 p.m. At 9:46 p.m., I will assume you have rejected this offer and will be completing your program. In that event, I wish you all the best and hope your time with the Guard is as fulfilling as possible."

Alfons gathered his papers and stood, casually lowering his glasses back over his eyes, as he rose. Looking Lukas in the eyes, he finished, "I would ask if you have questions, but I know you have many. I also know I cannot answer those questions, at least not currently. Our eight minutes are up, Mr. Dietrich. May God guide you, whichever path you tread."

With that, just as abruptly as he had departed the lecture hall earlier, he vanished, leaving Lukas alone, his head swimming with thoughts and

75

suspicions. He had a hundred questions and no one to ask save the birds resting on the eaves. Some of the more prominent: *Was this actually happening? Am I truly being offered a secret post as some security agent doing work a Guard could only dream of? Why did the job have to be draped in mystique? Were there not more appropriate ways to transfer employment inside the Vatican? What if this Alfons was merely a ruse designed to test my commitment? If I resign tonight, would tomorrow find me on the morning train back to Zurich?* Naturally, other, less profound questions were plaguing him as well: *Why can this guy not develop a more cordial way to exit a meeting? How did he have so much information about me – most of which would not be in a standard personnel file? How did he know I would come to this alcove at this exact time? What was someone like him doing watching "The Matrix" anyway?* Although questions flowed like waters released from a dam, answers were as scarce as water on the moon.

*   *   *

Friday, May 14, 1999 – Evening

Training had been typical and routine. He and his squad had performed perfectly despite the afternoon sun beaming down on them in full dress. Lukas' mind began wandering after a few hours. The responsibilities of a Swiss guard, before so crucial and significant, now seemed smaller, simpler. That talk with Alfons kept swirling in his mind. The harder he tried purging it, the more ferociously it returned to his forethought. *That crazy man is making me doubt myself, and I'm not sure about anything anymore,* he had thought. His life, which just this morning was so planned out and befitting someone of his aptitude, now seemed disorganized, confusing, and murky.

Naturally, Lukas had not given in to temptation and had performed perfectly during training despite his difficulty focusing. And now. Darkness had fallen over Vatican City, bringing with it a quiet calm. Oddly, not even crickets could be heard in the uneasy stillness of the barracks. Lukas sat on the edge of his bunk, unable to wrap his thoughts around this awkward and unexpected opportunity. If Alfons was to be believed, Lukas was being offered a chance – one single chance – to remove himself from the Swiss Guard program and join, well, something else. The nature of this alternative post was elusive – possibly the biggest hoax he had encountered. *The crazy guy mentioned 'The Matrix,' as though this was meant to be my own personal 'red pill – blue pill' moment. What nerve!* Despite his conscious mind's desire to forget Alfons' offer, he was still sitting in the dark, sultry quiet of the barracks –

76

a completed form 874 on his bunk and his bag unzipped, waiting to be filled with his few personal things.

Lukas wrestled desperately with his own personality. Although he had applied to the Swiss Guard for job security and its hefty pension, a much larger part of him had joined to belong. He had always felt like he simply watched life go by like a zoo's visitor watches chimpanzees through a glass veil. He had hoped that the Guard would open itself to him and he would fit in among its numbers, but he continued feeling separated. Lukas was certainly *with* them but would never manage to *be* one of them. Alfons' offer, though presented in the most bizarre fashion, made sense. God had ever been the one to understand him. The offer made life as part of the Swiss Guard seem smaller, though no less important, than he had viewed it – as though he were Gulliver suddenly awakening to discover how much larger the world was than the microcosm he had always occupied. His internal battle waged on as he sat beside his bed, unconsciously packing his bag. His conscious mind struggled between faith and reason, though his subconscious had already decided the issue. He looked down in awe as he packed the last bit of his things. *The 'red pill' it is, then.*

He made it to the alcove by 9:30 p.m., and Alfons, much to his relief, was sitting quietly on the bench. The stillness of the night enveloped him like a dense fog swallows a meadow's lone oak tree. He approached, not entirely sure what to expect. Alfons, without looking up, smiled. "You have made a brave choice, but that choice should be as fulfilling for you as it was for me. Before we continue, I need to ask one thing further – I need you to clear your mind of everything you thought you knew of life and the way things operate here. You will be re-taught many things from a different perspective, but that process will be far easier if you purge your thoughts of all those exercises, drills, and perfunctory speeches you have endured. While necessary for a Swiss Guard, they could be hazardous for one of us."

Lukas nodded silently in agreement. *What real choice do I have at this point?*

"Excellent. Come with me then."

Alfons rose and led Lukas to the School of Records building, where most of their lectures were held, but instead of the lecture center or testing room, they made a hard right, down a hallway Lukas had hardly noticed before. During their walk, Alfons freed up a few more details about this post. "Our job entails a blending of skills. We perform tasks akin to the KGB, MI5,

77

and FBI. Our duties often require investigation far outside of these walls and sometimes even within. We are a small and discreet element of the Vatican's security and state agenda. There are only eight agents at any given time, typically organized in pairs with a Senior Agent and a Junior Agent, although after several years together, that distinction diminishes." The dim hallway was terribly long with no decoration along the walls but covered with that same aged golden carpet with which he had become so familiar. At the end of the hallway, a door to the right led them downstairs. No one spoke as they descended.

The bottom of the stairs opened to a tiny office – empty and seemingly abandoned. A small desk sat in the corner, accompanied only by a rusted file cabinet. A small bulb dangled above the room, fighting the darkness, its pale light reflecting off the gray linoleum. The only thing visibly distinct about the room was a door at the rear with a magnetic card lock. Lukas couldn't help but notice, however, that unlike the rooms above used for lectures and exams, this room had far better air conditioning. Alfons removed a card from inside his jacket and unlocked the door, motioning for Lukas to follow him inside.

Once inside, Lukas found himself in a room far more advanced than he could have imagined for the Vatican. It was unoccupied, save for two women sitting at separate computer terminals. Neither of them bothered glancing up. A large monitor, at least ten feet across, mounted to the back wall displayed a map of the world and a series of apparently random colored dots. The other monitors and displays were of normal, working size, and there were several workstations around the room's perimeter. The only doors, other than the one they'd just come through, were two glass doors on a side wall, both of which were armed with the same magnetic locks. In the center of the room stood an impressive stack of data servers – all humming along smoothly.

Alfons strolled to the glass doors and paused, turning to Lukas. "This is our control room where missions are organized and evaluated." Alfons' German accent seemed ethereal against the data servers' humming in the background. "It is also a research lab. You will be assigned a workstation at some point, likely tomorrow, and gain access to all manner of public data in addition to the Vatican's extensive internal database. It covers centuries of human history, including much still unknown to the general public. The colored dots on the large monitor, you will notice there are seven of them, represent the Agents like ourselves. Your dot, the eighth, will be activated once you have completed some paperwork, again, most likely tomorrow. We are to be partners, Lukas. When a Senior Agent loses his partner, he is allowed to recruit his replacement. You will only be my third partner since I joined the department. My former partner is now a Senior Agent of his own. One of those two dots in Buenos Aires right now is his."

"And your first partner?" probed Lukas.

A short pause, the first he'd seen from Alfons, was followed by a solemn ". . . is no longer with us."

"Our department has existed for well over a century," mentioned Alfons, abruptly changing the subject. "Long enough to have evolved a method of handling most any issue that might arise. Have you heard about the assassination of Pope Pius XI in Venice in 1935?"

"No."

"Because it never happened. Our service got wind of the plot and prevented the assassin from getting within one hundred kilometers of the Pope. The bombing of the Peter and Mary Cathedral in Cologne, Germany? Did you hear of that?"

"No."

"Again, because it never occurred. Our agents, working with German authorities, apprehended the terrorist long before that bomb made it into the city. I could continue, but I think you are understanding my point about what we do here. Our victories are uncelebrated. Only our failures are known. The pay and other benefits are equally rewarding, but the real reward is being instrumental in keeping the Church safe. God has relied on humanity to achieve his ends here on earth for millennia, and we are a vital piece of that agenda."

Lukas' head was swimming, trying to soak in all of this. He was being recruited as a spy/detective/liaison for a secret department inside the Vatican. This was wilder than his dreams could have imagined but almost too wild for him to accept. *I have no training or exposure for this sort of thing. I can use a gun and stand at attention wearing heavy armor, but I would be lost sifting through computer databases or deciphering a coded message.*

"Enough of the esoteric – let us attend to more serious matters. In a perfect world, you would have a training period before tackling a live assignment. Our world is far from perfect, and the best training is experience. In two minutes, you and I are going to step through these doors," Alfons pointed to the ominous glass doors while finishing. "Tonight is one of our more shameful moments. Unfortunately, we are to interrogate one of our own, a Bishop from Dallas, Texas. You need not speak. In fact, I need you not to, but ask only that you do the following."

Alfons reached inside a nearby filing cabinet and pulled out a pair of black glasses and a rather worn folder crammed full of papers and assorted notes. "Please wear these and carry this file under your arm. Lukas followed instructions. "Gut. Lastly, You are to look at the suspect only and nothing else in the room. There is nothing worth seeing, at any rate. Do not sit, fidget, or lean against the wall. Just stand beside me casually, staring at the suspect. Got it? You can set your bag down here until we finish. Is your mind clear, Mr. Dietrich?"

Lukas nodded quickly. *Is this for real? We're going to interrogate a Bishop right now?* His heart started beating faster and faster as Alfons, without any further speeches, opened the door and entered the room.

The room was quite plain – simply a table with chairs on each side. A portly gentleman sat on the far side, nervously smoking a cigarette. Only an ashtray, a water pitcher, and a few plastic cups adorned the room. Alfons tightened the collar on his white shirt and adjusted his tie as he sat. Lukas, as instructed, remained standing and began staring at the Bishop.

"Bishop Hawkins, is it?" started Alfons plainly enough.

"Yes sir, and your name, if I might ask," quipped the Bishop, almost as a stimulus-response.

"My name is rather inconsequential, actually, but for courtesy's sake, let us agree that you can call me 'Albert.' Lukas was surprised hearing Alfons lie so freely, but he surmised there could be some good reasons for concealing your name from interrogation suspects. "Before I invite Mr. Rasmeld here to share his findings, I thought we might chat briefly. Do you know why you are being questioned?"

"They mentioned budget issues with my Diocese in Texas, but I'm not sure I am the proper. . ."

Alfons seemed uninterested in the full, "you should talk to my accountant" speech. "Excellent, then we might discuss a few things together," interrupted Alfons. "Is the name, 'Granzinas' meaning anything to you?"

"No. Never heard that name before. How does this relate to my budget?" The Bishop had become irritated, but his cigarette began trembling between his fingers.

He is hiding something and trying to work out how to keep it hidden.

80

Alfons continued, "Sehr gut. How hot are summers in Texas, if I might ask?"

"Huh? Well, they can be pretty scorching. Last summer, there were . . ."

Alfons, again interrupting the good Bishop, pressed, "So, I assume your parishes each have several air conditioning units?"

"Well, yes, of course."

"Who changes the filters on those units, Bishop Hawkins?"

"We have service technicians." Hawkins' answers had gotten terribly short again.

"Parish employees?"

"No, private contractors, I imagine."

"What was that word you just used, sir? 'Imagine'?"

Bishop Hawkins had barely finished smashing his cigarette butt into the ashtray before reaching in his coat pocket to retrieve another.

"Tell me, does each parish make its arrangements independently?"

No answer was given save a quick glance at Lukas, who had remained dutifully at his post, staring at the good Bishop.

Alfons refused to let this question go unanswered, but, surprisingly to Lukas, his tone transformed, becoming far more compassionate and less accusatory. Alfons removed his glasses, poured a cup of water, and handed it to the Bishop before leaning forward and softly saying, "You understand, of course, I know the answers already. I am not a police officer, Bishop Hawkins, and you are not under arrest. Our goal here is to foster understanding. You need to accept that your actions have been uncovered, and it is time for *your* confession. Things like this are far better handled privately than by outside forces. You understand, of course?"

A mere nod of the head without eye contact was the only response needed. Afterwards, Lukas watched in awe as Alfons worked the interrogation, manipulating the Bishop into admitting to hiring the Granzinas Company to maintain his buildings while they charged an outrageous premium. Granzinas would show up periodically, climb up on the roof, or examine the units outside, performing no real work. As bills were paid, Bishop Hawkins received half of their take. Over $160,000 had been siphoned from the Church.

Once the full confession had been recorded, Alfons signaled for Vatican officers to escort the Bishop out. He then motioned for Lukas to follow

81

him back into the control room. He inquired, "You have questions, I presume?"

Do I ever! "Why bring him in for questioning if you had the information already? Was it simply to humiliate him?"

"Hmm. . . I was expecting something closer to 'Why was an American Bishop in a Vatican basement, but alright. . . On the contrary, I had almost no information. I knew the name 'Granzinas' from some of his local parish priests and that his budget had significantly higher maintenance bills than most. That was all I knew for certain."

"Then, you *lied* to him?"

"Yes. Quite often. I used fake names; I led him to falsely believe you were a financial investigator with a full report prepared; and I am sure you could name several others."

"But. I thought we were doing God's will. Can God's will include deceit?"

"When Jesus entered the temple in Jerusalem, did he kindly ask the traders to vacate? No, he grabbed a whip and beat them until they removed themselves. God's will, at times, Mr. Dietrich, involves the use of tactics that might, on the surface, seem inconsistent with God's general character. Twice this evening, I have asked you to clear your mind of pre-existing notions. How many blissfully ignorant Egyptians suffered and died at the hand of God's plagues? Did David turn the other cheek when facing Goliath? How many innocent babes perished during the great flood? Our job also involves tactics that seem out of character with traditional Catholic principles."

Lukas considered Alfons' precept. *I guess it makes sense, in actuality. Why do the Swiss Guard carry a sidearm or even that ceremonial halberd? They are not completely for show.* He nodded in solemn, if reserved, agreement.

"This has been a long night for you, Mr. Dietrich. Grab your bag and . . ."

Before he could finish his thought, Alfons' cell phone rang from inside his jacket. Although Lukas could only hear Alfons' end of the conversation, the tone and look on Alfons' face betrayed that things were not going as planned.

Alfons finished his conversation and turned back to Lukas. I will show you to your room, now. You will want to sleep as quickly as you can – tomorrow, we have an early start. First thing in the morning, we make for Seville."

82

"It is not the critic who counts, not the man who points out how the strong man stumbled, or where the doer of deeds could have done better. The credit belongs to the man who is actually in the arena, whose face is marred by dust and sweat and blood, who strives valiantly, who errs and comes short again and again, who knows the great enthusiasms, the great devotions, and spends himself in a worthy cause, who at best knows achievement and who at the worst if he fails at least fails while daring greatly so that his place shall never be with those cold and timid souls who know neither victory nor defeat." – *Theodore Roosevelt*

Sunday, May 16, 1999 – Early Afternoon

Two large eagles soared majestically across the bright afternoon sky far above the hustle and bustle of everything seeming so important to those below, their dark feathers contrasting dramatically against the blue heavens. Sam gazed absently, through the taxi's open window, at the eagles dancing through the atmosphere. He was focused so intently, in fact, the driver twice had to alert him of their arrival at his hotel, La Gran Villa. His spirits sank as he turned from the pageantry in the skies above to the dilapidated ruin before him.

There was no longer anything "grand" about La Gran Villa. The aging pink exterior was flaking off in large chunks, revealing the faded stucco beneath, and several windows above had been boarded over. Graffiti adorned the entrance, but it was, quite naturally, in Spanish, so Sam remained blissfully ignorant of its profane message. Even the "G" in "Gran" had abandoned the hotel's front sign, likely judging the hotel as no longer worthy of its presence. *Great. This city is filled with such life and beauty – except for my little spot, naturally. Hope I don't forget to thank Gerard for pushing me into this ridiculous trip.* Sam gathered his things and paid the driver. He silently vowed to relocate soon, but today, he desperately needed rest.

Unfortunately, the decrepit hotel was the perfect companion for Sam's flight. That flight from Los Angeles to New York had been delayed when an angry flight attendant quit her job on the spot – storming off in a big huff. They had waited over two hours for a replacement. This delay made him miss his connection to Madrid – stranding him at JFK for five hours waiting on a later flight. The insult set delicately atop that injury was that since he was being accommodated on a different flight, the airline could not honor his first-class ticket – forcing him to make the long transatlantic voyage in coach. Sam grit his teeth when he discovered that losing his first-class seat also meant being assigned a middle seat between two decidedly inconvenient travel companions for an eight-hour flight. On the aisle sat a horribly oversized gentleman who had crammed part of his flab between his two armrests while the excess flopped over into Sam's space. The window seat contained a sweet older lady who, unfortunately, just loved talking. From the moment the plane pulled away until just before landing, Sam had been probed about every aspect of his small life.

Another crushing defeat occurred in Madrid where instead of Sam's brand new oversized suitcase, a large wad of clothes and personal items, along with a few shreds of the bag itself, tumbled down the baggage ramp enveloped in thick plastic and bright orange airport tape. Apparently, his luggage had gotten caught in a conveyor belt and was ripped asunder. The bulky wad represented everything the baggage handlers could salvage. Sam had mused; *good thing I brought that old letter and my research in the carry-on – whole trip would have been wasted. Heh! This whole trip was wasted before even getting started.* Things had actually started improving after Madrid. The train made the trip south to Seville quickly, and the taxi ride to the hotel had been quite pleasant. The Andalusian air was crisp and invigorating, and Sam had soaked in the beauty of Seville – at least, until arriving here.

Heaving a sigh of surrender, Sam toted his bundle of tape and plastic and two smaller bags inside La Gran Villa toward the front desk. After an awkward encounter getting his things through the hotel's heavy glass door, Sam noticed the interior was just equally as horrific as its exterior. Ancient and faded drapes hugged dingy windows along the atrium's rear, and dark red carpet, loose in several places, stretched across the floor. A large gash in the carpet near the elevator revealed the concrete below. Aside from himself, no one seemed to be about the place – no one sitting at a dinner table, no one at the bar, and no one at the front desk. La Gran Villa reeked of neglect and desolation.

Papers were scattered and strewn across the front desk, some serving as a coaster for a coffee mug that, from the dark, flat liquid inside, looked as if it had been sitting for some time. Sam rang the rusted bell on the counter reluctantly, dreading the demon it might conjure from the hotel's bowels. His fears proved well founded as an older, rather portly desk clerk, wearing the

84

faded name tag of "Javier" emerged, toting remnants of a tuna sandwich. He waddled over, sat his sandwich beside the coffee mug, and peered, uninspiringly, at Sam. Sam noticed that Javier's left eye was swollen and could only open a fraction as wide as his right. Sam was still distracted by that limp eyelid when Javier blurted out, "Ingles?"

Sam focused on Javier's right eye and responded, "Yes, please. No espanol."

"Thought so, from the look of you. You have reservation, yes?"

Sam wasn't sure exactly what he meant by "the look of you," especially since, at best, Javier only saw half as much as anyone else. *Yeah, good thing I have a reservation. Hate to be turned away from here.* Sam, checking his internal pessimism, politely responded, "Yes – Samuel Johnston."

Javier made a few rough keystrokes on an old computer and responded, "Yes, I have it here, room 28, for one week, yes?"

"That's right," answered Sam, hoping at least his room would be free of old coffee and half-eaten tuna sandwiches.

The rest of check-in went as check-ins typically go, except when Javier went to fetch the keys, those for room 28 were absent. Slightly embarrassed, he looked back, "Room 29 ok with you instead – larger bed and I will not charge extra?"

Larger bed sounds nice; hopefully it won't come with larger stains on the sheets. "Sure, I'll take it." With no delusions about summoning a bellhop, Sam lugged his things upstairs, as the elevator was out of order. His room, though not as dilapidated as he feared, was in rough condition. Coated with thick dust, it had likely been unoccupied for some time. The same stale drapes as below adorned his window, which overlooked the dismal brick of the neighboring building. The old, flat green carpet left footprint indentions as Sam walked across it, taking several seconds to bounce back into position.

Over twenty-four hours had elapsed since he pulled out of his driveway, and his body felt it. Though only late afternoon here, Sam needed to crash. He peeled back the bed's top quilt, and pleasantly, the sheets were clean. *One small step in the right direction – finally.* He crawled into bed, hoping to sleep through until morning. His meeting with Marta Vega was at 10:00 a.m. tomorrow, and he wanted to be well rested. He was fairly sure this meeting would only upset an old woman by surfacing painful memories, but he would at least be able to say he followed his own yellow brick road all the way to Oz, even if there was no wizard behind the curtain when he got there.

85

Though he slept soundly for a few hours, he awoke at one point in the night and found no rest thereafter. He begrudgingly arose at first light, got ready, and headed downstairs to find somewhere, preferably outside of the hotel, to celebrate this first morning in Spain with a nice breakfast. He found a small street-side café where he enjoyed a light, though delicious, breakfast with the sweetest, freshest orange juice he had ever tasted. Afterwards, with a full belly and a few granules of fresh hope, he set out on foot for Marta's apartment. *If I read my maps right, Marta is only ten blocks or so from here, and the walk would be refreshing.*

*   *   *

Thursday, October 15, 1959 – Late Evening

Ten blocks made an arduous trek through the cascade unleashed by the foreboding sky above, but that bus stop was the closest to Manuel's hotel, La Gran Villa. Each bootstep splashed into pooling water. While October was not traditionally known for such chaotic downpours, occasionally the rains came early. He gripped his umbrella firmly, struggling against a spontaneous gust accompanying the downpour as the sky lit up from a majestic lightning flash. With the umbrella in one hand and luggage in the other, he wrestled to occasionally wipe moisture from his glasses or swipe his drenched black bangs from his eyes. The hotel was now only eight blocks away, but they would be a challenging eight blocks.

Manuel had secured a room at the exotic hotel in the Santa Cruz section of Seville, where his family had lived before the war. The hotel was also small enough that they might not look for him there. While he still wasn't exactly sure who "they" were, someone was hunting him. No one in Spain, Italy, or anywhere else would care about the documents tucked in his luggage. Well, no one save the Vatican, but that made no sense. After all, no one in Vatican City believed him when he desperately pleaded about the documents' importance. *Why fight so hard to recover what they held so trivial?*

Turning the corner four blocks from the hotel, Manuel tried in vain to convince himself that it was simple paranoia – mind games from an overactive imagination. That mysterious brown sedan had haunted his thoughts, though, ever since boarding that first train in Rome. It was some distance from the train platform – shrouded figures inside with occasional puffs of cigarette smoke billowing from its windows. Naturally, he had shrugged it off. No one cares about a brown sedan with figures inside the first time they see one. He had been careful – no one would miss him for twelve hours at the earliest.

Regardless, when he switched trains in Monaco, he stepped onto the gravel near the platform, and there, just beyond the station's black fence, sat another brown sedan – complete with shrouded figures inside. *Surely, that was a different sedan,* he mused. No one thinks much about two brown sedans with figures inside. After all, people sit in brown sedans at train stations every day waiting to pick up passengers. In Madrid, however, as he hiked to the bus station, his fears materialized in earnest. There had been no brown sedans skulking outside the train depot, and he had convinced himself those earlier sightings were simple coincidence. But, as he neared the bus station and an all-too-familiar sedan drove up and parked nearby, his fears collapsed upon him. *Someone, somehow, is following me. To make matters worse, whoever it is knows my route and likely my destination.* No one wants to see *three* brown sedans, all with figures inside staring at them. That sort of thing would terrify anyone.

Manuel slogged down the last block, checking the side streets; however, he had seen no brown sedans since leaving Madrid. *Hopefully,* he thought, *my laying low for a day in Cordoba threw them off the scent.* The streets were clear, not only of brown sedans, but of all movement. No one wanted to be outside in this torrent. Manuel hadn't relished the storm either and was delighted upon finally reaching La Gran Villa. It was a vibrant, modern hotel, bright pink in color, with an elaborate street sign showcasing its name. A cheerful, though chubby, doorman met him, taking his bag and umbrella and helping him inside out of the deluge. The hotel's interior was alive, filled with people huddled around tables in the atrium – either eating dinner or just celebrating the roof over their heads on a stormy night like this. Bright golden drapes covered the atrium's large rear windows, projecting the subtle opulence of the Villa. Stained glass atop the atrium lit up sporadically as colossal lightning flashes ignited the sky, casting a brilliant kaleidoscope across the crimson carpet below.

Manuel shook off his boots and made his way to the front desk. A cheerful desk clerk met him with a large smile and cheerfully walked him through the check-in process. Once finished, he reached under the desk and pulled out a metal room key. "Here you are, Mr. Vega, sir, room 28. Javier!" Young Javier had been focusing on some young ladies near the bar. He grabbed Manuel's few things, and the two of them rode the elevator to the second floor.

"Here you are, Mr. Vega," Javier uttered, setting the bag down and handing Manuel the key.

After forking over Javier's tip, Manuel removed his soaked boots and overcoat, drew the curtains shut, and plopped on the edge of the bed. His exhaustion stemmed less from the long walk toting his luggage through wind and rain than from maintaining his constant vigil. That third brown sedan had petrified him, and from that moment, he had been maniacally scanning for anyone paying him any undue attention. Finally alone in his hotel room, with the door locked, he relaxed his senses and released his mind from the persistent fretting he had inflicted on it for almost two solid days.

Manuel bent down and opened his suitcase. Luckily, its contents were still dry. Aside from a few scraps of clothing and his translations, inside rested his cobbled document collection – some typed, some handwritten; some on paper, some on scraps of parchment; some only sixteen years old, while others were penned over a millennia ago. Despite this diversity, they all shared vital characteristics: the official seal of the Vatican had been impressed into their surface; they were all penned by Catholic Priests or Bishops; and each one described first-hand accounts of the most terrifying subject Manuel had ever encountered. He removed a few essentials and re-packed, assured that everything had survived the arduous journey. He sat the bag aside and laid back, hoping to get some desperately needed rest.

Rest, however, was in short supply. Despite repeated attempts, he kept dwelling on that abominable sedan. *Who had been inside it? If they had been dedicated enough to track me all the way from Rome to Madrid, surely they would not give up the chase so easily? They must know I would eventually come to Seville. If they are here in Seville, I have to keep running.* These thoughts, his only companions, made terrible bedfellows. He had only managed a shallow, superficial sleep when sun's first light crept through his tiny window.

Manuel sighed as he got up and started getting dressed. He even tempted fate and decided to have breakfast downstairs. Though breakfast, a simple cup of tea and two slices of dry toast, flowed uneventfully, Manuel's paranoia returned, swelling with each sip. He tried hiding behind his newspaper but felt as exposed as he did trudging through the monsoon last night. *I can't keep this up.*

After breakfast, he scouted outside the hotel for brown sedans or, indeed, anything looking suspicious. Unfortunately, much to his discomfort, the more he searched, the more *everything* looked suspicious. Last night's rain had delivered a heavy morning fog shrouding everything further than a block away, but everything he could see was overrun with eyes – all glaring at him. A newspaper vendor gazed far too long when he declined a purchase. *Why stare me down that way?* Three street urchins met his gaze as he turned a corner but did not approach to beg. *Odd. These kids hit up everyone – why leave me alone? I should be appreciative, but it feels wrong.* An older lady crossing the street at the same time stepped aside, giving him an overly wide berth. *Did she think I might attack her?* Either everyone was paranoid, or he was. Manuel knew it was him. As mid-day approached, the fog finally cleared. He had spent the morning dodging every shadow his mind concocted. No one had been spying on him from a rooftop; he had not been attacked from a dark corner; and, most importantly, there had been no brown sedans. *Is this what a delusion of persecution feels like? Enough of this – I came to Seville for a reason, and it is high time I got started.*

He headed south – home to his twin sister, Marta. Marta had returned to Seville when she was fifteen to care for their ailing mother, while Manuel had stayed with his aunt and uncle, going on to finish his schooling in England. He missed his sister, and while they wrote regularly (at least they had before he started working for the Vatican), he hadn't seen her for several years now. The sidewalks had gotten more crowded as the day progressed, forcing him to relinquish his paranoia for the time being. *Way too many people about to be suspicious of everyone.*

He crested a small hill and saw the old family home at the end of the street. Marta had sold it after their mom's funeral, using her share of the money to buy an apartment several blocks away. Manuel paused when he reached the place, lamenting its deterioration. He was walking the perimeter but stopped dead in his tracks when he saw them. Resisting the tears of long-forgotten memories, he was shocked they were still here after all this time.

The night his father died, fighting had broken out in their neighborhood. Two bullets pierced their wall during the skirmish. Though only six at the time, the memory of finding those bullet holes rushed back from the dark recesses of his thoughts –the tiny crevices where unwelcome memories get shoved. Neither young Manuel nor Marta shed a single tear. They merely sat in utter silence, glaring into the horizon watching the sun dissolve. Children, too, in their own way, come to know war.

89

Shoving the past's dark memories back into place in his mind, he trudged onward, even managing to forge the beginnings of a grin filled with excitement. However, as he turned onto her street, all excitement instantly splintered into tiny shards as he spotted, parked in front of Marta's building, a familiar brown sedan. His skin lost color, and sweat suddenly soaked his face and arms. Heart beats came harder and faster as he desperately struggled to do something – anything, but he couldn't will himself to move. He gaped helplessly at the sedan as the passenger door opened, and a gentleman in a gray overcoat, likely far more man than gentle, stepped out and faced him directly. The man did not move to give chase but simply stood motionless, meeting Manuel's stare.

While they stared for no more than thirty seconds, it was an eternity for Manuel. On the thirty-first second, however, he finally willed his feet loose, turned, and did the only thing he knew to do – run. Block by block, without regard for traffic, Manuel sprinted to the fullest extent of his will and physical being, never looking back. He was in mortal danger. *They found me!* He pressed on, full throttle, until finally collapsing from exhaustion beside the Guadalquivir River near Seville's bull fighting arena. He hit the ground hard, crushing his nose into the paved walk. His nose pouring blood down his face, he lay sprawled on the ground – too exhausted to continue. Resigning himself to his fate, he turned to confront his pursuer. No one was there: no sedan – no man in a gray coat. In fact, the only people about were a tourist couple, gaping in awe at this bizarre Spaniard who had just bolted to the river's edge and collapsed violently in front of them.

The woman pulled a kerchief from her handbag and handed it to Manuel as her husband helped him up. Still breathing uncontrollably hard and his heart pounding, he managed a thankful nod and limped to the river's edge. The couple quickly moved on to some, hopefully more tranquil, site while he leaned against the railing, gazing into the water. Gulls atop the nearby Triana Bridge squatted, gazing at Manuel, with no apparent concern for gray overcoats, brown sedans, or bleeding and exhausted Spaniards.

Marta! I only wanted to visit you for a moment, but these harpies refuse, hounding my every step. They must know I have these documents, but why go to such lengths for some field notes, unless. . . those bastards! Cardinal Hickman and the others – they did believe me! They understand the importance of these documents, but yet they want the truth hidden? Why deny the world such precious knowledge when it needs it the most? One thing is

90

perfectly clear. They just made their undeniable statement. If I publish the documents; if I share what I know, Marta suffers the aftershock. They parked at her house for one reason: to remind me that my actions carry dire consequences. Marta, my sweet sister, why have I gotten you wrapped in this web?

The bleeding had only just begun to slow as his eyes swelled. This time, he couldn't resist the falling tears. *How can something so noble wreak so much damage?* The river continued flowing southward as he pounded his fist against the railing in frustration. If he revealed his findings, the world would see, for the first time in nearly two thousand years, that there truly are wondrous powers greater than ourselves out there. If he returned the documents, he would save his sister any undue suffering. *How can I choose between my own sister and something so globally inspiring? How can I stand idly by, but a stone's throw from a crystal spring, watching a parched world die of thirst?* As he faced upstream, a soft voice from long ago whispered two simple words into his mind. Those words, at first echoing flatly against his wall of solemn determination, slowly coalesced into a potential solution to both spare Marta and rescue the world from fear and darkness. Manuel whispered those words to himself, managing a soft grin as he gazed into the Guadalquivir, "be courageous."

*   *   *

Thursday, May 20, 1999 – Mid-Day

Sam's mind kept returning to Marta's letter from her brother as the tour bus swayed and rattled its way across ancient streets. While he tried enjoying the tour, he was still fixated on this mysterious Manuel character and his discovery. Sam had strained to mask his disappointment upon discovering that Marta's letter contained no secrets, no clues – no leads – it had been, instead, a sweet letter wishing his sister well and, without revealing anything, defending himself. It mentioned problems with Vatican leadership but offered no hints about his discovery.

Still, there was something odd about her letter. Its last paragraph had a distinct, separate tone – as though not meant for Marta at all, but someone else entirely. Sam knew this was insane. Since finding that first letter under that desk, almost eight months had passed. He had, for almost the whole of those eight months, been fixated upon this bizarre mystery. *Who was Manuel Vega, and where was he now? What did he find that he supposed was so revolutionary?* The answers lay hidden forty years in the past and were still

91

hidden, despite Sam's efforts, including flying halfway around the world chasing them.

He had tried enjoying what remained of his vacation, visiting many of Seville's biggest tourist attractions and sights – the Moorish palace Alcazar; the Plaza De Espana with its fantastic fountains and architecture; and the Torre de Oro tower overlooking the river, to name a few. Seville's beauty and quiet, comfortable embrace had, over these past few days, transformed his trip into more of a deserved retreat than a pathetic fool's errand. Sam had felt alive and had even made a concerted effort to avoid ordering light beer.

The bus had just passed Plaza del Toro, Seville's famous bullfighting arena, en route to cross the Triana Bridge to visit the Triana district across the river, along with its myriad shops, clubs, and cafes. Sam had been looking forward to visiting the Triana district even before landing. Though none of it would darken his doorway, he was especially excited to check out Triana's great antique shops. This was his vacation and Triana would be a great place to unwind and have a few drinks – maybe even to forget, at least for a brief moment, this ridiculous adventure.

As the bus turned onto the bridge, Sam caught a brief glimpse of the street's name embedded into the corner building: "Cataliticos Reyes." While confident "Cataliticos" meant "Catholic," he was unsure about "Reyes." So, he flipped through the pocket dictionary every tourist packs, discovering that "Reyes" meant "Kings." Sam's arms suddenly sprouted goose bumps. He had heard the phrase "Catholic Kings" before. *But no – that wouldn't make sense. How could Manuel have written . . . unless . . .* Triana would have to wait.

The bus reached Triana and unloaded its tourists – a miniature throng of thirsty, eager souls looking to experience this nook of the city. Sam departed with everyone else but frantically hailed the first cab he found back across the river to Marta's building. Marta lived on the third floor of an older four-story condo. The buildings on either side of hers were only single storied, allowing upper floor residents, such as Marta, a spectacular view.

Sam climbed the few steps to the landing and rang the buzzer. A familiar meek voice eventually came through the intercom, "Bueno?"

"Ms. Vega? This is Sam again from California. I hate to keep bothering you, but I was hoping to see that letter of yours again?"

"Well, of course, son," came the reply. "I am not sure what you hope to find, but you can certainly have another look if you like." The front door

92

made a tired mechanical buzz as Sam pulled it open and made his way up the stairs to the third floor. The elevator was, quite naturally, out of order.

He finally made it to Marta's floor and limped to her front door, pausing to catch his breath. While excitedly bounding up stairs, he had tripped, landing on his right knee. It was still throbbing when he arrived, and he was breathing fairly hard. He didn't want to scare the poor woman. Marta was in her upper sixties – relatively short, with a mixture of silver and jet-black hair hanging just below her shoulders.

Sam, finally breathing normally, rapped at the door – just loudly enough to be heard. Eventually, the door opened, and Marta invited Sam inside. The apartment was immaculate, and, other than some cups on the counter, it seemed as though no one lived there. Marta, as she had explained, prided herself on keeping things neat and clean. "My son, it is good to see you again. If you would care to sit, I will get my brother's letter." Marta's voice in person was different than over the phone or through the intercom. Though kind, it was raspy, likely from decades of unfiltered cigarettes. Sam settled into the same worn spot on the sofa he had sat in just days ago.

Marta soon returned toting a small box. She placed it on the coffee table and sat beside Sam. Resting inside was that letter she and Sam had read and re-read earlier. Sam politely took it and, without removing the letter, examined the envelope itself. It bore a Spanish postmark, not an Italian one.

"Ms. Vega, have you noticed this? This was sent from somewhere in Spain, or am I reading this wrong?"

Her nose crinkled, and her forehead developed a few more creases as she looked it over. Her eyes began swelling with new tears as she confessed, "I . . . I never bothered looking at the envelope before. I guess I always assumed it was posted in Italy. You are right, but I am not sure how this can be. The letter was obviously written while my dear brother was working inside the Vatican. If he were already in Spain, why not come to me directly? Why travel the whole distance here simply to mail a letter?"

"Maybe he meant to visit, but things didn't work out. Maybe whatever caused his disappearance also kept him away from you?" Sam gently took the envelope from her hand and re-read Manuel's letter:

October 15, 1959
My Dearest Marta,

93

I am hopeful this letter reaches you in Sevilla and finds you well. I know it has been some time since I last wrote, and you surely anticipate something far more substantial than this tiny note, so I must apologize for my brevity. I have not much time for anything else right now. I am currently caught up in something, but if I can somehow see my way clear, I plan on having much more time to visit with you in Sevilla.

They are certainly coming for me, sweet sister, and I have little hope of evading them as they are proving to be extremely clever and resourceful, these Catholic Kings. I have uncovered something truly wonderful, but I dare not detail my discovery now for fear of putting you in danger as well. I am en route to the train station, but desperately needed to drop you this quick note before departing.

If I am unsuccessful, and they find me with my discovery in tow, they will surely destroy it. I yearn to share my experience and my discovery (both halves – the majestic and the horrific) with the world. It will shed wondrous light on the darkest of eternal human dilemmas, putting to rest so many trials, frustrations, and struggles. Despite my best efforts, having begged and pleaded – kissing the feet of twenty Cardinals – my pleas continue falling upon deaf ears. They have no right to keep it hidden from the world, Marta, and I will thwart their suppression!

In the garden, God punished the serpent by taking its legs and forcing it to slither on its belly for all eternity. Since then, we have always learned to treat evil with a distanced hatred – knowing that evil cannot help itself but act according to its true nature. Regardless of my fate, I must ask this one thing until we next meet: let us begin to forgive those who have injured us. It is perhaps the only true path to peace.

Your brother,

Manuel

As Sam finished, Marta lightly touched his shoulder and asked, "What made you think of that postmark? What is going on?"

94

Sam stared at her blankly. While he had heard her, his mind wouldn't stop racing. *Catholic Kings? Why call them Catholic Kings? There must be a connection here. And he sent that letter from right here in Spain. There's something about that street I saw, but what?*

"Sam?" Marta inquired again, not getting a response the first time.

He got the message and told her about the street named "Catholic Kings" – and how excited he was.

Sam caught a quick glimmer in Marta's eyes not there before. She began rifling through that small box, removing its odds and ends. "This is where I keep a handful of my brother's childhood things that were still in the old house when I sold it." As she was speaking, she continued rummaging until she pulled out a small, worn book. Though the cover was in Spanish, it appeared to be a collection of Aesop's Fables. Marta quickly thumbed through the worn pages until landing upon a particular tale. "Have you heard the fable about the farmer and the snake?" she asked as she turned to Sam, showing him the open page. "It was one of our favorites."

When Sam shook his head in the negative, Marta smiled a wry smile and began reading, in English for Sam's benefit. The story was about a farmer who found a snake frozen almost to death. Out of compassion, he placed it against his chest to warm it up, saving its life. Once properly thawed, the snake promptly turned and bit the farmer on his chest, inflicting a deadly wound. The moral of the story had to do with not expecting someone to ever act contrary to their true nature.

Sam recognized that message. He picked up Manuel's letter, pointing to that last paragraph. "This line about evil not being able to help itself due to its nature – he was somehow referring to this fable?"

"Perhaps, though I cannot imagine why. What could one have to do with the other? This is all confusing and not like Manny at all."

"Ms. Vega, I think he was writing in code, screening his message from anyone but you." After the briefest moment of silence, Sam's eyes widened, and he turned excitedly to Marta. "He hid his discovery! He hid it, and he hid it right here in Seville, somewhere near that Catholic Kings street! He must have been telling you how to find it if anything happened."

Marta's eyes, at first excited with this revelation, filled with hard tears at the painful reminder. She turned and wept, despite her best efforts to hold back the emotion. Sam's enthusiastic spark was drowned by her sobs, and he didn't quite know how to react, save to sit solemnly beside her. Marta's tears

95

slowed eventually, and she started timidly, "It is hard for me, you understand. This is but an adventure for you – uncovering clues and hints. I, too, want to know what my brother found, though not for the adventure or excitement. It is my brother's legacy – the reason he disappeared. I am torn apart between the sorrow of losing my brother and the joyful hope of finally fulfilling that legacy. That is why I cry, my son."

"I understand – though I can't imagine how difficult this all must be. I should probably leave."

Marta looked into Sam's face and must have noticed the morose veil descending across those brown eyes of his, smothering the sheer excitement from only moments ago. "No, son. Stay. We may yet discover something together."

Sam made an internal vow to choose his words more carefully as his mind gradually returned to the letter. "Why do you think he referenced snakes so often, Ms. Vega? Was your brother fond of them? He referenced this fable and mentioned God's punishment of the serpent."

"I do not remember him being fond of snakes. He loved spiders for a time for whatever reason but never snakes. Wait – our mother!" Sam's quizzical gaze was all he could manage. "She always referred to the river as a big blue snake slithering through the city." Marta walked over to the open window and gazed west. The Guadalquivir River, basking in bright afternoon sunlight, appeared far more golden than blue. "She would often say it was a monstrous snake winding through Andalusia on its way to the ocean for a drink. I think she did it to scare us from playing near there."

Sam limped toward the window and looked where Marta's eyes were pointed. "Well, that street, 'Catoliticos Reyes,' it runs right to the river. I mean, it ends at the Triana Bridge, right?"

"Yes, it does, though I am still not, how do you say, 'sold?' If Manuel hid something near that bridge, it certainly would have been discovered by now. Seville has changed much since 1959, Sam – so much construction. So many new businesses have come, new bridges – so much development. There is nowhere near that bridge where something could have remained hidden for forty years." Her voice more somber than before; she turned to face Sam, "If he hid something, it is there no longer."

Sam, still staring at the river, refused to surrender, "Didn't his letter say God punished the serpent, making it slither on its belly? If the Guadalquivir is the snake, its belly could mean the river's bottom. There's been no construction down there has there?" As Marta shook her head, Sam's heart leapt at what this could mean. *That discovery might still be down there!* However, as quickly as his excitement climbed, it plummeted again to the depths, and he said nothing further.

Minutes passed in awkward silence until Marta finally grasped what had happened. "The river bottom is a big place, no? Where would you even begin looking?"

Sam, growing more despondent, picked up Manuel's letter, gazing through it more than actually reading. As he neared the point of surrender, his eyes caught something his mind had blurred through earlier. He read aloud, ". . . kissing the feet of twenty Cardinals. . ." *It couldn't be that direct, could it?* Sam grabbed a nearby pen and paper and began doodling. He started talking aloud, partially to Marta and partially to himself, as he drew, "rivers have a current, unlike lakes . . . to bury something in a river, you need to account for that current, or you'd never recover what you buried. . . even swimming straight down from the surface you would deviate several feet before touching bottom." He finished his drawing and it looked rather like a clock's pendulum. Marta looked it over as Sam explained, "twenty feet – Manuel was describing the digging point," Sam was pointing to pendulum's bottom, "as being twenty feet away from his anchor point here," as he slid his finger to the top of the pendulum.

Marta's face betrayed her confusion. "I follow you so far, but where do you fix the top of the pendulum – where is this 'anchor point,' as you called it?"

Sam understood what she was getting at. Like any good treasure map, unless you knew where to start, it was worthless. He didn't have an answer for her. As Sam returned to the window and glared at the golden sunset reflecting off the river's surface, his mind raced. *Where would Manuel have wanted to fix the starting point of this "map" of his? He's compensating for the river's current, so the starting point has to be alongside or . . . above?*

He turned to face Marta. "The Triana Bridge! It must be the bridge itself. It stretches over the river *and* lies at the base of Cataliticos Reyes. The anchor point is the bridge, Marta!"

Marta smiled back at him. "Sam, my son, that bridge is long. Where would you attach the anchor point?" She obviously still carried her doubts and reservations.

97

Sam replied, "Manuel must have taken care of that already. I need to check out the bridge. Hopefully, he left some markings or signs. Ms. Vega, I am going to discover Manuel's legacy if it's still down there. If this discovery of his is as awe-inspiring as he claimed, the world will hear about it, and I assure you Manuel will get full credit!"

Marta fought back another wave of tears as she embraced Sam. "My brother is gone now, and all because he wanted to protect me somehow. I do not know if you will find anything, but I will pray." Despite her efforts, tears were falling rolled down her cheeks.

Sam's mind was afire. When he woke that morning, he assumed he had traveled the full length of his yellow brick road. But now, his road stretched on, and he had further yet to travel. Rather than despair at the revelation, his heart pounded with adrenaline. He finished meeting with Marta, bid his farewells, and left. As he turned the corner, he only casually noticed the brown sedan parked across the street with two men inside.

Later, physically and mentally exhausted, pumped with equal parts of excitement and dread, he welcomed darkness from atop the Triana Bridge, watching the sun slowly melt into the golden Guadalquivir River basin at the far edge of the horizon.

*   *   *

Tuesday, October 20, 1959 – Early Evening

Manuel stood, dressed in black, a gray box and a canvas bag at his feet, on the edge of the Triana Bridge looking down at the current. He had been waiting here for some time, and, while his eyes were transfixed on the emerald water, his mind kept going over and over the night's plan. It had been five days since he encountered the man in the gray overcoat, and he had not seen him or that brown sedan again. Instead, he had spent his days holed up inside La Gran Villa, constructing that box and writing.

In every story of buried treasure he had ever read, the treasure was always coins or jewels. The folks doing the burying never fretted about their treasure getting wet. He was not so fortunate. He was burying documents – and ancient documents at that. That box needed to protect its contents for perhaps a year or more until he could ensure Marta's safety and return to retrieve it. It had also taken the five days for the thick epoxy resin, the same used by shipwrights to seal a ship's deck, to set up and cure. Afterwards, he had wrapped the entire thing in duct tape and secured several weights to the exterior. Though not terribly large, just under two feet on all sides, its

98

construction had been a meticulous task. If somehow water reached these documents, he would not only have failed himself, but the whole world.

Tonight, once the sun finally faded beyond the horizon and darkness had again descended, he would dive into that river and bury his treasure at the bottom. As a contingency, should he be unable to retrieve the box, Marta would hopefully decipher the clues he had inserted into her letter. That was unlikely, however — not because Marta wasn't bright enough to unravel the clues; rather, she would likely never presume his letter to contain clues in the first place. He had been forced to gamble on that point, however. If his letter was too direct, and read by the wrong people, this would all have been for naught.

The river itself also presented a major hurdle. The burying of the box on the river's bottom would be particularly challenging, but this was the safest spot to avoid it being accidentally uncovered. In a field, a farmer might inadvertently plow it up. In town, a crew might develop the area for houses and find it, destroy it, or — even worse — unknowingly build directly over it. On the river bottom, it would remain undisturbed until he came looking for it.

At last, the sun retreated beyond the edge of the world, ushering in a new darkness. Manuel gathered his things and walked down to the eastern base of the bridge. The Triana Bridge was Seville's oldest, spanning the entire width of the Guadalquivir — well over 150 yards. Its underside was made of three large archways. Each archway was composed of rows of iron rings — the larger rings at the base and smaller rings near the crest. Manuel hid the box and other things and quickly changed into clothes better suited for swimming.

His first task was to secure his rope to the bridge's under belly. With his rope, pre-cut to forty feet, tightly around his shoulders and a can of spray paint in tow, he gripped the large ring closest to him with both hands and feet and began slowly crawling across. Ring by ring, grip by grip, he deliberately worked his way further and further out over the churning murky waters of the Guadalquivir.

Facing the night sky, his spirits sank as calm stars retreated behind heavy dark clouds. He had just reached the tiny rings nearest the apex when the skies opened. *This whole affair just became far more difficult, but there is no turning back at this point. I have been lucky not running into those Vatican goons for this long, but they could be desperate by now. Tonight has got to be my night — rain or no.*

99

Manuel hooked his left arm on the bottom beam, and, with his free hand, painted two orange snakes on each side of the center rings. Marta would need a decent starting point. The ache in his arms grew more unbearable with each second, though he had no choice but to power through. Securing the rope with one hand proved far more challenging than he had practiced. His left arm was already throbbing, and the darkness under the bridge was impenetrable. With sweat pouring down his forehead into his eyes, he persevered and finally, when it seemed his arms were spent, finished the knot. He dropped the rope's other end and clambered back down.

Once there, he plopped upon the rocks at the water's edge, unconcerned about the torrential rain. His rope, now dangling from the bottom of the Triana Bridge, would not go unnoticed long, but his arms refused to help him rise. No less than twenty minutes passed with rain pounding down on him until, at last mind overpowered body. He slowly pushed himself from the muddy stones and surveyed his situation as he wiped drenched hair from his eyes. The rope was holding, and, so far, no one seemed to be giving it or him much attention. *If just one nosey tourist questions why a rope was dangling from the bridge . . .*

Manuel stumbled over to his box. He tied a life preserver around it, anticipating the need to keep his prize afloat until the right moment. The wind picked up, and thunder crashed across the heavens as Manuel waded into the swirling waters, toting the box in his arms. The cold water was unforgiving as it quickly deepened, and wading became swimming – out to his rope floating lifelessly upon the river's surface. Since he had to hold the box afloat, only one arm was free to wrestle the swollen current, only allowing Manuel to trudge forward mere inches at a time. As one arm would tire, he would switch, using the other to hold the box aloft while the former took its turn treading water. He fought against both the downpour and the current – struggling to keep both the box and his head above water. Occasionally, his grip would slip – triggering a panicked scramble to save it.

After an apparent eternity, his outstretched hand finally grasped the rope. In the midst of the tempest, even breathing was arduous. Manuel rode the current until the rope was taught and cut the life preserver free, aside from a long secondary line, and the box sank at once into the river's depths. Bitter tears fell as he stared into the blackness. He fought the current and made his way back to the eastern bank.

100

Lightning scorched the sky, igniting the darkness, contrasting against ominous clouds overhead. His arms were jelly, and his neck muscles strained from propping his head above the raging waters. He was not done. Two tasks remained, and one of them had to be done now. His rope had fortunately not attracted much attention, but his luck wouldn't hold forever. *Must get back to the bridge and get that rope down before someone starts to care about it.* Manuel, crawling at first, forced himself back up the riverbank. As he neared the bridge, bright lights from far upstream caught his eye. *A boat – heading this way! I have to get that rope down from there – now!*

Manuel once again grabbed the rings under the bridge and scrambled upward, burning what paltry strength he had left. The unyielding rain pelted him as he climbed, but he dared not pause. He would need every precious second to untie the knot. As he climbed, the ship's lights loomed larger. He would, at best, have but the briefest of moments to free the rope before someone noticed him hugging the bridge's under-girth. When at last he reached the knot, he had mere seconds to spare – not enough to untie it. He pulled his knife and sliced the rope just below the knot. It fell harmlessly into the river. The boat was bearing down, but before he could decide what to do, his arms decided for him. They had, despite his determination, reached their limits and were now trembling terribly. They betrayed his grip, and he plummeted into the river below.

Cold water enveloped him. He closed his eyes. The current pulled him downstream fast, but his arms were spent. He kicked toward the surface. He felt the air on his face and took a quick breath before sinking back under. He kicked upward again. This time, luckily, he stayed afloat. He opened his eyes while rain stung his face. He spotted the bank. He kicked. He kicked again. Thunder shook the skies as he continued kicking, slowly, deliberately, creeping toward the bank. His arms floated lifelessly, but he had to get to land before his legs cramped or became as drained as his arms. Sand touched the tip of his toes. *Land!* A final kick and his body beached itself. He was exhausted and had nothing left.

For more than an hour, he lay there exhausted. No one came. He finally marshaled enough strength to sit up. All was quiet. There was no sign of that ship. *Is it over? No. Still have to bury that box.* That box, wrapped in dark tape, would stand out terribly against the river's pale bottom. It had to be buried below the silt. The thought of crawling to the river bottom chilled his soul. His arms still ached, though their trembling had ceased, and the

101

saturating rain showed no hint of abatement. Still, he had little choice in the matter but to see this thing through. He trudged back under the bridge, letting it take some of the rain off his head for at least a short while.

Hours passed as Manuel sat huddled under that bridge. At first, he had thought of nothing, content merely focusing on the moment. Eventually, as his adrenaline waned and breathing slowed, his thoughts wandered – at first, to his sister, Marta, sleeping soundly mere blocks away. He smiled, despite his condition, finding solace that her dreams would remain peaceful and her bed soft. Slowly, though, his thoughts turned from contentment to, well, something else. His jaws locked tight as he reminded himself that this entire scheme, while successful, was a far cry from what truly needed to happen. The world starved for this sacred knowledge – now sealed on the bottom of the Guadalquivir, serving no one. He had, in the end, only succeeded in moving the documents from one dark, desolate hole to another. These thoughts were pride, masquerading as martyrdom. His father died, not because has was a martyr, but because he was courageous enough to stand despite all signs compelling him to forfeit. Manuel shook his thoughts back into submission. These documents were not lost, and at least tiny shreds of hope remained that they may yet be recovered.

Though quite sleepier than when he started, his muscles had regained some of their former strength. He removed a spade from his bag and waded, once more, into the churning water. He spotted the life preserver floating atop the pressing current and made directly for it. The brief respite had served him well, and he reached the preserver without much difficulty. He closed his eyes, inhaled deeply, and, finding his own courage, dove into the cold depths.

With one hand on the tether, a thin rope still connecting the box and the life preserver, he dove deeper and deeper. Groping in the darkness, he finally felt the box resting along the river bottom as air bubbles leaked through his pursed lips. He began digging into the soft silt. As his air would expire, he would surface, always holding tight to the tether line. He repeated the routine, and as the hole at the bottom grew, his strength was sapped. He had wanted a deeper hole, but he was done. This dive would have to be the last. He reached the river bottom and found where he had been digging. He struggled against rocks and roots, digging as deep as possible. He kicked the box inside the hole and scrambled – back filling dirt to cover it. He floated to the surface and was again dragged downstream. He pulled until he found the

102

life preserver and worked his way to the riverbank for the final time. *It is actually finished.*

He had endured, and his discovery was hidden yet again, but it was no longer in the Vatican's clutches. Should fortune shine on his path, it could be recovered one day. He scrambled up the bank, not entirely certain of his next move. Tonight, or what was left of it, he would get some well-deserved rest. He reached the top of the bridge, still breathing heavily as the rain, ironically, slowed to mere droplets. He looked across the bridge, and his throat closed shut when he saw it – the brown sedan. It was perched on the far side facing him. Its headlights ignited. Debilitating dread smothered him. The small flicker of hope that had begun burning was snuffed out in an instant as his heart began fiercely pounding against his chest.

The headlights grew as the sedan crossed the bridge. Manuel started running once again. His muscles were shattered, and his running had not been great, even on the best days. None of that mattered now. The sedan sped up as he ran faster. *This is it – they have come for me. Hopefully, they haven't been watching me from atop the bridge this whole time!* Each breath came only in short, shallow spurts. *Where am I running? I can't go back to the hotel. They most certainly have it under lock and key.* His feet splashed in puddles as he tore through the city streets, making as many turns as possible. The sedan closed in. There was no hope of outrunning it. He turned a sharp corner, ducking behind a deli.

He knew instantly his mistake was fatal. The sedan's tires slushed through the water and stopped, sealing him in the tiny alcove. Unfortunately, he was walled in on three sides – a death trap littered with garbage amid several inches of standing slush water. The sedan opened and out stepped a dark figure in a familiar gray overcoat. Manuel let out a long overdue breath, resigning himself to his fate. As he walked courageously toward the sedan, his mind betrayed him, denying even the tiniest hint of accomplishment. *My clues in Marta's letter! They won't work! Everything was based on the river's normal depth, not its depth during this absurd monsoon. The river that has beaten on me all night has finally won. If Marta does decipher the clues in her letter, she will dig much further from the bridge than she should!* He stopped, cursing himself under his breath, fighting against tears he had been too exhausted to shed. *I have sent my sweet sister on a fool's errand! That letter should never have called for a forty-foot rope!*

*   *   *

103

Friday, May 21, 1999 – Early Evening

A Cardinal has two feet – not one. If Manuel kissed twenty Cardinals' feet, he would have kissed forty feet, not twenty. Sam grinned as he deciphered that final clue from Manuel's letter. It had bothered him all afternoon as he stared, confused, at the Triana Bridge. A mere twenty-foot rope wouldn't stretch from the bridge to the riverbed. He had been wrestling with that dilemma for some time now. Sam had even spotted Manuel's "anchor point" on the bridge earlier that morning. He had booked several tourist cruises up and down the river, and, as he passed underneath on his third trip, he noticed a pair of faint orange lines on the bridge's underside. Though weathered by time, they resembled snakes. *What was this guy's obsession with snakes anyway?*

Am I actually going to do this? I've chased this ghost half way around the world, and now, its trail leads under one of Spain's largest rivers. Will it end there? If I reach bottom and discover only an empty hole, what then? What if I find nothing at all? How many holes would I need to dig to convince myself there's nothing to find? Answers lay at the river's bottom, and tonight he would find them. Sam stood atop that bridge, watching Seville casually float through this Friday evening as it had the thousands before it. People passed by on foot, on bikes, in cars, and even below him on ships, and Sam couldn't help but feel separate, as though, somehow, their world had shrunk, becoming far more predictable than his. Actually, he knew it was not their world that had changed, but his – expanding into something far more chaotic.

Sunlight faded, and twilight swallowed the city as Sam felt the bridge's worn, rusted railings against his palms. While always having been a strong swimmer, Sam had done nothing like this before. He nervously turned to gaze across at the Triana district on the other side. Tourists and locals alike milled about – flitting in and out of various shops and cafes. One car, however, a lone brown sedan, was parked near a small store, with two figures casually sitting inside, apparently minding their own business.

Darkness finally descended, and Sam prepared for the most bizarre leap of blind faith he had ever made. *What if those orange "snakes" I saw are just random acts of old graffiti? What if this grand illusion had been concocted by an older woman desperate for anything to connect to her brother and me, a boring social worker yearning to feel just a little less normal?* Self-doubt had plagued Sam since first uncovering that letter over eight months ago, and tonight, there would finally be denouement, one way or the other. He would

104

either recover something under that water, justifying this wild pursuit, or he would find himself at the bottom, just as alone as he was back in Anaheim. Regardless, tonight would, at last, mark the end of this debilitating ebb and flow of excitement and uncertainty.

He returned to La Gran Villa, changed into swimming trunks, and gathered the few supplies he had scrounged up: a forty-foot piece of black nylon rope, a few carabineer clips, a knife, some diving flippers and goggles, a chlorine float usually found in residential pools, a small anchor attached to a long chain, a life preserver, a roll of duct tape, a camping shovel and a small case of multi-colored princess wands.

Sam kept walking into Seville's hypnotic night air and wound his way back to the bridge. Once there, he made his way down the steps on the east bank. He sat along the concrete platform, gazing at the calm water reflecting the illuminated Triana Bridge across its placid surface. He sat patiently waiting as activity died down further and took advantage of the time, making a few preparations. He covered the float in duct tape – using some excess tape to form a loop hole. He wrapped the rope over his shoulders and across his chest several times.

As he worked, his thoughts returned to a gnawing dilemma he had wrestled since leaving Marta's. *I think I know where the anchor point is, but where is the dig point – forty feet down to the river bottom or forty feet to a point on the river's surface and then straight down?* The most logical choice seemed to be an angle straight down to the river bottom, but Sam, playing against logic, decided to first try the dig site directly below a point on the river's surface. For that site, he would need the pool float.

Another hour shrank off the clock, and nightlife slowed atop the Triana Bridge and surrounding area. He had first to attach the rope to what he hoped was the anchor point Manuel had marked. He crossed his ankles over the iron beam running below the bridge's rings and grabbed ahold with both hands, so that he was dangling above the ground, his face staring up at the underside of the bridge. He craned his neck to peer at the archway and gasped, noticing how high it would take him above the river. He first slid his right hand upward along the beam and gripped it tightly, then slid his left hand upward to join it. Then, gripping with both arms, slid his ankles up further in unison. *This is what I have to keep doing. No matter how high this cursed arch goes, I just follow this pattern: right hand, left hand, ankles, over and over again. God, those*

105

better be freakin' orange snakes up there, and not remnants of a Spanish 'Kilroy was here'!

He kept at it, slower than he preferred but persistently. A few people had spotted him crawling under the bridge, but no one had stopped to ask questions or notify authorities. Sam had thought, *with this rope across my shoulder, they probably suspect I am merely a city employee.* As long that illusion held, Sam would take advantage of it, but it meant he had to look like he knew what he was doing. One slip or foolish hand gesture might prompt a call for someone to 'help that poor man under the bridge,' and this whole adventure would crash. He finally reached the top of the arch, and, to his dismay, the orange lines were too beaten and faded to truly interpret.

Having come this far, Sam held on with his left hand and quickly looped his rope through the small center ring several times, finally snapping a carabineer clip to secure it. The other end remained tied to his waist. Getting down would not be a simple matter, however. His options: either drop into the river, a twenty-foot plunge, surely to be noticed by nearby stragglers, or, his preference, turn around and crawl down the arch the same way he scaled up. He held on with all his strength and unlocked his ankles, allowing them to dangle. He made to move his left hand to the other side of the beam. He almost slipped but found a hold at the last second. This turning around was treacherous, and even the tiniest error would send him plummeting into the river. He saw the spot he needed his right hand to grasp and made his move. It worked. Only the ankles, the most challenging part, remained. He couldn't do many sit-ups on a good day without exhausting himself, and this one was vertical – twenty feet in the air. As he clenched his core muscles harder and harder, his feet continued rising. Sam knew he wouldn't hold much longer. Those ankles had to get locked back into place. He made one last big push. His water shoes barely grazed the beam, but no further. His core muscles released, dropping his legs. The pressure was too much. He fell.

Water closed around him as Sam plunged into the river. He pushed upward and broke through, grabbing a quick breath. The bank wasn't far, and luckily, the current was mild. He managed to tread back without much fuss. Though the nylon rope was still secure, that loud, public drop had forfeited all anonymity. The handful of people witnessing his tremendous splash when he impacted were pointing in his direction from atop the bridge. *What do I do now? Police or some emergency service would undoubtedly arrive any minute, and there's no way they'll just let me keep crawling under their bridge and falling into their river. I need to move – now.*

Samuel, deciding to play to the onlookers, stood on the bank staring up at the bridge with its host of onlookers and took a bow as he waved – drawing ripostes of applause mixed with insults and taking it as a good sign. His heart was pounding, and he didn't know quite what to do, but he couldn't stick around waiting to be picked up. So, he hurriedly tied the rope to the bridge's base, snatched his bundle of belongings, and left. *I can't believe I thought I'd be able to pull this off!*

Sam stormed off in the general direction of the hotel but, yearning to disappear, stopped at a small tavern – the sort no one pays any mind. The bar was not a festive, night life, meet others and be-seen sort of place, but rather, a drown your problems, avoid or help kill the roaches, enjoy the second-hand smoke, and don't flash your cash sort of place. Sam's first stop inside, however, was the restroom. Hoping to come off more "bar friendly," he lost the swimming trunks, dried his hair, and tried cleaning up generally. Afterwards, he headed to the bar and dejectedly ordered a light beer, doing his best not to look around or attract undue attention.

He nursed his beer for almost an hour before the empty stool beside him got an occupant: an older man, far older than himself, reeking of last week's garbage. His face was adorned with a dingy, silver beard, far thicker than the sparse patch atop his head. Frail and thin, likely counting each cursed day as a prisoner awaiting parole, he handed a crumple of soiled bills to the barkeep without a word. The barkeep poured some dark brown liquor into a glass and positioned it in front of the old man. He, like Sam, had come in alone with no apparent interest in seeing anyone or being seen and wore surrender and defeat about him like a heavy cloak. Sam finished his light beer and ordered another, but the two of them uttered not one word to each other for some time.

At least, that was, until the older man finally took a drink and, glaring forward, uttered in a deep baritone to no one in particular, "Mistakes tend to linger around, like a shadow, except they pile up on one another. Eventually, it is easier to just give up and lie down than keep toting them around."

A startled Sam glanced around to see to whom the old man might have been speaking, but no one was in ear shot but himself. The stranger was simply glaring forward, taking another slow sip. "Excuse me?" Sam spoke up,

107

not sure if he was the intended audience, but clearly confused that the old man had spoken English.

"Sorry. Just mumbling something I heard once." Still cradling his glass between his aged, rust-colored fingers, he turned to face Sam. "Never saw you in here before, son." His breath reeked of smoke and some variety of pickled fish.

"No, I'm from America – here on vacation, actually." Sam chortled slightly as the word "vacation" escaped his lips. *Not sure what kind of vacation this is.*

As though reading his thoughts, the man replied, "Heh. Well, if you are in here, your vacation is probably not turning out the way you expected. You blame yourself, yes?"

Sam, confused and clearly rattled by his directness but even more so at his accuracy, only managed a quick, "Guess so."

"Figured. Known people like you my whole life. Can spot them from across the street. I am very much the same, you know. Spent my life blaming myself for yesterday's sins – too timid to venture out and make new ones."

"Not me. I make mistakes all the time. It's only been an hour or so since my last big one, actually."

"I want to tell you a story. I share it from time to time with those who seem to have given up." He sat his glass down and, without seeking permission, began. "There was this pet store. Could have been anywhere. Had two hamsters in a cage. Typical hamster cage: little water bucket, straw lining the bottom, tiny wheel for the little guys to run on. First hamster climbs inside the wheel and runs. Does this every day, never going anywhere – just round and round inside the wheel. Second hamster notices this absurdity and laughs. He thinks to himself, 'Silly. So much wasted effort – for nothing. Well, you will not find me in that infernal wheel, I swear it.'

So, the second hamster lies down in the straw and falls asleep. Every day, it is the same thing; first hamster runs in the wheel; second hamster laughs at him and falls asleep in the straw. One day, the second hamster, now quite fat from lack of exercise, suffers a heart problem and dies right there in the cage. The first hamster sees this and is saddened to be all alone in the cage. But still, he keeps running in that wheel every day. Of course, like any good animal story, this one has a moral . . ."

Sam interjected before the stranger could finish, "Let me guess – never give up, right?"

The man shook his head. "No, that is not it. You give that first little hamster far too much credit, son. He knew nothing about exercise or health. Running in that wheel was, for him, never a question of whether or not he should give up. He was merely living the life he was given, that is all. Life gave him a wheel, and he ran in it." With that, the old man returned to his drink.

Sam made no response as this man's cold words pierced his thoughts. He just sat in silence. Soon enough, the man finished his drink and left without so much as a 'fare thee well.' Sam said nothing either, still mulling the strange man and his odd tale. There was truth there. Sam was always checking over his shoulder, scrutinizing his previous footsteps – never spending enough time focusing on making new ones. He couldn't leave Seville this way. He had to check out that river bottom. He resolutely finished his beer and headed back outside.

At the Triana Bridge, things had calmed down dramatically. No one was about – either walking on the bridge or on the walkway alongside the river. Deep night had fallen, and Seville was sleeping. His luck had held somewhat, as his rope was still where he tied it. He pulled out the pool float, fastening the anchor's chain to it. He also taped several princess wands to the anchor. It was more than a little emasculating using the princess wands, but they had been the only water-proof light-up trinkets he could scrounge. He secured the diving mask and snapped the wands' inner capsules, allowing each to fill with brilliant shades of red and pink. Sam sighed with nervous anticipation. It was now or never. With rope in hand, he trudged into the river.

Once he could no longer touch bottom, the current carried him gently the length of rope, and he dropped anchor. Sam took a deep breath and submerged. Through the haze, he saw tiny pink and red lights resting on the river bottom. He kept diving until he reached them. With the shovel, he began probing the silt. He wasn't able to dig but a few quick holes before needing to surface, but by keeping one hand on the anchor's chain as he made his way up and down, he kept his bearings well enough. With each strike of his shovel, soft dirt swirled into the water in a blinding cloud – a complication he hadn't anticipated. He was forced to wait as the dust dissipated before moving on. Between running out of air, lousy visibility, and constantly fighting the current, the search was mentally and physically exhausting.

He had been at it for quite some time before he began feeling confident that he had guessed wrong about his dig site. He gathered the anchor, still with glowing pink and red wands attached. Although he needed to move the anchor, his body was drained. Pushing it could be dangerous if something went wrong. Sore leg muscles cried in agony, strained from persistent treading against the current. So, he rested on the river walk for a brief respite. As Seville fell into an even deeper slumber, the river, Seville's great snake, as Marta had called it, slithered through it without a murmur. The night air itself seemed comatose as neither wind nor breeze stirred. Seville's silence, normally saturated in beauty and life, echoed only an unsettling emptiness and dread.

Eventually, the need to wrap things up subdued his need to rest. Sam changed out the princess wands for fresh ones, clipped the rope to the anchor, and waded back in. This time, however, he held the anchor while diving, trying to set a new dig site exactly forty feet from the bridge. He swam until the rope was taught and resumed digging. Feverishly, he dug, waited as the dust settled, dug, and waited again, occasionally surfacing for much-needed air.

His frustrations mounted, however, as all of his fears and self-doubt crashed around him, one empty hole at a time. His spirits sank deeper and deeper as, out of desperation, he dug further to the left, then further to the right. Both legs and arms screamed for relief, but he pushed them. When he had first started digging, his approach had been quite methodical, digging in a specific location before moving on to another. That discipline had, over time, been supplanted with hacking wild, deep gashes into the sand. The river bottom surrounding the anchor had been chewed up. He knew there was nothing there but couldn't stomach the thought of surfacing empty-handed. He blindly slashed at the river's bed.

His legs, fed up with this tyrannical oppression, finally declared independence and cramped up simultaneously, leaving Sam no choice but to surrender. He would need to surface for air soon. As he stopped resisting, the current pulled him downstream, and he took advantage of the opportunity to stab in new and wildly random spots on the river bottom – faster and faster, no longer allowing the silt to settle or to get his bearings. Exasperation had enveloped him, whispering in his mind that this time, after surfacing, he wouldn't return. At the last, when his need for air reached its crescendo, his shovel struck something hard.

Sam contained himself, as he had endured other moments of ill-fated excitement triggered by rocks, roots, and other debris lying beneath the silt. He struggled to discover what his shovel had struck, but with so much silt

110

swirling in the water, he was reduced to using his hands. His fingers traced, to his utter and complete astonishment, the edges of a box! *Unbelievable! Surely, this isn't what I hope it is!* Sam worked frantically to unearth it. He tried, but it was far too heavy to lift. He needed to get some air quickly. He groped and felt several weights taped to its surface. *This is actually it! This box was buried here intentionally!* Still not sure how he misread Manuel's "forty-foot" clue, he hacked at the thick tape securing the weights. One by one, several dropped away, and the box finally lightened. He was completely out of breath now and needed to surface. He grabbed the box and turned upward to ascend, but a dark shadow covered the river.

The night was already black as pitch, but this new shadow cut off all light – and hope. *A boat – and not a small one!* Sam's newfound exuberance suddenly took a back seat to this growing terror. This behemoth pushing upriver was the coffin's lid closing shut as he suffocated inside the watery casket below. He dared not surface near the ship as its rear propeller hung far below the surface. Sam had to abandon the area or risk being pulled inside the deadly blades. The box, now far lighter, might easily be chewed into pieces by that propeller if abandoned. He was going, and that box was coming with him. He desperately needed to breathe. The ship's underbelly already covered the water above, and its bow was almost to the bridge. Sam frantically started swimming along the bottom, tugging the box with him. The shadow above marched upstream as Sam tried to be free of its path. His chest stung from holding his breath. He needed to surface, but wasn't yet clear. He pushed harder, fighting the overwhelming urge to breath. *This is crazy! I could drown right here!*

With no options remaining, he treaded water – pushing with everything he had. In the sky above, he saw stars again. The ship's edge was just ahead. He willed his cramped legs into submission. He kicked again and again; nothing mattered now but breathing. He kept kicking. The zone of safety was coming but far too slowly. He began ascending, while still frantically pushing further away from the ship. He had to breathe, and now! He turned upward and kicked – hard. He broke through to the surface, instantly swallowing as much air as he could. One moment sooner, and he would have been sucked back down by the ship's undertow. Any later, he would have drowned or blacked out from asphyxiation. He kicked one final time, pulling further from the dark bulkhead. He had done it! He bobbed in the river, hugging that old box – exasperated, coughing, and gasping for fresh air. An exasperated Sam, dragging a mysterious box plucked from yesterday, soon writhed onto the paved walk of the Guadalquivir.

Time passed. The city continued its slumber. Sam's limbs screamed from overexertion. He had always considered himself a strong swimmer, but nothing could have prepared him for that. His heart pounded, adrenaline flowing through him, as he sat up. The dark river simply flowed downstream as though nothing had happened. The river cared nothing for discoveries, survival, the Vatican, or any of this he had put his life on hold to pursue. *Maybe,* thought Sam, *my life wasn't put on hold following this scant trail of crumbs. Perhaps it is only just now beginning.* Sam glanced at the box he had unearthed. It was a cube, roughly two feet all around and completely wrapped in rotted duct tape. He ripped off the few remaining weights as he sat resting. *What could possibly fit in so small a box with the potential to change the world?* The answer, despite his burning curiosity, would wait until after sunrise from the safety of his hotel.

More time passed, and Sam finally felt strong enough to climb the bank and return to La Gran Villa. With his bag over his shoulder and the box under his arm, he reached the bridge's surface and leaned one last time upon the railings, gazing down at the calm river surface. Not unlike the snake from the fable, the river had almost claimed his life. Sam scanned the desolate bridge. No one was around, except . . . he had not noticed it before, but a car sat quietly parked at the far end of the bridge. It was running as Sam could make out exhaust trailing from its tail pipe. *Why would someone be out here, unless . . . No!*

His heart, which had finally started to slow, began beating faster as his mind tried justifying the ominous vehicle. *Young lovers making out near the water?* Sam knew better. The longer he stared, the more the car resembled the one he had seen earlier. *This can't be. Surely, no one already knows about this infernal box? What the hell is inside this curse?* Headlamps switched on, shattering the darkness. *They are connected – the people in that car and this box. Need to make one last push!*

Sam ran – hard. The sedan's engine revved behind him, confirming his darkest fears. He hadn't gone through this ordeal only to have the Vatican, or whoever that was, rip this discovery from him just as he had vindicated himself. He pushed himself faster and faster through the desolate streets of Seville. *I'll never outrun them on open streets! Need to find places too narrow for cars – force them to come after me on foot. Need a place to hide!* Seville is

112

old, with many streets built before cars, with alcoves and alleys barely wide enough for two people to pass. *Those narrow streets behind my hotel would be great if I could make it!* Sam made a few quick turns and backtracks when he could – forcing the sedan to make wide circles and buying Sam a few precious seconds.

He was in a dead sprint. Faster. He pushed his legs beyond their extent as he approached the hotel. The morbid calm of Seville's streets was splintered by his feet striking the pavement and the sedan's engine as it closed on him. He reached La Gran Villa and tore inside. As expected, no one was about. Sam dashed through the atrium and out the back door into a maze of dark alleys comprising the block's interior. His heart was pounding against his ribs, and breathing was getting harder and harder. He couldn't keep running. *I need to hide now!* He wildly rushed through the alleys until he noticed an open door apparently serving an electrical room. He darted inside, slamming the door shut behind him. Luckily, it locked as it shut. *May not be able to get out right away, but they won't be getting in.* No sound penetrated the thick door, but Sam stayed immobile, squatting on the concrete floor, listening intently. Shadows passed across the tiny streak of light under the door, but no one attempted to force entry. Time passed until utter exhaustion finally came to collect its due. Sam passed out of consciousness as darkness took him.

PART TWO

"I paused, examining and analysing all the minutia of causation, as exemplified in the change from life to death, and death to life, until from the midst of this darkness, a sudden light broke in upon me--a light so brilliant and wondrous, yet so simple, that while I became dizzy with the immensity of the prospect which it illustrated, I was surprised, that among so many men of genius who had directed their inquiries towards the same science, that I alone should be reserved to discover so astonishing a secret." – Mary Walstonecraft Shelley, Frankenstein; or, The Modern Prometheus

Saturday, May 22, 1999 – Mid-Afternoon

Concrete is unyielding. When, at last, Sam Johnston stirred from exasperated slumber, his whole body ached. His back and hips ached from hours pressed against pavement in the tiny utility room. Muscles, pushed beyond their limits, cried out in agony as he leaned up and tried surveying his surroundings. Waves of pain pulsed with each tiny gesture. He blinked. Darkness consumed him, though his eyes were open. The air stank of mildew and grease baking in the room's intense heat. It was Saturday afternoon, and Sam had been lying unconscious since early that morning. The only light was a faint streak pouring from beneath the locked door. He was not injured, that he could tell, but he was in pain, reeling from a body strained far beyond its capacity.

Last night. His mind, previously occupied compiling a damage report of all his screaming joints and muscles, began remembering what had unfolded. What led him to this room basked in darkness? *They were chasing me.* He remembered that first. *Who was in that car, and even more importantly, where are they now? Whoever they were, they don't know I'm in here. Locked door or not, anyone that determined would have had me . . .* Sam stopped thinking as hushed voices passed just outside the door. He couldn't make out any words, but it was clearly serious from the tone. Once the voices had moved on, he allowed his mind to resume its voyage as if somehow someone might have heard his thoughts.

Sweat had consumed him throughout the day as he slept. The May sun was relentless, and the electrical room had no air conditioning or basic ventilation. He may have only succeeded in avoiding the bakers by hiding in their oven. He fumbled around in the dark nearby and felt his bag. *The bag – Thank God!* He took out his towel and wiped thick moisture from his face and

117

arms. His lips were parched and cracking, but unfortunately, his water bottle contained only drops. Regardless, he hurriedly spun the lid off and moistened his lips with tepid water. Such fleeting and paltry relief from the swelter bought him a few moments to remember. *It was dark. I was so tired. The river and that ship had almost killed me, but I found it. Didn't I?* His situation had become so bleak he had completely forgotten that cursed box he had plied from under the silt. He groped around blindly once more, and his fingers landed on something hard in the distance. *That must be it!* He lurched forward another foot or so and stopped short. His arms rebelled at the exercise, delivering a fresh, sharp wave of pain. He ignored their protests and reached out. *Yes. That's it!*

Sam felt the outside of the box as more memories of last night fell into place. The tape on the outside – he remembered that; he remembered cutting weights off. *Cutting! That's right, my knife is probably still here somewhere.* Though he wanted to tear into the box and discover what precious artifact he had forfeited his life for, he knew it would be for naught in this blackness. He had to either find some light or break free of this deadly snare. He bent over, rubbing his legs, slowly at first but faster over time, trying to get proper circulation working. They weren't doing well. He had pushed them – hard. First, they had cramped, and he had willed them into submission, despite their condition. He had forced them to kick, harder and harder, over and over again, working to break free of that overhead ship. Though he had rested afterwards, it wasn't enough for that dead sprint against the infernal sedan, through the hotel here into this alley.

His legs were of little use, but with luck, he could perhaps get them to support him upright briefly. Sam kept at it, trying to regain feeling and circulation in his legs, and it seemed to be working some. Rather than intense, dull pain, his pain grew sharp as blood finally began moving. He moved his legs – not at all once, but sections at a time, starting with the feet and working his way upward. There was pain, tremendous pain, but he dared not make a sound. There was no way of knowing what skulked just outside. Sweat was dripping down his face again, and he struggled to breathe the hot, thick air. He pulled his tender legs underneath him and attempted to stand. He collapsed onto the merciless paved floor. He tried again. *Just need to stand up and get my muscles working again. Nothing feels broken – just maybe damaged and over-strained.*

A few painful attempts later, and Sam was standing upright. The pain had not subsided, but he was growing more accustomed to it. He shuffled a few tiny steps, arms outstretched, in the blackness to the nearest wall. He searched for something to support himself and landed upon a wall stud, old and rotting from neglect, but it sufficed. *What are the odds I can find a light switch? If this is an electrical room, it could have a light.* He fumbled about along the wall, finding only wall studs until he had a revelation. *The wands! Did I still have any of those left or did I use them all?* He let go of the wall stud and tried kneeling. He fell.

From the ground, other than the pain of slamming into the pavement, it was far easier to locate the bag. He groped through it again, finding his knife and several unused princess wands. *My God! These stupid things might actually save my life.* Sam twisted the wand, snapping the tiny capsule inside, and the room transformed from a stuffy, pitch-black tomb to a stuffy, off-putting, hazy pink tomb, but finally, he got a feel for the place. The only door was on his right, with a knob requiring a key to turn. *Surely, there's a safety violation there somewhere.* There was no furniture – no chair, no desk, certainly no bed. The remaining walls were lined with electrical panels, conduits, mounds of loose cable, and more conduits. He saw why the room had been left open: a telephone panel was ajar with sundry wires jutting out the top of its metal casing. *Someone was working on this panel and left things unsecured. Why not come back today and finish?* Oh yeah, he answered his own question; *today is Saturday – no one's coming back until Monday at the earliest. Not sure I'll hold out until Monday.*

The only thing worth investigating was a bundle of cables and wires heaped in a disheveled pile in the opposite corner. He sighed at the dismal prospects and crawled over. With just the pink light, he couldn't tell much about the cables themselves, but underneath he felt something encased in hard plastic. *Buttons!* His excitement grew as he pulled out a lineman's handset. Though dark pink to his eyes, it was likely orange or red, complete with dialing buttons and two alligator clips dangling from wires below. It looked to be in good condition, but in order to use it, he had to stand back up and get a better look at that open telephone panel. He squirmed over and, with the handset and wand in one hand, attempted to stand. He made it, slightly less dramatically than before.

Sam hoisted the cover open to look inside. He had worked on panels like these during his college years, but those had English labels, and the wires were distinct colors rather than just hazy shades of pink. To make matters worse, sweat kept dropping into his eyes as he poked through the jumble of wires and circuits. It was slow going, holding the pink light in his teeth and using one hand to grab the panel's side for support, but eventually, he found what looked like a semi-solid lead wire with enough exposed cable for Sam to secure the alligator clips and attempt a call. He made the attachments and, to his amazement, heard a weak dial tone!

He dialed the code for a collect call and entered the only phone number he could think of that might be of some use to just then.

After accepting the charges, Sam heard a familiar voice. The voice was distant and staticky, but it was there. "Sam, my man! How are things in Spain? This dog of yours is ready to go home, man. . ."

Sam didn't know how long the call would hold and didn't have time to suffer through Gerard's typical tirade of casual banter. He interrupted, "Listen, Gerard, I may lose this call any minute, but I need your help. And when I say 'help,' I mean *your* help."

Gerard had his fingers in just about a little bit of anything, legal and otherwise. He had connections with folks Sam pretended didn't exist but always knew were there, lurking in the shadows. Their world existed alongside Sam's, the one most people train their minds to ignore, hoping that if they don't see it, it might not really be there – voices from locked rooms, mysterious unsolved shootings, money lifted from corporate books that never gets found. Gerard got the message loud and clear. "What's happened, and what do you need?" His tone shifted – suddenly all business.

Sam was whispering but whispering as loud as he dared. "I might have found what I came here for, but someone else is interested. I don't know who they are, but they have connections, and they chased me through the city last night. I got away, but I've locked myself in an electrical room near some shops behind my hotel. I'm mixed up in something I shouldn't be, and I'm scared, man."

Silence was all Sam heard from the other end of the phone. No breathing, no response, but also no dial-tone. He was still connected. *Gerard might still be listening!* "Look, this line is weak, and I can't hear you anymore, but I am hoping you can still hear me. Don't call the police or the embassy or anyone like that. That might even be who's chasing me. I need help from someone, *special*. You know people, Gerry; people you don't find in the yellow

120

pages. This little room is really hot with no ventilation, and the heat in here is killing me. I have no water, and it is really hard to breathe. I appreciate . . ."

He heard some intermittent static before the call went flat. Unfortunately, the handset was old and rusted – falling apart. The wires from the clips were hardly connected and brittle. Fixing them would take better lighting, patience, and more tools than he had in this cell. *That was my one phone call, I guess. Hopefully the invisible hand of Gerry's secret world reaches across the ocean.* He dropped everything and crumpled back down. Breathing continued to be a struggle. He looked around in desperation, but the longer he inspected the room, the more pathetic his situation became. He couldn't access any buildings' systems; the door was securely locked, and heat, sweat, and lack of water would only make things worse as time stretched.

He sighed and looked to that box at his feet. Sam pulled it over. Its outside was covered in molded, saturated duct tape. His knife cut through the tape easily, but, to his dismay, the box had no lid or hinges. Its entire surface was encased under a thick layer of sealant. As quietly as possible, he began chipping through the coated wood. Carefully, he sliced pieces from what he surmised was the top. The work went slowly as Sam avoided over-exertion. Regardless, bit by bit, chunks of wood broke from the whole, revealing a hollow cavity. Although working under pink light – courtesy of his princess wands, it was sufficient. Eventually, enough of the top had been chipped away giving Sam his first peek inside, and he couldn't believe what he saw. *Papers? That's what I've gone through all this hell for - papers? I hoped for the Holy Grail, Spear of Destiny, or another wondrous religious relic with terrific powers, but no. It's just a bunch of papers. I'm dying in here because some lunatic in the fifties decided to bury his homework rather than turn it in.*

Sam, fed up with this entire ordeal, shoved the box aside. He needed to save his strength and not push himself, certainly not for something as trivial as old paperwork. Time passed, and his wand eventually dimmed, ushering in a fresh darkness. The enveloping blackness blended with the darkness smothering Sam's thoughts. Every new step taken on this quest had only brought him new misery and misfortune. He had suffered wave after wave of disappointment and agony with the aspiration that something truly great lie waiting to be unearthed – something so magnificent that it could even prove the very existence of God. Cold tears formed in Sam's eyes as his wand's tiny bit of remaining light melted away. He had more princess wands but saw no point in igniting them. His bleak thoughts turned to Sarah – he had left her half a world away to chase this ghost's legacy, only to become a ghost himself.

What documents could have possibly been so important? God didn't write documents. To his knowledge, Christ was a carpenter before taking his show on the road and wasn't known for any real writing either. Even the Ten Commandments, arguably the only thing ever directly written by God himself, had not proven God's existence to the Jews in the wilderness. So, how could this character, this Manuel, a Cambridge graduate, presume anything written by mortal man could possibly achieve what he had alluded to? As time passed in solemn desolation, Sam's curiosity slowly began working its magic. In that box, resting merely feet away in the abyss, sat what he had sacrificed so much to acquire. That alone might not have been enough, but Sam recalled what Manuel sacrificed for those papers and how desperately the Vatican seemed to want them back. He owed it to himself to find out what was on these documents accompanying him in the darkness.

Sam snapped two more princess wands, enough to give sufficient reading light, and dragged the box closer. He diligently finished removing the top and extracted an old black binder marked "Read First." He flipped the cover open and began reading:

"Dearest sister, your reading of this letter testifies that my plan has unfortunately gone horribly wrong. I am hopeful at least that you are safe and have found everything in this box intact. I had intended to publish this information for the benefit of all, but outside forces intervened, and adjustments had to be made. Please know I have done everything in my power to protect you and guide you to my discovery if I was somehow unable to recover it myself. I love you, Marta, but your finding of this box likely means we will never see each other again. I am terribly sorry, but hopefully, the impact of this discovery will, in some small fashion, justify the cost.

The documents accompanying this binder are authentic Vatican papers spanning centuries, each bearing the Vatican's official stamp, verifying their authenticity. I am enclosing sixty-two separate original documents and in this binder, a separate English and Latin translation of each. Before you dive in and begin scouring through them, please understand: these documents are old, some of them dramatically so. They are fragile, requiring extreme care, and some of the ancient parchments are now quite brittle or

122

faded. Once you have gone through everything and convinced yourself of their critical importance, please make arrangements to deliver them to a friend of mine, a Mr. Jonathon Halpert, now living outside of San Luis Obispo, California, in the United States; he will ensure all of this is given the proper attention.

There is a preferred method to review everything. Following this method might help you grasp the central concept more easily. Dearest Marta, these documents contain evidence documenting the existence of a God that is quite real. I have forsaken our relationship, perhaps even my life, believing this truth. These documents relay the experiences of Priests throughout history engaging dark spirits or demons, and through their strife, the hand of God has been revealed. Though hard for me to grasp as well, these experiences validate demons, and the God they tremble before. Know that I love you and am relieved that you have found my work and that, at the least, my sacrifices have not been completely in vain:

Sam sighed as he squinted. *Demons? Did he actually say 'demons'? How ridiculous! How could some old papers prove demons exist?* Sam believed in a God, and in a hell populated with evil. He wasn't sure about demonic possession, though. Most books, descriptions, or movies about possession he had seen were either cliché and theatrical or so trivial and mundane that the 'victim' could easily be faking. Still, the concept was intriguing, so he readjusted his eyes and turned the page:

"I recommend that you first read Emmet's account. I have catalogued this as document #47. Once finished, return to this letter, and I will guide you further. Please read no further until you have first read Emmet's encounter."

*   *   *

Saturday, May 22, 1999 – Evening

Sam played along and rummaged through the box to document #47. It was an old, yellowish-stained paper with a script penned in hand. It was impossible to read the slanted scrawl in the poor light, but he remembered Manuel referencing a translation of each document resting in the binder. He found that translation and began reading:

"1888 A.D. – Philadelphia: This August has been far hotter than normal. My mention of the heat is more than an

123

opening pleasantry – it will become pertinent later. I was asked to visit with a patron, a Mrs. Emmet Johansen. Mrs. Johansen came to me early Thursday morning, clearly fraught with despair, describing the horrific condition of her husband, Emmet. His skin was brittle, chapped, and cracking, leaving open wounds of exposed blood between the crevices. His hair was falling out and he had lost his powers of speech. He remained, however, very much aware. She described his eyes as reflecting pain and frustration from not being able to speak. A final condition, which intrigued me most of all, was that his toes and fingertips had begun rotting.

Several doctors had called and each one, in turn, had retreated, shaking their head in disbelief. Her situation tore my heart asunder, and I volunteered to visit Emmet despite strong suspicions that I could do nothing beyond comforting a poor woman who was soon to become a widow. Regardless, I stopped by that afternoon and instantly smelled a powerful odor throughout the house. It smelled of decay, similar to infection. As a younger man, I recall the same stink in medical tents on the battlefield. It is powerful, and can make you wretch if hit with it all of a sudden.

When I first saw him, he was still, simply lying in bed wearing customary red long-johns covering his body. Mrs. Johansen pulled back the blankets to show me his feet. His toes had turned almost black. The same effect was noticeable on some of Emmet's fingers. At my request, she made to unbutton his top, as I wanted to examine his skin. When she reached for the top button, Emmet reached up, grabbing her hand. Though he didn't speak, his eyes reflected a great terror. She rubbed his forehead gently, whispering something inaudible and his arm lowered. He looked away so as to not bear witness to my reaction.

She unbuttoned the top of his long-johns and flapped the panels apart. His skin looked parched and dry. It was cracked and broken, much like dead earth, exposing blood and sores between crusted flakes of dead skin. Some cracks in his skin were dangerously deep. Gray puss oozed across his chest from several ruptured sores. Despite my efforts to maintain a Godly composure, I stepped backwards in fear and shock, pulling my collar over my nose and mouth.

Knowing his bizarre condition was beyond anything I could hope to give any meaningful advice on, I wanted to at least pray for them. Still with my collar over my nose, I made to place my hand on Emmet. When I touched his forehead, he jerked away violently, like I'd hit him. It made no sense. Others had touched him with no such reaction. I began praying but was interrupted when Emmet, having not made a sound earlier, howled out, 'Stop! Have mercy.' My heart broke. I motioned with my free hand for Mrs. Johansen to button Emmet's top and cover his feet, and I stepped out to regain my composure.

The stink was not as powerful in the main room, and I could breathe freely. My thoughts grappled with what I'd seen. Emmet's condition made no sense, based on my trivial grasp of medicine. However, something odd jumped into my mind. As I mentioned, this August was terribly hot. Oddly, however, I felt no traces of the summer heat in that house. I did not sweat or need to fan myself. That notion triggered another question: Why, during such intense heat, was Emmet covered with blankets and wearing long-johns?

Mrs. Johansen explained that Emmet was actually quite cold. Though it wasn't logical, it brought up another possibility regarding his toes and fingers. In the coldest parts of winter or high in the Appalachians, occasionally, some unfortunate soul falls victim to exposure. Extreme cold can cause frostbite, which blocks blood flow. My cousin, Gertrude, lost her right foot due to extreme frostbite, and that foot was the same dismal color as poor Emmet's digits. The blanket, the long underwear, the blackened toes, and the oddly comfortable temperature inside the house led me to a confusing theory that somehow Emmet had frostbite, although that wouldn't explain his hair loss or his reaction to my prayer. It might, however, explain the cracked skin on his chest, and God only knew where else.

For days I continued to check on Emmet and tried to track his condition. Each time I visited, however, his reaction to my presence became more violent and angry, and the temperature inside kept dropping. After a week had passed, I began to suspect something supernatural: some sort of spiritual attack. Though authentic demonic possessions are extremely rare, I had encountered such a thing once in the past, and some of the characteristics and violent reactions to Christian authority were present there as well.

125

On the eighth night, I returned to the Johansen household. Once I had her consent, I bid her to remain in the living room and, no matter what she heard, to not enter. Demons are apt to use any advantage at their disposal, particularly the suffering of a loving spouse.

The events of that evening still haunt me. I performed the ceremonial rites as well as I could, and Emmet resisted each attempt, growing more violent each time. At first, his resistance was mild - just some flailing of his arms and legs amid loud cries for mercy and pity. When that failed, the devil got more desperate. He put his arm up to his mouth and bit into Emmet's flesh, inflicting a gruesome wound and tremendous bleeding. His howls afterward grew much louder, followed by renewed pleas. I paused to try bandaging his wound, but each time I touched him, he fought as though my touch somehow burned him. Emmet's chest wounds ripped apart with his wild twisting and wrestling, causing more gray puss and blood to ooze forth from his cracked skin.

After praying quietly in a corner for some time, I again attacked the demon. I demanded its name. Prior to that point, the only sounds from Emmet were cries for mercy. However, when I demanded the demon's name, Emmet's eyes changed from a pitiful reflection of pain and misery to glares of hatred and venom. He stared through me and began shouting obscenities. I see no need to recount his actual words, but such horrible profanity was quite out of character for someone as mild-mannered as Emmet.

Regardless, I kept at it switching between supplicatory pleas and intercessory demands. After much turmoil and strife, Emmet placed his blackened fingers on his head and dug his fingernails into his scalp. I wept like a babe but continued demanding the demon's name, even as the blood pouring from Emmet's scalp ran down his face. My insistence finally paid off as Emmet screamed one final word to me - that of 'Thentul'!

Once I had the demon's name, I commanded it to depart. It resisted for another hour or more, but eventually, Emmet shifted violently, and his bed crashed apart, the mattress falling to the floor. When that bed frame splintered, it knocked me off my feet and pressed me against the wall. After that, Emmet passed out. The room felt hotter almost instantly.

126

It has been over a month since that night, and Emmet is recovering some. He doesn't speak anymore, and the color never returned to his fingers and toes. Most of those have since been amputated, but despite some big scars, the cracks in his flesh are closing, and the wounds are scabbing over.

I am hopeful that I will never again face such horror.

Sincerely,
Bishop Durmett

* * *

Saturday, May 22, 1999 – Evening

Sam shook his head with disbelief, not so much that the events described in document #47 were truly supernatural, but that those events actually happened in the first place. He replayed the horrid details, trying to wrap his mind around the reality of it, but something was still unsettled. Even if he acknowledged the horrific details, the little Vatican seal in the document still didn't prove anything. Perhaps the priest witnessed an epileptic attack or some other psychological phenomenon. Maybe he saw bedsores or leprosy instead of skin mutilated by some mysterious force.

Regardless of all the possible alternative explanations for what the Bishop had witnessed, not everything could be easily explained. Perhaps the greatest of these would be Emmet's healing and recovery after the exorcism. Unless the Johansens were performing high theater and choreographed the whole thing, there was no logical reason for Emmet to recover after the exorcism. However, no one, especially not someone in the late 19th century, could use epilepsy, bed sores, and the loss of frostbitten digits to pull off a possession hoax. The cost seems far too great, and the tale only made sense if the victim suffered a legitimate malady.

Sam was ultimately unsure what to make of the Bishop's account, but curiosity was prying at his mind. There was no way to dig further into Emmet's story. Over 100 years had elapsed, and all the characters had long since passed. Sam, left with nothing further, returned to the binder and Manuels's instructions to his sister:

"By now, hopefully, you have read the account of Emmet's possession, and, most likely, are far from convinced that this account reflected a true possession or exorcism. The difficulty lies in the fantastic. Think of the most trustworthy person in your life, our aunt or

127

uncle, me, or someone else important to you. If that person told you something truly fantastic, like 'last night the moon was green' or 'the dog in the street was smoking a cigar,' you would not be convinced - despite your complete faith in the one doing the telling. So, when I present a written account of something as fantastical as a demonic possession from over seventy years ago, I expect nothing but skepticism.

However, before we venture on, I would like to highlight some details. First, that letter is an authentic document received by the Vatican in 1888 - the Vatican seal impressed into the original document testifies to this fact. Second, it was genuinely penned by a Catholic Bishop, with no apparent need to fabricate its contents. Sweet sister, you may be suspect regarding Catholics, but even at my most skeptical and hedonistic, I always held some notion that Catholic Priests generally care for their parishioners and would most likely relate stories of their misfortunes truthfully. Finally, if the details regarding Emmet are true, I can think of no scientific explanation explaining them.

Like you, I would still be unconvinced. After all, our inability to understand how all the facts fit together does not necessarily justify resorting to the supernatural. Pagans used the supernatural to explain lightning and earthquakes, and those rudimentary beliefs are shattered by today's second-grade science books. With that being said, I ask only two things further: one, that you not wholly dismiss the possibility of Emmet's tale being true, and two, that you now read the translations of documents #12, #22, and #7. Feel free to read the whole documents if you like, but the passages I marked should suffice. Please do not read these passages out of order. It is particularly crucial that you not read any of document #7 before reading the others! Please stop reading until you have, at the minimum, read the marked passages."

Sam couldn't help but stare through the hazy pink light at Manuel's words. Manuel echoed his skepticism and completely understood, even agreed, with Sam's reluctance. Sam knew the Bible referenced demonic possessions, but it also contained tales of the Red Sea parting, worldwide floods, people rising from the dead, and numerous other events that Sam wasn't sure were meant to be literal. Sam obliged Manuel, and turned to the translation of document #12, and found the marked passages:

128

"1526 A.D. - Cordoba: I embarrassed myself by vomiting as I entered. Never before have I encountered such a stench. Ponce's aging skin appeared broken, like glass buckling under pressure. Dark-red, web-like fissures covered his chest, arms and legs. His blood was exposed by the cleavages in his flesh. In addition, sores and pustules pocketed his chest and would occasionally rupture, leaking their foul ooze upon him . . ."

"Several toes had become almost black in appearance. They were awful to behold, and Ponce seemed to have no feeling in them. I must surmise from his facial expressions, as he seemed to have lost the power of speech, that he was alert and aware of his surroundings. Ponce could nod or shake his head in response to questions, although such movements seemed to pain him. His swollen eyes reflected suffering and sorrow enough to melt the hardest of hearts. . ."

"The office of the Inquisitor was not informed about Ponce's condition. I must apologize on that count, but after my investigation, this was clearly not a case of witchcraft or heresy. Ponce needed help, not judgment. I wanted to hold his hands, but upon contact, he screamed in agony and pain. Being unable to touch him without invoking such reactions, I decided to withhold direct contact. . ."

"I noticed an odd coolness about his room, despite the overbearing heat affecting the whole region this summer. It was at first a relief, but soon became unnerving and a source of much confusion. There was no logical explanation for the temperature inside his hovel, and, as if the mystery had not yet become confusing enough, the temperature grew cooler the closer I stood to Ponce as if he, himself, was the source of the phenomenon. . ."

"The exorcising of this demon was difficult, requiring the greater part of the week, and only, as dawn approached on the sixth day, did the demon finally reveal its name - that of 'Thintewl.' It was loathe to speak its name, but the demon seemed able to control Ponce's vocal abilities, shouting profanities and curses, in addition to numerous and pitiful cries for relief. . ."

"1753 A.D. - Boston: Thentle, as the demon reluctantly called itself, was stubborn beyond reckoning, clinging to young Earlene desperately. I had read of exorcisms but had never performed the rite myself and did everything I could to convince myself Earlene's plight was not supernatural in nature. Despite repeated prayers and demands to the contrary, it refused to depart, leaving her deformities as intact as when I first saw them. Her torso and back had a horrid distortion in that the skin appeared separated, not unlike dry, dead ground, with gaping crevices cleaving it apart. Blood could be seen between the crevices, appearing as red fissures. . ."

"Her fingers and toes had turned black, as would frostbitten extremities. In addition, as with frostbite, the poor girl completely lost all feeling in those blackened digits. Though unable to speak when I asked about her condition, she howled in protestation, hurling vicious profanities, when I touched her. Earlene's parents were reluctant to leave me alone with their daughter, and I fear their presence may have emboldened the spirit within her, resulting in the prolonged exorcism . . ."

"July is typically sultry, but this particular July had been almost unbearable. Many local farmers' crops had wilted under the intense swelter. I only mention the heat in passing, to describe a further oddity. There was an unsettling coolness in the child's bedroom that, while slightly relieving, was quite uncomfortable - like a dismal wine cellar or basement, smothered in dankness with the scent of mildew in the air. More striking still was the almost immediate flood of warmth once the demon had been driven out. . ."

Sam's stomach turned as he read. The drapes shielding his psyche from truly accepting these occurrences as actual demonic possessions were being violently ripped from their sconces one by one. His skin began feeling uncomfortable, like wearing a suit two sizes too small. He was a grown adult, college-educated, an intellectual, but he was being dragged, like a maddened criminal, down a path promising to unravel precious childhood presumptions so many take for granted. *There really is a boogeyman. There are monsters under the bed. Dark forces do lie in wait inside your closet. What point is there*

130

in rescuing children from domestic abuse when beasts like this lurk in the shadows?

Darkness had fallen, and the sounds of night filled the room. Crickets chirped, and the lamp's humming drowned the silence. The pink light was holding somewhat, though slightly dimmer than before. He stretched his arms, and twisted around slightly to relieve tired muscles. Although he might be forced to concede that demonic forces do actually exist and have been possessing folks throughout history, he was not sure this revelation fulfilled Manuel's great promise. Sam had followed this trail around the world, searching for something claimed to prove the existence of God. Instead, he seemed to have, at best, only uncovered proof of demons. The world was dark enough already. Did a world filled with violence, despair, and isolation need proof of these evil beings skulking just beyond reach, waiting to strike and inflict such pain? He had still not read the marked passages from Document #7, so he returned to the binder:

Document #7 – Ponce; Liverpool, England – 1934

"1934 A.D. – Liverpool: I am no stranger to the exorcism ritual, but my visit last month with Chauncey still weighs heavily on me. Luckily, Father Cowell had prepared me for Chauncey's physical deformities: cracked and bleeding skin, blackened fingers, and loss of speech, to name a few. Unfortunately, no written warning, regardless of how well drafted, can properly prepare one's nostrils for that putrid scent. It was overwhelming, similar to the stink of a festered wound, and I wrestled that odor the whole time I was in Chauncey's flat . . ."

"The demon did ultimately give its name – calling itself 'Thintul.' Although my past experiences qualify me as an 'expert' on these things, one event makes this utterly unique. The demon, enraged at my persistence, howled that it had abandoned the young American girl, the decrepit Spaniard, and the one called Emmet, and it would, therefore, not forfeit Chauncey. There seems to be no record of a demon recalling its previous attempted possessions, but this 'Thintul' was adamant that its claim to Chauncey was permanent since its prior hosts had been denied, but through Jesus Christ, we were eventually able to persuade it otherwise. . ."

131

Sam slammed the binder shut and closed his eyes. *Demons are very, very real! I don't want to hear any more of these horrid accounts! This demon took normal, everyday people as hosts – not criminals, not people playing with Ouija boards, not pagan or Satanic worshippers.* The longer he sat, refusing to read further, the more terrified he grew. Horrors clearly existed outside our realm. Eventually, the frail pink light faded, and total darkness enveloped him once again. Outside, Seville was sleeping again, but Sam sat wide-eyed, staring into the black. Even the thought of sleeping terrified him – dreading what might come for him in his dreams.

Sam's paranoia continued for some time, with Sam envisioning every tiny noise as some fearsome creature piercing the thin veil between worlds. He would only go mad if he kept this up, so he broke open his last two wands and continued reading:

"These four separate accounts span centuries and reach across the globe. There was no possible way for the four separate priests to have known each other or corroborate their tales. This demon, Thintul, seems to strike during periods of extreme heat and wreaks such similar inflictions upon his hosts, there is no other explanation save the veracity of these priests' accounts. I cannot explain my excitement when stumbling upon Chauncey's account; for what better proof than to have one account of Thintul actually reference possessions from prior documents! This demon, and you will see evidence of several others, truly exists.

If this were the end of the tale, this collection would be a dismal proposal indeed – only serving to condemn us to a darkness plagued with evil spirits while we crawl but a stone's throw from complete damnation. This is not, however, the story's end. Rather than focus on the existence of the demon, focus upon something marvelous which might at first escape your attention. Each of these cases ended with the demon being purged from its damaged host. You see, these tales not only prove that demons exist but also that a far more powerful God exists. This collection is not a window into a horrible reality where demons manifest and wreak agony upon humanity at will, but a window into heaven where God rules over all and protects his subjects. Perhaps those protections are not so omnipresent or demonstrative to avoid all demonic activity in the first place, but humanity should elect, rather than weep at the exposure to harm, to triumph in the knowledge that God has power over these demons and will scourge them at our moment of most dire need."

Manuel spoke, almost to Sam directly, pointing out the obvious truth: these writings, by disparate authors, written without knowledge of one another, and across the whole of human history, prove not only that demons exist but that God, too, exists, and that in a conflict, God's will is superior. This truth was the comforting blanket Sam needed to stave off the terrors from the shadows – allowing him to close the binder and fade off.

*   *   *

Saturday, May 22, 1999 – Late Evening

The cell phone rang, shattering the night's silence along the Monaco pier. Victoria sighed as she pulled her attention from the gentle waves ferrying the moon's reflection until casually crashing upon the beach. It was Hector. She struggled to mask her anger over his poor handling of the Athens job, but she knew better than to bite the hand feeding her, even when deserved. She needed to know what he wanted. "Hello, sweetie, where've you been?" she asked in their mutual coded greeting.

"In hell, darling, awaiting your return," he responded in perfectly coded response. The codes, which she hated, let them both know they had reached one another, and they were free to talk openly.

"What do you want?"

Hector, likely detecting her contempt, replied, "Listen, let's put Athens behind us. That business got sorted out in the end. I have a new job for you, but you'll have to move quickly."

Victoria wasn't entirely ready to launch into another big crisis right now and had been enjoying a few days on the Mediterranean. Still, she was close to paying Hector off from that business all those years ago and could hardly afford to refuse. She turned and started briskly walking toward her hotel as she continued, "Where is the pick-up?"

"Spain, darling – Seville, actually."

133

"Your wickedness makes you as it were heavy as lead, and to tend downwards with great weight and pressure towards hell; and if God should let you go, you would immediately sink and swiftly descend and plunge into the bottomless gulf, and your healthy constitution, and your own care and prudence, and best contrivance, and all your righteousness, would have no more influence to uphold you and keep you out of hell, than a spider's web would have to stop a fallen rock." – Jonathon Edwards; Sinners in the Hands of an Angry God

Sunday, May 23, 1999 – Mid-Morning

Lukas couldn't help feeling responsible. This was his first real assignment, and things had done anything but go according to plan. He had seen this "Samuel" character climb onto the bridge. There had been no way to know he would take off when Lukas turned on the headlights. They had been watching him for days, and aside from an unhealthy addiction for the Guadalquivir River and Triana Bridge, he had behaved much like any common tourist, until Friday night. They had parked on the far side of the river to keep an eye on Sam – especially curious was his long pause atop that bridge. Sam was contemplating something more, well, involved. Alfons, despite Lukas' urging, refused to take Sam earlier that evening. Alfons had simply, in his own plain manner, replied, "Not until he has done something worthy of being taken." So, they had waited and watched. That night had dragged, and at one point, Sam even abandoned the bridge for hours. Lukas had assumed this temporary crisis had run its course when Alfons insisted they continue waiting. "Be patient," had been the only explanation.

Lukas, though terribly excited about his new post, had not been afforded any training prior to being brought on this assignment. Alfons had apologized on that point, but apparently all agents are trained "on the job," and Lukas' time had been educational. He had watched Alfons' surveillance techniques, seen him tap phone lines and obtain hotel records, the whole time under strict instructions to "watch, learn, but fight the urge to intervene." Alfons had a particular manner and way of doing things and Lukas assumed he needed his new partner to at least watch the swimming video before plunging into the pool.

On Friday, Lukas had finally gotten the chance to be more involved when Alfons invited him to drive. Lukas had figured Alfons' invitation was more likely based on Alfons' desire to be the, "jump out of the car and grab him" guy, rather than the "bring the car close enough" guy. That lone decision, the decision for Lukas to drive, had been the undoing of their efforts. When Sam crawled back upon the bridge, hauling a bulky box under his arm, Alfons, peering through infrared binoculars, quietly uttered one word, "Follow." Lukas, not thinking, had turned on the headlamps and was shocked to see Sam sprinting away. Alfons had said something then, but Lukas was already committed and sped up chasing Sam across the bridge and through the streets of Seville. Lukas smiled as Sam turned into the hotel. "We have him," he thought jubilantly to himself, but before he could share his enthusiasm, Alfons leaped from the car and tore after him. Lukas had screeched to a halt and hurriedly parked, following Alfons less than a minute behind.

Everything since then had been utterly unexceptional. Alfons had seen Sam running out the hotel's back door, which opened to a labyrinth of alleys, home to a storage facility and a defunct motorcycle shop, amongst other things. By the time Alfons had reached the back door, Sam had vanished into the night, but Alfons was able to get a read on the few exits from the block's interior. Sam had temporarily eluded them, but he did not escape. There were only four exits, and Alfons could monitor all of them simultaneously from one helpful vantage point. Sam was cowering somewhere in the interior, though they had no way of knowing where. Alfons had called for local officers to show up and help search the buildings and streets along the perimeter. Alfons mentioned that searching the perimeter ensured those four exits were the only way in and out and that no "ratte hole," as he phrased it, existed for Sam to slip through. Once satisfied that he had, at a minimum, successfully cornered Sam, he released the local police, and he and Lukas began their stakeout.

They took turns watching exits from the vantage point while the other worked the more intricate search. The most likely hiding spot would be inside one of the storage units, and that was where they had focused their initial efforts. With a meager two-hour sleep in the back of the sedan before dawn, Lukas was exhausted, and the sweltering heat beaming down didn't help. If Alfons was tired or hot, Lukas couldn't tell as he wore his coat throughout the day and never stopped to rest. Either Alfons was simply showing off or was, perhaps, empowered by God himself. They got through most of the storage units on Saturday with no sign of Sam or that box of his. At Saturday's end,

Alfons declared that they would take shifts sleeping in the sedan. Lukas had drawn the first shift and had agreed eagerly.

Sunday morning was already warming up by the time Alfons returned from his rotation in the sedan. He approached Lukas. "Morgen," he sputtered crisply.

Lukas turned to face him, "and to you, too, Mein Herr."

"Anything unusual?"

"Not really – some vagrant woman showed up today, but I thought little of it. They move around a bit, do they not – vagrants?"

"Some. Describe her, bitte."

Lukas tried remembering the poor woman, but it was harder than it probably should have been. Lukas made a mental note to work past his civilian temptation to avert his eyes from homeless folks. Civilians see a homeless person or vagabond and turn away to avoid the guilt confronting their less fortunate brethren, but an agent should be paying attention – to everything.

"Well, she was in a wheelchair, terribly dirty, average build. She had fairly long black hair, I remember that."

"How were her teeth?"

"Pardon? I was not really close enough to . . ." Lukas couldn't help but be confused by the question, and it must have shown.

"Teeth, Mr. Dietrich, provide excellent evidence regarding the authenticity of a gypsy, street urchin, homeless person, or anyone of that ilk. Homelessness is drudgery coupled with despair. Oral hygiene does not typically make the list of things one keeps on top of after finding oneself on the street. A true homeless person generally has unkept, uneven, and rotten teeth, and even if new to their plight, the teeth will still be likely stained."

Lukas had never considered how much information you could get simply by looking at someone's teeth, but that would only be the latest revelation Alfons had shared with him since joining him last week. Alfons had shown him things like ways to order food to engender confidence in the wait staff and how to walk while masking your footsteps. This job was a whole new world, and Alfons was his guide, but still his mistake on the bridge haunted him.

Alfons had, at one point, tried to assuage his guilt. He had whispered sternly, "I will only mention this once. Mistakes happen, and we go on. The only mistake that truly can remove you from the game is the mistake of dwelling on prior failures instead of letting them be the growth opportunities

137

they should be." Lukas had tried taking those cold words to heart. Chasing Sam across that bridge had landed both of them in this situation. There were still a hundred little holes Sam could have scurried into, and their job now was to face another day peering into each one. He turned to Alfons, "I'll get started if you like?"

A curt nod was Alfons' response.

*   *   *

Sunday, May 23, 1999 – Mid-Day

While only a mild hindrance, the rusted wheelchair's left wheel was tighter than the right. At first, it was merely an adjustment, but as the morning wore on, it had become burdensome. It was likely rust or something that could be easily cured, but crippled vagrants don't typically leap from their wheelchairs to operate on them. She had to maintain her cover as a poor vagrant living on the streets, and that meant enduring that defective chair. One of her first purchases upon arrival in Seville had been a shiny, new wheelchair, which she promptly exchanged with a poor, disheveled man. A brand-new chair would only draw undue attention.

Two agents, she had discovered, both wearing suits, kept a diligent eye over the interior of this block. Many sections of Seville were like this – a perimeter of shops and apartments with a maze of alleys and trashier establishments in the interior. These two men didn't fit in here. They weren't police. *Not even Spanish detectives would drive that shitty brown sedan. But who do they work for?* They had clearly been lying in wait and had come upon Sam unaware. *How did he escape them anyway? Hector said this Sam is a simple tourist with no street time at all. How could a . . . ahh . . . a rookie. One of these two is new and tipped him off somehow – maybe a revving engine, a slamming door or even headlights suddenly igniting. Any number of amateur moves like that could have flushed their quarry.*

Victoria mulled this over as she quietly closed the storage closet. This little gambit would only buy her a couple of minutes, but in her line of work, that was an eternity. She knew which door Sam was behind, and unfortunately, it was near where one of the two had taken up sentry duty. *Good spot for that, too. From there, he can see down every exit corridor. Hope he flinches and rushes to inspect my diversion, when it finally goes off.* This was a reliable diversion. A small leaking propane tank, a traditional rat trap with a light sponge on top serving as trigger, some ice melting into a funnel perched above the sponge as the detonator. As the ice melts, water droplets would

138

descend through the funnel and onto the sponge – gradually making the sponge heavy enough to spring the trap. The tiniest bit of powder on the trap should ignite the gas.

The chaos of the explosion and ensuing flames should distract these two long enough to get Sam out of there and into this wheelchair. The wheelchair, in addition to helping her blend in, would also double as an assist for her cargo, an adult male American who apparently got in way over his head. He had been trapped in there for over thirty hours, and Victoria had no way of knowing his condition. He would likely be dehydrated and unable to walk out on his own. Of course, she would also need to slap her wig and blanket on him. *He needs to pass as me – at least from a distance. Won't be time for me to coach him on his mannerisms or even blacken his teeth. I'm going to kill Hector one day! He knows how hard it is to smuggle a living human, and into the United States, at that! The pay is good, though, and will almost settle my debt. I could actually be free of him soon!*

Through her micro-binoculars, she could tell that the younger agent, most likely the rookie, was currently checking potential hiding places, and the older, a serious-looking gentleman masked in determination, watched the escape routes. Luck, it seemed, might be on her side with this arrangement. Once the explosion triggers, the veteran agent would likely leave his post to assist the rookie, giving her time to get Sam free before either agent knew anything was up.

She was rolling forward, replaying this scenario in her mind's eye, when it happened. A thunderous "BOOM" echoed behind her, telling her the game was now afoot. She spun around, watching and waiting for the older agent to take the bait. Remarkably, and to her astonishment, he stayed put, doggedly maintaining his post. *This guy is beyond professional – no way he works for anyone in Seville, maybe part of Spanish Civil Guard Intelligence. What sort of trouble has this Sam character gotten into – to have someone this professional hunting him?* As she was revising her plan to be a little more direct, the agent got a call. While she couldn't hear any conversation, his body language spoke volumes. The rookie was checking out the explosion and had called for help. Apparently, despite his better judgment, the explosion proved too great a temptation and he ran to assist.

Black smoke billowed her as she quickly rolled to the utility room door and pulled out her tiny lock-pick gun. Victoria usually prided herself on her basic, low-tech approach, while her competitors leaned toward sophisticated

139

gadgetry to counter the eyes and ears of those in their way. She avoided complications by thinking things through rather than relying on technology. However, when it came to picking locks, nothing compared to a high-end lock-picking gun. She could pick most locks quickly enough, but manual tools leave marks and were sometimes cumbersome with wet or slippery hands. She marked her watch. *Here we go. No turning back. Twenty-five minutes to make this whole thing happen.* Sands were already slipping through the hourglass.

Victoria placed her ear to the door jam and listened. Nothing. *Not great news, but might not mean anything. This guy's been trapped for a long time and there's no way of knowing how much water he's had, if any. He could be passed out (or worse). Hopefully, he's not injured – that would be an unpleasant wrinkle.* Softly, she spoke into the door jam, "Sam. I am coming in. Gerard sent me." *Last thing I need is this guy pulling a gun just as I open the door.* She placed the pick-lock gun against the lock and gently squeezed the trigger. A slight whirring was the only sound as the tiny pins inside writhed into place and turned the lock.

Potent sunlight poured through the open door. Sam was awake but not moving. He had a knife in his left hand, and loose papers and odd little plastic wands lay scattered about. His eyes were wild and red – likely swollen from tears and agony. He was soaked in sweat, and his lips were parched. Near his head was a wooden box with its top shredded away. Any pity she felt, however, had to take a back seat as those agents would soon return. They had to be on their way before that happened. Plus, the sands kept slipping – *only twenty-four minutes now.* She knelt down and sternly began, "Your name is Sam. You are from the U.S. You are in real trouble. We have little time, so you need to cooperate without question – and without delay. Nod if you understand."

He managed the slightest head gesture, proving he was at least alert and responsive.

"Fine. Drop the blade."

He laid the knife on the floor. Judging from winces of pain when he tried shifting his weight, she knew he wasn't mobile. She removed her wig, letting her auburn hair fall around her shoulders. Victoria then hoisted Sam into the chair and placed the wig on him. She also laid the sand-colored blanket over him. It wouldn't fool anyone up close, but perhaps from a distance. He let out a muffled cry from the move. *Muscle strain? Must be – nothing appears broken or bleeding. Perhaps internal injuries, but no time to*

140

diagnose right now. She spun the wheelchair around to leave, and Sam protested. He opened his mouth to speak, but his voice was gone, and his throat likely scorched. He pointed to the papers and the tattered box on the floor.

So, that was it then. The agents wanted those documents. She was inclined to oblige them, but common sense got the better of her. Until she knew more, she couldn't just leave them behind. She swore under her breath as she collected everything and placed the box in Sam's lap. *Twenty-three minutes now, and we've got to move fast – they've probably figured the fire was intentional by now.* Sam gripped the box as a mother clings to her child but didn't utter a sound. His face wore a mask of weariness, but not purely physical – there was emotional exhaustion as well.

She quietly locked the door behind her and wheeled Sam along the broken walk toward the opening at the back of the block. She had to hurry! Victoria forced the old chair over the uneven and cracked stones. The end was drawing near. She shut her eyes and listened. Scattered cars buzzed about in the street ahead of her, but she focused on the world behind her. Only a few steps further and she would turn on a smooth modern sidewalk – free from prying eyes. Boots clapped onto stone in rhythm behind her. *Almost there – do not look back. Twenty-two minutes left – still on track.* Those steps behind her had remained steady, not speeding up – a good sign. She felt the stones under the wheelchair give way to smooth pavement. A sharp right and she was no longer in sight of anyone in the interior. She listened – no footsteps.

Victoria knew that wouldn't hold for long. They knew the explosion was rigged and would come out to the street. She opened her eyes and focused on the brown sedan parked curbside just ahead. Sam had seen it also and started getting fidgety. "They aren't in there right now. Relax." He seemed to calm a little at her reassurances as she reached into her pocket and pulled out a small knife. She hurriedly jabbed the right rear tire. She put the knife away and pushed Sam gracefully to a van parked nearby. It was bright yellow and looked like it had enjoyed a far brighter past than its present. It had a white top with its entire underbelly coated in rust while random stickers and graffiti decorated its exterior.

The van had a rear wheelchair ramp, and she had Sam loaded in short order. She yanked the wig and blanket from him before locking the chair's brakes and slamming the rear doors. She was soon in the driver's seat, pulling forward into the main flow of the street, when she squealed her tires loudly.

141

One of the agents had just emerged onto the sidewalk. Sirens in the distance were closing in on the mysterious explosion and fire. Victoria, satisfied that things were going as expected, reached between the two front seats and handed Sam a bottle of water. "Here. You are dehydrated. Try to drink. Not too fast, now: slow, deliberate sips. Got another one when you're ready." Sam eagerly took the bottle and drank. She switched on the air conditioner – such as it was in the old van. *Twenty minutes left, and I've got to get in position.*

*   *   *

Sunday, May 23, 1999 – Mid-Day

Several blocks later, she pulled over and parked. Sam, the second water bottle in his hands, managed a quick grin before noticing the small hospital nearby, and his face again became confused. Victoria noticed those wrinkles on his forehead. "It's ok. We're not staying. Just need a few supplies and a new vehicle, but we need to move! Time is against us." She got out of the van and threw open the rear doors, but instead of the old, decrepit wheelchair Sam had been sitting in, she unfolded a new one. She pulled out a dark leather bag and placed a hand on Sam's shoulder. "This is important, Sam. I'm going to shave your head now, and we have little time. My job is to get you home safely, and sometimes we need disguises in this line of work." She saw distress in his eyes, but behind that fear and apprehension was a mind that understood.

He gave a muffled, "OK".

She removed some cordless shears and got busy. *Eighteen minutes* more, she thought to herself as she hurried through, scooping large wads of reddish-brown hair into the blanket. She stopped short of a perfect job, leaving occasional small patches of thin hair sprouting from his scalp and blew any excess hair away. His face showed the despair and despondence of someone being adding the proverbial "insult to injury," but that pitiful look would come in handy soon. "Ok. Good. Now, we have to get you changed. Let me help. She removed his pants and shirt in no time and wrapped him in a hospital gown lying at his feet. Sam's face betrayed his amazement at the tricks Victoria had stashed in plain sight. Once finished, she hoisted him into the new wheelchair outside, disposing of the old one, along with the blanket, hair, and sundry articles, in a nearby dumpster. She hopped back inside and turned back. "Give me a quick second." With that, she closed the van doors.

142

A moment later, she emerged sporting nurse's scrubs, and the fake rot and stains had been wiped from her teeth. Victoria grinned as she saw Sam's shock. Her uniform was a perfect match for the other staff, including a badge. "I do my homework," was the only explanation offered. She gave the old box of documents back to Sam and whispered, "Not sure what's on these, but you hang on to them for right now. We'll talk later, but you should do your best not to say anything for now. Nod if you understand."

Sam nodded in response, and she pushed him up the curb and into the hospital. Though not terribly large, the hospital was frenetic, especially for a Sunday. Doctors, nurses, and other staff darted up and down hallways and in and out of rooms, running their assorted rounds. A receptionist looked up before opening her mouth to question her and her odd patient carrying a wooden box. However, before she could manage to speak, Victoria, in perfect Spanish, asked for her to fetch Dr. Christobol to the cancer ward for an urgent patient consult. Sam's look of distress and pitiful condition, coupled with their authentic clothing gave her no choice but to comply.

Victoria didn't wait for the nurse, pushing Sam past the counter into the belly of the hotel. A quick dart down one hallway ended at a supply room. No one gave her a second thought as she quickly unlocked the door and gathered supplies – a needle and kit to start an IV, some surgical tape, and four bags of Saline – rehydration fluid. All of the equipment went into a plastic bedpan that she tucked into the pouch on the back of the wheelchair. *Only fifteen minutes to be in position*, she reminded herself as she checked her watch. She spun Sam around and ducked back down another hallway – toward the rear exit.

Victoria rolled Sam through the Emergency Room toward large electric double doors. No one in the waiting room bothered paying them too much attention. After all, who notices a nurse pushing a cancer patient through an emergency room? The doors slid open, basking them once again in bright sunlight. Just off to the side of the building sat a bank of parked ambulances. No one seemed to be milling about or watching them too carefully, so she headed straight for them, wheeling Sam ahead of her and tucked between two ambulances. The door lock was easy enough, and the ignition wiring was only a bit trickier. As she was loading the ambulance, she checked her watch again. *Only thirteen minutes left. They are finishing changing their tire right about now, and they'll be here in short order."*

143

She pulled away from the hospital and headed back south. She was looking for a particular complex, *Los Sabios Del Rio, or "The Sages of the River."* Befitting its pompous name, it was an oversized compound with two lower floors of high-end shopping and five floors of residential lofts above. While the stores in the high-class plaza were more upscale than average, there were a number of restaurants and pubs inside as well. None of that particularly interested Victoria, however. She was only interested in one particularly helpful feature: the plaza's multi-level parking garage. The garage covered both customer cars and the loading dock, where deliveries were made throughout the day. Victoria made two calls en route – one to confirm a cab waiting for her and another to Hector, confirming a different vehicle.

Only eight more minutes. This is going to be tight. Everything better be in place. She had known this rescue was a long shot the moment Hector explained it last night. *Sam's lucky to still be alive,* she had thought when she first opened that small locked door and saw him lying on the floor. There was a story behind this; she had figured that much, and it involved that rotting box Sam was hauling. There would be time for stories, but not during these eight minutes.

She pulled into the garage and drove straight ahead, parking beside a yellow cab. *At least this piece of this puzzle was OK.* The cab driver's window lowered as she approached. She pulled out a wad of cash and crossed her arms, leaning on the edge of the window. "Listen. There is no time. This is going to be 'different.' I need you to drive yourself to Madrid as fast as you can without getting caught speeding, and then turn around and come right back home. You will have no passengers except for this money I am handing you. This should be three times the normal fare to drive all the way to Madrid and back. Are you with me?"

"Sure, Senorita. Am I going to get in trouble?"

"No. Ask no more questions. I do need one further favor. If you do get stopped, they will ask who hired you. You have never seen me – understand?"

"Si."

"Just tell them it was a tall, thin man with reddish hair – an American. Now – Ándale!" With that, she slapped the driver's side panel, and the cab driver pulled away quickly. *With luck, he gets at least halfway there before getting snapped up – depends on how connected and dedicated our friends in the brown sedan are.*

144

Victoria made it back to the ambulance and, without anything further, opened the door and rolled Sam out the back, still clutching his wooden box. She rushed him through the garage to the loading dock. Sundays were usually slow, and that worked in her favor. However, no amount of luck or fortune would help her if Hector hadn't delivered. She made her way to the far end where, as requested, sat a *Mohau Light* delivery truck, complete with slide-ups on each side stocked with cold *Mohau Light* beer bottles and cans. Its outside was covered in vinyl depicting a cold *Mohau Light* can glistening with beads of sweat. She didn't quite understand why, but Sam chuckled as they approached the truck. She pulled the handle on the driver's door. It was unlocked with no one inside. The truck keys were in the ashtray, as promised. Victoria ran to the rear of the truck and opened it up. The interior also looked like it was stocked with cold *Mohau Light*, but Victoria grabbed a hidden handle, and the rear panel pulled out, revealing a hollow cavity inside. Sam's face, again, betrayed confusion.

Victoria, noticing his concern, explained, "This truck is used to smuggle people: usually, dragging people away from their homes to somewhere else. Today, though, it is helping you return home. There are no creature comforts. It will be dark and probably a little scary. I would love to sit here explaining until you are convinced, but we have no time. You have to get in this truck right now!" As she was finishing, she reached down, grabbed the wooden box, and sat it on the ground. Then, she hoisted him upward, again with whimpers of intense pain, and laid him in the back. While the hidden space stretched about twelve feet, it was but three feet high and wide with no light. "Once we get out of the city, I will stop and help a bit more. For now, you need to lay in there and make no sound. Here is this box you care so much about." She quickly tossed in the box, bedpan, and other supplies and slammed the door.

Very little time remained, and the clock was ticking. She hid the wheelchair and yanked off her scrubs, revealing a khaki shirt and shorts – the kind typically worn by people driving *Mahou Light* trucks daily. Her hair she pulled into a ponytail jutting out the back of a *Mahou Light* cap she bought last night to complete the look. She pulled away from the hulking garage, once again, into the ever-present Andalusian sunlight. The beast handled terribly, and the right turn signal was on its way out, but she and the truck soon learned one another. *This is it. Time's up. I need to get set.* As the last grain of sand fell from her mental hourglass, she pulled beside a ratty convenience store – just one block from the hospital they had visited only moments ago.

145

The brown sedan was, expectedly, parked just behind that abandoned yellow van. The van's doors had been plied open, but no one seemed about. *They are still inside, likely asking questions and making phone calls. Just hope they're smart enough to connect that stolen ambulance.* The pieces were still in motion, and she had orchestrated this last part of the plan banking on her adversaries: on their intuition and tenacity. Traffic cameras around the city would easily show that ambulance pulling into the parking garage. They, hopefully, would take the bait and scurry after that cab.

Victoria sat patiently for twenty more minutes before there was movement. The agents bolted out of the hospital, jumped into the sedan and sped away. She couldn't help but grin as she stayed a comfortable distance behind, shadowing them as they wound through the city and eventually onto the freeway heading out of town — toward Madrid. *This may have worked perfectly. When folks chase something ahead of them, they seldom bother checking their rearview mirror.*

She trailed the sedan for some time after leaving Seville. Once reasonably sure they were heading to Madrid, she pulled over to check in on Sam — as promised. She stopped at a fuel station and, after running inside for a few scattered items, went to the rear of the truck and opened the rear doors. He was doing fine, though not terribly comfortable. "Here, Sam." She handed him a threadbare blanket she had found behind the truck's seat. "Listen, Madrid is over five hours away, especially in this rig. I want to get an IV started to help with your dehydration, understand?"

Sam nodded slowly.

"Ok, great. Let me take a look." Victoria crawled inside and got to work jury-rigging an IV to drip saline into his system, intended to keep him from losing much more fluid and start his recovery. "Here is another bottle of water. You should be doing a little better by the time we reach Madrid. I did find a few more things inside." She held up a small blue two-way radio. "I'm going to tape this thing open in here. You won't be able to hear me, but I'll hear you. If you need to stop for some reason — bathroom, problem with the IV, whatever, just tap the handset, and I'll stop shortly. If you have a bathroom emergency, well, bedpan's right there. You are in my care now, Sam, and I don't flush my deliveries." Victoria made sure everything was as comfortable as she could make it and shut the back panel once more, got back on the freeway and made her way cautiously north around the mountains toward the capital city of Seville.

146

*　　*　　*

Sam felt every bump as the truck jostled along. His head was spinning. Had he merely escaped one dark pit to be shoved into another? *Damn, how long was I stuck in that infernal utility room? I was able to move before, but now – so much pain! Can dehydration affect sore and stretched muscles? Everything hurts. Hopefully, rest will help. Who the hell did Gerard send to help, anyway? She seems smart – always got things figured out a few steps in advance. Still, she seems so unconventional. Why couldn't I be rescued in a private jet and whisked straight home? Instead, I get rescued in the belly of a truck used for human trafficking. Figures.*

"You know a conjurer gets no credit when once he has explained his trick; and if I show you too much of my method of working, you will come to the conclusion that I am a very ordinary individual after all." – Sherlock Holmes in "A Study in Scarlet" by Sir Arthur Conan Doyle.

Sunday, May 23, 1999 – Early Evening

Pink sunlight fell lazily through the branches of the park's, larger than really necessary, magnolia trees. As the light worked its way in and around the leaves, some descended onward to the stone: a roughhewn pink granite block sitting quite apart from the others scattered along the otherwise dense copse. A light breeze careened through the park, granting momentary relief from the May sun, and slightly jostled the magnolia branches, rapidly flickering sunlight off and on again several times. If that momentary strobe-like effect bothered the black rhinoceros beetle, slowly plodding through the grass alongside the stone, he didn't let it show. With each step, he cautiously pecked through grass and moss in a deliberate northern march, the long pointed horn atop his nose warbling from side to side as he went. There was no way of knowing what to the north justified such a journey, but it must have been vital as he continued marching without so much as a pause. It was odd that the beetle even elected to march at all, as rhinoceros beetles possess the gift of flight.

Unbeknownst to the beetle, his sojourn northward was a potentially fatal mistake, for high in the magnolia branches perched a hawk casually minding her own business. Well, she was minding her own business until that breeze swayed the tree branches and reflected pink sunlight off the beetle's back. That tiny, flickering sparkle in the grass caught her attention. She gazed at the oddity far below and cocked her head first to the right, then to the left. At first, it was pure curiosity, but upon further study, that curiosity morphed into a whetting of the appetite. There are, as it turns out, few birds that aren't always ravenously hungry. In fact, if birds could speak, they would have little use for the phrase, "No thanks, I'm full." So, as hungry as this hawk was, a rhinoceros beetle crawling, with grim determination no less, through the grass was a tremendous temptation. The hawk launched from the branch and dived aggressively toward the beetle, beak open and ready for the kill. The stoic beetle continued his northward journey, sparing not one moment of thought on the approaching hawk. Just as the hawk closed in, the ground beneath the beetle's eight legs suddenly gave way, exposing what, from a beetle's perspective, would have seemed a massive crevasse. The beetle plummeted downward, and the hawk, disoriented by the sudden disappearance of its prey, forgot to pull up and slammed violently into the pink granite stone. Several minutes later, when the rhinoceros beetle finally crawled from the crevasse and continued northward, the hawk still lay limp behind him, her shattered body basking in what few rays of lazy pink sunlight remained descending through the massive magnolia trees.

Lukas was entranced by these goings-on and had only managed a few bites of his bocadillo sandwich when Alfons, surprisingly, broke the uncomfortable silence with an atypical chuckle. Lukas, surprised by a chuckle coming from his serious partner, couldn't help but turn from the rhinoceros beetle toward Alfons' typically stoic expression. But it wasn't particularly stoic just then. In fact, it seemed almost cheery, with hints of a grin at his mouth's edges.

Alfons pointed toward the hawk and began, "Sorry. This little scene here . . . fascinating. Animals so often inadvertently paint elaborate truths. You watched that episode unfold, yes?"

"Yeah – hope that bird makes it."

"That bird overcommitted. She created a situation where either she or that beetle was going to buy it. Agents often pursue their targets with such zeal and enthusiasm that we, too, set up deadly 'us or them' scenarios that often do not work out. There was no reason for that hawk to swoop in so fast. Those beetles are not particularly agile. Her greed and voracious appetite eclipsed everything else in her environment."

Lukas wasn't sure he agreed. "So, the bird, excuse me, hawk, made a mistake? I saw nothing unusual about her attempt – just unfortunate she failed to approach from a different angle."

Alfons, returning to his cold, plain manner, responded, "I think you imply too much. I never said the hawk did something especially different from what any other hawk might do in the same situation. That particular hawk is no more dimwitted than her brothers and sisters. I was simply commenting on the nature of hawks, and most birds for that matter. Like agents, they get so worked up in their missions and objectives that they box themselves and their prey into an 'either/or' scenario."

"I am not sure I completely understand," came Lukas' only reply.

150

"Well," Alfons returned, "let us revisit the episode on the bridge in Seville. When you turned on the headlamps, you created a scenario with only two outcomes: either Sam would be 'captured' or he would 'escape.' That dramatic chase through the streets of Seville should not have been necessary. I had been hopeful I might coax that box from him rather peacefully if given the opportunity. When we sparked that chase, we were just like that poor hawk lying there. We overcommitted, leaving no room for opportunity."

Alfons had, without insulting Lukas, put the events on that bridge in perspective, and it made sense. Lukas took another bite from his bocadillo and couldn't help but grin. His partner had forgiven him, and hopefully, he could, in time, use this small token to begin forgiving himself. Several minutes further passed without a word until Alfons, finishing off his bocadillo, asked, "Why yellow?"

His question was asked seemingly to the wind rather than Lukas or anyone else in particular. Lukas replied, "Pardon?"

"Why a yellow van? This morning, when Sam escaped, why escape in a *yellow* van?"

"He likely had little choice in the matter. It might have been the only vehicle available."

"Mr. Dietrich, we should never assume anything 'just happens.' Should we not be vigilant and at least consider that everything our adversaries do is intentional? For example, why drive a yellow van as an escape vehicle? It is bright and does a terrible job of blending in. For that matter, why squeal the tires? I could assume the squealing tires were just the by-product of a hasty escape, and I could assume the van's color was just a coincidence, but what if they are not?"

"That would mean Sam *wanted* us to notice him. But why would he want that? He knows we intend to catch him."

"Yes, but perhaps this situation is more complex. I am wondering now why only one of our tires was punctured. Again, if Sam wanted us disabled, he should have punctured more than one. That would be the conventional way of looking at it."

Lukas, struggling to keep up, said, "Maybe he was afraid that he had no time to do more damage?"

"Perhaps, but play this out. If you or I emerged onto the street to see him driving off in that yellow van, and then saw several tires punctured, would we stop to change the tires or radio local police for assistance? For that

151

matter, we have but one spare. Even two flat tires would have triggered a call for help. By only slashing the one, Sam molded the perfect opportunity, buying himself as much time as possible."

"Interesting. You are right, of course." Lukas felt awkward openly complimenting Alfons. He had no need for Lukas' accolades.

Alfons spent another moment in silence before announcing, "Mr. Dietrich, this was not Sam's doing. He now has an accomplice."

Lukas wrinkled his brows considerably at this accusation. *How would he know that? We have not seen another soul in any footage or evidence.* "Where do you get that, Mein Herr?"

"Do you remember the old Polaroid cameras, Mr. Dietrich?"

Lukas nodded confusingly.

"Well, what we are doing here is not unlike assembling a series of Polaroid instants to try making sense of what we know – like working a jigsaw puzzle without knowing what the final picture is supposed to be or if you even have all the pieces. Let us begin with a brief inventory if it were. What 'pictures' or facts are we certain of? An explosion was triggered – minor, but sufficient to draw our attention. That explosion occurred in a storage unit we had cleared the day before. During the exact time we were investigating that explosion, our captive escapes. You noticed a street woman earlier this morning who was not there yesterday. You mentioned she was in a wheelchair. Sam escaped in a van, a vehicle large enough to accommodate a wheelchair quite easily. Also, we examined inside that van. There were no rear seats – it had been modified to haul cargo. It has been excruciatingly hot since we cornered Sam, yet he did not escape until Sunday. By then, depending on what supplies he had brought with him, he was getting quite desperate."

Lukas, becoming excited, chimed in, "I think I see what you are driving at. If you arrange these pieces chronologically. . ."

Alfons nodded as he continued over Lukas, "There is no way a tired, likely dehydrated, man with no appreciable talent or record of 'street skills,' for lack of a better term, pulled this feat off. I would also add one more Polaroid to the menagerie. He did not attempt escape at night while we took shifts sleeping. His chances were certainly higher while we were at half-strength, but he waited until Sunday morning, when we were both awake. Why? I would posit that it was an unfortunate turn of events that his 'helper' did not arrive until sometime early Sunday morning."

Lukas was amazed at how quickly this sweater had unraveled by merely tugging on a few errant threads. Still, the whole picture hadn't fallen completely together. He glanced at Alfons and asked, "I understand then that the explosion was a diversion, planted by his helper. When it goes off, she finds Sam and gets him into that yellow van. But we still do not know why she drove a yellow van or squealed her tires, no?"

"Partially." Alfons continued in his tight, German accent. "First, I would caution against using the label 'she.' Are you certain that was a woman in the wheelchair this morning? To unravel the rest of the riddle, we must ask the correct question. So far, we have been asking 'why someone would choose such an ostentatiously colored van and make so much noise.' However, we should likely be asking, 'why someone trying to escape would want our attention?'"

Lukas answered plainly, "She. . . I mean, they, *wanted* us to follow them to the hospital?"

"I think so, yes. This behavior has been consistent, has it not: an ambulance – such a vibrant, easy-to-spot, get-away vehicle; after that, a speeding yellow cab, so simple to track and follow? Do you have a mental picture yet, Mr. Dietrich?"

Lukas was still mulling it over but rose when Alfons did and walked along the edge of the copse back toward their brown sedan outside the Parque de Retiro. Neither agent spoke until their path took them alongside a grand statue in the center of a fountain: a large statue of the angel Lucifer falling from grace. Alfons broke the silence as he stared at the statue, the sun quickly disappearing into the distance. It was over twenty feet tall, depicting a lone angel, wings still attached, lying upon a rock gazing toward heaven. Its bronze color had tarnished over the years, resembling a dark iron hue. "The Statue of the Fallen Angel. Magnificent, is it not?" Alfons continued without waiting for a reply, "You know, this is one of the only, if not the only, statue in the world devoted to a 'Pre-Satan' depiction of Lucifer. Tragic: the ramifications echoing throughout all of time stemming from just one corrupt heart."

Lukas, his thoughts interrupted, was so taken with the statue's grandeur he stopped to take it in. He couldn't help feeling a sudden and distinct chill running up his spine. It was the mouth. Lucifer has just been evicted from heaven, but his mouth did not reflect the perfunctory anger nor even defeat and surrender that might be expected. Instead, Lucifer seemed surprised, perhaps even saddened, being driven from God. As they walked

153

further away, Lukas turned once more and looked back. He could barely make out the outline of the angel's wing as the last bit of pink sunlight descended from view, ushering in a new darkness.

Once inside the sedan, Alfons started the engine, pulled away, and turned to Lukas. "So, have you figured it out? Why strut as a peacock with plumes of vibrant feathers instead of crouching as the chameleon, lying quietly unnoticed?" The silent pause must have been all the answer Alfons needed. "Not to worry. I suspect our answer might be rather elusive. Earlier, we watched that hawk crash into a stone chasing a little beetle, yes?"

"Of course," Lukas replied.

"Well, perhaps the answer to our riddle lies not with the hawk but rather with the beetle. As did I, you likely watched that little scenario unfold from the perspective that our little friend was simply minding his own business and marching toward his doom. What if, instead, the beetle knew of the hawk and diligently made for that hole, intending to foil the attack? What if the beetle *planned* to fall in that hole instead of *accidentally* falling in?"

Lukas grew more confused, a reaction with which he was becoming accustomed. "Are you suggesting the beetle used himself as bait to lure the hawk into committing possible suicide?"

Alfons couldn't help but let a muffled grimace and quick giggle escape before replying. "No. I do not think our little friend brewed such an elaborate scheme at all. I am simply referring to this beetle, Mr. Dietrich, to illustrate a metaphor. Occasionally, might the machinations of predator and prey be more 'evolved' than a coyote and a road runner?"

The sedan maneuvered through Madrid quietly until Lukas dared to speak up again. "So, if I may ask, does this metaphor about the beetle explain the yellow van, squealing tires, and ambulance?"

"It is merely a theory at this point, but perhaps our prey has a more complex agenda than simply flitting off to Madrid with us nipping at their heels." Alfons left it at that and continued driving through Madrid's dark streets.

*   *   *

Sunday, May 23, 1999 – Evening

Plush gray carpet lined the hallway inside the Interior Ministry headquarters, running from wall to wall for the entire length. Lukas had at first wondered why such a drab color, but the part of him that couldn't care less about carpet easily quashed his curiosity. Although Alfons had not hinted at

154

their destination, Lukas assumed they were visiting the head office of the National Police Corps – the Spanish equivalent of the FBI.

They finally reached the Police headquarters, and two glass panels slid quietly apart, revealing a smallish office space. At a service desk sat an officer. Alfons introduced himself, "Alfons Schmidt, at your service, Senor." He handed his Vatican credentials to the circumspect officer. While the officer was eyeing Alfons' badge and papers over, Alfons finished his rather terse introduction, "We are needing assistance. Could we speak with someone in surveillance, por favor?"

The officer motioned for them to sit, and they humbly obliged. Lukas was still curious. *Odd that the bizarre encounter with the hawk and the beetle sparked such a strange revelation. I am not entirely sure there is any more to this story than a simple chase that got away, but why is Alfons doggedly pursuing this theory? Perhaps pride has taken hold.* Lukas had wondered how Alfons maintained his stoic composure. *Are we not admitting failure to the Spanish police and pleading for help like beggars rather than returning to the Vatican empty-handed?*

The small room they were in was still – a stillness that unnerved Lukas. There was no cheesy, piped-in music, no computers buzzing, and no overhead lights humming. Lukas' sense of dread grew with each muted second.

The silence was soon broken, however, by the light "ding" of the elevator along the back wall, followed by its chrome doors parting, revealing a smiling agent. He was not in uniform but wore a charcoal gray suit with matching tie, and his olive-skinned head was void of any hair. He stepped out and walked over, extending his hand. Lukas noticed that he put his hand forward, but it was not pointed directly at Alfons or himself. *He wants to know who is in charge.* The good Inspector was not in suspense long as Alfons quickly reached forward, shaking his hand.

"Good evening, Sr. Cruz. I am sorry to bother you so late." Alfons apologetically began.

"This is no problem, Sr. Schmidt, was it? We are always happy to help our Vatican friends. If you do not mind, I would ask that we save any details until we get down to the floor."

So, we will be going down. I wonder how deep the real headquarters of this place are buried. Lukas also shook hands quickly with Inspector Cruz before following the two of them into the elevator. As the doors closed, the Inspector entered a code on the elevator panel, and the elevator descended.

155

Eight or nine floors, Lukas mulled to himself as the elevator repeated its muted "ding" and opened upon a very different scene.

Rather than a quiet, professional office, the station "floor" was a gymnasium-sized, chaotic wad of cubicles, computer monitors, and stacks upon stacks of files and papers. Though Sunday evening, the station was littered with people scampering here and there, with almost no one sitting quietly at their desk. The entire scene was reminiscent of a hectic stock trading pit. Inspector Cruz, once Alfons and Lukas had stepped out of the elevator, leaned over and, loud enough to be heard over the din, belted, "Follow me. We will find somewhere a little quieter, yes?"

Alfons nodded in return as they weaved across the sea of activity to a wooden door on the far side. That door opened into a petite conference room. There were no adornments to speak of, save a long table with ten chairs lining its perimeter. Each man took a seat, and Inspector Cruz blurted out as he sat opposite Lukas and Alfons, "So, you had asked for surveillance, yes? What exactly were you wanting surveilled, if you would not mind sharing?"

Lukas, slightly surprised by his sudden directness, was even more surprised by the extreme serenity on Alfons' face as he responded, "Actually, my subject has likely already been surveilled. We just need to see the footage."

"I assume this relates to that business in Seville this morning? My branch there tells me you asked for help yesterday checking out a city block and again this morning sought street camera footage?"

Alfons plainly replied, "That is correct. What we need to see now are the next few minutes of that same footage. This morning, we stopped watching when we saw a taxi speeding out of that garage, but we discovered later the cab was a ruse. The real vehicle likely left the garage shortly afterward. This film may go a long way to helping us corner our suspect."

"I see," was the Inspector's only reply – at first. After the silence from such a short answer had sunk in, Inspector Cruz, his voice climbing an octave, peered across the table at Alfons and laughed. "Perhaps you would prefer to hand over your case file and let us catch this suspect for you? You seem outgunned here, Sr. Schmidt." The Inspector's haughty condescension dripped slovenly from each word.

Alfons, still calm, coolly replied, "I don't think that is necessary . . ."

Inspector Cruz, rather than allowing Alfons to finish, continued, louder than before, "You have already bothered us twice with this matter and now

156

have your hat in your hands for a third time. I had heard rumors of the Vatican agents, but none of them spoke of agents posing as Oliver, meekly begging for 'more.'" The Inspector chuckled, impressing himself with his own wit.

Alfons, maintaining his demeanor, made only one curt response. "It is a *'Mahou Light'* beer truck, and it will pull out of that parking garage within three minutes of the cab's departure. It will make a right turn. If any of this is inaccurate, we leave your country on tomorrow's first train."

Lukas was spellbound. Alfons had divulged none of this to Lukas earlier. When that cab pulled from the parking garage, they were in front of the hospital, just finishing up their inspection of that van. There is no way Alfons knew what vehicle Sam had escaped in. *The old man has lost it. He is betting our whole case on a wild guess?*

Inspector Cruz, just as surprised with Alfons' statuesque demeanor as his response, chuckled again and replied, "I see. I will take that wager, Señor. If you will remain here, I will retrieve the film."

As the door closed behind the Inspector, Lukas opened his mouth, but Alfons interrupted, "Offer no opinion or question, Mr. Dietrich. I assure you this room is highly bugged with many ears listening."

Lukas, not having considered that, reluctantly shut his mouth. *God, he better know what he is doing, or we are done right here, right now.*

Minutes passed, roughly twenty of them before Inspector Cruz returned with three others in tow, the last of which pushed a media cart with a monitor on top and a tape player below. Rather than quickly hitting play, as Lukas expected, the Inspector spoke, "My team says you were several blocks away during this filming. So, you see, there is no way you could know when or if a beer truck might pull in or out of that garage. Would you like me to show you out now while we merely think you delusional, or would you rather wait until we prove it?"

Alfons placed his hands flat on the table in front of him and turned to one of the other officers, a female standing beside Inspector Cruz, and asked plainly, "Pardon, Señora, might I borrow a business card?"

She glanced at the Inspector and, seeing no objection, obliged. Alfons, without looking at its face, flipped it over on its face, took a pen from his jacket, and scribbled something Lukas couldn't make out on the back. He laid the pen down and handed the officer her card back. "Please put this aside and try not reading it until I say. Would you be so kind?"

A head nod was all the reply he was granted, and with that, Alfons turned to Inspector Cruz. "You have not yet watched the footage. In fact, you are likely stalling while you finish pulling it. If you had seen it, you would either have discovered I was wrong and eagerly pushed the 'play' button, or you would have found that I am right, and you would likely not wear as big a smirk as you do now. When should the footage arrive?"

"Shortly." The Inspector's grin began to melt, confronting Alfons' calm and controlling demeanor. The four officers sat opposite them, and for several minutes, no one spoke.

At last, a clerk arrived with a large cartridge. Without a word, he inserted the tape, pressed play, and, after nodding to the Inspector, departed. The monitor flickered, and soon Alfons and Lukas, along with the Spanish officers, were watching traffic footage from earlier that day in Seville. *Los Sabios del Rio* was not terribly active, and vehicles were sparse. Soon enough, as the little white numbers on the black-and-white image read 10:23:46, the all-too-familiar taxi cab pulled out and sped away from the garage. At this point, Alfons and Lukas had stopped the tape earlier but now allowed it to continue. White numbers continued advancing. It was soon showing 10:24, quietly clipping toward 10:25. Lukas felt sweat building on his forehead as no one made a sound in the room, and all eyes remained glued to the screen. 10:25 came. The Inspector leaned forward, watching the silent footage depicted only a barren exit to a parking garage. As :58 and :59 rolled away, turning the time counter from 10:25 to 10:26, lights poured from the garage and grew brighter; something was coming. No one in the room, but Alfons, was breathing. With only fifteen seconds remaining, a stubby *Mahou Light* truck pulled forward and, as predicted, turned right.

The room was bathed in silent awe. The female officer paused the recording showing the fuzzy gray image of the truck's side. Lukas, astounded by the prophetic accuracy of his partner, stared at the Inspector, waiting for the inevitable apology. The Inspector started tapping his pen on the table. As soon as he smiled and opened his mouth to speak, Alfons cut him off. "Inspector, this is no time for reconciliation or pleasantries. We can deal with that another time if you like. Right now, we need to find that truck. While this footage is far from clear enough to give us a shot of that driver, we should have a great shot of those plates."

The Inspector nodded in agreement and, along with his team, stood up to leave. As they neared the door, the female officer stopped, turned back to Alfons, and asked, "Can I read this card now, Señor?"

Alfons, with the driest of smiles, replied, "Of course."

She took the card out and read its message to the group, "The truck will fail to signal when making its right turn?"

The Inspector laughed aloud, apparently realizing he had been beaten by a true professional.

*   *   *

Monday, May 24 – Several Hours Before Dawn

The ten of them bounced along in the truck's dark interior. The eight Spanish officers, armed with automatic weapons and decked out with kevlar, tear gas, and other sundry weapons and gear. While the Corps had allowed them their side arms, everyone knew they were merely guests, tagging along with the unit. No one spoke to Alfons or Lukas. Lukas noticed that Alfons, rather than getting whipped up in the adrenaline-soaked fervor bathing the team, had his head bowed in quiet solitude. *He is praying.* Lukas had gotten so caught up in the assault that he had forgotten his ultimate purpose was to serve the Catholic Church and God himself by extension. Lukas, taking a queue from his partner, likewise bowed his head and began whispering: *"Our God in Heaven, please hear my prayer. I pray first for safety during this crisis. We work diligently and I ask only that you bring us home again. I would also offer a prayer for the brave souls accompanying us, that your protection might shield them also."* Lukas repeated his prayer twice, never asking for victory or that evil be brought to justice.

It was now early Monday morning, and they had been quite fortunate. The tags on the *Mahou Light* truck were connected with several sightings of the same truck frequenting a machine shop outside the city. Witnesses had reported hearing shots and soon afterward seeing this truck drive by. The machine shop allegedly specialized in refrigerated trucks and was owned by a Frenchman, a certain Francois DeCurtaine. Francois turned out to be a fictitious name but a popular one. It had been used to acquire a house in Sao Paolo, Brazil, inside which local police had discovered a heroine distribution hub. "Francois DeCurtaine" had also been a partner in a land deal outside of Salt Lake City that became an illegal dump site for hazardous waste. In fact, the international nature of this Francois, coupled with the Vatican's interest that allowed them to proceed under Interpol rules rather than the more

159

lethargic Spanish procedures. Interpol, Lukas discovered, had rules for swift crisis intervention with only the scattered bits of evidence they had cobbled together.

The other officers had been standoffish throughout the ordeal, except perhaps for Hanso. Hanso was a young recruit, fairly new to the unit from the academy. Though not especially tall, he was stocky and seemed in great shape. Hanso had spared a moment before loading up to chat with Lukas. His first comment straight away was directed at Lukas' weapon. "You charging in there with just that little 9mm?"

Lukas couldn't help but grin. After all, Hanso had no idea how many awards Lukas had earned with just his "little 9mm." He leaned forward and offered, "Not exactly. I plan on *walking* in long after *you* have charged in. I am just a guest here, remember?"

Hanso wiped some sweat from his neck with a kerchief and gave a curt reply, "In the blender, none of the ice is a 'guest.'" He grinned back at Lukas before asking, "Who is your partner, exactly? Some of the guys are saying he is psychic?"

Lukas, secretly harboring the same reservations and suspicions, offered the only response he could manage, "Not sure – only know that once every so often, blenders break down before crushing all the ice."

Hanso smiled at Lukas and loaded up, but had said nothing on the ride over to the site. When the truck finally came to a halt, the captain, a gaunt figure going by Mendoza, opened the rear doors and leaned in, saying, "No drill. This is live. Follow my lead. High profile here – Interpol and whatnot. Any heroes sit the next one out. Good luck. Move!" Before turning back, he looked directly at Alfons & Lukas, "You two stay put. You can get out when we say. No one wants an incident with one of you two on our soil. Understand?"

Both Lukas and Alfons nodded silently and stayed seated. Luckily, the doors were left open, allowing them opportunity to at least hear some of the goings on – at first, only shuffled footsteps in the dust, trailing away to the right. After moments of silence, there was some light clanging – metal on metal. Then, more nothingness. No gunfire, no explosions, no shattering glass. The whole affair was akin to eavesdropping on an Amish SWAT team raiding a Quilting Bee. After languishing, far longer than likely necessary, in the truck, Mendoza returned, ducking down and leaning his forehead against the truck's frame. "Sorry to disappoint, guys. Nothing here. Found your truck, but nothing inside. We are heading back . . ."

Alfons interrupted, asking, "Might we at least inspect the facility? I know your team would have checked every inch already, but I need some sense of the place so I can write up this failure in my official report."

Mendoza thought for a moment and returned hesitantly with, "Alright. Go on. We are still taking photos and squaring the place up. You have maybe twenty minutes."

Lukas, followed by Alfons, clambered out of the van and headed toward the large metal building. It had a bulky sliding door in front with large stenciled letters, faded from time, spelling "DeCurtaine." A smaller door on the side had been pried open and was dangling from one hinge. Both men stepped through into a spacious chamber: three stories tall and more than three times as wide. Apparently, only the rear contained smaller rooms or substructures. Inside were parked several vehicles, some on jacks and some on the ground – all in various states of repair. Their *Mahou Light* truck was completely intact. Alfons headed toward the truck, and Lukas followed. When he noticed Lukas, he turned back and quickly mentioned, "We have little time here. I need you to go check through the offices and storage in back."

Lukas obliged and made for the rear of the shop. Assorted work tables, shelves, and bins were littered throughout, covered with various parts and tools, mostly covered in rust. Large shop lights dangled from the ceiling, casting their pale hue downward. The concrete shop floor was weary from time, revealing large cracks and chips in the pavement. It seemed, at best, that they had caught whoever ran the shop by surprise, but their crew just happened to be away. At worst, the owner had gotten wind of the raid, evacuating, leaving nothing but trucks and random machine parts in their wake.

When Lukas finally reached the rear, he noticed one corner had been converted into a series of small rooms – mostly offices and a restroom. He carefully wound through the offices, thumbing through loose papers and drawers, but everything seemed appropriate for a machine shop – old invoices, part orders, client records, and the like. He continued looking until he finally entered the far corner and found Hanso also rifling through papers.

Hanso looked up when he came in and, naturally, started a conversation. "Never seen a place this clean. You?"

Lukas, truthfully, could only shake his head in response. *No need to tell him this is my first assignment.*

161

"I mean," continued Hanso, "even an ice cream parlor has *something* out of place. This place looks *too* legitimate, *too* perfect, if you get my meaning."

"I do. Scary thought – if this is staged, how sophisticated is the organization that pulls this off? The Vatican itself would not look this clean if we had a month."

Hanso smiled and kept looking. Lukas, too, continued to snoop around until his eyes landed upon the concrete floor. It was clean and smooth, not the same worn and chipped monstrosity from the shop floor. He darted out and checked the floors in the hall and some other rooms. Their floors were of the same aged and cracked concrete as the rest of the place. Only this back room where he and Hanso were now had a new floor installed. *Odd. Why would someone only replace the floor in one small back office? They would not – at least not just for the floor's sake.*

"Hanso, was it?"

"Si," came the answer.

"Something is wrong here. The floor in here is newer than everywhere else. Something is underneath. Look around."

The two of them poked around until Hanso discovered a seam in the concrete tucked under a stack of cardboard file boxes. Once he noticed the seam, he waved Lukas over, and the two of them quietly cleared the area revealing a suspicious metal hatch in the floor. Lukas pulled his sidearm and stepped off to one side while Hanso grabbed the handle and pulled upward.

An ear-piercing "Pow!" rang out as the first sound Lukas heard. The second sound was Hanso's body slamming wildly backward into the pile of cardboard – blood pouring from his face, neck, and hands. Lukas hit the deck, fearing the worst, but no one emerged from below. Thundering footsteps of squad members pounded toward them. Lukas crawled over to Hanso, staying clear of the now-shut hatch. Hanso had been blasted by a shotgun at close range to his face and chest. His face was non-recognizable, and blood poured from apparently every inch of exposed skin his upper body had available. Lukas knew he had nothing to offer in the way of medical care. Hanso needed an ambulance and lots of morphine.

As footsteps entered, Lukas turned to face Mendoza – he had been the first to arrive. His face turned pale at the gruesome sight of poor Hanso writhing in agony. Lukas pointed toward the hatch in the floor, and Mendoza motioned for him to back away. As he moved aside, more squad members

162

arrived, and Lukas watched as two of them grabbed Hanso, dragging him outside. The remainder of the squad encircled the door in the pavement. Mendoza grabbed the handle and jerked the door up – this time, no one stood in the opening – and no gunshot rang out. Lukas, his ears still ringing, noticed a cord dangling inside – *a rigged door.*

The door gun was only rigged for one shot – apparently meant to stop only the solitarily curious. The team pulled flashlights and headed into the darkness below. Five men disappeared before Alfons arrived and, after checking quickly to make sure that none of the blood was Lukas', helped him up. Lukas quickly relayed what had happened and his role in everything. For some time the only thing escaping that open hole was a powerful reek Lukas had never smelled before. He started to cover his mouth and nose when Alfons gently pushed his arm down. Lukas turned to ask why, when he heard it: footsteps heading upwards. Mendoza emerged first carrying a wafer thin, teenage girl. Covered in her own filth, scratched and matted, she seemed hardly awake. A second officer just behind Mendoza was toting a naked toddler in his arms, malnourished and likely only a few days from perishing. Eventually, twelve children were rescued from that hole, some naked, but all exposing their terror and relief at being found. Lukas had uncovered a lair for temporarily hiding children taken from their homes. There was no way to know, at least not right then, how long they had been down there, nor how many would have been "distributed" further down the chain had Lukas not come along.

The rest of the morning slowly fell into place. Sunlight spilled over the horizon as ambulances, fire trucks, and hordes of police converged. Alfons, undoubtedly proud of his protégé, kept the two of them out of the spotlight while making arrangements to get them out of there. Eventually, a lone officer volunteered to escort them back to the Ministry. En route, Alfons called a now quite humble Inspector Cruz. While Lukas couldn't hear the Inspector's end of the conversation, Alfons' part went something like this: "Hello Inspector, I assume you are aware of what transpired?" . . . "Yes. I will tell him. Quite intuitive: noticing that business with the new flooring. Well, at any rate, we are pleased to have dealt a blow to Sr. DeCurtaine's organization, but that truck we found – while the truck we were looking for, it was missing one driver and one passenger.". . . "I see. I appreciate your continued efforts, but I would like to offer you a proposition. Conduct your search. Lock down your borders and ports, but allow me to take care of the airport here. I can manage with the airport team already in place, but I would appreciate you letting whoever runs airport security that I am in charge for a few days, yes?". . . "I am confident our fugitives will depart Spain shortly, if they have not already.". . . "Thank you again, Inspector."

While Lukas' head was still reeling from everything that had happened, a few questions kept coming back to him. He looked to Alfons sitting beside him and asked, quite plainly, "How did you know Sam escaped in a *Mahou Light* truck, and more to the point, how did you know the truck would not signal for its right turn out of the garage?"

"He was in your rear-view mirror for over an hour after leaving that hospital yesterday, and that truck's right blinker must be busted. While diligently signaling for every left lane change, they never bothered signaling for the ones to the right. Mr. Dietrich, our beetle avoided its hawk by hiding in plain sight, less than a few cars behind."

". . . as if millions of voices suddenly cried out in terror, and were suddenly silenced." – Obi-Wan Kenobi in Star Wars by George Lukas

Wednesday, May 26, 1999 – Early Morning

The clock tower outside the flat chimed its seventh time, and Sam knew he needed to get up. Things had, at first, moved quickly once Victoria and he got to Madrid. They had only just arrived at that machine shop when Victoria hurriedly switched them to that green compact and whisked him here. The flat was a cramped studio on the third floor devoid of any comforts other than cold running water. Mattresses resting on the floor had served as their beds these past three nights. The place had been relatively clean, but several mice had taken up residence, stubbornly refusing to vacate despite Sam's efforts. Their lone window happened to face a clock tower of the local parish – a nice view, actually, but for the obnoxious chimes reminding Sam how long he'd been asleep.

Sam was no longer on the IV and was feeling far better than on Sunday, but for overwhelming boredom. He had been instructed to "never – ever" go outside while Victoria was out. She had been fairly closed-lipped about what she did while she was away, but whatever it was took considerable time as Sam had been holed up these past two days with spacious intervals of quiet solitude. Lack of activity combined with fear of capture provided marvelous incentive to remain quiet and allow his muscles to recover. In particular, his legs, strained from over-exertion, had regained much of their former mobility. He could now walk around without crutches and could even reach inside the top cabinets without more than a slight whimper.

What truly occupied Sam's time more than anything, however, had been those papers he had plucked from the river bed. At first, he had re-read and even re-read again the accounts of Emmet and the others invaded by an evil spirit calling itself "Thentul." His awe and emotional reaction were just as strong in the second and third readings as in the first. His initial paternal sense of pity melted into terror each time his mind began grasping that these accounts weren't fiction but authentic recountings of dark forces.

Eventually, he had managed to press onward through Manuel's collection. Of the sixty-two accounts, he had originally only become familiar with four. The remaining fifty-eight were all accounted for and waiting to be

165

explored. Using Manuel's instructions as his guide, he had, for two days, covered every entry in the macabre collection. In the end, there was no longer any room for doubt. Manuel had truly discovered, discarded and forgotten in the bowels of the Vatican, records of demonic possession with details so strikingly similar they would have been impossible to fabricate. They detailed possessions all over the globe and across millennia, some dating back to the Middle Ages. Sam struggled to maintain his composure but often found himself weeping as he combed the dark passages, imagining the horrors inflicted on these poor souls. No one was immune, it seemed: male or female, athletic or disabled, rich or poor, the young or the elderly. Church patrons were as likely victims as pagans, and no ethnicity or culture was off limits.

Though the emotional roller coaster consumed his mind, life in the flat was itself a challenge. Any food had been cooked on a portable camping stove, and his reading had been done by lantern. Victoria's absences grew longer with each disappearance. This morning, she was already gone before he woke up, leaving only a cryptic note on the stove, reading, "Meet me downstairs at 8:00." *That's it? What's waiting downstairs? She's acted strangely ever since we got settled in, and why is she always so . . . distant?*

The one distraction Sam had discovered was an old trunk – wooden and hinged with antique iron – buried under some debris. This journey had, for all of its misfortunes, provided Sam a tremendous diversion from his affinity with antiques. There had been pieces inside palaces and historic sites, but they were locked away and secured. This trunk, however, while not particularly historic, was unique and clearly assembled by hand. *Naturally, I've got no way to get it back to California. Ha – not even sure I'll get myself back!*

Victoria, however, was his best chance to get home and, at a basic level, had taken care of him. She pulled him from that utility room in Seville and got him safely here. She cured his dehydration and had provided food and clothing. She had not spoken much to him about that brown sedan nor for whom she was constantly checking the window. It was now Wednesday, and he would have otherwise been flying back home today. He had a new passport and fake name to travel under: "Rodney Hamilton." Sam didn't feel like a "Rodney," but he had not been consulted in the matter. With his head now clean-shaven and his new name, it had taken him a moment to recognize the guy staring back at him from the passport photo.

This cryptic note from Victoria today mentioned meeting him downstairs, but he hadn't tackled stairs since the incident. They might be

166

challenging for his recovering leg muscles. He was just finishing breakfast, dry toast and warm juice, as the chimes rang out. It was eight o'clock. He had to get downstairs. Sam squinted as the bright morning sun hit his eyes. He looked below but couldn't see Victoria, or anyone else for that matter, so he grabbed the railing and began descending – one step at a time. His muscles were stiff and sore, but he managed. He wasn't yet strong enough to climb normally, but by laboriously having both feet land on each step.

Victoria was surprisingly nowhere to be seen at the street level. So far, she had honored every promise. Perhaps the church clock was early, and it wasn't quite eight yet. Just as his mind began cycling through horrible scenarios, he heard a plain-spoken "Good morning" from above. He looked up and noticed Victoria squatting on the second floor landing with her arms folded across her knees. *How did I not see her as I came down?*

As if inside his thoughts, she offered, "Don't worry. I wasn't out here when you passed. How do you feel?"

"Fine," was his perfunctory response.

"No, you misunderstand. This is not a casual conversation. I am speaking medically – how do you *feel*?"

"Oh. Well, I'm tired. That climb was more challenging than I expected."

Victoria simply nodded her head and replied, "OK. That's expected. Do me a favor. Come back upstairs as fast as you can bear without hurting yourself. I'll meet you inside." With that, she rose and bounded up the stairs.

Sam sighed, dreading the likely far more difficult upward climb, but he resigned himself to obey. He made good use of the handrail, letting his arms help as he ascended. Each step was challenging, pushing muscles yearning for relief. His mood grew darker with each successive step. *What sort of rescue is this? I should be home already instead of skulking about, being tricked into climbing up and down stairs. Who the hell did Gerard hire anyway?*

Sam was still brooding when he finally reached the flat. Victoria was squatting on the floor, her legs crossed in front of her with her arms resting quaintly atop the antique trunk. A pen and some crumpled paper lay on the trunk lid as well. "Good job. You can lie down now if you like." She jotted a few notes. Apparently, she had been timing him. "Today's a big day. We are catching a flight tonight and going to see about getting you home. Maybe even scrounge up some food from a real kitchen?" Victoria had a content grin as she waited for Sam's response.

167

Sam, exhausted from his ascent, noticed her grin and hint of satisfaction, and it was more than he could quietly bear. Sam inhaled deeply as his face grew more serious, and he glared at Victoria. "I'm sorry, but I have to know. Exactly where have you been these last two days? You were hired to take care of me, but you're out carousing . . ."

Victoria remained sitting, merely smiling as Sam continued his tirade, stopping just short of calling her negligent. Eventually, as his monologue wound down, she softly replied, "Sam. I understand what you must be feeling, but please know your impression is due to your not grasping the relevant facts. I won't bore you with all the sordid details, but I will share a few. First, we are in a race. The chase that started on that bridge in Seville is not over. Each day we cower here is a day *they* draw closer to storming through that door. However, it is also a day your strength returns, improving our chances."

Why is she so calm and chipper? Can't she see how angry I am about this whole thing? Sam couldn't help but interject, asking, "Then why haven't you been here caring for me – helping me heal?"

Victoria, ignoring Sam's interruption, continued. "The second fact you may not be aware of, as you seem content cuddling under your blanket of self-pity, is that with me gone, you've been forced to make do for yourself – moving about, fetching your own things, making your own food. All of this required you to really *use* your muscles. Ideally, you could have recovered quaintly, resting in a hospital bed while your muscles healed through rest and expensive meds. That ideal is far from here. I needed you to improve far quicker by using those tender muscles. In fact, that was the point behind this morning's little exercise. Stairs were a big concern, and I needed to know that you could handle a few. Congratulations, you passed."

How humiliating! The worst part is that she's probably right. By leaving me to my own devices, I've likely recovered far quicker than I would have lying up here with her feeding me chicken soup – if they even make chicken soup in Spain. Sam meekly gave the only response he could think of, "Do you know who's chasing us?"

Victoria quickly brushed some strands of light brown hair from her eyes as she answered, "Two men. Not sure who they work for, but they probably aren't Spanish. I can promise you, though, they are absolute professionals. Maybe we'll put a few pieces together on our drive."

"Sounds good. When do we leave?" His anger had melted back into determination.

"In about ten minutes. Gather what few things you have – you can put them in here." She flung an empty backpack at his feet while continuing, "Those papers you cherish can come too. I need to know more about them, and I've got a good long drive to Barcelona to get all the details."

*   *   *

Wednesday, May 26, 1999 – Mid-Morning

"You're serious, aren't you?" Victoria peered over the top of her sunglasses suspiciously toward Sam, her forehead wrinkled. "You honestly believe that scattered wad of papers proves, I mean conclusively proves, that somewhere out there, a God truly exists?"

Sam nodded in affirmation, "That's what I'm saying. Listen, it was really hard for me to grasp, too, but I've gone through all of this several times now – what, with all my free time lately – and these notes and journal accounts really prove demons, and the God they fear, are very, very real. And when I say 'real,' I mean it literally, not some vague metaphor or analogy where God personifies nature or some nebulous value like happiness or contentment."

Instead of amazement or even curiosity, her expression dulled, poorly masking what could only be interpreted as pity. Victoria turned back, gazing at the highway stretching out before her. "So, these stories – they were written by whom, men? Humans, right?"

Sam, apparently unnerved by her blatant lack of sincerity, answered politely, "Yes. Priests, specifically. But they weren't writing for an audience. These journals are internal – reports of the priests' activities. They were not conspiring to prove anything. In fact, the only person to read them, prior to forty years ago anyway, was likely some Vatican officer or Cardinal – likely giving each only a cursory glance before tossing it."

Victoria was unconvinced, but Sam seemed so unabashedly wrapped up in this fiction she couldn't crush his dreams, not after all he had endured. *Poor guy. Suffered such agony for this, this fantasy. Pity – he seems so confident. In fact, the only real evidence in his favor is . . .* "Say, Sam," Victoria interjected, changing the subject, "any thoughts on who was in the brown sedan?"

Sam, likely still trying to work out how he could convince her about his document collection, responded plainly, "They probably work for the Vatican. They were watching me from that bridge in Seville and only made to grab me once I had this box in my arms. These papers were stolen from the Vatican

169

forty years ago by a translator named Manuel." Sam relayed to Victoria his story – from stumbling across that cryptic letter under the writing desk to following the trail of discordant breadcrumbs leading to the bottom of the Guadalquivir.

Victoria listened intently, partially admiring his dedication but mostly questioning his sanity – pursuing these shadows with such scant evidence. Not unlike Don Quixote, Sam had found his windmills to tilt at, and it had almost cost him his life. *Hector once mentioned these secretive Vatican agents. If memory serves, he was actually afraid. Didn't think Hector was afraid of anyone.* Victoria turned to Sam, "That's not good news, Sam. If those guys are the same Vatican agents I've heard of, we might hit a brick wall getting you out of the country. However, that is your best evidence for the importance of those documents. Pretty sure *I'm* not buying what you're selling, but they're obviously valuable to the Vatican for some reason. They wouldn't bother sending their prized agents after something trivial."

Sam bit his lip solemnly before responding, "I hadn't thought of that, and I'm glad you think the documents might at least be important. It's sad, though, that you think the best evidence for my claim is that someone important wants to steal it. I can understand, though, I think. Been arguing with my dad about God for decades. Imagine the most trustworthy person you know excitedly calling you up, saying they'd seen a UFO. Do you believe them, truly? Or do you only believe they saw something that they think was a UFO? I think some people have distanced themselves so far from the notion of God that He is as fantastical as a UFO or the Easter Bunny. The only way to break through is for you to experience some of this for yourself. Could I read some of this to you while we drive? Maybe if you hear some of these stories, you might come around."

Victoria, resigning herself to the inevitable, replied, "Sure. Convince me." *So now I get a sermon – great! It's either this or refuse, and he'll think I don't "get" his quest. He needs to know I'm in his corner – even if that means letting him spew these fantasies he's concocted: be they devils, angels, Santa Claus, or even the Cubs winning the Series.* Victoria relaxed her arms, settling back into a slightly more relaxed repose.

Sam seized the opportunity and snatched the binder. "I've gone through this thing twice now and this one section, for me, is especially persuasive. It's about a massive Chinese flood in 1931. Even if it doesn't convince you, it should at least get your attention."

Sam opened the binder and began reading aloud: *"My sweet sister, if you are still following along, you have read some of humanity's darkest moments, but the accounts so far have mostly described physical inflictions – horrifying wounds and deformities suffered by the victims. It bothers me greatly, but demons apparently possess knowledge of the future and other hidden facts. This often manifests through the victim speaking an unknown language or describing something the victim could not possibly know. While no doubt fairly persuasive in person, details like that have little value in a written collection like this. It would seem as though the scribe was simply concocting the details. However, I have discovered an utterly remarkable group of accounts from three priests. Each had no opportunity to conspire with the others nor familiarize themselves with any accounts penned before theirs. The three accounts are numbered as documents 46, 2, and 57. I recommend encountering them chronologically, starting with document 57."*

Sam took a sip of soda, the first he'd had in days, turned to the English translation of document #57, and continued:

"1872 A.D. – Amsterdam: On Wednesdays, I check in and pray with the sickly members of my flock: shut-ins that get out no longer; those in hospitals or the local sanatorium; and a few that have simply taken ill and remain behind closed doors. Nikolina was of the latter variety. Once I arrived, her mother led me down the back hallway. She opened the door to the girl's room, but rather than enter, she stepped aside and warned me of her deteriorating condition.

Nikolina was asleep but breathing heavily. Each exhale was laborious and loud – far louder than even that of a normal adult, much less from a young twelve-year-old girl. I walked to her side and lightly rubbed her cheek. Her eyelids sprung open at my touch, revealing red, bloodshot, and swollen eyes. I tried introducing myself, but the girl made no response. I then inquired about her condition but again, was denied any response.

When at last I asked if she found speaking with an old fool like me tremendously dull, she answered with harsh laughter – a deep guttural laughter so wholly unnatural that my words failed me. She sat up, still staring into my eyes, grinning maniacally. My compassion melted into terror with each passing second. It must have been her eyes, now that I think back. They glared straight through me: past the Priest, even past the man. They pierced straight

171

through my adult façade to the little boy cowering inside, the one we all spend our whole adult life hiding from the rest of the world. Imagine – a grown man of the cloth, terrified by such a young girl!

I marshaled my courage to try and at least act like the man, the Priest I was supposed to be. I cautiously reached for her hand to pray with her, but she yanked it away viciously. Suddenly, and without provocation, Nikolina, or who I thought at that time was Nikolina, began speaking, although her voice was not that of a young girl. It was masculine, mature – hard and heavy with saliva. I remember its words distinctly, "You will not touch the girl. I will take her if you try touching her even once more."

I asked with whom I was speaking if not young Nikolina, and the voice responded. "My name is inconsequential, especially to one as pathetic as you."

As I pried further, the voice became less vile and more refined, though still deep and masculine. Where moments earlier it was monstrous, it was now crisp and pure – as if speaking with any intelligent man in Amsterdam, complete with perfect Dutch pronunciation. Eventually, it tired of my inquiry, answering, "Some things are far too intricate for your human mind."

I had begun to fear that poor Nikolina might have become possessed by a dark spirit, but wild conclusions like that require far more study than I was prepared to undertake. I stammered over my words, asking why, if it was not human, it appeared so much like one.

The voice chuckled at that – again, not the laughter of a twelve-year-old girl, but the mature laugh of a grown man. "You play coy with me, Priest. I can smell it, you know – your fear. You cower behind inquiry and exposition while exquisite terror filling your soul oozes from your pores."

Those bloodshot eyes were still trained on me – staring through my thin exterior. I had read of possessions but never encountered one firsthand. I pretended to remain calm, asking more questions.

The spirit's response sent my mind reeling. "You fear mortality, Priest. Death will surely arrive at your doorstep, yet you dread its arrival with such juvenile and pathetic cowardice. Your eyes see this little girl's body, but you sense . . . something greater: the iron grip of

172

despair, the futility of your worthless life. Shall I relieve you now? Take your life right here where you stand? No, I thought not. You prefer draping your whimpering fear around you like a filthy rag until your final moment. Am I right? Speak!"

That last demand bellowed from this being's depths, and I jumped backward, stumbling over my chair and tearing my cassock.

"So, you would flee and embrace your cowardice? Relish your decision when the flood waters come, and you gasp for just . . . one more breath, desperately struggling to cling to your bleating, cringing life."

This foe was beyond my abilities, and, by rights, I should have immediately sought more experienced help, but that mysterious reference to flood waters piqued my curiosity. I gathered the few morsels of courage I had left and righted the chair as I rose. When I foolishly asked to which waters he was referring, the demon burdened my mind with horrors I would never purge.

"You would know of your demise? I tire of you, Priest. I will answer, but then you flit away and leave me with my petite trophy. It is bad for you - in the end. Two score and four years from now, as you humans mark what you call 'time,' the floods come. Millions perish as my Master, the Lord of Water Dragons, basks in blood and agony. As the torrent breaches its pathetic barriers, death and anguish visit the throng. Screams of the innocent fill your final thoughts - cries of souls extinguished in but a moment as raging water sweeps through in the middle of night, catching thousands completely unaware. Most have only the briefest of moments to scream out into the darkness before succumbing. Others survive the initial pulse only to be taken in the aftermath. Babes cling to their parents - wives to their husbands - settling for the pitiful comfort of not dying alone. You are not so fortunate.

You will try, Priest. You try outwitting the torrent, but you fail miserably. You scurry upon a rooftop as the rising cesspool rages. The dead race by - pale and bloody. Many have missing limbs, oozing dark pools of blood around their corpse. You foolishly try comforting those in anguish, but your pathetic efforts enrage a distraught father. He beats you, kicking you mercilessly into the waters below. Your options dwindle away. All is lost.

173

You struggle to stay afloat in the morass, but it is in vain. Your throat fills with water as you gasp for even the tiniest morsel of air, but there . . . is . . . none . . ."

I cried out, 'Stop!' for as it spoke, my throat tightened. The air became thick, and breathing was nigh impossible. I had waded into something far deeper than my meager talents could handle. Fortunately, the demon sneered and released me, returning my breath. I gathered my things and, without another word, cowardly abandoned that poor girl in the clutches of that devil.

In the end, Father Durbin was eventually able to help young Nikolina purge the dark spirit. The exorcism stretched several days before the devil eventually capitulated. Father Durbin has likely filed his own recounting of the exorcism itself, so I will not bother detailing that here. I will likely never have a night when those dark words do not echo in my dreams - smothering me with regurgitated terror and dread. I only pray for God's continued care and guidance - Bishop Hinsch."

Victoria offered no response as Sam finished — her eyes fixed on the highway ahead. She made a conscious effort not to roll her eyes or reveal other subtle hints of disapproval. Without discussion, Sam quickly turned to document #2 and continued, this time apparently skipping ahead a little:

"1917 A.D. - Hankou: The walls began buckling as immense pressure mounted outside. Thick, cloudy water had already found its way in through first-floor doors and windows. The timbers of the house creaked and moaned under tremendous strain. It would be over soon. My assistant and I, along with the Chinese family, all crouched atop tables and cabinets - anything that would support a person. The youngest, clinging to her mother's soaked gown, would not stop wailing. It was dark. Nothing could be seen but rising waters and the flame from our two tiny lanterns. The deafening splinter of the walls and shrieking terror-stricken cries filled the night. Hope vanished.

I have never known such intense fear. Being caught in any terrible catastrophe would be harrowing, but timidly crouching on the anvil's surface waiting for the hammer-fall, with no way of escape or hope for survival - that dread is unimaginable. Eventually, I wished for the end to

174

come. If I were to be smashed in the inevitable collapse of the hovel or drown in the depths below, then let it be done. I felt moisture on my bare feet. I assumed the water had risen above the table's surface, but my young assistant had wet himself, and urine streamed across the table, soaking my feet and the hem of my soutane. I turned to scold him, but the expression in his eyes told me he was beside himself in despair.

None of it was real, of course - this terrifying vision inflicted upon me by the monster inside Shen. Regardless, the sense of reality was too great - the details so vivid - the vision overwhelmed me. While my body lay prostrate on the floor of that decrepit hospital, my mind huddled in terror inside this tiny house.

Water was coming. It had poured in for hours. I tried to wake, but I failed. This vision had ensnared me, forcing me to endure. I tried covering my ears, but the screams were far too loud, penetrating my soul. A desk toppled, plunging the brothers backward into the abyss. Their father reached out, but they were swept quickly away by the current, their bodies smashing violently into debris. I heard bones break and flesh ripping against jagged glass.

When, at last, the hammer did fall, it fell hard. The walls' groaning became a deafening 'boom' as their timbers splintered in a thousand directions, one large piece puncturing my right calf, and I dropped the lantern. I cried out to the darkness in agony. My heart pounded inside my chest, faster and faster, as I struggled to stay above water. The house was gone, and the rain poured. I no longer heard the babe's cry. I searched for her or her mother, but they were gone. Everyone was gone. Nothing remained but water, shattered debris, and blood. I grasped for something, anything, to use to stay afloat. Nothing was available. The current dragged me under, and I descended into darkness. The vision shattered.

I was back in the hospital, staring up at Shen, or at least Shen's body, for whatever was inside him was no longer Shen at all. My head was dripping wet and my clothes stank of sweat. He grinned, the most mischievous and horrible grin, drool dripping from his bottom lip onto my chest, as he glared. I frantically worked to catch my breath, finally asking why it had inflicted that vision upon me.

175

Its response was loud and violent, "You are a fucking pig! You and all your kind, Priest! You wear robes and rings and look down on all the swine in your herd – as if you are so special. You saw how special you were when the waters came, yes? How many are baptized in pain when those floods come, and your God abandons them? So much swine for the slaughterhouse – Leviathon will be pleased! Go now, pig! GO!!"

I hurriedly fled out of fear for my life. Shen was young and strong, even without that thing inside him. Together, they could strangle me instantly. I had exorcised demons before, but never had I been tormented through a vision. I pray to God I never will again."

Victoria, having patiently endured these stories so far, mustered an inquiry, "So, these tales – you believe them? I mean you actually believe something supernatural happened simply because of a few flood predictions?"

"Well, yes. The flood did happen, you know. Manuel included an article about this terrible flood striking inland China in 1931 – millions perished; one of the deadliest natural disasters in human history."

Victoria glanced over at Sam with a smirk and responded, "Kind of elementary, right? I mean, you know what they call the Yellow River in China?"

"No, I don't, but . . ."

"They call it the 'River of Sorrow.' They call it that because of its propensity for severe flooding. Apparently, silt gets carried downstream and builds up along the river bottom – raising the water higher and higher against the levees until they eventually burst in these periodic violent and catastrophic floods. All the big major inland Chinese rivers do the same thing. So, some people predicted a flood in 1931 in China . . . big deal. Had they predicted one in Libya or Nigeria – I might be impressed." She smugly grinned as she turned from Sam's confused stare back to the road.

Not giving up so quickly, he offered meekly, "Would you mind listening to this last flood entry? It might help."

"Fine with me. We've got nothing else to do until we get to Barcelona."

Sam turned to the third entry:

"1930 A.D. – San Francisco: "I dread these visits – long, empty hallways echoing each bootstep; stained and worn paint flaking from the walls; muffled cries of despair behind thick closed metal doors. The end is always the

176

same – some poor soul suffering from gruesome years of psycho-therapy, sedatives, and shameful neglect. I had come to examine Judah, a man in his early thirties who had been admitted ten years ago when his erratic behavior turned violent.

Ten years and no one was any closer to understanding Judah's 'episodes' – as the staff had taken to calling them. Judah never remembered anything during the episodes except his visions. Sometimes they reflected images of the past – detailed images and not always from his own life. Some visions of the past reflected actions of hospital staff otherwise unknown to Judah. The details had been meticulously verified, but my friend Nathan had a greater concern. Occasionally, Judah's visions were of future events.

Periodically, Judah would awaken after an episode speaking of a massive market crash. That particular vision first occurred in 1922. Though not terribly educated, he described the events of Black Tuesday (October 29, 1929) perfectly: over 16 million shares traded, with the Dow closing at 230 points. This same vision had occurred three separate times over the years, and always with the same details. No one had taken Judah's vision seriously until the crash. That was when Nathan called me.

The hospital had jostled Judah's diagnoses several times – from schizophrenia to frontal lobe problems to epilepsy. Oh yes – I haven't yet told you of 'him.' While Judah is 'away' during his episodes, an alternate personality comes over him, horrible and vile. Nathan said the staff wrestles with "him" while Judah retreats into his visions.

When, at last, I arrived at the examining room, I rapped at the door and Nathan opened wearing a tired smile. After the perfunctory greetings and salutations, I turned to Judah. He was strapped into an oversized iron chair on one side of a thin table. I sat opposite him but did not speak – being content to merely observe. He did not seem to mind my presence. He may not have noticed me at all as he was transfixed on the ceiling high above the room. He was humming an old children's tune – something vaguely familiar but one my conscious had long since forgotten.

I sat my note pad down and went to grab my pen from my shirt pocket, but it was gone. I thought nothing of it at the time. After all, how often is a simple ink pen

177

misplaced? When, at last, I asked his name, he ignored me and continued humming.

However, after several attempts at conversation, I asked him about his visions. The humming stopped. Judah looked down at me. He smiled seeing my bald head, apparently taking satisfaction to finally not be the only one in the room with no hair. His teeth were blackened and worn to smallish points, and horrid breath reeked from his open mouth. He spoke. 'My visions scare me. So much blood.'

I asked if the blood was his.

His eyes watered as he replied, 'Not my blood, no. But so much blood swirling in the water. The faces have funny eyes - the floating faces.'

Nathan whispered they had also heard this vision before of a future great flood in Asia.

'The river takes them all. Judah's smile faded when tears began falling from the corners of his eyes. 'Some know the waters are rising and flee, but many stay behind. Nowhere to run. The waters rise. No place to escape. Some in boats get away. Others try making boats. Bathtubs, barrels, crates - anything. Some use coffins, dumping the bodies of their dead into the waters before climbing inside.'

I asked if he knew where the flood happens.

His response was cryptic, 'I hear some screaming about the Hwai swallowing Hankou. They don't scream for long. Metal sheets in the rushing water slice their bellies, and their blood joins the blood of others in the dark water.' By then, Judah was blubbering.

I sensed he would soon shut me out. I quickly pressed for a bit more information, asking if he knew when the river would rise. I was too late as his eyes slowly glazed over again. There was nothing more - at first. Soon, however, his arms began twitching. Nathan pulled me back and warned that 'he' was coming - the other personality I mentioned.

He became more violent as his chair rattled against the stone floor. There were no words, only malevolent growls, and guttural babbling interrupted periodically with pained gasps for air. The orderlies delivered a sedative, but it only enraged him further. His fingers grabbed the bottom of Judah's tunic and ripped it off, revealing vicious scars and burns betraying years of injections and

178

painful electroshock therapy. Howls of anguish poured from Judah's mouth, and he began gnashing his teeth together. This was no longer Judah. The creature glared about the room – stopping once it noticed me. I tried to look away, but my gaze remained fixed. It smiled before biting hard into Judah's bottom lip – sending a wave of red pouring down Judah's chest. Afterward, I was promptly ushered out.

While not entirely sure what to make of Judah's condition at first, I now suspect I may have witnessed a demonic possession. I will fill out the requisite paperwork to request an exorcist examine him, assuming the hospital cooperates, though I remain skeptical on that count.

As a side note, a few days following those events, Nathan called on me producing my lost ink pen from that afternoon. When I asked where he found it, he replied that Judah told him he saw me set it down at the attendant's desk. While I was at that desk, Judah was secured several hundred feet away in a sealed room. There is no way he could have known this. Nathan, a trusted friend of mine for years, assured me the pen was precisely where Judah had described it."

Sam closed the binder and looked over at Victoria eagerly, likely hoping this last account would generate more interest.

Victoria, primarily focusing on driving, offered one small remark, "That was certainly something."

Sam must not have completely caught her cynicism as he continued, "Yeah. There are dozens of stories in here, but these three are cool – accurately predicting the future like that: three unrelated accounts from priests encountering victims of demonic possession where the demon predicts this same flood. That article I mentioned? It's from the American consul describing the flood's aftermath. It estimates up to four million people perished – our greatest natural calamity, short of the black plague. There's no way these predictions are that accurate unless something supernatural was at work, right?" He stopped, studying her face, likely looking for the slightest hint of vindication.

She offered none, meagerly replying, "It is strange, though."

"Yes, who would have thought that . . ."

"I'm sorry – I wasn't finished." She interrupted, her voice a bit terse. "It is strange, though, that you take these accounts of this dreadful deluge–

179

you take these accounts and have the naiveté to point to them, claiming they somehow prove that a God exists! Do you hear how that sounds? You're saying you can prove God exists because millions of souls were snuffed out in a tragic flood! I would say that a devastating flood like this – destroying homes, crops, animals, along with millions of people – is potent proof that God does NOT exist!"

*   *   *

Wednesday, May 26, 1999 – Mid-Day

Sam's excitement dimmed. He was not prepared for this turn at all, but for everything he didn't know about false passports, smuggling, and picking locks, his expertise was people. Victoria was emotional and emotion shares no space with logic. He may eventually convince her of the miracle staring at her, but not right now.

Sam tried hiding his disappointment. He had hoped for a little curiosity and wonder – possibly a hint of excitement. To his dismay, however, she showed none of that. Her face at first showed no emotion whatsoever and now reflected only frustration. Her mind was sure there was no God. This conversation went as many before it had between him and his father. Like a tiger chasing its tail, their arguments about the existence of God circuitously spiraled, fueling a rising tempest that would eventually rupture, further fracturing their ever-fragile relationship. He had hoped that such convincing proof could break through even the hardest heart, but Victoria's was withstanding his onslaught, dimming his hopes of ultimately persuading his father.

Sam remembered something his grandfather used to say whenever a conversation got around to topics about life such as work or money. He'd spit a dark wad of chew on the ground nearby and offer the following advice to anyone in earshot, "No one can move a mountain. But, if you put your back into it, you might just move a rock. Thing is – you move enough rocks from the same big pile, eventually that mountain might just get moved after all." *So simplistic, but there's a kernel or two of truth hiding in there. This first rock would move, but Victoria has to be willing to listen.*

*   *   *

Wednesday, May 26, 1999 – Mid-Day

The journey had been quiet afterwards, both Sam and Victoria doing their best to cool any tension. Sam only occasionally commented on the beautiful Spanish countryside. In Sam's eyes, Victoria saw boyish wonder at

180

the rolling hills and valleys. She almost chuckled at one point when he became mysteriously transfixed on two large eagles circling overhead. Though fairly common in Spain, Sam mentioned having only seen them before in zoos. Victoria gradually realized how Sam seemed to live inside a protective bubble – insulating him from, while simultaneously denying him access to, anything surprising, challenging, or truly unique.

Just as the eagles disappeared across the afternoon sky, traffic grew dense, eventually stalling altogether. Soon, they were merely inching along – the way one does when traffic snarls. Victoria, at first, thought nothing of it, but a sudden terror gripped her mind. *Roadblock! The Spanish police might by now consider Sam a criminal mastermind.* She had to think quickly. She had shaved his head and made fake papers, but that wouldn't matter if a good cop compared "Rodney" up close to his picture. "Sam, can you reach my bag? Quickly! We may have a problem."

Sam snapped out of his daydreams and turned to comply. "What's going on?" he asked nervously, reaching for the bag.

"There's a roadblock ahead – likely looking for you."

"Me?!"

"Yeah. Listen. No time to explain right now. Let's just say your Catholic friends are more inventive than we thought. Find a tube of brown make-up. There are several in there – get the darkest shade you can find."

Sam rummaged around but found a tube soon enough. "This stuff?" He asked.

"Start rubbing it on your face, hands and arms. Lightly, we don't want to run out. Cover all visible skin. Try to avoid it looking uneven or smeared. We want you to look not so – white. Don't forget to cover inside and behind your ears and your eyelids. Understand?"

Soon enough, she saw it: a barricade checking everything heading into the city. It was still far ahead, and traffic moved like sludge. Sam would have time to finish his make-up job, but it wouldn't be enough. *I have to think. I'm missing something. Roadblocks are easy to beat if I have time to prepare and know one is coming.* Her palms began sweating against the leather steering wheel as she glimpsed something in her rearview mirror: a truck. *A slight opportunity, but it might work.* There was nothing particularly noteworthy about the truck except its cargo. It was pulling a flatbed trailer loaded to the teeth with huge glass jugs of drinking water. The bottles were ridiculously stacked on their sides into each other like a pyramid. Each heavy jug

181

supported the weight of those above it. Canvas straps stretched across each stack secured them, keeping them from toppling off the sides. *No one in their right mind stacks bottles that way. If those canvas straps were to burst . . .*

I'm relying too much on luck. Hector will never let me live this down if Sam gets killed, or worse: caught. Still, it was a chance she would have to take. Victoria glanced at Sam unapprovingly. He had tan cover smeared everywhere as he furiously tried masking his skin. His make-up had no chance. It wasn't Sam's fault. Few can mask their skin thoroughly without a full mirror and at least an hour to work. She could have helped him, but she needed to drive. *So, it's going to be the truck.*

Victoria, her voice calm and reassuring, turned to Sam. "Sam. Stop. We have to work together now. I'm going to stop the car up ahead and get out. When I do, I need you to follow my instructions exactly." Sam nodded as Victoria spelled out her devise to the last excruciating detail. She wasn't sure if Sam liked this plan, but that didn't matter. He was cargo, and she had to get this package delivered in one piece.

Victoria closed her eyes, listening. She slowed and heard the water truck's breaks squealing behind her and little else – Sam rustling against the leather seat, and . . . breathing? He was breathing heavily. This might be too much for him, but there weren't many choices left. That make-up would only confuse the police and draw extra attention. She opened her eyes and put the car into park, whispering to herself, *"Now."* She opened her door.

The door swung open, and Victoria stepped onto the highway's sunbaked pavement. Traffic was at a virtual standstill, so no one seemed particularly bothered. Immediately, she started waving her arms and yelling in Spanish as the passenger door opened, and Sam leaped out and rushed over, apparently to calm her. As he approached, she yelled for him to get away and pushed him aside. He stumbled backward. They were creating quite a spectacle. Sam regained his footing and came at Victoria again – still more out of apparent compassion than anger. He drew closer, but she stormed away from both him and the car. She made it roughly half the length of the water truck before stopping.

The truck's driver seemed amused. Victoria and Sam were now screaming at each other in English. The driver, though not understanding a word, could hopefully recognize a lover's quarrel in any language. He chuckled at Sam's pathetic efforts to calm her down.

182

Sam noticed the driver's interest in his dilemma and motioned for him to roll down his window. Sam's face was still one of worry and compassion. The driver's pity must have gotten the better of him, and he obliged. Victoria, in the meantime, made herself puke onto the roadway while leaning against the trailer. Sam, only knowing English, plead for directions to the nearest hospital. Although Sam's desperation was gibberish, the hapless driver knew the word "hospital," and pity supplanted his amusement. Sam nodded as though understanding the directions and yelled back to Victoria. Her "sickness" had passed for the moment, and she capitulated. She wiped her mouth with the hem of her shirt and returned – this time to the passenger door. Sam went to the driver's seat after repeatedly thanking the driver.

Victoria looked over at Sam and nervously bit her lip. She knew this gambit was risky. She had partially snipped those canvas straps toward the front of the trailer. The pressure of those heavy bottles would have to finish the job at just the right moment: too soon – the ensuing chaos would only highlight their scandal; too late – it would accomplish nothing. By then, the police would already have identified Sam and his pitiful make-up. They would hear about the highway injuries while handcuffed in a squad car.

Seconds became minutes as they slowly crept forward. There was no way of knowing how those canvas straps were holding up. Victoria turned to Sam to break the nervous tension. "I'm sorry about all of this, you know. It's always hard smuggling something alive – especially people."

Sam chuckled, "I've never considered this smuggling. I guess I think of you as my bodyguard or escort."

"Smuggling is much more subtle. Imagine a circus clown, a well-dressed executive, a muscle-bound James Bond sort of guy, a midget, and a normal dock worker in jeans. Each one has a key of cocaine to sneak past security. Who has the best chance?"

"Well, you are probably going to say the dock worker."

"Fine, smartass. But, why?" Victoria couldn't help but smile for the first time since they left Madrid.

"I'm not sure."

"Well, the others have a gimmick or angle that might help, but they share a common weakness – they attract attention. The best smuggler is the one no one notices: the guy that strolled right past the security guard might even have tipped his hat and threw a curt 'Good Morning' as he did. *That* guy is the smuggler – which brings me to why I'm sorry. This scheme might work

183

with a little luck, but it is not professional. We drew attention to ourselves. Everyone back there saw our little theatrics, and when those straps break, and chaos erupts, they will all remember us and our car well."

Sam replied, "You know, that's the most you've spoken to me since this started. I appreciate what you're saying, but despite everything, it is more thrilling than anything I've ever done before. I went on this blind date several months back that talked on and on about all the exciting things that had happened in her life, while I was stuck mostly just eating bread and pretending to be enthralled. One story, in particular, involved this monkey in Costa Rica stealing her beer before running off into the trees. Well, we've seen no monkeys, but this story beats anything she had to offer." A short pause elapsed before he finished, "Of course, stories won't impress my cell mates in a Spanish prison." His crooked smile faded once more.

Time inched forward, as did Sam and Victoria. The roadblock was only a few car lengths ahead now. The truck behind them still carried its full complement of bottles, and Victoria grew more nervous. She had hurriedly made strategic incisions and slices into the canvas straps with no way of knowing if it had been enough. It was a fool's quest, she knew, calculating how much damage to inflict so the straps would snap at just the right moment. Right about now would be perfect for her "incident" to occur. Once those bottles started falling, the ensuing chaos and confusion would force the small police detachment to investigate and help restore order. Their absence from the roadblock should create an opening for them to slip through without any inspection of their car or Sam's pathetic make-up. *Good thing the boy wore jeans.*

The officer checking their lane finally motioned for the SUV to pass. As they pulled forward, neither Sam nor Victoria spoke a word – their eyes were fixed on the rear-view mirror, looking for a miracle. Nothing happened. It was their turn. Victoria concentrated on hiding any apprehension or fear. *This is going to be a disaster.* Sam let his foot off of the brake and the car had idled forward only inches when it happened. A loud "Twang!" echoed from behind them, followed immediately by a second. Those straps had snapped, and with only seconds to spare! Victoria hoped it wasn't already too late. She, as would anyone else, turned to see what had happened.

She turned just in time to see the first bottle tumble, shattering against the scorched pavement, shooting glass and water across the roadway. There was no time for anyone around to understand what was happening before the second bottle hit. Two large stacks of bottles had broken free and began toppling off the trailer. Glass flew in all directions as cars scattered to get out of harm's way.

Suddenly, a terrible thought occurred to Victoria: *what about those poor souls in the other lane?* It was horrific. Bottles fell not only from the driver's side onto an empty shoulder but also cascaded from the passenger side into heavy traffic. One small compact's windshield was crushed under a falling bottle, and cries poured from inside: not only cries of fear but pain also. Someone had gotten hurt. Heavy bottles continued falling, rocketing shards of thick, broken glass into tires and car windows like bullets from a machine gun. Some foolishly abandoned their car to escape destruction as glass splinters ripped through their clothes and into their flesh. As more and more bottles toppled, cars rammed each other violently – people desperate to get clear.

Victoria denied herself any tears or remorse as she turned around. This was her doing, and it had worked. Officers rushed back to help the injured and get that truck out of traffic. "Sam. Drive, but not too fast."

Sam was speechless – entranced with silent awe at the gruesome scene taking shape. He didn't move.

Victoria repeated herself, louder, "Sam! Let's go!"

Sam blinked and sighed. He likely knew there was nothing they could do for those people now but pray. For right now, though, even prayers had to wait. He turned and drove through the roadblock, away from the destruction they had inflicted.

"Fly, you fools!" – Gandalf in *The Fellowship of the Ring* by J.R.R. Tolkien

Wednesday, May 26, 1999 – Afternoon

The empty glass clinked against the bar's dark wooden surface as Lukas finished his drink. Although airport drinks were usually watered down, they suited Lukas fine. He and Alfons had met in this bar at 2 P.M. each afternoon since they began choreographing airport security, but today's meeting had been particularly solemn. Today, Alfons had uncharacteristically ordered nothing but water. For the first time since Lukas had met him, his face betrayed concern. Something was wrong. Since joining Alfons, Lukas had known his greatest need was to learn. More often than not, this meant keeping quiet and doing as he was told. It had been this way Lukas' whole life: first with his father, then with school instructors, the commanders at the Swiss military academy, the Commandant in the Swiss Guard, and now with Alfons. However, one of a student's most delicate lessons is learning when to break with custom – when to defy the rules.

"You are troubled, Mein Herr?" plied Lukas, balancing his tone closer to meek inquiry than intrusion.

Alfons, gazing blindly into his water glass, responded, "Yes. I fear we have failed again."

"Again? Are you referring to Seville?"

"No. This is not the first time Vatican agents have been dispatched to retrieve that box, and we have likely failed just as did those agents of the past. This airport has been under our careful scrutiny for over two days. We have meticulously checked every international departure and have had no activity: no leads, no clues, not even a piece of suspicious luggage. I just spoke with our friend, Inspector Cruz, and a highway checkpoint was breached today outside of Barcelona. If one roadblock failure has been reported, then five others have been breached quietly. I hate to abandon hope just yet, however. It would be a shame for the cat to give up just before the mouse crawled into the open, no?"

Alfons' dedication seemed to Lukas more and more like desperation. Lukas had felt the same at the Ministry Office before this twisted game of hide and seek ballooned into a national manhunt. Lukas had read Sam's bio. Sam was not involved in human trafficking, but if that motivated the Spanish Police to help catch him, who was he to protest? Still, one gnawing question kept returning, and Alfons' reference to a previous failure only fueled that fire. *What did Sam have that they were so desperately trying to recover?* Lukas had not pushed Alfons on this issue since they took the case, but the pressure had become too great. He turned to Alfons and asked, "What does Sam have that is so important?"

"It does not truly matter, does it? Let me explain simply. The Church is the body of Christ, yes? Bodies, Mr. Dietrich, come with no spare parts – no bits to blindly toss aside. Our piece, the tiny little function we are given, is to serve as a muscle. You know how a muscle works? The brain sends a signal, and the muscle has but two choices – contract or expand – flex or release. Muscles have no capacity to ignore instruction. They always, *always*, respond immediately. So, you ask what Sam carries? It is irrelevant. Bowl of fruit, jewelry, or perhaps the Holy Grail – the distinction is meaningless. We are but a muscle – a muscle with a command."

Lukas teetered on the brink. If he pressed and Alfons took offense, he could be finished – this post with the Vatican gone and he on the next train back to Lucerne. He bit the inside of his cheek as he reluctantly decided. "With all the respect possible, I think you have missed something, Mein Herr. Your analogy of the muscle seems fine, but I am unsure about the brain. In the body, the brain instructs and muscles obey, but *how* does the brain instruct? It uses neurons, little tiny connections running from the brain through the nervous system to the muscles. Is it not possible that, on the rarest of occasions, neurons misinterpret the signal? When you recruited me, you mentioned sometimes, our job is to protect the Church from even its own leaders? How can we know our orders are truly divine without understanding them?"

"Certainly, events like those are quite rare, so incredibly isolated and difficult to identify. Can you even name one example?"

Lukas thought for a time and almost conceded, when something surfaced. "Are you aware of the Edgardo Mortara case?" In a rare moment, Alfons remained silent with his eyes trained on Lukas. *Really – something he does not know?* "Well, in the late 1850s, Catholic Agents, presumably folks like ourselves, were dispatched to Bologna to kidnap six-year-old Edgardo. The boy was Jewish, and so was his family, but the family's servant girl was Catholic. Apparently, the servant girl had, without the family's knowledge or permission, baptized Edgardo after the Catholic fashion. This same servant girl, you should

188

know, had been begging the Church for a dowry for some time and was the only witness to the alleged baptism. Bologna was a Papal State at the time, and under Catholic law, it was illegal for a Catholic to be raised in a non-Catholic home. So, the agents met with the Italian Grand Inquisitor and orchestrated the kidnapping. They barged into the Mortara home and ripped the child from his father's arms as the child and father wailed in desperation. The mother had been so overcome with grief and terror she had collapsed."

"That does sound horrific, but is it so morally abhorrent that. . ."

However, before he could finish, Lukas continued, "Little Edgardo, now an unwilling convert to Catholicism, gets shipped to Rome where Pope Pius IX raises him under the guidance of the Church. His natural parents are denied visitation for a long time, and finally, when they are granted visits, it is only under supervision. The Jewish Mortara family felt the Church had robbed their son of the Jewish rituals and practices necessary for salvation. The Church suffered as well. The international community was outraged at the deliberate kidnapping, and it played a large role in the collapse of the Papal States."

"Those agents, those 'muscles' as you call them, were irresponsible. Their 'brain' was acting on questionable evidence, consequently destroying both a family and a nation. They should have paused to consider perhaps their instructions were not Godly. Regardless of where an order originates, does not the person executing it bear some duty to at least weigh the ethics of the command?"

Alfons stared blankly at his protégé but soon smiled – not a broad, boisterous smile, but a smile nevertheless. "Very good, Mr. Dietrich. There is truth there – though perhaps only a parcel of it. This line of thinking triggers a failure in the chain of command. If the muscles no longer trust their instructions, do they then become their own commanders? Who, then, polices the police, hmm? Also, while the muscle wanders off contemplating the divinity of its instruction, is not precious time lost?"

Alfons continued, "Regardless, I commend your instinct. You will make a fine agent in time. For now, though, I will share what I know of this mysterious package." Alfons ordered a real drink and a second for Lukas and shared everything he knew about Sam's collection of papers. He knew it was a collection of Vatican translations regarding demonic possession: field notes and letters from Priests battling dark spirits. He told Lukas of how Manuel had discovered, translated, and compiled these documents. As he finished, he leaned closer and uttered just above a whisper, "You see, Mr. Dietrich, these

189

documents connect dots, much like those in children's puzzles, that no one previously knew existed. Manuel Vega accidentally stumbled across something humanity has searched for throughout history: Proof of God."

"We caught Mr. Vega, in the end, in Seville back in 1959. My mentor was but a junior agent at the time. He always lamented not securing those documents, and the cloud followed him for decades. Manuel refused to reveal their location, and there are limits to our methods – ultimately. When you and I were called to Seville that night, I hoped this was the target: that we were getting another chance to fix our mistakes."

Lukas' mind was spinning. *How was this possible? I have always believed God was real, knowing it could never be proven. There must be more to this story. If there is a way to prove God's existence . . .* He whispered back to his partner, "You are still concealing something. It sounds like this Manuel discovered not only the Holy Grail but also the Ark of the Covenant wrapped inside the Shroud of Turin, and our job is to take this precious light, a light humanity would use to climb out of spiritual darkness, and snuff it out forever. You are saying God wants us to *prevent* a spiritual renaissance the likes of which humanity has never experienced!"

Alfons finished the final swallow of his drink, stood, and put his hand on Lukas' shoulder. He had one response before leaving Lukas to pay the check, "What is God without Faith?"

*   *   *

Wednesday, May 23, 1999 – Early Evening

Several hours had passed, yet those final words still echoed. *What exactly did Alfons' mean? Does God exist if no one believes in Him? Surely. God existed before humans, after all. So, if God does not need people to believe, why would it matter if people came to believe based on pure, blind faith or based on a foundation of unequivocal proof? Perhaps Alfons' was being more figurative. Perhaps if . . .* His thoughts ran circles, dancing between raindrops, struggling to grasp something far beyond his reach.

The echo of his footsteps against the tiled floor of the long terminal was suddenly interrupted by his radio's buzz. He snatched it from his belt and answered, "This is Lukas. Go ahead."

The voice on the other end was staticky, but he made it out. It was Sergeant Jollo. "Hola – Senior Dietrich. Just swept the luggage conveyors in terminal two, and everything checked out. Will check back when I finish the central plant, Si?"

190

"Good work." Though no one was about, Lukas couldn't help but roll his eyes. Jollo, unlike any other member of their team, reported constantly. Lukas had tried explaining that he only needed a report if something was wrong or when completing his shift. Regardless, Jollo's reports rolled in. Though Lukas wasn't sure how Jollo made Sergeant, he understood perfectly why Alfons had him transferred into Lukas' division after only a few hours.

Airport congestion was normal for a weekday with few problems from their new security protocols. The passengers most affected were those flying internationally. Alfons and Lukas had established a special checkpoint to verify every passenger entering Terminal One (servicing all international flights). The checkpoint scanned passports and faces against photos they had of Sam. It was a final fail-safe measure, as Alfons had secured the airport's exterior as well. It would be impossible for Sam to get inside the airport without a guard laying eyes on him long before he reached Lukas' checkpoint. Some entrances had been temporarily closed, while those remaining had extra guards and even more eyes posing as passengers, creating centralized choke points.

Still, Barajas, Madrid's airport, was a large place, with infinite crevices where someone could possibly wriggle through. Alfons had warned Lukas several times about the sanitation docks, in particular. Alfons had spotted them almost immediately upon seeing the layout drawing. Each Terminal had at least one sanitation dock – essentially a dead-end hallway where rubbish was deposited in large bins to eventually be toted to oversized dumpsters. When their roll-up freight doors were raised, an opening was created, allowing anyone outside access – passage into the terminal beyond the metal detectors and screeners. To shore up this weakness, they had required a guard to be on call for each dock to oversee things while the trash was off-loaded. It still wasn't perfect. Some guards didn't come right away when summoned, and airport shopkeepers and custodians had no motive to patiently wait for them. There were also some guards that had been incentivized not to look quite so carefully as certain contraband made its way into the country through those docks.

Lukas was walking toward the sanitation dock in Terminal One. Fortunately, it was outside his new checkpoint. Even if someone breached the sanitation door, they would still face the new guarded checkpoint before reaching any flight gates. That arrangement was fortunate, as they didn't have enough guards to man each gate separately, and Sam would be just as "out of reach" catching a plane to Frankfurt, Milan, Vienna, or Tokyo as he would a

191

non-stop flight to Los Angeles. Lukas reached the door to the sanitation dock and swiped his badge, opening it. Dull fluorescent bulbs flooded the wide corridor with their pale grey hue. He reminded himself to breathe shallowly as the dock odors could be especially pungent.

At the end of the corridor, something caught his eye. A lone woman was leaning against the wall. She wore a uniform similar to those worn by airport sandwich and coffee shop employees. She had a trash tote beside her, loaded with black garbage bags. *Maybe she's waiting on security so she can unload.* Lukas decided, having not much better to do, to help out. As he got closer, however, he realized something was wrong. She was cradling her left shoulder. *She is injured!* Blood ran down her arm, and her shirt was ripped. He called out in Spanish, "Señora, let me get you some help!" Lukas rushed closer.

She was older than Lukas, though perhaps only by a few years. Her brown hair was tied back in a ponytail and she seemed in good, physical shape. Lukas made sure there weren't further injuries and radioed for someone to bring a wheelchair immediately. He looked into this woman's face. It was sweaty and exhausted. "What happened, Señora?"

She seemed reluctant to talk at first but eventually gathered the courage to answer. "It was so fast. I come to unload the trash and call for guard. No one came. I not want trouble with my work, so I raise the door myself. I had only gotten the door up a few feet or so when he slid underneath – some wild man with red hair. I never see him before. He push me down, but I no like being pushed. So I kick him, and he gets mad. He stands over me and cuts me with this knife. He ran away after, maybe about fifteen minutes ago."

Lukas was amazed. *Red hair? Could it be Sam? It didn't matter if it was Sam Johnston from California or Yosemite Sam from Warner Brothers; Terminal One had an intruder!* Lukas was excited. He stepped away for a brief second and radioed Alfons.

Alfons responded, in his typical calm, crisp tone, "First, contain the situation. I will move two squads into the connector between Terminal One and Terminal Two. You call an additional guard to our special checkpoint. Find out if anyone fitting this description has come through recently. The flights are our highest priority. If we keep him from boarding a plane, we will have him. Tonight, when things get quieter, we search inch by inch."

"Understood, Mein Herr."

192

As Lukas was making to call his checkpoint, he heard Alfons' voice again, "Mr. Dietrich. How is the girl?"

Lukas was ashamed. He had left her in pain this whole time. He turned and saw her sweat-stained face grinning half-heartedly back at him. "She is one piece. I have a wheelchair coming."

"Good work. Today might be a good day yet – even if this villain is not Sam."

As Lukas was again getting ready to call his security checkpoint, the wheelchair arrived. "Señora, would you be so kind as to sit? We will get you looked after. Do we need to contact your work?" Lukas smiled as he helped her into the chair.

"No, gracias. I was finishing my shift. I go home once I finish with the trash. I will tell them all about it tomorrow."

What a break! The fewer people know about this, the better. Lukas quickly made sure the roll-up door was locked, and the three of them turned to leave. They had gone only a few feet when the woman turned and asked, "Pardon – inspector? I forget my bag. Could you get it? It is by the trash cart."

Lukas smiled and sprinted over to retrieve her purse. Once there, he thought he heard something rustling inside the trash, but rats and other vermin in a trash cart are fairly common, and he had no time to root through the garbage. He returned with her bag and sat it in her lap. She looked up at him as they started moving again. "Thank you for everything. Truly. I had no idea how long I would be waiting down here." She tried her best to smile, but Lukas could tell she was masking her pain.

They cleared the sanitation dock, when Lukas remembered he never called for the extra guard for his checkpoint. He picked up his radio, but to his dismay, it was dead. Nothing worked: no lights – no static – nothing. He scowled and turned to the guard pushing the wheelchair, "May I use your radio? Mine has given up." The guard looked sheepishly and admitted that his was only a junior posting, and he was never issued a radio. *I can handle this – just need to reach that checkpoint. From there, I can make the call.* He motioned for the guard to follow him, and they moved onward.

En route, the woman asked, "Pardon, Señor. I have worked here many months and have seen no one dressed as you here. You work for Barajas?"

Lukas grinned. "No. Señora, I am but a consultant. We are organizing a search effort for a fugitive."

193

She smiled before probing deeper, "What sort of villain are you searching for? With this much effort, you would think they had attacked a Minister or something."

"I am not at liberty to say, but he has done some pretty bad things." *What should I say? Oh, nothing; he found some papers we lost forty years ago, and we want them back? They could prove the existence of God, but we cannot have people knowing for sure that God exists. We are the Church, after all.'* Lukas rolled his eyes, still unsure about their entire mission.

The checkpoint queue was not terribly long, with passengers calmly going through before reaching the flight gates, with additional shops and restaurants beyond. Lukas stopped at the checkpoint and leaned down. "Señora, help is just down that corridor. I will leave you with this good man here — what is your name?"

"Jaime Gamete."

"Very good. Sr. Gamete will escort you until you are safely back in your car or train heading home, yes?"

The woman nodded in agreement, gripping her handbag with her good arm.

Lukas leaned in and whispered to the officer, "Senor Gamete, the Health Center is past this security checkpoint. You understand that normally no one goes through this checkpoint without proper paperwork?"

"Si."

"She needs that doctor. Do not let her out of your sight until she is once more outside of security. You understand?" Officer Gamete nodded.

The two of them rolled away as Lukas walked to the checkpoint. He came in close, "Excuse me, Marco. How have things gone these last thirty minutes or so? Anything unusual?"

Marco shook his head as he replied, "No, Señor. Why do you ask? Something happen?"

"Yeah. Marco, call upstairs and ask for an extra guard for the rest of the night. Also, I need everyone to watch for a male with red hair. Might be our guy; might not. Someone snuck in here about 25 minutes ago with red hair. He injured a shop worker in the sanitation dock. We need to catch this guy, but even more importantly, we need to keep him from getting to those airplanes. Understood?"

Marco quickly responded with a strong, "Si, Señor. I would hate to have red hair and try catching a flight out of *this* airport tonight."

194

Lukas smiled, remembering his radio. "Marco, do you have a spare battery for my radio? It died on me in the trash dock."

Marco searched but came up empty-handed. "I am sorry, Señor. Do you want to borrow mine?"

"Fine. Call for backup first, and tell them you need another radio."

Marco made the call immediately. "Here you are, sir."

Lukas thanked him curtly before walking away. *Alright, you. Where did you hide? The only reason to break into an airport is to catch a flight. That means getting past security. Might you break in to retrieve luggage? No. Baggage claim is unsecured. Why sneak into a secured area only to grab something unsecured? This has got to be about a flight . . . unless he is after a person – someone arriving on an international flight. No, again, no. Incoming passengers get routed through passport control. They are never mixed with departing passengers. This must be about a departing flight.*

Lukas found a good spot on the upper level where he could monitor his checkpoint and keep an eye up and down the corridor. Nothing exciting was happening down there. He desperately needed to keep this suspect away from those departing planes at all costs. *But which plane – which flight?* He pulled out a copy of the flight list and perused the remaining international flights. There were twenty of them. Two, one to Paris and one to Tel Aviv, had boarded and were already pulling from their gate. That left eighteen. Six flights would depart within the hour – flights to New York, Calgary, London, Prague, Egypt, and Johannesburg. *New York?* That caught his eye. *Sam was American, and this breach happens only forty-five minutes before a flight to New York is scheduled to lift off? Seems convenient.* Still, something didn't set right. The Spanish Police may think Sam a vicious child kidnapper and slave trader, but Lukas knew better. Sam was a social worker who earned a meager living *helping* kids. He was not the sort of violent animal that would barge through a sanitation dock and stab someone.

Then it happened. Smoke – coming from the bend in the corridor just out of sight. He snatched the radio and tried calling Marco, but it warbled and buzzed. *Dammit! I have Marco's radio. I have to get down there! Now!* He tore off, sprinting downstairs toward the smoke. As he ran by, he noticed Marco had also left his post to investigate. Marco's new helper was currently running the checkpoint alone. *Damn! That was just what I needed to avoid!* Still, he tore down the corridor. Smoke poured from an open utility door. *What was behind that door? Air handlers?* His feet pounded on the floor as he

195

rounded the corner and closed in. Smoke alarms had been tripped, but only the local automated system. Emergency services would be standing by, awaiting confirmation before notifying the fire brigade.

Lukas reached the room. Inside were two security team members, one of which was Marco. They had an extinguisher and were squirting white foam over fairly large machines. "What happened?" shouted Lukas over the din in the room.

Marco stopped the fire extinguisher and looked up. "This unit caught on fire, Jefe. Not sure what started it."

"Marco, I need you back at the checkpoint now! I will secure things here." Lukas switched on his radio. "Emergency? Si. We contained the threat but need an investigation crew. Right – we used extinguishers. A large unit – air handler, I think – it was mild. It only took one extinguisher . . . no idea how it started, that is why I requested the investigation crew. We will lock it down and make sure no one comes in or out. Right – Gracias." Lukas turned to the other guard in the room, ". . . and you are?"

"Officer Montez. I was heading to Terminal Two and saw the smoke."

"Gracias, Sr. Montez. Looks like you caught the fire in time. Secure the room if you would?"

Lukas turned to go back, and standing in the corridor was Alfons. He opened his mouth and made a dreaded proclamation, "We have lost them, Mr. Dietrich."

*   *   *

Wednesday, May 26, 1999 – Evening

Lukas and Alfons jogged down the corridor and past the security checkpoint before another word was spoken. "What do you mean, 'lost them,' if I might ask?"

"They most likely boarded that Air Canada flight that pulled away six minutes ago."

Impossible! Alfons is going too far with his soothsayer routine. There is no way Sam and any helpers got past me and onto one of those flights. Lukas stopped, turned his quizzical expression toward his partner, and asked, "How can you be so sure?"

Alfons, not stopping for discussion, threw back a response, "I can explain, but seconds truly matter right now. If we are not on-board the London flight in five minutes, we are beaten."

196

London? Why, if Sam is on his way to Canada, did Alfons need a flight to London? Lukas had only two options – refuse to follow and abandon his partner or follow blindly, trusting everything would make sense in time. With little hesitation, he ignored all logic his mind screamed out, and instead followed his instinct. Once he caught back up, they jogged toward the British Airways flight in unison.

They reached the British Airways gateway just as the attendants were nearing the end of the boarding queue. Alfons wasted no time flashing his badge at the women working the counter. "Pardon, Madames. We have to get on this flight; it is serious police business."

The two girls looked at each other confused before one of them made a few keystrokes on her terminal and announced, with a lazy attempt at sounding disappointed, that the flight was "completely full."

Alfons, catching his breath from the lengthy jog, leaned in closer, "I tell you this is official. You see my credentials, yes? You have two choices – get us on that plane somehow, even if you have to bump someone – or refuse us. Please know, however, that if you refuse, I will be forced to impound this flight until things get straightened out with your superiors. So, choose: inconvenience a few or inconvenience all." Lukas had not seen Alfons so pointed before, especially since he was flaunting authority he did not have. Their consultant role gave them no right to interfere with flight schedules. By the time Alfons could call Inspector Cruz for authority, this flight would be in the air en route to London.

Both girls grew timid and backed away. The girl who had been working the terminal picked up her phone and made a quick call. Lukas could hear his heart beat as they waited to see if this bluff would work. The girl hung up and looked at Alfons sheepishly, "I will get you on board. Just a moment." Lukas did his best to hide his grin.

A few moments later, as they stepped onto the plane, Alfons turned to the head of the flight crew and asked for the captain, again providing his credentials. The captain promptly emerged from the cockpit, a hefty gentleman with a jolly demeanor. "How can I help you two gentlemen?"

Alfons smiled in return and handed the captain a small note as he answered, "Please communicate this authorization code to the tower. We desperately need to get airborne and cannot afford to wait in the queue line to taxi."

"Would you at least tell me *why* the hurry?"

197

Alfons looked back at the happy, though sweaty, face of the captain and answered, "I would be happy to oblige you and tell you everything I know, but it should wait until we are airborne. Explanation, itself, is a delay."

"Fine. Take your seats, and we'll get going."

What does Alfons hope to accomplish? If he is so sure they are lost, and that they are on a flight to Calgary, Canada, then why are we so desperate to catch this flight to England? And why the hurried take off? What could we possibly accomplish that ten minutes of taxiing on a runway will jeopardize? He is going to have to explain himself, and it better be good. This is too bizarre.

Lukas was sweaty and growing more frustrated. Luckily, an entire row had been cleared for them at the rear of the plane. Lukas took the window seat and wasted no time adjusting his vent as Alfons got situated. Lukas turned to Alfons and, before one question could escape, was greeted with a raised finger. *Is he serious? He is hushing me now? Fine. Fine.* Lukas turned toward the window in frustration. The evening sun was still bright, but there was enough reflection to see Alfons staring at his watch beside him. *He is nervous about something.* Lukas's rage turned again to curiosity.

Things continued at a frenetic pace for the flight crew. They rushed through the safety speeches and, much to Lukas' surprise, skipped the taxi line and made directly for the runway. The plane soon picked up speed, and he could see distance growing between them and the ground. They were in the air! Alfons let his head collapse back against the navy cushion as he sighed audibly. He closed his eyes for what amounted to an inordinately long blink before opening his mouth and turning toward Lukas. "I must apologize. I assure you there was no time to explain without squandering our chances. We have, I presume, roughly ten to fifteen minutes before that captain confronts us. While I will only be as forthcoming as I can with him, I would prefer transparency with you. You have many questions, yes?"

Lukas' mind raced to all manner of questions regarding how Alfons presumed to treat him as a partner while concealing vital information. However, none of those venom-filled questions escaped. Instead, noticing for the first time strains of fatigue and worry on Alfons' face, sweat on his forehead, and a reddish hue on his neck, Lukas asked, "How are *you* feeling, Mein Herr?"

Alfons smiled contently, "I am good. I have not run in some time, and time has a way of exposing our frailties. I will be ready to run again once we reach London – and so should you, by the way."

198

Lukas, only slightly comfortable that his partner was still in control, asked, "How do you know Sam and his helper are on that Canadian airplane?"

Alfons smiled. "Well, the credit for that starts with Sargent Jollo. You remember Sargent Jollo, yes?"

"Of course, but . . ."

"Well, Jollo tried radioing you to alert you about his completed sweeping of the central plant. With no answer from you, he called me. I got rid of him quickly and tried reaching you. I also failed. It seemed far too coincidental that your radio went down just after we spoke about important security changes. So I considered it, and guess who crossed my mind?"

"That woman? You think she is part of this? She was injured . . ."

"Did you see her injury firsthand?"

"Well, no. I started to and got distracted with the prospect of catching her attacker who might be our guy. By then, I wanted to get her to a doctor so I could get on with it."

"Which doctor did you take her to? It was inside — beyond the checkpoint?"

"Yes, but I sent her with a guard."

"That poor guard is likely unconscious in a restroom stall as we speak."

"OK — assume she was Sam's helper. How could she disable my radio? She never touched it."

Alfons smiled wryly. "Go back in your mind and listen. Do you remember anything odd?"

The odd rustling noise inside the trash cart rushed into his head. "There was something rustling in her trash cart. I assumed it was rats."

"I would imagine you were actually hearing a small microwave oven, likely running on batteries. Do you know what simple microwaves can do to electronics?"

"That seems like reaching. How could you know she had a rigged microwave?"

"I do not. In truth, many devices could have fried your radio, but it was definitely fried just after you spoke with me and while you were alone with her and that poor officer."

"Did you contact her shop?"

"No. It was the end of her shift, and I saw no need."

"Listen. This woman is a professional in every sense of the word. I am sure she is the same one you saw in the wheelchair in Seville, and I am sure she

199

drove that Mahou Light truck. You read Sam's file – no way he makes it this far on his own. He has secured professional help, most likely a smuggler or mercenary. Let us stop pretending Sam is calling the shots. She is young, fast, and extremely clever."

"Even if she is the evil genius behind the whole operation, how did Sam get inside the airport? He was not in the sanitation dock and no one got a hint of him coming in from the outside."

Yet again, Alfons smiled. "When Sam arrived at the Barajas Airport today, he was already beyond security."

"What!? How does that happen? Other than the sanitation docks, there are no other entries other than those used by airport staff, and we threaded those with security. There is no way he posed as an employee."

"You are correct; he did not."

"Then how?" Lukas approached indignance with this last question, concealing his amazement at Alfons' dizzying intellect and how he could see facts from a thousand angles simultaneously.

"Mr. Dietrich, there are almost one hundred unsecured doors leading to the interior of those Terminals. People pour through them all day without any inspection or even a second glance."

Lukas thought for a second before he stumbled upon it, "The jet ways! You think he *flew* into the airport? From where? Wait . . . Barcelona? The report we got earlier about the roadblock – that was en route to Barcelona!"

"It was." Alfons couldn't help but exude pride at his young partner for putting that together.

"Wait, so they drove all the way from Madrid to Barcelona? Just to fly *back* to Madrid? Why not simply fly somewhere safe out of Barcelona? It is like a fugitive trying to hide inside a police station."

"A rigged microwave; an understanding of our security; fake papers for Sam; a small fire in a nearby air handler – she had spent days setting that up. She has not been in Barcelona to set things up; she has been in Madrid. She had no tricks to get Sam on an international flight from Barcelona."

Lukas sat back, trying to let all of this sink in. *He is right; she is clever, but there are still missing pieces. Only international flights fly into Terminal One. Sam would have arrived at another terminal, past general security, but still needing to get past my final checkpoint. Also, what makes him so sure they were already on board a plane, and why did we have to leave so quickly – and to London, no less?*

200

"Still questions, I presume? Or have you pieced the rest together?"

Lukas started to ask but decided to try this riddle himself. "The fire in the air handler room. That took Marco from his checkpoint. That was when Sam slipped through. The new guard was so focused on red hair that he likely did not even look at Sam's photo. Sam has likely changed his hair color?"

"Or removed his hair altogether, yes." The plane continued ascending into the heavens on its northern heading toward London. The flight attendants were busy preparing the drink cart for its inevitable trek down the aisle. "Go on," Alfons encouraged.

"So the fire created a chaotic window to sneak Sam through the checkpoint. From there, I am assuming he sprinted to the closest flight just completing boarding – the Canadian Air flight, I presume?"

"Good job. But why, then, are we on a plane to London?"

Lukas was stuck on that one. "Well, the problem is that London was never a part of this. This flight was chosen randomly or through happenstance." He accepted a whiskey from the flight attendant and begrudgingly forked over his Spanish Pesetas. Lukas took a sip and placed the glass on the plastic tray. "We had to run to catch this plane. You chose it based on time. It was simply the next flight leaving Madrid, yes?"

Alfons, still grinning as he cradled a watered-down diet soda, corrected his protégé. "Close, but actually, it was the first flight leaving Spain. It was not Madrid I wanted out of; it was Spain."

"The real question, then, is why you wanted out of Spain so desperately."

Lukas continued mulling the problem as Alfons' attention turned to the aisle. The captain, now on a steady flight path, was on his way back to them. As he finally reached their row, he stopped. His formerly cheerful demeanor had disappeared and had been replaced with a concerned expression of dread. "Now, why did you two need on my plane so badly?"

Alfons, looking into the pilot's face, offered the answer Lukas had not yet arrived at. "We had to get out of the airport, out of Madrid, and out of Spain before the airports were shut down."

What? Why would the airports be shut down unless . . .

The captain's expression only grew more somber as he peered into Alfons' cold eyes. "Why should I not . . ."

Before he could finish, Alfons interrupted and finished his sentence for him, ". . . detain us and return to Madrid? It is your prerogative, but I assure

201

you, we had nothing to do with any fire, explosion, or chaos that might have happened in that airport tonight – neither the first nor the second."

The second?!

Alfons pointed to Lukas, "You see, one fire, a small isolated incident in an air handler room, gets treated like an industrial accident – nothing more. At least not until it is investigated. But a second fire or explosion – within minutes of the first? That creates a pattern. Patterns are not accidents. The assumption becomes that the airport is under attack. In an attack, no one waits for an investigation – the airport gets immediately shut down; no traffic allowed out, and only emergency flights allowed in. Afterward, our limited authority would not get a plane in the air – no matter who we called. Had we waited, we would now be hopelessly stuck in Madrid – prey to one of the most elaborate traps I have ever encountered."

Both the Captain and Lukas were in awe – their mouths wide open as they tried catching up. Alfons had pieced together these sundered events at a lightning pace, keeping the tiny embers of their search smoldering. "Now, Captain, if you would be so kind, I need to make some fairly confidential phone calls – might I use the cockpit's radio?"

"And he answered, saying, My name is Legion: for we are many." – Mark 5:9, New Testament – King James Version.

Wednesday, May 23, 1999 – Evening (Local Time)

Air blew through the vent against Sam's face as he sat gazing silently at the wispy clouds outside. They had been airborne for over an hour, and the sun was struggling to descend beyond the horizon. While this flight to Calgary required they be in the air for over nine hours, time would seem to stand still. Their plane took off around 6:30 pm and, due to changes in time, would land around 7 pm on the same day in Calgary. The entire flight would be spent chasing the sun westward across the globe in a seemingly perpetual dusk. While none of this was lost on Sam, he had spent his time simply staring outside. He was finally heading home, and this dreadful adventure could close, but the screams and cries of those injured on the road that morning haunted his thoughts, like an itch he could never scratch.

Victoria sat beside him, comfortably nestled into her middle seat, doing a remarkable job of ignoring the sweaty gentleman in the aisle seat. Sam was unsure what, if anything, to say to her. Her instructions in Barcelona had been explicit. "Don't look at me or speak to me – we don't know each other." He had complied fully thus far but didn't know if her instructions applied just to the airport or included the flight. Eventually, tranquility overwhelmed him, and he had to speak and turned to Victoria. "Excuse me, miss," he started, awkwardly pretending he didn't already know her. "Have you taken this flight before? It's a long time to be cooped up in these tiny seats, isn't it?"

Victoria turned to face him and couldn't help grinning at his juvenile attempt at subtlety. "No. I've not taken this particular flight, but I've been on long flights like this before." She leaned and barely whispered, "These seats are far more comfortable when there's an empty in your row." Sam caught a hint of something behind her eyes but not scorn nor rebuke. *At least we can talk now.* Sam lifted the tiny plastic beer cup in front of him, his fingers smearing beads of sweat on its exterior. He took a drink and noticed Victoria closing her eyes as her breathing grew deeper. After a few silent moments, she cocked her head sideways and began making a hacking sound – softer at first but gradually louder. When she started coughing toward the sweaty guy, he pretended not to notice at first. As her coughs became more dramatic, some landing directly over his V-8, he had no choice but to confront her.

He leaned further away but turned to face her, "Do you mind? Maybe you could step into the bathroom or something until you're finished?"

Victoria shot back an injured look. While continuing to cough, she managed a few words, "I'm really [cough] sorry. I'm allergic to [gag followed by a convincing nose-blowing] certain colognes. Is that [another loud cough accompanying a few drops of spittle] Polo you're wearing?"

"It is. I had no idea. I am so sorry."

A few moments and a hushed conversation with the flight attendant later, Victoria and Sam were sitting comfortably with an empty seat between them. Sam couldn't help himself. He grinned, remembering his flight into Madrid and the old woman denying him even a moment's peace. In many ways, Victoria was everything Sam wished he was. She made things happen; forcing open doors that were closed to most everyone else. His grin faded quickly, though, as the screams from earlier returned. The doors Victoria opened had a price, and he couldn't forget that.

Sam casually sipped his beer for a while before reaching under his seat and pulling out a brown leather briefcase. It was far more functional than that old box he had been toting about. He started thumbing through the pages inside – pretending to be reading for his own edification. *Victoria shut me out before, but she was under more stress back then. She might be more receptive now – we're on the flight home and we're out of Spain. Plus, if that second fire went off as she described, those Vatican agents are stuck in Madrid.* Sam leaned over, quietly asking, "Look, I don't want to bore you again with this stuff, but would you mind if I just went through some excerpts – just a few passages about a demon called Gyllou?"

Victoria sighed in resignation before answering, "Fine. Let me in on this Gyllou character, but you shouldn't get false hope. Nothing written on these pages is going to convince me there's a real God out there somewhere. Understand?"

Sam agreed quickly, taking her words as more of a challenge than the warning they were likely meant to be. He started off with some background. "Well, Gyllou is a demon of ancient Middle-Eastern origin, usually referred to as a fertility demon. Legends describe her wreaking havoc on unborn . . ."

Victoria interrupted, "Where is this from? Did you research demonology on your flight from Barcelona?"

204

Sam grinned as he answered, "No. Manuel described a few of the demons in his notes. He didn't do that for all of them – probably couldn't find information. Remember, he was writing this in the late 1950s, before the internet and when the subject of demons and spirits was far more taboo. Anyway, Gyllou is said to infest infants still within the womb, drinking their fluids and other unspeakable acts. Well, Manuel came across three instances where a demon, calling itself Gyllou, was exercised. Before getting into the details of the individual accounts, you should know that all the victims were pregnant at the time of their exorcism! Isn't that remarkable? A demon associated with fertility and infanticide is encountered during these exorcisms, and all victims are pregnant women?" Sam paused for a moment, waiting for any hopeful sign from Victoria.

Instead, he heard a distinct sigh before she interjected, "I'm not sure it's all that remarkable. If we're honest, these priests likely had access to the lore around this demon and could have just thrown that name in their letter or whatever. You might be crossing your chicken and your egg." After that, she leaned back, poorly masking the smugness in her eyes.

This time, however, Sam was ready and immediately shot back, "I think your assumption has more holes than you realize. You assume that these Priests knew about Gyllou. That is the real stretch. Demonology is not a heavily publicized field. Even Catholic training on exorcisms doesn't likely describe individual demons. You also seem to assume Priests are lying – that they performed an exorcism and either heard a name other than Gyllou or heard no name at all, yet wrote Gyllou in their correspondence. I admit I always tend to assume that Priests are truthful, but you're making the same error in reverse."

"Well, this conversation is going to be pleasant," rebuffed Victoria. "Look, there's no way that you and I sitting in a plane 35,000 feet above the Atlantic are going to resolve this. Why don't you just continue preaching and perhaps the precious light will pierce the heavens and open my poor, blind eyes."

Her tone was sharp and sarcastic, to be certain, but without hostility – at least not yet. Sam could tell Victoria had strong feelings about this and didn't want to risk pushing her over the cliff. Regardless, she had opened the door just a crack for him to continue going over the writings with her, and he intended to take advantage of it.

He flipped to document #33 and ran his fingers along the page, searching for a particular passage. His eyes widened as he landed upon the section he was looking for. He began reading, loudly enough for her to hear but not so loud as to share with their neighbors. These details were no good for children:

"1874 A.D. — Columbia: The experience thus far had been unremarkable — almost textbook for an exorcism. So much so in fact, that I questioned the authenticity of the whole affair. After all, you know better than I there is nothing routine or textbook about a true exorcism — no matter how banal it might first seem. As I continued my prayers and supplications, it happened.

At once, Inez cried out in anguish — a piercing shriek shattering the night. Amidst her wails, I noticed blood soaking her bed-sheet and motioned for Montes to turn her over. To my disbelief, her back had somehow been punctured twice, and dark red blood poured from fresh open wounds. The wounds were roughly three centimeters in diameter and equidistant on each shoulder blade. The emergence of such horrific wounds would by itself have been enough to shock my intellect and shatter my confidence; however, that paled in light of the next discovery. The wounds, my friend, they were clearly made from the inside — out! Excess skin and bits of hewn flesh protruded grotesquely. To this day, I have no words to truly capture what those wounds looked like. Even more mysterious, upon later inspection, there were no matching holes in the mattress, although Inez was lying on her back at the time. It sounds suspicious, I know. But my duty is to describe what I saw, my friend."

Sam stopped and looked up. "I want to skip to some other victims of Gyllou rather than read the whole thing. Sam flipped backward through the translated pages, stopping at Document #4. Before starting, he looked to Victoria again, "This one is from Egypt in the 10th Century. Writing was kinda formalistic back then."

He scanned until his finger stopped at the desired passage, and he read:

"995 A.D. — Cairo: Madame Jendayi was with child, and I took all care to protect her and the infant. The statues and adornment in the room were constant reminders

206

that we Christians were but visitors here. Although the Power of God ultimately prevailed, banishing this foul beast, it inflicted grievous pain upon Jendayi. Chief among these, aside from the tragic loss of her unborn son, were two large wounds on her back. I dropped my cane and inspected more closely. The pain was immense, and, judging from the wounds themselves, the injuries seemed to have been caused by something protruding from inside her back outward through her skin. My limited knowledge of science affords no physical explanation to account for these phenomena; the wounds appeared as inverted punctures, as though she had been gored.

Rather than waiting on Victoria's cynicism or sarcasm, Sam continued directly to the final document referencing this Gyllou – Document #17. He found the passage and quickly continued:

"1722 A.D. – Tuscany: Maria was swollen by this time, being only a few short weeks until her baby was due. When the injury hit, blood poured from her back, soaking the mattress and spilling onto the floor. I was in the midst of wrestling with her demon, a villainous sort calling herself Gillau. As such, I was not expecting such a scream just then.

When I noticed the dark stream coating the floor, I rushed to her aide. What I saw on Maria's back could not be. There were two holes in her back as wide as broom handles, gaping wounds from which blood gushed. There is more. The holes appeared to be made from inside her back. The skin was poking outward around each hole with bloody bits of tissue dangling. I have seen such a thing before. During the war, before I was a man of the cloth, a friend of mine was nearby when cannon fire splintered the deck. Shrapnel pierced him from the front, and the wooden shard ran him through. Maria's skin looked as though she, too, had been run through, but twice. There were no marks in her chest or in the mattress."

Sam closed the binder and waited a heartbeat before continuing. "There's more in these three passages, more similarities, but you probably don't want to sit here while I read them all. All three women suffered horrible fevers that wouldn't break, they all shout vile obscenities at the Priest in a foreign language none of them knew, and they all suffered a terrible

207

miscarriage either before or during the exorcism. This Gyllou is powerful and unrelenting: three different victims, three separate continents, separated by centuries – all with such exacting similarities. How many 'coincidences' do you need before accepting that they're not actually coincidences at all? There is absolutely no way these three separate exorcists knew each other or had some sort of 'cheat sheet' telling them what to write. All the victims were female. All were with child. All of them cry out the name of "Gyllou" when pressed for the demon's name."

Sam leaned back at last – mentally replaying what he had just said. *The argument is strong. The facts are there, and I don't see much room for interpretation. I don't expect her to have a soul-changing experience right here mid-flight, but she should at least acknowledge the facts. Her mind's closed door should have a few glimmers of light peeking in around the edges. Still, need to keep expectations low. She's too much like my father and particularly stubborn on these issues.* He played his argument in his head, patiently waiting for a response. What he got surprised him.

"You know what, Sam? Your facts make sense, although you seem to be rushing to a conclusion that's not entirely supported. You've got a whole stack full of these connected scenarios in that briefcase. Also, it would be pretty naïve for anyone to assume that the entire history of Catholic exorcisms has been either a great conspiracy or a bizarre exercise in creative writing."

Sam, unable to contain himself, interjected quickly, "Thanks! I knew once you saw the facts, you'd come around. This is astounding that you've seen . . ."

"Hold on. I think you misunderstand." Victoria's voice became more serious and pointed than earlier as she countered Sam's exuberance, "I haven't 'come around' or 'seen' anything. I only said your facts look solid, but your conclusion is shaky. Did several priests, performing rituals they felt were exorcisms, experience similar things? I think your facts justify that. But that is as far as I go. Does this mean the victim was actually possessed by a dark spirit? Not necessarily . . ."

Sam's exuberance melted. *How can she see the light and deny that it comes from the sun?* He cut her off mid-sentence, "So, you are saying that you see that I've shown you a '2' and another '2,' but you refuse to believe they add up to '4?' Wow, I don't know what you've been through in your life to so vehemently refuse to consider that something wonderful, though

208

supernatural, might actually exist out there! You acknowledge these Priests' experiences but deny their wonder. I just read you descriptions of these women being gored from the inside - out! Three separate priests experience that, and you refuse to believe anything supernatural happened? That's ig . . ."

Victoria tightened her lips and held up her hand before Sam finished his sentence. It worked – as Sam stopped talking. Both of them sat silently while Victoria kept her hand aloft. When she finally lowered it, almost a full minute later, she calmly said, "I warned you from the beginning that nothing in this assortment of old papers would convince me that God exists. We should stop before one of us gets emotional. I admire your passion, Sam, but this path you're on ends with an argument you don't want to have. I can assure you of that. So, let's just be quiet for a while, hmm? Maybe even get some sleep. It's still a long flight yet."

Sam, deflated and frustrated by Victoria's dismissiveness, tossed the briefcase back under the seat and turned back to the long dusk outside his window.

*   *   *

Wednesday, May 26, 1999 – Evening

The room smelled sweet – not sweet like catching a whiff from the cotton candy machine at the circus, but rather sweet like the aura of stargazer lilies intertwined with the scent of highly overpriced perfume. It was intoxicating. Sam weaved in and out amongst men in tuxedos and women adorned in flowing evening gowns. The room was dark – almost black, in fact, and the ivory from the few desert plates and coffee cups contrasted starkly against black tablecloths. Sam was confused. He had never been invited to a party like this, and in some odd way, he wasn't really at this one either. Though wearing an appropriate tuxedo, and nothing seemed truly out of place, the whole room seemed engrossed in countless private discussions. None of the faces looked friendly or familiar. Everyone either ignored him completely or shot him contemptuous glances masked behind paper smiles. He was the only one not a part of some small circle and everyone knew it. He stopped near windows overlooking the dark streets several floors below. That was when he saw her.

She was at first merely a reflection in the window pane. He didn't know her, yet something about her tugged the chords of his memory. He spun around to face her. She was looking back at him. Though others dressed

209

in dark – blacks, blues, and purples, not her. She wore a long, form-fitting yellow gown cut low in the front, with a slightly longer than appropriate slit running up her right leg. Her flawless olive skin melted against the gown. Dark hair in long, wavy curls draped about her shoulders and down her back. As their eyes met, she smiled. Hers was not the nervous smile of habit but the sultry smile of forbidden temptation. She made no gestures or motions other than taking a slow sip from the long-stem crystal glass cradled between her delicate fingers.

The milled conversations, which moments ago had filled the room, faded. Sam found himself walking closer. His mind struggled to place her but came up empty. As he neared, her smile melted, and she stared in complete contentment. From the corners of his eyes, everyone else seemed to dissipate into nothingness. They must still be there, but Sam dared not look away. They were now the only people in the room. She was sultry and seductive – everything he'd ever fantasized about. And she was within arm's reach.

Neither spoke. He struggled to come off as sophisticated as someone like her deserved. His mind raced, searching now for some introduction that was as debonair and distinctive as she was beautiful and exotic. Still, his mind produced nothing. She finally broke the tension by stepping forward – their faces now mere inches apart. He gazed into dark, entrancing eyes. Anticipation hung desperately in the air until . . . everything went wrong. It was light at first – that taste. He had eaten nothing – drank nothing. Yet a foul taste grew from the back of his throat. He did his best to mask the discomfort. She stared into his eyes and smirked. *Could this be happening? Why is she grinning?* The taste was now unbearable and was almost sulfuric in nature. Sam was forced to turn and gag. It was so strong now! He doubled over and heaved, trying to purge this plague. He looked back. She was smiling now – a devious, satisfied smile. Sam was bewildered. *What is this?* He wanted to ask who she was, but the taste was now so potent he could manage nothing but involuntary gag reflexes. She looked down at him as he knelt at her feet in pain. He glanced up only to watch this fantasy become a gruesome nightmare.

In an instant, her smooth, dark skin faded to pale white and became pocked with hideous bloody scars. Her dark eyes became as bright amber. She opened her mouth and spewed a piercing, high-pitched shriek. Where split seconds earlier lay gorgeous dark curls, now horrible, twisted gray horns

210

sprouted straight from her back. There was no relief from the sulfuric taste, and he retched far more violently than before.

So hard, in fact, he awoke, still sitting in his navy blue seat. Sweat covered his head, and his shirt was soaked. *A dream? It seemed so horribly real. That taste – was that sulfur – so vile and metallic?* Victoria was still sitting beside him, fast asleep. He wiped beads of sweat from his face. *I've been so engrossed in these writings, I'm dreaming about them now.* He managed a sip or two of his now tepid beer when something clicked in his mind – something about "Gyllou." He yanked the briefcase from under the seat and began scouring. *That taste . . .* He happened upon Jendayi's exorcism first. **"My assistant had to help me on more than one occasion once I had engaged the spirit in earnest. I am still uncertain what caused me to retch so, but I managed through and was able to continue after some time."** Sam could hardly believe what he was reading. *Did he – this priest in the 10th century – experience that same awful taste?*

He found Maria's account next. **"I found myself in need of something to wash out my mouth. The putrid wine available did little to assuage my need, but I persisted for the sake of this sweet young girl."**

There it is again! Manuel completely missed this when he compared these accounts! Likely because it was suffered by the Priest, not the victim, and it's not described explicitly. The Priest in Egypt described it as being sick, while the Priest in Venice only mentioned needing to wash his mouth. I need to see if the exorcist for Inez mentioned anything like this. He thumbed further back to document #33 and read the passage. Twice, he scoured it, but there was nothing about the Priest being sick or suffering a bad taste. *This can't be a coincidence. First, my dream and then finding similar effects in these Priests' writings!* As he went back over the dismal story for the third time, he caught something. *Wait a minute! At the outset, it read,* **"When we pulled up to the Cortez villa, I was forced to squint my eyes as we got out of the carriage. The sun in this cursed valley is brighter in February than on any summer day back home, my friend, I assure you."** *Then, they go inside and confront the demon. But there's another passage . . . where was it? Here it is.* He read in silence, **"Hernan stumbled on the threshold in the pitch of night. However, once more we had our composure and were prepared to return**

211

inside and face this dark one."

Sam re-read both passages, noting the differences in time. They were clearly outside twice – once in the bright afternoon sun and again under the dark of night. It also mentioned regaining composure. While far from conclusive, the scant facts allowed for the possibility. There was a moment, not accounted for in the text, where the Priest and the victim were separated. They could have been smoking, praying, playing Parcheesi, or retching helplessly into the sand.

Sam was astounded. His subconscious had caught something he had missed and revealed it to him in a dream. His excitement swelled. He needed to share this revelation, though Victoria would likely not be moved. Sam stretched his left arm over to press her shoulder when a short "beep" interrupted him. He pulled his hand back quickly. *What was that?* He cautiously tried once more. He was almost there when again a "beep" rang out, and again Sam yanked his arm back nervously. He looked over at Victoria as she opened her eyes and looked back at him.

"What's wrong with you? Are you sick? You're soaked – even your clothes." She pointed at large dark spots on his shirt where he had been sweltering from his dream. She opened her mouth to make another comment when the "beep" rang out once more. She reached down and pushed a button on her watch.

An alarm! Sam felt foolish, making a mystery of something so benign. *Why set an alarm for now, though? We're hours from Calgary.* Regardless, Sam had given up quite some time ago trying to decipher the inner workings of Victoria's mind. It conceived the plan that freed him and got him out of Spain. He was on his way home now, and he owed it completely to Victoria. However, he was still excited about his discovery.

"Victoria, listen. Something incredible happened while I slept."

"Ok, Sam. You can tell me all about it, but I need to take care of something first. Be right back." She opened the overhead bin and, after rustling through her small bag, slipped something into her pocket and headed toward the restrooms at the plane's rear.

The line was over four people deep, so Sam sat back and replayed his dream. It was terrifying watching that gorgeous woman transform into something so awful, but the sulfuric taste in his mouth? *That was remarkable!*

In about fifteen minutes, Victoria returned. She was smiling, but it

212

was a different smile. It was nervous – masking something. She had set something in motion. "What did you pull from your bag, if you don't mind me asking?" Sam wanted in on this new plot.

"Just a little something extra from that medicine closet in the Seville hospital. It won't be pleasant, but you'll know a whole lot more in about twelve minutes." Victoria was speaking in riddles, and Sam decided it wasn't worth the effort to try deciphering. The last time he got involved, he had helped her injure dozens of people whose only sin was driving to Barcelona. The screams, the smoke, and the chaos from that awful incident started resurfacing, but Sam had something far more critical to discuss than to rehash that.

"Alright then, I have twelve minutes to tell you about this bizarre dream." Victoria rolled her eyes – as would anyone forced to endure the sordid details of someone else's dream. Sam ignored her indignation and told her the whole thing. From the moment he first saw the gorgeous woman at that party to her terrible transformation. The horns, the look in her eyes, and finally, the awful taste on his tongue were shared in vivid detail.

Afterward, Victoria sighed before commenting, "Let me guess. You think this hot girl in your dream turned in that demon from the letters?"

"Well, I wasn't thinking that far into *her*, actually. I guess she might have become what my mind pictures as Gyllou, yeah. But that's not the exciting part. I'm talking about the sulfur."

"The taste you were gagging on? What about it?"

Sam's anticipation started building as he walked Victoria through the passages in Manuel's collection. When finished, he looked back at Victoria and asked, "Isn't this incredible? Not only are the experiences of the victims identical, but so are the attacks against the Priest! Words can't easily describe that taste from my dream, but it was horrendous. Surely, you can't deny any supernatural influence now!" He looked eagerly into Victoria's eyes but still saw no gleam of understanding. He braced himself for her response.

"Sam, your passion is amazing, but you are jumping at shadows. You have a dream where some hot girl gets twisted into a nightmare and you think it relates to these old manuscripts? I have to say I'm getting tired of listening to these tales of yours. I'm glad you find them engaging, but they're nothing more than scary bedtime stories. They gave *you* nightmares, right? They do not prove that demons are real. They don't prove exorcisms are real. And they most definitely do not prove that some God is out there running the

213

show! I hate to break it to you, but there is no God!"

Sam was in shock. *No God! Is she insane? Even if she had no spiritual connection before, there's no way to keep denying it now!* As calmly as possible, he offered his counter, "I see through you, you know. You act intellectual, but you're fueled by emotion. You accuse me of grasping at straws or rushing to conclusions when, in fact, it's your mind that's closed. You are so convinced that there is no God, you will stare at a mountain of evidence and still deny the possibility. What happened to you, anyway?"

"Leave it alone, Sam."

Sam pressed further, "No, seriously. What has convinced you so thoroughly that not even rational, objective proof can penetrate your thick skull? These are writings no one has seen in decades. They've been compared to similar accounts across the centuries, with incredible details in common. I could read you the accounts of Hyllum or Jacobitul if you need something far more gruesome? I've got more on top of those in here. Why, when I show you a table, do you insist it's anything but a table and deny any possibility of it being a table? I have to know. What stained your soul?"

Victoria was visibly upset, and her face flushed as she exclaimed, "My life is none of your damn business! And we don't have the luxury of sitting here psycho-analyzing each other. Let me just say this: what you claim is a table is little more than a pile of disheveled planks masquerading as a table – a desperate illusion concocted by someone so eager to believe it, he belittles anyone claiming otherwise. This emperor has no clothes and, apparently, will crucify anyone speaking up." As she finished, she nervously checked her watch.

Sam opened his mouth to retort when a loud gurgling sound suddenly erupted from three rows in front of them. In short order, the gurgling swelled – becoming a scream. Most everyone had turned to satiate their curiosity. Apparently, a woman had become violently ill. She was doubled over, crying out in pain. Her screams chilled his skin like nothing he had heard before – shrieks blended with horrible gurgling gasps for air. *So horrible! What could possibly be . . .* Something occurred to Sam as he looked down at his watch. He slowly turned to Victoria.

She didn't look concerned. Instead, she was watching the flight crew intently. Sam had no doubt that whatever was happening to this woman a few rows ahead had something to do with Victoria. He leaned over and whispered in a somewhat less than cordial tone, "What did you do to her?"

"Not right now, Sam," was her only defense.

Sam didn't care to be brushed aside this time. Echoes of those screams from the roadblock added to this poor woman's wailing was unbearable. His face flushed red as inside he fumed. It was then that he remembered Victoria pulling something from her bag overhead. "What the hell was in that vial?"

Victoria sighed, apparently growing more and more frustrated by his repeated questions, but Sam cared little of her frustrations. "Look, Sam. I have to keep an eye on this right now. Sorry it bugs you, but it'll have to wait."

The flight crew had by now arrived, asking the other passengers in that row to move so the woman could lie down. She was now heaving loudly, and Sam heard whispers of convulsions. One of the attendants, a frantic young blonde, ran to the front of the plane, and in moments, her quavering young voice came over the intercom pleading for anyone with medical training. Her voice carried a tragic earnestness. The sick woman was not faring well. Her family, apparently a husband and daughter, were distraught.

Soon, an older gentleman with salt & pepper hair pulled back into a ponytail arrived at the scene. Sam had no idea of the guy's qualifications, but hoped he could get the situation under control. The crew allowed him to examine his patient. Victoria studied the situation earnestly but made no attempt to help or offer Sam any explanation. Finally, after a few minutes of medical diagnosis, the volunteer whispered something to the flight attendant. Afterwards, they left, heading toward the cockpit.

Sam could bear it no longer. He turned to Victoria as wailing and dry heaving continued echoing throughout the cabin. "You did this, and you don't even care! Have you no conscience? In the few days I've known you, you've exploded a storage unit, stole an ambulance, shoved me into a hold used for human trafficking, injured who knows how many with flying shards of glass, set off multiple airport fires, and now this! What's next? What are you saving for your finale: a plane crash? You're a whirling dervish, wreaking havoc everywhere you go with no regard for anyone!"

Victoria had allowed him to prattle on until he made that last remark about not caring for anyone else. She leaned over and got in Sam's face as she whispered, "Listen here, you little self-righteous prick! I've tolerated your preaching and your bumbling about for days. *I* wreak havoc? You should know that other than that unfortunate business with the roadblock, not one

215

person has gotten truly hurt. And, while no one is getting permanently hurt, do you know what *has* happened? Your ungrateful ass has been inching closer to home – with your infernal cargo still intact. I have performed remarkably! This woman you're suddenly so concerned with? She'll be just fine. The little cocktail I injected her with is just a means to an end. She's going to be sick for a few hours, but then she'll start recovering. By tomorrow, she'll be fine. I wasn't hired to get your damn documents back – only you. That shit has done nothing but cause me a world of hurt. I should have left them scattered on the floor of that electrical room back in Seville."

Sam was shocked at Victoria's turn on him. She unleashed a fury likely pent up for some time, and he had no response. But when she dismissed those documents like trash, it triggered an unknown emotion. He felt cold. He didn't yell back. He didn't hit her or do anything, really. He simply faced forward and put his head back. *I hate her. That woman up there is dying, and my 'protector' is the killer. How do I deliver precious light to a dark world riding in a chariot soaked through with blood and misery?* The awful sounds continued pouring from the woman's row, but Sam no longer heard them. His mind was elsewhere.

Minutes later, the pilot came over the intercom with an announcement shocking everyone, except apparently Victoria. He announced, "Ladies and Gentlemen, I apologize, but we have an emergency situation involving one of our passengers requiring immediate medical attention. We will be making an emergency landing in Toronto. Everyone will need to de-plane, and gate agents will guide you through customs, assisting with any hotel or alternate flight arrangements. This flight will continue to Calgary en route to Vancouver tomorrow morning once the plane has been inspected and cleared. We apologize for any inconvenience, but each passenger's safety is our number one priority at Air Canada, and we appreciate your understanding. We are starting our descent now. Please return to your seats and fasten your safety belts. Thank you."

Sam knew it was there and had no need to turn to see it. Victoria was grinning from ear to ear. *She wanted to land in Toronto the whole time. The whole thing was engineered from the outset – even back in Seville.* Sam had heard of expert chess players who anticipate multiple moves ahead in the game, sometimes as many as twenty or thirty moves in advance. *How many moves ahead is Victoria?* He tried purging her from his mind. She had gotten him into Canada and locked those Vatican agents down in Madrid. *She can't help me anymore. My journey is spiritual, and I don't need a devil as my guide.*

Neither Sam nor Victoria spoke for the remainder of the flight. The plane eventually touched down in Toronto. Everyone stayed seated until the woman and her family had been escorted off the plane and were en route to a local hospital. Afterward, passengers began gathering their things – most grumbling about this unexpected change in plans. Victoria stood up, grabbing her bag from above, a small gray backpack. Sam could only speculate at the horrors tucked away inside. Once the aisle was clear, she walked forward as Sam picked up his briefcase and stepped into the aisle. The plane was large, with two aisles separating a middle bank of seats from those on the outside. Victoria, playing the part they had discussed, didn't look back or check on him. After all, they weren't technically supposed to know one another. *Funny. For all of our pretending, we really don't know each other after all.* Sam, quite contrary to plan, suddenly darted across the center bank of seats to the far aisle.

Sam's aisle happened to move faster than Victoria's, and he reached the exit first. Victoria's eyes met his briefly as he darted out the door of the plane while she was stuck in line – forced to calmly wait her turn as Sam continued gaining ground on her down the long gangway into customs and passport control. Sam felt more liberated and whole with each hurried step. By the time he reached passport control, he had almost convinced himself that this trail of destruction he had tread this far was now over. *Soon enough,* he mused, *I'll be back in Anaheim working on my caseload, trying to figure out how best to share this information with the rest of the world.*

He was actually grinning as he approached the passport window. That grin soon melted as the agents behind the glass discovered a problem. They came out of their booth and asked Sam to step aside. A thousand fears bolted through his head as he tried feebly to talk his way through the impossible situation. His passport contained a flaw that no one in Spain had caught. None of Sam's answers checked out, and with each conflicting lie, the agents' patience grew thinner. As the sun finally dropped beyond the horizon in Toronto, Sam was being escorted to a holding cell somewhere in the dark bowels of the Toronto airport.

PART THREE

"The man who persists through the bad luck - - who keeps right on going - - is the man who is there when the good luck comes . . ." – Robert Collier

Wednesday, May 26, 1999 – 11:03 PM, Toronto

"Well, Mr. Rodney Hamilton," the immigration officer snarled, *"my* information says you died eight months ago in Quebec City. It also says here that you are over two meters tall and have brown eyes. Yet here you sit, presumably – alive, well short of two meters, and with green eyes so cute, you'll make lots of friends in prison. You have already lied to those helpful men from passport control, but now tell *me* your lies – or you can go for originality points and give me the truth. Well?" The officer glared back at Sam, bushy eyebrows arched high with circumspection.

Sam started in on his obvious cover story. "Look, I don't know why your database has this mixed up. My name *is* Rodney Hamilton, but I live in Vancouver. I'm returning from a business trip to Madrid, but our plane made an emergency landing here. I don't know how this got so mixed up. I really need a hotel room and a shower . . ."

The officer's eyebrows flattened into a scowl as he let out a dramatic sigh. Though not a large man by any measure, he was imposing. He glared at Sam as he muddled through the cover story. He flipped open a small notebook and began taking notes while, ever so slightly, shaking his head. Once Sam finished his poorly rehearsed tale, the officer responded with, "Fine. I needed to hear that myself, you see. Apparently, it's too soon in our relationship for honesty. I understand – honesty is hard between strangers." He flipped the notebook closed and continued, "I will take the first step and be honest with you. I am a decision-maker. My job here is to evaluate your story and the facts and issue a decision. Officially, I have three options. I can let you go free and enter my great country unfettered. I can hand you to the Royal Canadian Mounted Patrol where you will most likely be interrogated and, if your true identity remains elusive, be returned to Spain. Finally, I can opt for immediate criminal sanctions and route you straight to jail. But here's the thing, 'Rodney,' none of those options should concern you. You *should* be concerned about my decisions that are *not* officially sanctioned. Do you understand, 'Rodney'?"

Sam mumbled a nervous, "I think so," placing his hands on the table, fingers crossed.

221

"It's so sad," the officer sighed, "your refusal to be honest. You know damned well you have no idea what I'm talking about." The officer, without warning or provocation, leaped up, grabbed the back of Sam's head, and slammed his face downward into his clasped hands. The move was swift and hard, and immediately, Sam's nose spewed blood across the table. The officer calmly sat back down as though nothing had happened while Sam cried out in pain. "I assure you nothing is broken. You're an undocumented illegal immigrant sneaking into Canada. My few superiors don't really care what happens to you here. I apologize, but I needed to demonstrate my honesty. Now that I've shown I can be trusted, I am hoping you can reciprocate, yes? Will you be honest with me?"

Sam, still reeling from the attack and bleeding profusely, nodded.

"Good – finally, an honest response. I believe you. Shall we start over?"

His brute tactics had worked, and the conversation afterward flowed freely. Sam spilled everything: his real name, details about his trip, about finding the letter under the desk, and how it led him to those documents. He mentioned being pursued by Vatican agents and how he had help from a smuggler. The blood had finally stopped before Sam finished, and he was pleading frantically. He desperately wanted the officer to believe the earnestness of his quest.

When he finished, the officer sneered back a wicked grin. He rose and replied with a curt, "pity," before turning to walk out.

"Wait! Rewind that bit, if you would," Lukas blurted out. Though disappointed Sam had somehow escaped custody, they had been allowed to view his interview tape. Alfons could see his partner enthralled with Sam's story – the passion with which he begged and the absolute candor he shared. The Inspector, growing weary of the same tired footage, obliged, but not without letting a sigh of frustration escape. "There!" exclaimed Lukas, ignoring the Inspector's sigh and pointing at the monitor. "Pause! Look at his eyes!" Both the Inspector and Alfons looked into Sam's bloody face, frozen in the monitor. "He believes it! He was not lying to you, Inspector. Whether true or not, in Sam's mind, he absolutely believes everything he said. His responses are direct and without hesitation. He is looking you directly in the eyes. He does not stumble over his words. He passes every test we are trained to look for."

He is right. For the first time since Seville, Alfons had seen Sam. His head was shaven now, and he was hurting and bloody. *Poor lad. He simply fails to understand.* "Good catch, Mr. Dietrich." Alfons turned to the Inspector. "Sam is being as honest as he knows how in that 'interview,' Inspector. Can we discuss how he got out of that room?"

The Inspector wilted and quietly uttered, "We opened the door."

"Sorry?" Alfons asked incredulously.

"In custody, mind you. We handed him to Immigration Officers from the RCMP. They had been called to escort this 'Samuel' or 'Rodney,' whichever it is, to a holding cell until they could do a proper work-up."

"I see. What made you call the Mounties?"

Sheepishly, the Inspector replied, "I didn't call."

"I am confused. If you did not call the RCMP, who did?"

The Inspector looked up at Alfons. "I wish I knew. At the time, we assumed it was someone in passport control, but they swear they didn't. We now know that no one from airport security phoned it in."

Alfons, more than surprised at this turn of events, knew exactly who made that phone call. He grinned a wry, frustrated grin. "Inspector, have you noticed a woman skulking about? Possibly half an hour before the Mounties arrived?"

"No. Not really. . . except. There was one, younger woman, but I wouldn't say she skulked about. She just borrowed a sheet of paper. Why?"

Alfons, jerked his notepad from his jacket pocket and jotted something down. He tore the page and gave it to Lukas. Lukas read the note, promptly excused himself, and darted out the door and into the terminal. He could still be heard jogging away as Alfons turned back to the Inspector. "Sorry about that. I needed to put some things in motion. You said one of the RCMP officers became violently ill before getting Sam to their car?"

"Yes, but what has that to do with . . .?"

"How long did you hold Sam before handing him over?"

The Inspector quizzically answered, "Around two and a half hours."

"And he has been gone about thirty minutes, you said?"

"Roughly."

"Good." Alfons scribbled more notes as he questioned the Inspector. "Now, I assume this woman borrowed a sheet of department letterhead?"

"Well, I don't know for sure, but I can check. How could you . . ."

"Never mind about that, Inspector. Time has suddenly become quite critical. Sam's plane – what triggered the emergency landing?"

"A sudden illness onboard – pretty severe from the sound of it."

Alfons smiled a satisfied smile. He could now see the dominoes falling in sequence. He replied, "Thank you, Inspector, I appreciate your help. I assume Sam escaped with his bags or anything he brought with him?"

"Yes, but he carried only a briefcase – no luggage."

"His fake papers: he has those as well?"

"No. Fakes are marked and stored here unless the RCMP needs it for their investigation. We have those."

"Thank you again." Alfons turned to leave but abruptly turned back facing the Inspector. "Oh. I almost forgot. What I saw on that video monitor violates every human rights treaty your country has ever signed. You may feel you are king of this castle, but I can assure you that if I ever hear of further brutality, I will report you and make it a personal vendetta to see you bear the full measure of punishment and scrutiny. You will disgrace your department, country, and family. I am in an awkward position, I realize. However, such brutish tactics sicken me and will not be tolerated. Understand?"

"I . . . but you can't waltz in . . ."

"Never mind. I am going. Once you assemble your witty retort, email me."

Alfons turned and walked out into the hallway beyond, heading back to the main terminal. He needed to connect with Lukas and try capitalizing on the abundance of luck he had been served. As he walked, his heels echoing off the linoleum, he kept mentally replaying that video. *Unbelievable! He could have broken Sam's nose with that pathetic display! Poor American – plunging, like many Americans often do, into the water without first finding out how deep it might be. He is in over his head, but we are finally quite close to catching up. I do hope this does not end badly for him.*

The long hallway sloped upward before finally emptying into the lobby. It was late now, and there was almost no activity: a few people milling about, gathering luggage, and calling cabs or hotels, but no one at the airline counters. Alfons waited. Lukas would be along once he completed his assignment. While waiting, Alfons thumbed absently through a flimsy map of Toronto. In about ten minutes, he made out Lukas' hurried footsteps echoing through the empty chamber.

Breathing heavily, Lukas started, "Mein Herr, I did as you asked, and in fact, there were several cars rented to female drivers following that emergency landing. We filtered them based on age and passport information, and we found a match! A compact was rented to a Shirley Thompson, matching the description of a Shirley Thompson on that flight. Even more exciting, according to the manifest, she sat in the same row as our Sam! Unfortunately, she rented it over two hours ago and could be anywhere by now."

"Mr. Dietrich, you disappoint me. Do you think she left without her cargo? Sam has only been out of custody for forty minutes. We are actually quite close. We need only deduce their most likely destination."

"How? We have nothing to go on this time."

Alfons grinned sheepishly. "So certain?" He rose and headed toward the exit, Lukas following close behind. They passed through the revolving doors into the warm night air. The overhead sky was calm, but ominous spotted clouds hovered above. Alfons looked left and right before spotting a cab about a kilometer down. He began jogging and holding his arm aloft. His efforts were successful, and soon, he and Lukas boarded the lime-green cab. Alfons peered through the plexiglass and spoke up, "1155 Yonge Street, please."

*   *   *

Wednesday, May 26, 1999 – Late Night, Toronto

The drive over was uneventful. Lukas had spent most of it on the phone with the Toronto Archdiocese. Alfons had delegated to him the unenviable task of arranging for a car. Alfons, himself, continued poring over that flimsy map he found. Neither spoke much to each other until they arrived. Once they stepped out, Alfons paid the driver while Lukas looked around. Yonge Street was a commercial street lined with multi-story office buildings full of retail shops at the street level. While the street likely teemed during the day, at this late hour, the sidewalks were barren and the street quiet. Though there were no indicators on the building, 1155 Yonge Street housed the Archdiocese offices.

Alfons and Lukas found the entrance. Heavy glass doors, routinely sealed with a magnetic lock, slid open. *Gut – someone is inside waiting! That is a welcome relief. Seconds matter.* Within minutes, they found themselves standing in front of a Director Chrier. Chrier was imposing, standing well over six feet, not a hair on his head and a muscled torso hidden beneath his heavy brown suit. Chrier was not the official director, and his name likely wouldn't

225

appear in any directories. Alfons had met these Under-Directors, as they were known, before and had no desire to know what he was working on this late.

Chrier didn't wait for pleasant introductions before beginning, "I am understanding you need a car. How long?"

Alfons offered a curt, "Two days at the most — hopefully sooner if we catch another break."

"A 'break,' you say?" answered Chrier. "From what I can tell, you have had no breaks since you began. I am tempted to decline and spare the Church any further embarrassment."

While Lukas' face betrayed them, Alfons maintained his collected composure despite the threat. *Within minutes, this Chier has detailed information about our case? This makes no sense — our active files are sealed — even from other agents. I wonder . . .* Alfons, in his typical cold manner, replied, "Director, I beg your apology, but time is vital, and this child will likely perish during the night without her mother. We beg you, please grant our humble request."

Alfons could almost feel Lukas' confusion but hoped he maintained his composure. The Director glared at Alfons first and then at Lukas, likely searching for any hint of . . . well, something. At long last, Chrier mumbled something indiscernible under his breath before tossing Lukas a set of keys. "Go out the way you came." His baritone voice revealed no emotion. "Silver Chrysler at the back of the lot. It has a full tank." Director Chrier lumbered away without waiting for any sort of response.

Lukas made to hand the keys to Alfons, but Alfons waved them off. He needed his hands for a few phone calls. They did as told and discovered the car where it was supposed to be and in good shape. When Lukas started the engine, he turned to Alfons. Alfons looked at him, grinning, "I suppose I should give a little direction, yes? Make a left on Yonge Street and head toward the lakefront."

Lukas nodded and pulled away. Thanks to an unforgiving time change and two long flights, they had been denied quality sleep for over twenty-four hours now, and if Alfons' hunch was right, things were only heating up rather than cooling off. *Those few hours of shallow rest on the plane would have to serve. Luckily, our fatigue is shared equally by our prey. In fact, they have likely suffered more this day than we have.* Lukas drove at a normal clip toward Lake Ontario at the southern edge of downtown. On the lake's other side rested

Buffalo, New York. Alfons clung to hope that Sam and his helper had not somehow crossed the border already.

In a car, it takes almost two hours to drive from Toronto, around the Lake, and into Buffalo. They fled the airport barely an hour ago. Which would mean they were somewhere in the middle right about now. But that makes no sense. Sam has no papers now. They cannot cross without papers. We have both his original and forged papers with us. That delays her and forces her to adapt. They are tired and want to cross the border quickly. She would not want to drive further west across Canada to another crossing only to still lack papers. She is looking for another way across this border. Alfons reached in his jacket and pulled out that map of Toronto from earlier. There it was – *a train track:* a rail line running international trains across the border and into Buffalo. *That has to be her way in! Everything else requires papers or additional nights in hiding.*

Alfons grabbed his phone and called Amorette back at the Vatican. She seemed cheerful as always, though nearing the end of her shift. Alfons explained their situation and that he needed any information she could scrounge on that train. As usual, Amorette delivered in short order. Alfons had just finished thanking her when Lukas found a quiet parking spot near the water. "Fate has finally smiled on us, my friend. You may turn off the car. In fact, come; let us see if we might grab a drink."

A few short blocks away, they stumbled across an Irish pub along the waterfront. From their seats outside, they could see the water and hear gulls crying out to one another for no particular reason. Some animals just cry out a lot. A street band was playing some fairly awful music nearby, but they weren't close enough to be a problem. The pub wasn't crowded, it being Wednesday night and the midnight hour fast approaching. Alfons was the first to speak after they'd ordered. "We have been fortunate. When we flew to London, I had no idea what sort of connection we could garner to get us to Canada. As luck would have it, there was a single flight, but it landed in Toronto. I was hopeful we would then find something to get us to Calgary or Vancouver or that our pleas to those airports would have sufficed and Sam would be waiting in handcuffs when we arrived. However, Sam's companion triggered an illness on that plane, forcing an emergency landing in, of all places, Toronto. In her attempt to land outside of our net, she touched down exactly where we were headed."

"That is remarkable, Mein Herr, perhaps our only break in this case."

227

"Oh, we have had more, and tonight's fortune is not yet spent, it seems. I do not understand why, but Sam abandoned his helper and attempted to go through passport control on his own. The poor guy cannot lie his way out of anything. Luckily, they held him for two hours – just long enough for us to arrive in Toronto close behind them. In fact, his helper only got him out of there about thirty minutes before we arrived. So now, all four of us are in the same city once again, and our biggest break: Sam now has no papers. She cannot get him across the border without them – at least not openly. She will have to smuggle him across. For that, she has three viable options: on foot, across the lake, or by rail. I am betting against a footcrossing. It is dangerous, and the trek from the city to a good crossing point would be arduous. Water is an option, but I had Amorette check. There have been no Canadian reports of stolen boats nor any U.S. Coast Guard reports of illegal traffic. If they did cross by water, it is too late. We have missed them. Rail, however, presents a fresh opportunity.

There is a train scheduled to pull from the freight yard soon, but we must resist the urge to scamper over there. If they see us milling about, it could scare them off. We need them to climb aboard and settle in. That rail line passes through checkpoints on each side of the border, and that is our window."

Lukas barely touched his beer as Alfons detailed his plan. Although a bit of luck would be involved, luck seemed to be smiling on them at the moment. When he finished, Lukas remarked, "What fortune! We come halfway across the world and now are only an hour or two from victory. Tell me most cases are not as trying as this!"

If only he knew what a trying case actually was! Alfons' face betrayed him, and Lukas looked at him as though he knew something was wrong. Alfons could not honestly respond; the pain was still too near. Memories of that night in Copenhagen still haunted his thoughts, but he couldn't share them with his young partner. Horrors of that ilk were best left unspoken. He shoved the painful memories back into the dark corner of his mind where such things typically skulk. Lukas, however, would expect an answer of some sort. So, he ventured down an alternate path.

"Fortune. I even said it myself, did I not? Luck, fate, fortune. We sometimes forget that we are the very hands of God. Are we certain these events are mere happenstance? Is it not more likely that God has intervened on our behalf? Where is our faith?"

228

"You mentioned faith earlier today as well, in the airport. How did you phrase it, 'What is God without faith?' What exactly did you mean by that, if I might ask?"

Alfons took a slow sip of his beer and leaned back. "Mr. Dietrich, faith drives the whole engine: faith that God exists, faith that He is good, and faith that He is in control. Faith is the magic that gives the miracle meaning."

Lukas thought quietly for a second before replying, "So. These papers Mr. Johnston plucked from that river would *prove* God's existence? Thereby denying us the opportunity to believe through mere faith?"

"Correct. Our duty here is to ensure everyone has a chance to make their own leap of faith."

"But Christ walked the Earth, did he not? He performed miracles, fed thousands from mere scraps, rose from the grave, and ascended into heaven on clouds. Everywhere he went, he gave people *proof* of his divinity. Those believers did not have to follow through blind faith – they bore witness to his power and followed with no doubts whatsoever. If faith is so essential, why perform miracles?"

Alfons laid a few worn bills on the table to cover their drinks as he rose. "Mr. Dietrich, even discussing your question requires faith. Had Christ not risen from the grave and ascended, there would be nothing to have faith *in*. As for the healing and other miracles, I would ask you to look through your New Testament. With few exceptions, prior to each miracle, Christ sought some element of faith. Whether calling for an extended hand, a statement of belief, or a simple touching of his cloak, he almost always demanded an expression of faith *before* performing his miracles. In fact, Mr. Dietrich, there are far more instances where Christ, placed in a situation where one group or another demanded He prove Himself, consistently *refused* to prove His divinity even to his own death."

Alfons could tell from Lukas' expression that he had never truly considered this nuance of Christianity before. *If we can prove God exists, as simply as you can prove that water becomes steam as it boils, the decision to choose Christ is no longer truly a decision at all.* Lukas offered no response as they walked outside into the stale night air.

*   *   *

Thursday, May 27, 1999 – Just after Midnight, Toronto

Alfons paced along the boardwalk, staring absently across the bay, barely listening to the ringing of buoys bouncing rhythmically atop the waves.

Unfortunately, the street band had now moved closer, and their music muddled the night. Doing his best to ignore the band, he looked upward. Heavy, dark billows had formed, masking the crescent moon and occasional starlight over Lake Ontario to the south. Unfortunately, south was their destination, and those clouds weighed on Alfons' mind as heavily as they did the evening sky. Though Lukas presumably had little to no helicopter experience, Alfons had flown one frequently in the military. Clouds, alone, posed no problem, but rain falling from them would. Back in the Vatican, Amorette was hard at work finding them a pilot willing to give them a lift across the border. Any pilot that saw a hint of rain, however, would refuse immediately. Descending rain, like heavy fog, wreaks havoc on visibility. Avoiding obstacles and landing safely become almost impossible. Pilots can't easily discern when to reduce rotor tilt or by how much. Hopefully, they would reach the border checkpoint before the skies opened.

Each passing second brought Sam closer to home. Although Sam's documents were stolen property, once the world got wind of their message, formal demands for their return would matter little. It would start small – a few friends, a handful of intellectuals and scholars. Soon enough, the results would get published, and the world would discover what they had so desperately fought to conceal.

Several minutes passed in worried silence until his phone rang. It was Amorette. "Herr Schmidt, I have a pilot, but you must hurry. He has a 'bird' fueling now, but he mentioned an approaching storm. I still need clearance from the U.S. should that time come, but thought you should get going in the meantime. Here is the address." Alfons scribbled down the address quickly before hanging up. Amorette would be a remarkable agent in her own right if the Vatican ever allowed for that sort of thing. *Later we can mourn the inequity of gender bias, but right now was for more pressing matters.*

"Mr. Dietrich," Alfons barked into the still night air, "we must move!" Without a further word, Alfons turned from the handrail and made for the car. Lukas navigated Alfons' clumsy oversized map while Alfons drove as quickly as he dared. *There are two checkpoints for this train – one on each side of the border. If our luck holds, we reach the Canadian checkpoint ahead of that train and secure those documents before they reach U.S. soil. Once they cross that border and we lose sight of them, it is over. Our fortune has in large part been due to Sam's awkward stumbling about in foreign lands. Once unleashed in his*

230

home country, those documents will be out of reach. We will not see them again until they get published in The Journal of Anthropology.

They reached their helicopter pilot in short order. Alfons wasn't exactly sure what to expect as he rang the farmhouse doorbell. A portly man with a smile as large as his belly answered. He sported a faded gray, big one-piece coverall, with a Molson baseball cap. Through thick lips clinching what was left of a Camel, he introduced himself as Haygoode, mentioning repeatedly how happy he was to be helping the Church. Alfons struggled picking through Haygoode's strong Canadian accent, but soon got the hang of it. After brief introductions and pleasantries, their gracious volunteer escorted them out back where his 'bird,' as he called it, lay in wait. It was rather smallish, but would seat four uncomfortably. The bright orange hue of the fuselage only added insult to the injury. Lukas was less successful hiding his disappointment than himself, but Haygoode seemed oblivious. The three of them scrambled aboard, with Alfons and Lukas in the rear. Lukas had relayed their situation, giving Haygoode their destination. Their pilot knew well enough where to go, but was quick to mention those dark clouds in the southern sky. Although Alfons had expected as much, Haygoode explained he had no intention of flying across Lake Ontario as there would be no place to land in the event of an emergency. After fumbling about with the controls and seatbelts for a moment, the engine was soon whirring and the overhead rotors spinning. They ascended into the dark skies, the nearby city lights of Toronto shrinking as they climbed.

The higher they flew the more wind they encountered. At first, the helicopter swayed from side to side struggling to stay on course, but after a few adjustments, things got more stable. Haygoode was forced to fly lower than he'd planned, and to mitigate those strong crosswinds, he had also changed their approach. They would reach the border checkpoint from the northwest rather than the more direct route. Haygoode explained the details and Alfons, though disappointed, understood. A quick glance at his watch confirmed what he had already deduced: their twenty minute window had just lost twelve minutes. Haygoode didn't notice, however, an even greater problem: that wind and this new course correction would, by the time they drew close to the border put them on the opposite side of those clouds. If it did start raining, Haygoode would have nowhere to go but further south – into U.S. airspace. Alfons could do nothing about any of this, however. He didn't control the wind. He didn't control the rain. And he certainly couldn't control that train.

He had been doing his best to maintain his composure as they sped toward the Canadian checkpoint. No rain had yet fallen, but the weather was worsening. Alfons bit the inside of his cheek as he peered at tree limbs swaying harshly below. Things seemed far calmer inside than they appeared outside. This pilot was good, despite his unconventional demeanor and relaxed attitude. They were en route, and at this pace, would beat the train to the checkpoint. They needed only to stay on target and avoid any . . . *rain*. Haygoode and Alfons cursed under their breath as heavy drops began splashing against the helicopter's rounded glass. The drops started slowly but picked up their pace quickly. Haygoode looked around likely noticing what Alfons had predicted earlier – their way back was blocked by fierce storm clouds.

"I'm sorry friends," Haygoode shouted into his headpiece, "we're going to have to set down before this gets out of control!" He began steadily descending into the blackness below. Haygoode struggled against both wind and rain keeping things steady until suddenly, and without warning, the sky lit up.

Alfons craned his neck to see what happened. *That could not have been lightning. Lightning has far more grandeur.* When he saw what lay just outside, however, he would have readily accepted traditional lightning. In the dark pitch of night, Haygoode had inadvertently dropped the helicopter directly between two large electrical towers. Alfons grit his teeth as he realized their simultaneously fortunate and unfortunate predicament. They had been remarkably fortunate in that their descent had not dropped their rotors into invisible power lines. That would have sliced the lines hurling the helicopter violently into the ground. A terrible explosion just west of Lake Ontario would have been Alfons' last impact on this world. Their fortune in avoiding that calamity, however, was splintered when the sky ignited. A massive limb had broken free from a nearby tree and dropped onto the lines, snapping them. The two fragments of that line now flailed like spaghetti in the wind. These lines were live and extremely deadly.

Alfons was not the only one to notice. Haygoode also realized their precarious situation. Rotors were churning between two strands of wild electrical line. No one spoke. Lukas may not have grasped the situation's gravity as he continued looking out the side window towards the distant storm clouds. Alfons offered a silent prayer for their protection as Haygoode tried gaining control over the deadly game. He would have to fly backward out of danger, but that would be far harder than it sounded. He had to stop the 'bird' from creeping forward, causing it to hover in place. Then, without veering to either side, deftly back away from danger. Haygoode's small helicopter wasn't designed for backwards flight, but Alfons was hopeful Haygoode had done this maneuver before. When they came to a complete mid-air standstill, Lukas, noticing the momentum change, turned to speak, but Alfons signaled for him to remain silent and calm. Lukas' eyes grew wide with terror as each piece of this delicate balancing act triggered in his mind. The process would be like navigating a mine field, but one where the mines flailed about wildly and unpredictably. No longer moving forward, the rain had caught up and was now upon them fully, pounding heavy drops against the glass bubble at the helicopter's nose.

Haygoode began. He tilted the 'bird's' nose upward slightly and it responded with a slight backward motion. Alfons knew this must be done slowly – too large of a tilt, and the updraft would create a deadly suction drawing the power lines into the rotors themselves, again, resulting in a fiery explosion and a quite painful death. Alfons was surprised at Haygoode's graceful maneuvering. Each hint of movement was countered by an equally slight adjustment keeping them centered. Haygoode fought both the elements and the natural proclivity of the helicopter itself as he quite literally danced between raindrops.

Bit by bit, however, his plan was working. Alfons and Lukas sat with their eyes glued to the lines whipping in the wind. A nervous sweat built up on their faces as they dared not move or even breathe. Alfons tried containing his dread for the sake of his partner, but it was more challenging than he could manage completely. At one terrifying moment, they all jumped as a hapless bird hurled violently against the fuselage. The thud echoing against the hull made their hearts leap fearing the grinding of a rotor and beginning of their end. *Earlier Lukas mentioned this case being challenging. Wonder what he thinks now?*

The remaining maneuvers were performed as delicately and masterfully as Alfons could have hoped. Small adjustments coupled with short timid spurts of reverse flight and eventually they were free of death's snare. As the helicopter hovered above the trees, Haygoode wiped his forehead and finally spoke into the mouthpiece, "Guys, I don't dare set this thing down here.

With it being so dark and all, there's no way to know if the ground is level. We can't go back, either. The storm over Toronto looks wicked. So, we have but one option: forward."

As Haygoode ascended once more, Alfons tried relaxing, but a nagging thought crashed forward. He didn't need to look at his watch. He knew the answer. He pulled the microphone closer to his mouth and said, "It's too late for Canada. You should have your clearance by now. We need to get to the American checkpoint in Buffalo. If you push it, we might still have a chance."

"When a train goes through a tunnel and it gets dark, you don't throw away the ticket and jump off. You sit still and trust the engineer." – Corrie Ten Boom

Thursday, May 27, 1999 – After Midnight, Toronto

Victoria stared blankly ahead into the pitch, light only occasionally piercing her peripheral. She and Sam sat quietly inside the truck, rocking gently from side to side as they journeyed south. Sam's nose had finally stopped sporadically bleeding out as it had earlier. Naturally, however, he couldn't breathe through his nose, and the miserable inhale and exhale of hot breath was the only noise in the truck's cabin. Neither spoke much as contempt for their plight continued to weigh heavily.

Victoria knew though, despite everything, most of this was her fault. Well, not technically *her* fault, but certainly not Sam's. He was an unfortunate pawn in a repugnant game being played by her demented boss, Hector. While pride had kept her silent so far, silence and the nothingness ahead merged with the heavy, black shroud smothering her conscience. She grabbed the water bottle from the cup holder. The water cooled her tongue and throat. She was exhausted, and poor Sam was, no doubt, in far worse shape. Their mad dash was far from over, and there was little time for compassion. She shoved her pity aside.

Victoria nestled the water bottle back into its holder and leaned back against the soft gray leather before finally turning to Sam and breaking the silence. "I'm not sure what you're brooding about, but I'm assuming your silence means it's pretty negative. You have a lot to be upset about, and I don't know which is at the top, but I would like to, for my part, apologize for my tantrum on the plane. That was unprofessional, and came from a place of pure emotion. This whole business with demonic forces and exorcisms is unnerving for someone like me. You see, my life is guided by three basic principles. The first two aren't an issue right now, but the third one? There is no God. Listen to the way I said that. I didn't say 'I don't believe in God' or 'I'm not sure if there is a God.' There is no God. So you come along with, I'll admit, some pretty strong evidence that one of the three solid things my life is built on might be wrong. That pisses me off. I want to not only to dismiss your evidence, but to rip it into shreds. I tried ignoring you and let you prattle on as

235

I've done with countless Bible thumpers. Problem is, you're not thumping a Bible and you never quit."

Sam gave a rather shallow smile. "Thanks. That was hard. But, while I'm still pretty upset with you, you're far from the top of my list. That asshole Inspector earned that honor a couple of hours ago."

She sighed mumbling, "Yeah. About that . . ."

"Don't tell me you . . .," Sam interrupted.

"Don't be ridiculous." She interrupted back. "I had nothing to do with his piss-poor tactics. However, you should have sailed through passport control. Your papers should have been flawless, especially for the price I paid. You should understand, our worlds are different, Sam – very different. Ever lift a rock or log from a bit of soft earth and catch a glimpse of all the activity under there you never knew existed? You get only a quick peek before the worms, bugs and other critters scamper away. This journey you're on is a bit like that. You've experienced things normal people aren't meant to experience. Will you ever look at beer truck and not wonder if stolen children are inside? If a future flight makes an emergency landing, what horrors will float through your mind? The flaw in your passport created another moment where you were forced to peer behind the curtain when you shouldn't have.

I paid for your paperwork in Madrid, using a guy I've used for years. He does incredible work, and charges you for it. He made a mistake on Rodney's passport. That never happens. You would likely have been nicked in Spain, but we avoided any serious passport screenings. That is why you're breathing through your mouth right now. Even more unfortunate, is 'why?' Fredo never screws up papers like that. He *wanted* you to get caught. Since you don't likely know Fredo, this probably has far more to do with me than you."

Sam faced Victoria with a confused glare.

She sighed as she took another drink and continued, reluctantly. "My boss wants me to fail. Under *my* rock, things work differently. You don't get a boss by submitting a resume and filling out a stack of papers. Bosses come in two varieties. The first is a mentor, someone higher up the chain than yourself. Those guys tend to be bosses just long enough for their underlings to make a deal with someone even higher to get rid of their mutual middleman. The second type become bosses only by exerting control. This is my guy. I owe him a considerable debt from a job that went wrong some time ago and have been working since to set things right. I'm not far from hitting my mark. He

236

knows it, and it scares him. I make him a ton of money, but if I went solo, I would keep what I kill, instead of sharing it with his greasy ass. So, you see. If you get caught, and he has to make good with your friend, my debt starts all over again. That's why we're huddled in this dark, infernal box instead of a diner somewhere in Buffalo quietly sipping a cup of coffee."

Victoria checked her watch and leaned back again. They had been fortunate at least to a small degree: finding this international train leaving at the right time. Their luck jumped from morsel to full bite when spotting this boxcar. Four sport utility trucks pre-loaded as if put there especially for them. Her lock gun made quick work of one on the upper level and – viola! What could have been a dismal, bumpy trek hiding under grain sacks or between chemical drums had become a quiet excursion resting in contoured leather seats.

While Sam was being "interviewed" by the customs inspector, Victoria had made a few arrangements. Grabbing water, some NoDoz tablets and a couple of day-old sandwiches had been part of her rather short "to do" list. There was no way of knowing if her scheme had unfolded properly in Madrid or if those agents were still trailing them, but she couldn't afford the comfort of leisure. Time was still quite vital and everything hinged on getting Sam across the border. From there, it should be easy to reach her grandparent's old farmhouse in Pennsylvania. She was hopeful the place still stood and they could finally get some much needed rest.

Sam had been relatively quiet, but after a moment of soaking up her revelations about Hector, started talking, "I know a guy back home. Name's Gerard. Great guy, if you're on his good side. We've been friends a long time. He runs a mechanic shop, but everyone knows there's a lot more going on around there than just fixing cars. He lives under this same rock you mention and is careful about never letting me see any of that. He screwed up once a few years ago, and I saw more than he would have liked. I stopped by to pick up my car, and as I was paying, a mechanic crawled out from under a massive pick-up carrying what looked like two bricks of cocaine. I turned my head real fast, you know – pretended to be tying my shoe or something. Gerard knew I saw it, though. We never talked about it, but I never saw that mechanic again. I knew better than to ask. Not sure what that story means, really. Just saying I might understand a little something about life under your rock, and how much I don't belong."

237

Victoria responded in a somewhat hushed voice, "It's not a blessing, you know – more of a curse. Once you crawl underneath, and bathe in the darkness, it stains you. Sooner or later you can only *remember* life outside in the sun. You forget the excitement you thought you craved and lose all thought of glory or adventure. Instead you grasp for the tiniest shreds of life in the light, but you never reach it again. You try enjoying a beach somewhere, pretending you're no different than the tourists strolling along the boardwalk. Difference is, your eyes and mind have to keep moving. Is someone you hurt yesterday coming from behind? Maybe some cop you never met is investigating and his case leads him to you just at that moment. What trash is ok to throw away? Does it have prints? Will it matter? I've met people like you; thinking they live an insulated life where boredom and predictability tend to crush hopes and aspirations. There's also warmth and peace of mind inside that bubble; things like families and relationships; children laugh there." *Well, some do.*

"Sorry, I know I come off cold and distant sometimes. I do that on purpose – not to isolate you. It's to protect you. You need remain a stranger to the darkness. Life underneath is not for you, and shouldn't be for anyone. I want you as good natured as you were when you landed in Spain. I want you to put things like airport fires and exploding glass behind you and focus on *your* life. You save children and nothing's more important in the whole world."

Victoria felt emotion building in her – pain from long ago. Thoughts of heading to her grandfather's farm must have triggered memories that needed to remain forgotten. She abruptly changed the subject. "We will be in Buffalo soon. Quite a ways from California – but crossing that border, with you and those documents intact, will be a big victory. Unfortunately, this night is far from over. We may still be followed and several hours stand between us and rest. We're both beat, but we can't nod off now. I'll make you a deal. I know you truly believe in those papers. I see it in your face each time you plead for me accompany you on your journey. Read a particularly interesting set of records, and I promise to keep an open mind." *Need to keep his mind occupied.*

*   *   *

Thursday, May 27, 1999 – After Midnight, Toronto

The tiny light shone onto Sam's lap from the rearview mirror. He opened his briefcase and thumbed through pages until reaching Manuel's letter to Marta. *I don't know if she'll stay this open-minded. So I should read*

238

her the Hamlin accounts now. These are some of the darkest tales in here, but the similarities and revelations are incredible. He found the selection he wanted and started reading:

"Sweet Sister, by now you have slogged through the majority of these dark, horrific accounts and re-tellings. You have read the realities faced by the possessed and witnessed several examples of these patterned incidentals: demons bearing the same name inflicting damage on victims centuries apart with such specific and exacting similarity leaving no room for doubt regarding the authenticity of their existence. Thank you for journeying this far, but now I beg you to journey a bit further. I should inform you that during my research, I came across a distinction that is not well publicized: there is an unholy distinction between a demon and a fallen angel. Most experts mention simply that demons are a dark spirit and there is no such distinction. However, these next few accounts reflect something far more devastating. While demons are dark spirits with an evil will and a confused sense of self awareness, fallen angels are princely and noble. They are the self-same angels who rallied behind Lucifer in the rebellion in heaven. Their failure resulted in them being cast out of Heaven for eternity.

The horrifying truth is that, while demons and fallen angels can both possess a host, fallen angels exert a far greater degree of control than a demonic spirit. Demons seem intent to merely tasting life, occupying their host and inflicting as much damage as possible to the victim's family and loved ones. Fallen angels, however, have a more far-reaching agenda, using their host to twist human events and pervert society according to their own designs. These next few accounts are from a set of fallen angels and, were it not for their pride, nothing coincidental or similar would have stuck out from their exorcist's report. Please read documents 13, 5, 27 and 43." Sam flipped to document 5.

Otto – Trondheim, Norway – Early Nineteenth Century

"Cardinal Santara – Please excuse this report, as I am but Bishop Francis' assistant. I was present during the events described herein and can attest to their authenticity. However, the Bishop can no longer write under his own strength. Last week's ordeal has left him paralyzed from the neck down, and he has asked that I transcribe this letter for him, providing details where his memory might have lapsed. I will include a small notation when I interject:

239

There was to be an exorcism. I have performed exorcisms before, but neither training nor experience could possibly have prepared me for what lay in store. In a standard exorcism, if there is such a thing, there is screaming and anger; spitting and vomiting; cursing and gnashing of teeth. There would be none of that this time. I had answered at the behest of the local Priest due to a strange anomaly with a townsperson, specifically a giant of a man named Otto. Otto ran the local blacksmith shop. He was respected and well liked, but was often referred to as slow of mind and speech. He stammered over his words and relied on his cousin to handle all business matters. However, for his failing, his skill with the hammer and anvil were legendary.

Otto had been arrested and charged with arson and murder, specifically setting fire to the local orphanage taking the lives of several children and caretakers. We arrived at the local jail in Trondheim and were immediately escorted to Otto's cell. Surprisingly he exhibited none of the classical signs of possession we are trained to identify: no dual personalities; no random obscenities; no speaking of unknown languages. In fact, Otto's cogent behavior made others suspect something supernatural. I had been given papers showing Otto's illegible hand and obvious illiteracy. Even his signature was the "X" poorly scrawled across the bottom of the page. However, the Otto I met was quite fluent, speaking with sophisticated eloquence.

[Side note.] Otto greeted us with outstretched arms as though expecting us. His omniscience was puzzling and frightening. He greeted us not only by name, he had the presence to ask about my mother's palsy – something I had not shared with anyone openly.

When we discussed the attack on the orphanage, he responded with jubilation. He argued that the spawn of Adam had spoiled creation and these discarded orphans would only grow to adults with an even larger appetite for destruction. Otto claimed he was doing society a favor. What struck me as even more odd than his adherence to his bizarre logic, was his persistent exuberance. He was truly thrilled to have set that fire, and even more so knowing orphans had been burned alive. Otto continued, mentioning how Adam's spawn had been a plague for all of eternity and

240

he had always strived to balance the equation. It seemed he wished to confess to previous crimes, so I pressed onward. By now, the cell's candles were running low and the tiny cell shrunk around us. Even the air grew thin and breathing grew more labored. Otto stopped smiling at once and stood.

[Side Note.] Father Francis may not remember this specific detail, but just before Otto stood, he glared at Father Francis with utter contempt and everything went silent. The popping of logs in the fire, even the crickets' song fell completely still. That painful silence continued for some time before Otto eventually broke the silence, but I remember that terrifying quiet feeling very much not of this world.

Our discussions then turned more to the supernatural. Otto stood glaring through us. He began speaking and his words still follow me like a shadow. "You know what humans fail to grasp about their young - their capacity for pain. Being smaller, their tiny nerve endings are packed tightly together and their tender skin is far thinner than it will be later on. A child's pain is exquisite." He drifted a moment, as someone might trying to recapture the decadence of a sweet desert from long ago.
I asked how he found the pain of a defenseless child so intoxicating. In a blur of motion, he pulled a loose, rusty nail from the table and pierced my left hand, pinning it to the table's surface. As I cried out, he smiled. He then leaned forward and whispered into my ear saying, "Your pain, Father? Is like eating two day old bread. Had I done this to a small boy, his cries of agony and confusion would have been a fine wine dripping from my tongue."
There was clearly more, but apparently Otto needed goading. I pressed, asking how he could speak with such authority while only drawing from the death of these few children. He smiled down at me and said one word, "Hamlin - a small town in Germania. They lost their children, too - far more than this paltry handful."
"Friedrich was the name, then. Though six centuries ago, I remember that name fondly. Friedrich had opened the doorway just enough, so I obliged him and entered. It was quaint at first - life in the monastery, routine upon routine - masquerading as the simple Friedrich. Soon I was

241

able to shepherd more of the brothers into worship of the old gods. As additional doors opened, my colleagues slipped through: first Kasyade, later Bataryal. Our trio began our reign of exquisite destruction, and in a short time, our threesome controlled the monastery.

We dug a pit. It was vast and deep – the bottom invisible from the surface. Though it pained us greatly, we introduced ourselves to the children of Hamlin with treats and candies while telling stories of Odin and Thor. Secret agreements, dark words and promises of wishes granted enticed the children to follow us to the monastery. Close to one hundred in total followed us into the trees that night under the forest moon. They would not return.

Their screams were orgasmic. Their petty cries upon realizing their plight as they were herded into dwarfish cells like veal awaiting the slaughter paled to the shrieks to come. Some were victims of delectible mutilations. A tongue jerked free from a tiny mouth with blacksmith tongs, a brother beaten to death with the bloody, severed leg of his younger sister as she was forced to watch – this ilk were but our first taste. We threw our waste into the pit and scorched any remains to dust, purging any earthly memory of the bastards and whores of Hamlin. Mutilations are exhilarating, to be sure, but they dull the pallet over time. We hungered for something new. We first looked to the hunt; setting a child loose in the woods with some token to rekindle their lost hope. The fresh cries of that renewed hope crushing under our heels were savory. Their cries as they descended into the pit grew distant but lost none of their seasoning.

As supplies wore thin, a final solution presented itself. The young swine were bound to a cart as one of their starving brethren was forced to dine on their raw, living flesh. The horror was decadent. Discordant sobs of despair and starvation poured from one as screams of pure agony spewed from the other. Tiny teeth pierced the living flesh of their prey tearing away blood-soaked mouthfuls. Young breasts and genitals were typical morsels chosen for the feast, but the jowls, for myself, were such a delight – forcing the wretches to rip away living meat while staring into the horrified, tear soaked eyes of their prey. Blood and tears covered the faces of the young bitches as they were forced to satiate themselves through the pain of their

242

brethren. Screams of the most scrumptious anguish filled the air with wonderful despondency."

[Side Note] Father Francis on more than one occasion wretched as details of this dark past were unveiled. At the end of his tale, Father Francis wretched again and Otto leaped backwards and grabbed up the small wooden chair smashing it into the head of Father Francis, collapsing him into a pool of his own retched bile and vomit.

Regardless of the certainly dubious authenticity of Otto's tale, it was not a tale Otto could have told. The man known as Otto could not read or write and had likely never left the confines of Trondheim. There is no way he could relate such horror or despair with anything close to this creature's eloquence.

Sam stopped and looked over at Victoria. Instead of the anticipated catatonic look of someone enduring an insurance seminar, her eyes were wide. "It goes on to describe the exorcism itself, but that isn't all that helpful for our purposes."

Victoria wasted no time responding with, "So, the demon possessing Otto wasn't a 'demon' at all? It was what: a fallen angel?"

"Exactly. Christian theology and mythology holds that Satan led a revolt in Heaven organizing a large contingent of angels to rebel against God. God prevailed, and expelled Satan and his supporters to Hell. Most people, including me before I read these passages, regard demons and fallen angels as one and the same. Those possessed by mere demons seem to wind up in a psychosis — no longer functional. Eventually, they are bound in bed, exhibiting horrific signs of possession, but unable to continue a daily routine. A fallen angel's victim moves about as normal. To an observer, they act and sound like themselves from before, but inside they are prisoners forced to idly watch as their body commits dreadful atrocities — living inside a perpetual nightmare."

"That sounds terrible. It does. But I am assuming you have a follow-up to Otto's story? Surely, Manuel wouldn't have compiled something like this based on just this one tale?"

Sam smiled. *I'm not sure if she's really interested in this or is just placating me, but let's see how she reacts to Magdalena.* He flipped further back to a different account and began:

Magdalena – 1902 – Bolivia

243

"I had visited this valley before, but never have things been so despondent. All four villages were shadows of their former selves. Bodies lay rotting in disheveled mounds and animals lay slaughtered in the fields. Many homes reduced to smoldering ruins. I had been warned, but my limited imagination is not that flexible. By the time I reached the chapel, I already had my kerchief over my nostrils to block the stench. I was greeted by two men with rifles strapped to their backs who escorted me inside with little conversation.

As I slogged forward, I encountered the source of the stench. The corpses of dozens of children lay side by side, baking in the late afternoon sun pouring through gaping holes where magnificent stained glass once stood proudly. I asked why their bodies had not been properly buried, and was told simply there were only so many shovels. What seemed to the outside world to be a localized feud, had, in fact, been a genocidal tsunami, triggered by one person – Magdalena.

Downstairs, I saw her. She was bound to a chair in a locked room in the cellar accompanied by an armed guard and Father Javier. I made my hurried introductions with few pleasantries. The Father told me how she had manipulated her husband, a wealthy merchant in town, into a trumped up squabble with a competing merchant from a neighboring village. Fighting escalated, each side grew more armed and the death toll climbed. Magdalena eventually murdered her husband, blaming the other side. She was calling the shots and nothing was off limits. Unspeakable remains of so many tortured victims had littered her hacienda before Father Javier had ordered it scorched.

Most unsettling, however, were tales of Magdalena before the fighting. She had been a teacher, loved by the children – the same children that she peeled the skin from their backs while they howled in agony. She was a beautiful, sweet woman and a loving wife. No one could fathom her transformation until the tide had finally turned against her. Her rampage had become too dark, too terrible for even her hired thugs. They turned bringing her to bear.

When Father Javier had attempted a conciliatory prayer for her soul, the true nature of her condition became exposed as she laughed and ridiculed God. The more intimate the prayer or ritual, the more repugnant and

244

hateful her rebuke. She could also detect hidden things she could not have known. As an experiment, Father Javier had placed a crucifix to the underside of her chair while she was out of the room. When she returned, she refused to sit in that chair - the same one she had sat in for days. When compelled to sit, she struck him across the face screaming that she would not fall for such trickery. In repeated events, she always knew whether or not the crucifix was under the chair without having seen it. Father Javier described her as almost clairvoyant.

When, at long last, I was alone with Magdalena, I performed a small experiment of my own. I began to pray out loud for her soul. I made sure to mention her madness - her delusional behavior. I specifically mentioned her husband's murder and the mutilations of the children, asking for God to pour forgiveness upon her soul. As I prayed, I listened. I wanted to hear beyond her laughter and cajoling. I listened to her breathing and body movement. They spoke volumes. While her voice scoffed at what she called "pathetic" and "worthless" supplication, her breathing became more and more labored, shorter and harder. I finally asked with whom I was speaking. She looked up with disheveled and sweat-soaked hair draped across her face and said one word: 'Death.' "

Sam stopped for a drink. As he paused, Victoria turned to him. "I think I see where you are going, though I'm not saying I believe you. You're saying that a fallen angel has a lot more control over its host than a run of the mill dark spirit or demon?"

"Seems that way. The internal struggle between a typical demon and its host is so intense, the demonic force only manages to disrupt its host's daily life and make a handful of gestures, obscenities or the infliction of dreadful physical wounds. These fallen angels, though, are another matter entirely. They could manipulate someone into becoming a serial killer or assassinating a President."

"One question: do you have any basis for this distinction? I mean, if fallen angels were originally angels in Heaven, where do you suppose demons come from?"

"Honestly, I don't know. I have a lot of research to do before going public. I didn't know what would be on these pages before I read them a few days ago, remember? Other than having seen 'The Exorcist' several times, I

245

know nothing about demonology. I'm eager to start once I'm back to my normal life." *Normal. What does that even mean anymore?*

"Was that it or was there more on this Magdalena?" Victoria inquired.

"Quite a bit more, but I'll spare you the lengthy journey." Sam scanned through the next page or two before coming across the piece he wanted. "Here. I do want to read this bit, though."

"I remember the monastery, Priest. I remember that pit and the misery we heaped upon those insufferable sons and daughters of whores. It was deep within a Germanian forest. Although Armaros took great pleasure in orchestrating his complicated machinations, my delights were far simpler. He would laugh as he tortured them, but my laughter was strongest merely observing the swine in their cells. The bastards had agreed to leave a back corner of each cell as a latrine of sorts since we had no incentive to make accommodation for that sort of thing for their kind. Having overheard arguments between two older boys, both trying to be chief of their pen, as they slept, I quietly slid a bit of fresh sheise near one of the boys' face. I hid nearby and watched as he rolled over into it and immediately assumed it had been the other boy's doing. That fight was delightful. The second boy was beaten close to unconsciousness as feces and urine were strewn about during the scuffle.

Engineering feuds was joyous, but there is also such amusements simply transferring captives. A strong willed boy could be isolated and thrown into a cage with only girls. Inevitably, he would attempt to exercise control and the girls would resist violently. A girl could be thrown into a boys' cell. I would watch as she was ravaged repeatedly or as the boys tore themselves apart claiming her as their own. Such tinkering, deliciously destroyed morale and kept the rats from growing comfortable in their cages.

Although most victims were hurled into the void of that massive pit, occasionally I would spirit one back to their cell to see the horror on their cell mates' faces. Those recently marred, mutilated or even missing precious bits with bite-sized chunks ripped from their flesh, crumpled into a corner, bleeding and trembling only to look into the horrified and repulsed face of their fellow wretches."

246

Sam closed the binder and sat silently staring ahead. It wasn't long until Victoria broke the stillness. "So these fallen angels possessed several monks at once? And worked in concert torturing those children? Wow, that is really grim. Let me guess . . . these accounts detail such similarities, the children, the pit, the forest, the monastery, etc., but they were written almost a century apart on opposite sides of the world. How am I doing?"

Sam rolled his eyes at her sarcasm while answering, "Good – though I know you don't believe it. I'm not pushing you."

Victoria quickly changed the subject. "Sam, what was the name of that village again, Hamlin?"

Sam's face lit up. "Yes! I can't believe I forgot . . ."

"Do you mean the same Hamlin with the pied piper?" Victoria interrupted.

"The same! Listen to this . . ."

"Marta, you may have caught the name of Hamlin in these most recent documents. I, too, could not help but recall the tale about a town of Hamlin that hired a piper to rid the town of rats. After completing his task, the town refused to pay the piper. In retribution, he led their children away to either drown in the river or fall from a cliff. Different versions have different endings for the poor children. I did a little research and discovered something remarkable, while tragic. The town of Hamlin in Germany is real. One of the oldest town records is from the fourteenth century which sadly reads, "It has been over 100 years since our children have gone." While the mythology of the pied piper is assuredly a fantastical addition, the odd disappearance of Hamlin's children seems quite real.

I was so intrigued by these tales I tried researching the monastery itself. At first, I found nothing. There were no references to an old monastery near Hamlin. However, one afternoon I was able to sneak some research time in the older records in the Vatican Archives and found a note about a German monastery lost due 'to misfortune.' That scrap led me to another volume detailing a monastery becoming infested with pagan worshippers. The Church had destroyed it and tried wiping away all traces of its existence."

*   *   *

Thursday, May 27, 1999 – After Midnight, Buffalo

Victoria had not seen Sam restrain himself like this before. He had just shared arguably the most convincing, while simultaneously the most heinous, bits of that entire ensemble, but wasn't forcing his conclusion down her throat. She had to admit, *his silence is working*. While she was nowhere close to acknowledging a God, these last couple accounts kept rolling around her mind. Previously, Sam made passionate arguments about how no one could deny the authenticity of these experiences. Those arguments gave her something to fight. She had resisted religion her whole life, but how could she resist her own mind. *What do these accounts or stories, or whatever they are, prove? I wish Sam would plead his case again. Sam – I can fight, but these little threads of doubt? They float aimlessly around my mind and I don't know why I can't ignore them.*

Her inner debate was cut short as she felt the change. Though subtle at first, the seams in the rails were coming a touch slower. "Sam," she whispered. "Gather your stuff. We'll going to hit the border inspection soon."

Sam obliged while Victoria gathered their few random bits of paper and water bottles. They were riding in a new Ford Expedition, one of four in their boxcar. She had picked one on the top row to minimize the chance of a physical inspection. The intermittent rail seams were quite a bit slower now and she definitely felt the train slowing. By Victoria's estimation, they were less than a mile out and would stop any minute. Once they came to rest, each car would be inspected, and there was no way of knowing how thoroughly someone might look through theirs.

"Ok Sam." Victoria continued whispering, "I need you in the back seat floor board. If someone looks in the cars up here, they'll look in the front and possibly the rear stowage. Back there is your best bet for staying hidden."

Sam turned to crawl back when he noticed Victoria pull a smallish revolver from her bag and start loading it. "What are you doing?" Sam yelled as loud as he possibly could while still whispering. "I don't want any shooting, blood or death! Have you already forgotten our argument on the plane?"

"Have you?" came her response. "I don't want shooting, blood or death either. If I fire this thing, it will be loud and will draw lots of attention. I really need you to trust me right now. Guns can do a lot more than shoot people. I've gotten you this far, and will finish the job, but you need to trust me and get your ass back there, right now!"

248

Sam turned sullenly and got into position. Just as the train pulled to a complete stop, he asked, "How did you even get a gun anyway? You didn't bring it on the plane. You're a good smuggler, but no one is that good."

She rolled her eyes while opening the truck's front door. *Like he has any idea what I could get onto an airplane! I could have brought a live grenade onboard if I wanted one.* "I took advantage of your time in custody to get a few things. Even when *your* journey stalls, things for me keep right on moving. Now, Shhh . . . I think someone's coming." She stepped outside of the truck to the platform, closing the truck's door as gingerly as possible behind her." Rain pelted against the heavy sheet metal above, echoing throughout their box car. The rain would help to mask any accidental sounds she or Sam might make, but would also mask sounds from the border guards. *This could be a huge mess. Let's hope these guys are in a hurry to get back out of this weather.* Victoria closed her eyes, listening.

Footsteps . . . moving slowly. Their owner was just outside walking along a metal platform. They stopped at the car's sliding door. *The door's release creaked downward smoothly. Those releases are not as easy as all that; this guy's strong as a bear.* The door slid open a few feet before she heard the faint click of a flashlight being switched on. She was crouching on the back side of the truck, feet perfectly hidden behind the front tires. She resisted the urge to open her eyes and kept listening. Her heart sank when the heavy stomp of a wet boot landed on the boxcar floor. *Breathe slowly, Victoria. Sam – please keep still.*

The second boot landed with a solid thud. Victoria had heard all she needed. She opened her eyes and looked down. *Dammit!* The upper deck was metal, but full of small rounded roles. *If this guy walks over and looks up, he'll see me like it's nothing.* Still, she couldn't risk moving and inside the truck she would have been helpless. This was her only play. The heavy bootsteps slogged around the inside of the car with the dull greenish flashlight beam darting sporadically. The flashlight's owner eventually began looking around toward the back. She slowly reached in her front pocket and found the revolver's grip. It was solid and cool to the touch. She delicately pulled it from her pocket not daring even to rattle the bullets in their chambers.

The pale light flickered off suddenly, but the boot steps continued – toward the small ladder extending to their deck. *Shit, here he comes.* Soaked boots landed on alternating rungs. *It's only a matter of time now.* She aimed toward the rear and steadied herself. *I can't kill this guy, can I? No. I won't.*

But I may have to hurt him if he keeps climbing, goes for a radio or his own gun. Victoria's grip on the trigger tightened as she trained her eyes to focus in the pitch black. A second sound suddenly closed in. In mere moments, a new set of footsteps stopped at the half open door just as the first neared the top of the ladder. *Dammit! If there are two of these guys to deal with now . . .*

"Hey, Paul! Get down and seal this one up!" shouted a high-pitched nasal voice fighting for breath after an apparently long run. "Boss says you can go drool at the dealership! Line's gotta break free, now!" After that, the second steps resumed running toward the train's front.

"Cripes," muttered a deep, gravelly voice. After a short pause, she finally heard it: the rungs of the ladder. He was climbing down. She sighed, releasing her grip. One rung after another, he descended to the floor and back out the door. The rain was slowing down, helping her hear more clearly. Unfortunately, what she heard sounded dreadful. The release bar that had slid so effortlessly opening the box car was stuck. He struggled a bit before radioing for help. Two more agents showed up and together they finally shoved the bar into place. That release bar itself didn't concern her. What did, however, was the grinding sound the door made as it jolted into place. *A ball bearing in the door is out of place and jammed against another. It'll take an ox to open that door now!*

She cracked open the truck door and whispered, "OK, you can crawl out now, but keep quiet. We haven't pulled away yet. Just as Victoria finished her warning, the train lurched forward. Sam crawled out, toting his briefcase. Victoria shut the door behind him and took a quick second to wipe away any finger streaks on the truck's exterior while contemplating her next move.

Sam looked at her confusingly and asked, "What took so long? I thought something had gone wrong."

Her fingers skimmed the metal grip of the pistol in her pocket. "It almost did. We're fine though, but we've only got a few precious moments. Let's get down." The two of them, Sam following behind, walked to the rear of the platform until she felt the metal ladder against her foot. "OK, Sam. Hand me the briefcase and get down there. Hurry." The international rail line crossed the U.S./Canadian border by spanning the banks across the Niagra River. The U.S. checkpoint would be just on the other side of that bridge.

Sam obeyed, scrambling down. After handing the briefcase down, she followed. Once down, she inspected the freight car door. It was as she feared. Though the lock would release easily enough, the door itself was stuck. *If we*

250

don't get this open and soon, we'll be trapped. Roaches in a roach motel, no way to check-out. She looked for any chains or lever, but none were to be found. *To come this far only to be beaten by a decrepit box car door.*

Victoria was frantic and began pacing, the void around her was suffocating. In frustration, she leaned against one of the trucks on the bottom level. *The trucks!* There wasn't much time, but it was the only idea she'd had. She hurriedly pulled out her lock gun. Racing against time, she popped open the back of the first truck. She yelled out to a confused Sam standing near the immovable door, "Come here and get the jack out now! I'll get the other one!"

As Sam raced over, she scrambled to the other truck. They worked frenetically. In moments, she had the front truck open and was retrieving its jack as well. Both jacks were the customary "scissor" variety typically accompanying a new car. While smaller and less powerful than a standard hydraulic jack, they might suit their needs. She called out into the darkness, "Sam! Bring that jack to the door!" He shuttled to the door and Victoria wedged both jacks between the door jam and the heavy inoperable box car door. "OK Sam. Take the one on top and start cranking. Give it all you've got! Go!"

They started working in concert. The jacks were hard to turn, especially as drained as they both were. As pressure built, Victoria felt it: the change in the track. *They were approaching the bridge!* They had mere minutes, and Victoria knew it. She had seen the maps. This part would be tricky, even without a jammed door. A tiny island lay just across the border – Squaw Island. That was her target. The ground was natural, not paved, with no houses or construction – no one would see their jump. *Occasionally, a border control agent sits watching as trains cross the threshold, but with this darkness and hopefully a quick dart out the door, that won't be an issue tonight. The track there is level with the ground: no treacherous elevation issues. We've got to hit that island to make this work. But we won't hit anything with this infernal door closed!* She pulled with everything she could muster. "Sam, let's do this in unison. Ready?! Pull!!" They both strained desperately as she felt the lever give. *The door moved! Every inch will be this way.* She yelled out again, "Good! Again! Faster!"

Like a rowing team captain, calling "stroke" repeatedly, Victoria screamed as the two of them, through brute force, shoved the door open, fractions of an inch at a time. She felt them near the end of the bridge. The rush of night air, still moist from earlier rains, pressed against her face as they

251

cranked the jacks open. The piercing shriek of metal grinding against metal pierced the night. They had opened it some, but it would be tight. It would have to be enough. "Ok! Grab your briefcase and get into position!"

They were crossing Squaw Island now. Sam squatted at the edge of the open door mustering the courage to jump. Indecision would cost them the moment. "You know that leap of faith you talk about, Sam?" she screamed into the black night.

"Yeah!"

"You first!!" With that, she shoved him out with her foot and leaped out a split second afterward – blindly into the void.

"Alice came to a fork in the road. 'Which road do I take?' she asked. 'Where do you want to go?' responded the Cheshire Cat. 'I don't know,' Alice answered. 'Then,' said the Cat, 'it doesn't matter'." Lewis Carroll, *Alice in Wonderland*

January 20, 1973 – Mid-Day

Blended aromas of hamburgers sizzling atop the scorching griddle and cold strawberry ice cream filled young Sam's nostrils as he stared blankly down to his uninspiring grilled cheese sandwich. Though Woolworth's lunch counter was not especially crowded, the few gathered seemed to be enjoying themselves and their meal, far more than he was. His mother, engrossed in conversation, allowed Sam to bask in his own boredom. He had tried acting interested at first, but those initial efforts failed miserably once their discussion turned to church and charities. Henny, his mom's guest, was hard for Sam to endure anyway, as she was Marvin's mother. Sam couldn't stand Marvin. If bullies were graded, Marvin would earn a "C" – the kind of bully that readily annoyed and frustrated Sam but posed no real threat. Eventually, Sam resorted to spinning himself quietly on his barstool while absentmindedly nibbling on the grilled cheese.

It was a cold Thursday, and most folks in the business center of Anaheim were at work rather than hanging out at Woolworth's. Sam would have otherwise been at school, but for a teacher's meeting, forcing his mother to drag him along. This winter had been far colder than most. While Anaheim is typically known for its mild climate and picturesque summers, this chill had forced people to fetch seldom worn coats and jackets from storage. His mom had forced him to wear that itchy, orange sweater his grandmother made him last year. Although he hated that sweater, it was good he had worn it as the store was chilly even inside. Sam hadn't noticed the chill much as he was preoccupied watching Henny's bleached "bun" hairdo bounce in rhythm as she talked. It was funny the way it seemed to dance atop her head, but Sam contained his laughter well enough.

At some point, well after Sam began poking holes through the grilled cheese with his finger, he saw the man. He was a big man, and wore funny sunglasses even inside the store. Truly, it wasn't the man catching Sam's

253

attention – it was the man's dog. The man and his dog had come inside together, completely catching Sam off-guard. *Dogs aren't supposed to be inside!* He tried getting his mom's attention to ask permission to go see the dog, but Henny's non-stop conversation left him no openings. Despite being dismissed twice with a raised finger by his mother, curiosity eventually over-powered his internal sense of duty and he jumped up following his own path.

By the time he arrived, Sam's friend Richard was there kneeling, talking to the man and petting his dog. Sam hadn't even known Richard was in the store, but was happy having a friend there. The boys soon discovered that the dog, a beautiful white lab wearing a yellow sash across its back, was named Shep. They weren't alone with Shep for long, however. Soon, several kids had flocked around. After all, it's not every day a big white dog walks inside a department store. The man was friendly and hadn't stopped laughing since Sam, Richard and the others showed up.

Sam and Richard laughed with the man and Shep for some time until Sam's conscience returned to his mother. He had known better than to run off that way and needed to go back and check in. Maybe she would let him come back. He skipped carelessly across the shoe department back toward the lunch counter. When he got there, however, his mother and Henny were gone!

She is looking for me! This is bad; I have to find her before she finds me. Sam raced to the toy department. *She'll go there first, I'm sure.* He frantically checked down each aisle, even the "pink" one, but there was no sign of her. Not knowing where to go next, he randomly searched different spots: pets, sporting goods, even the restrooms. He didn't find his mom, but he did spook a timid young girl rolling a joint in the back stall. Sam eventually resigned himself to his fate. He would return to the nice man and his dog and wait for his mom. She would eventually search everywhere – knowing he would never leave without her. He would be in trouble and suffer whatever that meant.

When he returned, he was breathing heavy from his running, and fresh sweat irritated his chest far worse than that annoying orange sweater could have on its own. However, the others were still there and in mere seconds, it was as though he had never left. The children laughed and talked with the nice man until a slightly older girl asked, "Why are you wearing such dark glasses? It's not sunny and you're inside."

The man chuckled as he turned to face her, "Oh child, I have a problem with my eyes and these glasses just help me get along." His smile faded, however, as he sniffed the air. The children must have thought it strange since they smelled nothing, but the man's frown and wrinkled forehead pushing away his laughter and jumbo smile seemed to worry them.

Sam didn't notice the mood change straight away. He was too focused on Shep, but when silence reigned where only moments ago poured boisterous laughter, it caught his attention. The man stood up facing them. "Children, please come outside with me – right now. We can play with Shep in the parking lot, but we can't stay here." He made a clicking sound with his teeth and Shep calmly backed away from the children and the two of them made for the front. Some of the children, including Sam, turned and followed.

As they approached the door, his thoughts returned, once more, to his mother. He couldn't leave without his mom knowing. He separated from the group and paced nervously by the check-out lanes. He waited there timidly for several minutes before smelling something akin to the disgusting foulness of rotten eggs or spoiled cabbage. He walked along the storefront trying to escape the smell, but had only managed a few steps when it happened.

Color faded to white. There was a shattering boom, but only for the briefest of moments, and then – silence. Pain. Silence. Nothing.

Sam couldn't move. He was lying on the ground – outside. The silence was overbearing. He tried opening his eyes. Everything was out of focus – like peering through cheap binoculars. He wanted to cry out, but his throat refused. Even swallowing was a tremendous challenge. Sam felt the sting of salty tears pouring down his cheeks. Boots and shoes all around him sprinted in every direction. Some things came into focus gradually. He saw glass and twisted metal first. Then blood. So much blood. *Is the ground falling? Wait – that doesn't make sense. I'm rising. Someone's picking me up.* More pain – sharper, more intense – not deep and dull like before. He tried again to cry out in agony. Though his mouth opened, and he thought he screamed, the world remained quiet.

Moments later, after hovering awkwardly above the pavement, the ground rose again. This ground was not cold and gray, like before, but yellow. Bright yellow. *And soft? A blanket.* The world twisted. Pain surged again. More tears. Focus was returning, unfortunately. Beside him lay Richard. Richard was still and his eyes were closed. Though cut all over and bleeding, he wasn't crying. "Richard," Sam tried mouthing his name. Instead of silence, this time he heard ringing. The ring was distant at first, but crept closer, growing incrementally louder. *Where is mommy?* Sam cried out for her, but

255

still heard only ringing. He tried again. "Mommy!" Still ringing. *Maybe she can hear me even though I can't?* Severe pain pulsed through him, far worse than before, but more concentrated. *My arm?* He shut his eyes.

The ringing continued growing. What started as a distant, high-pitch tone swelled until it surrounded him. It grew deeper. He kept his eyes closed. He thought he heard voices and sirens out there somewhere beyond – like listening to something while under water. New pain. His ears started throbbing sending wave after wave of deafening tones careening through Sam's head – each more dreadful than its predecessor. The pain from his arm was excruciating. He remained alone on the yellow blanket. He began sobbing uncontrollably. *Where is mommy? Where am I?*

He felt something. Something cold touched his forehead. He opened his tear-filled eyes just in time to see a pink tongue lap the bridge of his nose. It was Shep! He couldn't reach up to touch him, but Shep remembered him. The white coated lab was laying down on his belly, with his snout pressed to Sam's head. Sam was happy to see Shep, but couldn't muster a smile. *Where was the nice blind man? He needs Shep.* Sam tried turning his head to look for Shep's owner, but only hurt his neck. More pain. Fresh tears.

Eventually, though the pounding in his ears ushered in fresh waves of pain, the ringing stopped and sounds cleared. Everyone buzzed about frantically. Broken glass lay everywhere being crushed underneath heavy fireman boots. Amidst all the sirens and chaos Sam heard one word repeatedly: boiler. *What was a boiler?* Sam desperately cried out again, "Maaaaawwmm!" at the top of his lungs. Shouting hurt all over, but he couldn't fathom where she was. His right arm still hurt the most, and he was, gradually able to look down to see why. It was bandaged, but the wrapping was soaked through with blood. The orange sweater was charred and cut up. Footsteps approached and Sam wistfully looked up. He was disappointed.

A man in a blue uniform knelt beside him. "Can you hear me, son?"

Sam tried answering, but his throat was scorched.

He smiled with compassion and continued, "Tell you what kid, if the answer is 'yes,' blink once; blink twice for 'no,' got it?"

Sam blinked once in response.

"Do you hurt?"

Blink.

"Where's it hurt most? Your arm?" he asked, pointing down.

Blink.

256

"Ok. Let me see . . ." He pulled out a small syringe and stuck him with it – just above the elbow. "Son, in a few minutes, you won't feel much of anything. Before then, answer a few more questions?"

Blink.

The nice man started changing his arm bandage while asking, "Were you in the store alone?"

Blink. Blink.

He stopped smiling but kept working. "Were you there with your dad?"

Blink. Blink.

"Mother?"

Blink.

The man became even more sullen and touched the top of Sam's head. "Just rest, son. We're gonna get you to the hospital."

By the time Sam was being loaded into the ambulance, Richard still hadn't moved, but Sam could see him breathing. Shep had stayed around, lying quietly at his side. The nice blind man wasn't around, and Sam worried for Shep, but what could he do?

His mother never showed.

* * *

February 13, 1976 – Early Evening

"I don't buy it, not for a minute, Victoria! You can't sit there, look me in the eyes and tell me math's all of a sudden gotten 'too hard'. You always get good grades, and now – a 'D'? What's really going on, young lady?"

Victoria sat mindlessly gazing out the front window, wishing she were anywhere else but right there. The trip from Butler to Mt. Jewett took several hours, thanks to the twisted, windy roads through the country and Allegheny forest.

"Well?" her mother continued, like a harpy tormenting Phineus. Victoria took a sip of soda, a grape Nehi that had grown progressively flat as the trip dragged on. Her mother, not waiting for the prolonged silence typically following Victoria being asked a question she didn't want to answer, pressed, "You are smart. We both know you're smart. This isn't about being smart. It's about being diligent. Math's not something *you* struggle with. It's always been one of your strongest subjects. What happened to suddenly make you lose interest? I need an answer, Victoria! The real answer! Right now!"

257

Her mom's voice was rising, and Victoria's game had run its course. *I can't come clean on this – not this! I've got to give her something – but what? It has to be believable. She knows I'm too smart for drugs. It can't be about Miss Jacobs. She's the nicest teacher in the whole school. Maybe – another student? A bully? No – no good. She would either know I was full of shit or believe me. Both bad. If she buys it, she'll call Miss Jacobs, and everything gets worse. If she doesn't buy it – she'll blow a gasket. Hmmm . . . maybe . . .*

"It's a boy, mom – OK?" Victoria raised her voice just enough – walking the fine line between being respectful yet convincing. "Are you happy now? I didn't want to say anything, but there's this boy in math class. Victoria quickly turned away, blankly gazing out the side window. She also started thinking of the saddest moments she could conjure. When she turned back around, her eyes needed tears for this to be truly convincing.

Outside, snow began falling harder and apparently had been for some time. They were less than an hour from Kane, and the trees' limbs sagged under a suffocating white blanket. The road was becoming saturated with snow and slush. The sound of snow being crushed under their tires was drowned out by the silence lingering in the air following Victoria's confession. Her mother was likely struggling to absorb what she just heard. Victoria had never swooned over a boy before, no more than the occasional nervous glances kids exchange before learning better tactics. Then again, Victoria was eleven. Things might be changing on that front, and her mom needed to consider that. A few moments more slipped by before Victoria's mom finally broke the tension with a surprisingly concerned, "What's his name?"

It worked! She thinks I've got the hots for some guy in math. Unfortunately, Victoria had been so preoccupied with figuring out how to react if her mom saw through the charade, she was not prepared to flesh out the story if she bought in. "Freddy," she replied meekly, still not wanting to appear too comfortable with the subject.

"Freddy? How long have you known him?" An unmistakable undertone of concerned compassion carried her words.

Victoria knew deep down the diversion wouldn't last, but with luck, it would hold until they reached her Grandfather's farmhouse. For the façade to last, she had to play along. "He just started here this year. Moved in from somewhere."

"Is he cute?"

258

"What? Mom!" Victoria couldn't help but face her mom directly. She was uncomfortable enough concocting her mythical Freddy, but now? *Am I going really going through with this?*

"Well?" Victoria's mother continued. "If some boy's distracting you from your schoolwork, he better be good-looking." As she finished, she turned to look Victoria in the eyes.

Her mom's face had shifted from frustrated anger into a wry, but curious, grin. As their eyes met, Victoria noticed a hint of something beyond compassion, but she didn't yet know the word to describe it. Later in life, Victoria would not only learn the word she didn't yet know was 'empathy,' but she would discover how rare it really is in its truest form. Even without the word, she knew her mom felt something *through* her. *She must have had a real crush like the one I'm making up.* Victoria felt guilty lying to her mom, but there was no way out now but to see it through. She opened her mouth to concoct more details about this Freddy but got no more than a syllable out before everything went horribly wrong.

Victoria's mother, having turned to face her daughter, didn't notice the sharp bend in the road. Their old Studebaker slammed into the snow-covered guard rail before twisting violently and flipping over it. Though there were no dramatic cliffs or embankments, the car rolled before coming to rest, luckily, right-side up. *What just happened? We hit something?* Victoria was stunned; so stunned she didn't notice the glass chips embedded in her forearm; so stunned she didn't see the crushed windshield; and so stunned she didn't notice the steering wheel crushing her mother's chest.

She tried sitting up, but everything hurt. Her head had come to rest against the side window, and it took some doing just to look around. She fought through the initial pain and raised her head off the window before noticing her mom. "Mom! Wake up, mom!" Before she could finish even those few words, tears started. Bitter, salty streaks poured from her eyes as she slid across the bench, ignoring her own pain, to wake her mother. *My God, My God! What is happening? Why won't she wake up?* She screamed out, "Mom!" There was no response. Victoria saw her mom still breathing, though only short, shallow gasps. She put her hands on her shoulder and jostled her – hoping she was just unconscious. Though her mind knew better, her heart kept fighting.

"Mom, mom. Wake up. It's ok. We can get out and flag down someone. We'll be alright. You just have to wake up first!" Victoria grew

259

more frantic as the breaths grew shorter and shorter. "Mom, wake up. Come on, just open your eyes." Victoria bowed her head, offering a silent prayer: *Dear Jesus. Please help. She goes to church. She's always there for everyone. She even feeds people down at the mission. She talks about you with patients at the hospital. She doesn't deserve this; you know she doesn't. Give her back her strength. Give her back her breath. I know I don't pray to you like I should, and I'm so sorry. But this is really important!*

It took almost an hour, but ultimately, her breaths stopped coming altogether. Victoria was helpless. All she knew to do was hold her mom's hand in hers – hopefully letting her mom know she wasn't alone. Victoria kept rubbing her mom's hand for a long time afterward – resisting wave after wave of bitter tears. She lost each battle as fresh tears followed the trails blazed by their predecessors across her blistered cheeks.

It was already dark when they hit that guardrail, and several hours had slipped by afterward. Night settled in, and the temperature, already bitter cold, was dropping dangerously. Victoria, still holding her mom's cold hand in hers, noticed her breath pouring steam from her mouth. She was cold, and getting colder. She thought first of giving up, giving in. There was nothing for her now. Her mom was her world, and now Victoria's lies had betrayed the one person she truly believed in. The notion of being left alone with *"him"* was far worse than dying out here in the deadly chill. As she sullenly sat beside her mom, something inside her, once warm and full of light, grew cold and dark. She turned to her mother and softly said, "I'm so sorry. I'm sorry I lied. You never knew the truth about Daddy, but I know you wouldn't want me to freeze out here. I love you more than you ever knew – more than I would ever show. Love kept the truth from you. It would have hurt you so much to know the truth about him, Mom. Things will be really hard for me now, but God doesn't care. It's going to be up to me. I've got to start fighting harder. And I have to start now."

With that, she let go of her mother's hand and looked around. The bitter cold was creeping inside, mostly from the front windshield. The impact had shattered and ripped it from the car in several places. Snow continued falling – large, heavy flakes piling on the hood. *We'll be covered soon. Need to move.* She slid over and tried opening the door. It wouldn't budge and was crushed. *Ok, I could make a small fire to stay warm, but that doesn't sound smart. How do I light a fire inside a car without burning the whole thing up? Need something to keep the fire in. Ashtray? That might work, but the fire*

260

would be awfully small. Glove box? No. Too far away, and who knows what's leaking in there. So, what, then? Victoria searched around and found her cousin's "Holly Hobby" lunch box in the back. It was tin with pictures of three little girls on the front and trimmed in lavender. *This might work if I keep the fire from getting too big.* She dumped out the rotted contents which had lived inside for several weeks now.

OK. I have a container, now I need fuel. I'm in the middle of a forest and can't get to any firewood. Go figure. I could burn Mom's clothes, but that's not right. Surely, there's something else to burn. She saw nothing but a few napkins tucked under the front seat. *Maybe . . . the seats themselves? They're covered in cloth probably have foam underneath. Can't get the seat cloth into the lunchbox without a knife.* She scanned around while her mind raced. *No. No knife, except – glass!* Victoria removed a particularly pointy-looking shard from the windshield and leaned back, slicing the cloth from the back seats. Once she had hewn several large strips, she sat back to think.

Now – how to start the fire? If "he" had been in the driver's seat, I'd have a fancy cigarette lighter. Wait! The car has a cigarette lighter. She pushed the lighter and waited with fingers crossed until it popped back out. The coils inside were bright orange.

Victoria lit her fire, and it worked – at first. She had not anticipated the smoke. As the fire flickered, billows of hazy black smoke quickly filled the interior. Victoria coughed as she used snow to snuff out the flame, shoving her nostrils against the gaps in the side window to grab quick breaths of fresh air. *That was ridiculous! How did I forget about the stupid smoke? I could have killed myself! I have to start thinking things out ahead of time. How many second chances will I get? Maybe if I kept the fire near the front windshield, the smoke would drift outside.* Unfortunately, this meant holding the fiery lunch box in her hands. She had her gloves, but they were thin and wouldn't hold up against a metal lunch box with a scorching fire smoldering inside. She used everything she could to protect her hands – even wrapping them in her mom's scarf when she could no longer bear it.

It was hard. Her body and mind craved sleep, but she dared not succumb. *I would either wake up with flames licking my skin – cooking me alive; or I would fall into a deadly frozen sleep once the fire dwindled to nothing.* All night, she resisted the temptation. Occasionally, she would pack snow into the glass Nehi bottle, holding it beside the fire – melting the snow. It did give her passable drinking water. Throughout the night, she fought sleep, thirst, fire, and cold. She needed to live. For her.

Morning eventually came with a dull whimper. Bright sunshine did not pour through the pines bringing fresh hope. Rather, the dark pitch of night merely faded slowly into the dull gray of morning leaving Victoria empty as she dreaded her next move. Snow hadn't fallen all night, and the car was not completely buried. In fact, it was only covered up to the bottom of the car body. However, the blanket packed atop the car's hood had buried her most likely escape route. Victoria fought through the pain, laid on her back and kicked with everything she had against the side window. It wouldn't budge at first, but after several strong kicks, the cracked glass shattered. One particularly jagged shard pierced her right shin as she rammed it through. She cried out in pain. No one heard. No one came running. *I suppose I can stay and cry or I can get going.* She pulled herself up and used what remained of the blackened lunch box to break any remaining glass. She placed her mom's jacket over the small jagged bits along the window's bottom edge and pulled herself through the opening and into the fresh blanket of snow outside.

She fell hard, knocking the wind out of her. Soon she pulled herself up and limped slowly up the embankment to the highway. *There are tracks in the snow! The road's not impassable!* Victoria sighed with relief at this tiny bit of hopeful news. She turned toward Kane and started hobbling. Each step on her right leg sent a fresh wave of agony searing through her, but she pressed on, refusing to award this tragedy any further victories. She pecked along, fighting a blistering wind and immense pain from her bleeding shin, leading a dark trail of crimson resting atop white powder in her wake. Some time later, a deep rumbling behind her caught her attention. Victoria turned to see the outline of a logging truck approaching. She smiled.

*   *   *

April 9, 1981 – Late Afternoon

Laughter and excited voices echoed throughout the gymnasium, blending the cacophony of conversations, giggles and exuberance into a dull roar. Children joked, jumped rope, and played basketball along with a host of other amusements while bouncing around with the sort of carefree spirit only children fully embrace. Sam's team looked at each other, grinning to see the place so alive. They made up a small squad, five people in total, who had drawn this program as their partner for the "Community Contact Project": an opportunity for college kids to engage the community and work directly with

262

the children. Each of them, originally full of hope and aspirations, had seen their spirits dwindle as the weeks progressed. The children, most of them in middle school, were distant and aloof, seldom willing to share anything beyond casual banter.

Sam had struggled to connect for some time, but had become little more than a chaperone for a pick-up game of dodge-ball or basketball. His instructor had been encouraging – telling him how delicate kids at this age are. They're expected to handle adult situations, but they hadn't yet developed the necessary tools. In particular, Sam had been trying to connect with Larry, a heavy-set sixth grader who was alone more often than not. Sam had tried engaging Larry for several weeks before noticing something he had missed previously.

Larry periodically kept watch on a small group of three other kids. They were all boys and glared at Larry often. Sam wasn't sure what to make of this until he caught something in the eyes of the tallest boy, Billy. It was neither curiosity nor confusion – it was contempt. Billy's sidekicks didn't seem to share such strong emotion. Sam recognized the pattern. They were bullies, and Larry was their target. Sam had determined that today, with some help from the squad, would be different.

Sam, Chuck and Jorge grabbed a basketball and started assembling a makeshift game of 21. Several boys joined in and were having a great time. The three bullies were playing with them, while, naturally, Larry sat by himself quietly. After a few rounds, Chuck and Jorge began strategically pulling the boys into secondary games until, as luck would have it, Sam was eventually alone with Billy. He suggested changing the game to something slower, like HORSE. Billy agreed, especially as his buddies were involved in other games. *Good leaders don't go crawling to his followers begging for inclusion. They should crawl back to him.*

Talking a bully out of bullying can be harder than talking the sun out of being hot, but it was worth a shot. "I'm Sam." He offered the first line, hoping for a positive return.

"Billy." The truncated response and the fact that he responded without even looking Sam in the eyes spoke volumes.

"Which did you lose, Mom or Dad?"

He caught Billy in mid-shot and the ball went wild as Sam's question hung in the air for several moments. Sam recovered the ball as Billy stood in shock.

When Sam returned, Billy tried playing it off. "What are you talking about, man?"

Sam took a shot from just beyond the free throw line as he smiled and responded, "Oh nothing. You remind me a lot of someone I knew once. Great kid, but he lost his mom. I just wondered which one you've lost?"

Billy, his mind likely trying desperately to keep up, missed his shot terribly.

"That's an 'H' for you, Billy." Sam took the ball and smiled again as he went for a simple layup.

Just before he jumped, Billy shot back a quick, "My Dad. How did you know anyway?"

The ball bounced into the net as Sam faced Billy. "Just a theory. It's not the end of the world, you know."

Sam went to fetch the ball, leaving Billy to think a little. *Need him to engage me now. This won't work if I push.* He tossed the ball back without another word.

The game went on for several plays before Billy spoke again. "You're wrong. It *was* the end of the world – *my* world."

Sam, relieved Billy had climbed out on that limb, resisting pushing too hard too fast. "I felt the same way when my mom was taken."

"Taken?" Billy seemed confused by Sam's word choice.

"Well, she wasn't kidnapped or anything like that. She was killed in a massive explosion. A boiler exploded in a department store. Whole place went up."

Billy's eyes bulged at the mention of an explosion. As Sam was trying for a simple free throw, Billy finally opened the door. "My dad was everything to us – my mom, me and my brothers. He got in a fight at a bar about a year ago and got hurt real bad. Everything changed after that – everything!" Sam noticed the water in Billy's eyes and the anger behind his voice. "He's the one that's dead, but we all lost our lives. Now mom has to pull two jobs, and my kid brothers? Who do you think looks after them? Me! What chance they got? None! Nada!"

Sam sunk his free throw and let the air settle before going any further. He did, however, eventually try offering solace. "You still have a father, you know?"

"What?"

"I don't know what you believe, Billy. But I believe that we all have a father in heaven constantly watching over us: over me, and over you – even over your brothers."

Billy laughed at Sam's response – not a deep, hearty laugh, but a cordial chuckle of disapproval. "You really buy that? My mom believes that, too. She prays to God, and he sits there watching her work herself to death!"

There is a hard truth inside there and I need to tread lightly or this thing turns south fast. "I watched a nature show the other night on TV. You know the kind where they go in and capture wild animals to move them to other areas. You know why they do that?"

"Not really."

"Well, it's to help them. These animals, the other night it was a bear, find themselves in bad places, places where people are or where there's no real food for them. Anyway, they set out some bait and when this big black bear came out to get the food, they shot it with tranquilizer darts and put it to sleep. What do you think that bear was thinking in those last few moments before he fell asleep?"

"I don't know what bears think, man!"

"Well, I don't either, but if he were a person, he would probably have been thinking about how unfair life was. He was just minding his own business, and out of nowhere, some idiots shoot him with painful darts. He had done nothing to them! As he drifted asleep, he probably thought life was over, right? "

Billy offered no response, merely taking his shot from under the basket.

Sam didn't wait for the invitation to keep going, "Thing is – this bear? Woke up hours later in a safer part of the woods where he could go on with his life. There were more ways to look at the situation than through the bear's eyes. There might be more at work in your life than you realize. Perhaps you'll be stronger as an adult from having to look after your brothers. Perhaps you will respect your wife more knowing how much work it is to raise children. Perhaps your mother is gaining strength and independence that will benefit her one day. Perhaps your brothers are learning things they never would with your mother watching them. There could be hundreds of reasons for why things are the way they are, but you can't see them because you're only looking at the situation through your eyes. So, don't make the mistake of

265

assuming that God is not there or that He does not love you because, from *your* perspective, things seem crappy."

Billy hung his head down, and replied, "Never thought about any of it that way. Everything just seems so unfair since dad's been gone."

"You know what's really unfair?" Sam responded.

"What's that?"

"See that kid over there sitting by himself?"

"You mean Larry – He's such a nerd, man. Nobody likes that guy."

"Know why? He's alone so much he's forgetting how to get along with other people. You take this anger from your own life, turn it on him and push him away. Do you think he *likes* hanging out over there by himself? How many times do you have to kick a dog before he stops coming around? Who knows, one day he might embrace all this rage and hatred everyone's pushed on him and take someone's life in a bar fight one dark night? Some folks treat God as something they take out for certain holidays, Christmas or Easter, but ignore Him the rest of the time. God is with us always, but it's up to us to decide if we cling to Him or pretend we're on our own. The belief in God is like a warm blanket we can curl up under to shelter us from all the horrible things of this world. It doesn't make the cold go away, but you'll get through far better than without it."

That was the point beyond which Billy could not return. His tough exterior melted away, one tear at a time. He stormed away to the bathroom, but Sam already knew he had broken through. When Billy returned, Sam apologized for getting so personal, but let him know that he would see him next week. Billy didn't offer much, but his return smile was all Sam needed.

*   *   *

November 17, 1982 – Midnight

For months now, she and Joseph had been on their own. Autumn had faded, and as winter crept upon them, food had grown far scarcer. They had been reduced to rummaging through restaurant garbage bins, wolfing down any bits they could find. Joseph had resisted at first, but hunger spoke louder than his ego. The plan had originally worked well enough. Pittsburgh was large, so if they kept moving, there was no jeopardy of being caught pilfering through the refuse decent people left behind. Problem was that plenty of other starving folks had the same notion. To discourage the throng, more and more places starting locking the dumpster lid. It was also becoming more fashionable for people to take home uneaten food rather than leaving it for

266

the trash. Naturally, this translated into Victoria and Joseph going to sleep occasionally listening to their stomachs' grumbling their unique, particularly discordant lullaby.

Tonight, as the bitter northern wind swept over the sleeping city, Victoria's thoughts wrestled with solutions to this most pressing dilemma. She remembered back to her much younger childhood where her mom ensured she attended church regularly. While any lessons drilled into her by overbearing teachers had been purged over the years, few memories of time spent with her mother persisted. One memory, in particular, surfaced: she was sitting with her mom as a room full of hungry church-goers sat stuffing their faces with turkey, dressing, mashed potatoes and pumpkin pie. Victoria didn't remember the joy everyone felt or the jokes shared by the pastor. She did remember the food and the church pantry. While fairly certain most of the food was brought in by church members, she remembered never seeing the church kitchen and cabinets bare.

Joseph's face melted when she revealed her plan. "You serious? Break in to a church to *steal* food?" He shoved his hands into his jacket pockets and peered up at her from the curb where he was sitting.

Victoria didn't like being challenged by someone four years younger than her. She had sheltered him from weather and hunger since running into him that night several months ago after escaping from the Schmidts. He was new to the streets and would likely have perished if not for her. She defended herself, "Yes – absolutely serious. Look, churches have weak security. No guards, no alarms."

"But, but . . . it's a *church*, Vicky! Don't you go to hell, stealing from a church?"

"Joe, hate to break it to you, but there is no hell. There is no God, nor heaven for that matter. Don't get me wrong. Churches aren't bad; they teach people to be good and do good things. But guardian angels aren't protecting any of the churches in Pittsburgh, and they all have food. It doesn't get any simpler."

"No God? But, all those people – millions of them – go to church every Sunday. They're all just crazy, and *you're* the one who's got it figured out?" Joseph's nose crinkled like someone had suggested he leap from a bridge to test out his invisible wings.

"No – not crazy. Just wrong. I've seen the truth right before my eyes. My mom and I were in a car accident, and she got hurt really bad. I sat beside

267

her, watching, as she took her last breaths – the whole time begging for God's help. My mom was *good,* Joe. She went to church. She helped people. It took me a long time to understand why God stepped aside and watched her die. I tried figuring out why he didn't care about her. What had she done to deserve that?" Victoria fought against yesterday's tears – refusing them passage.

"And. . .?" Joseph seemed intrigued as Victoria never spoke about her past.

"I was tore up for a long time. My mom always said God loves everyone. Well, I was never certain about the 'everyone' part, but I did think God at least loves moral and decent people. Well, my mom? She was both decent and moral. She probably had plenty of issues that I was too young or stupid to see, but from my seat, she was a saint – a saint whose chest got smashed in by a steering column. I was holding her hand, Joe. I felt it grow cold. I got pretty messed up. How could this loving 'God' figure just let my mom die like that? I was praying, too, dammit. I was praying hard. I *needed* God to hear me. He didn't."

"Wow, I'm sorry. I never knew about your mom."

She smiled thinly. "It's alright. I try not bringing it up – still hurts, ya know? Anyway, I know why I was so confused and angry. If you believe in God, you spend your whole life justifying how a 'loving God' inflicts such horrible things upon such undeserving, faithful and upright followers. The truth is much simpler. There is no God." Victoria's eyes swelled, but she would not allow a single tear to flow. Pale moonlight traced the silhouette of dark clouds hanging low in the skies behind her as she reached her hand out to help Joseph up.

He smiled uneasily and took her hand. "I don't know if I agree with you, but my stomach agrees with getting some food. If there is a God, He'll understand."

They walked for some time searching for a likely target. It needed to be a nice average church. One too small would likely not have much in the way of a kitchen, while a big church might have bigger, better locks or even night workers. Eventually, they found it – a Lutheran church just the right size. They skulked about outside looking for the right place to enter. This was, after all, a new challenge entirely – breaking in to a functional building. Kitchens wouldn't be near the main entryway, and they weren't likely to be near lots of windows. A small side door looked perfect.

"Ok, Joe. Keep watch, got it?"

Joe just nodded in response, clearly growing more nervous as minutes passed.

Victoria checked the door. *Locked – figured.* She tightened her grip on the metal rod they'd brought for just for this purpose. Wham! She struck the metal knob hard. The impact's echo reverberated throughout the night air, but Joe gave no indication that anyone noticed. She had dented the knob, but the lock held. Wham! Wham! She slammed the rod against the door knob twice more. She looked back at Joe. All was still fine. The knob was loose now – loose enough for her to use the rod to pry the lock free from the door frame. They were in.

As it turned out, the door opened to a cluttered storage room stuffed with a thousand sundry items. They fumbled about until, eventually, they pecked through the debris and found their way to a large hallway. Occasional light pressing through draped covered glass led them to a likely prospect: a large room – covered in peach colored linoleum tile. Victoria didn't want to risk turning the light on, but moonlight shining through a couple uncovered windows helped them get around without much fuss. A closed door opposite those windows looked promising and, once opened, they saw it – the refrigerator.

Joe shot a quick smile to Victoria. She had stumbled across a gold mine. The fridge teemed with food. While mostly ingredients of food, like condiments or seasonings, there were drinks and several half-eaten desserts lurking inside. Additionally, the cabinets on either side held several cans, large commercial cans, of vegetables. Just as Joe reached into the fridge, they heard a "click" and light flooded the room just outside.

Someone's coming! Only seconds stood between them and capture. Footsteps echoed against the linoleum closing on the kitchen door. Victoria darted into the corner just as the door opened. She was now behind the door, as light poured onto an unsuspecting Joseph. The footsteps were those of a middle-aged man – presumably the pastor by the look of him.

He entered the room cautiously, but once his eyes landed on Joseph, his hands clutched around Joseph's wrist, and he turned far more vicious. He leaped upon Joe in an instant, grabbing both of his hands before Joseph could react. The pastor twisted an arm behind Joe's back. Joseph cried out in pain as the pastor began berating him. The pastor used all manner of vile insults, accusing Joseph of crimes against the church and himself. From Victoria's hiding place behind the door, she caught the rage and anger in the pastor's eyes.

Then something happened. As the pastor tightened his grip and Joseph cried out once more, Victoria's vision blurred. A cavalcade of long-forgotten memories rushed upon her. Nights when her father, mad drunk, snuck into her room. Bruises when his drunken passions took another form. Lies to her mother hiding the truth. The betrayal of Pastor Schmidt, her foster father once the state finally took her away from her natural one, as he preached love and forgiveness from the pulpit but slammed her to the floor for the mildest indiscretions. The blind hatred and cowardice smothering her until she forged the courage to break free – choosing the streets over bondage and humiliation. Victoria's mind saw red. She reached out grabbing an oversized can of green beans. Her fingers clasped the edge of the can as she hoisted it high above her head.

She stepped forward and slammed it down. She brought it down violently on the back of the pastor's head. He released Joe as he fell sideways to the floor. She leaped down and kept pounding him about the head where he lay sprawled. It wasn't until Joseph finally screamed "Victoria!" at her repeatedly that she finally realized what she had done. She dropped the can, now covered in blood. She was breathing hard and had no memory of what had happened. She regained control of her thoughts and noticed at the Pastor's feet a zipper bag, the kind typically used by banks. She helped herself to all the cash inside, ignoring the checks, and turned to leave.

Joseph was in shock. He opened his mouth to protest, but she ran out without waiting for his plea. He followed. She led him to the edge of the street outside, and turned to him, handing him a quarter. "Joseph, take this quarter to that pay phone. Call the police and tell them what happened. Tell them to send an ambulance and then run. Do not follow me. My path is mine alone. You're better than this – stay that way. I know you probably still think God exists, even after tonight. Belief in God is just an illusion, a myth people cover up with to shield them from the cold while they slowly freeze to death."

270

"All that most maddens and torments; all that stirs up the lees of things; all truth with malice in it; all that cracks the sinews and cakes the brain; all the subtle demonisms of life and thought; all evil, to crazy Ahab, were visibly personified, and made practically assailable in Moby Dick. He piled upon the whale's white hump the sum of all the general rage and hate felt by his whole race from Adam down; and then, as if his chest had been a mortar, he burst his hot heart's shell upon it." – Herman Melville, Moby Dick

Thursday, May 26, 1999 – Early Morning, Buffalo

The faded Buick's engine rattled as they left the city lights of Buffalo in the distance. With no more surprises or delays, in a few hours they would reach the old farmhouse outside Mt. Jewett. At least that was what Victoria had told him. He didn't care much anymore. It was after 2 AM and Sam was beyond exhausted. His legs were still rubbery from that business in Seville; he hadn't gotten any quality sleep for over thirty hours; his nose still burned like fire from being bashed into a metal table; and his forearms had just been forced into servitude sliding a busted, half-ton freight car door. He desperately needed to find a bed and collapse for about five or six days.

Victoria was driving, doing her best to avoid any attention. With any luck, something apparently in short supply, their stolen Buick would survive the journey down highway 219. The road was riddle with small towns and curves through the hilly countryside, but it was far more isolated that any other route. The older model was easier to lift and far less likely to be tracked. Choosing any car from that parking lot had been risky, though. The bar had been just on the other side of the channel from Squaw Island and only a few cars were parked outside.

They had both trekked through the muddy sod of Squaw Island to reach Buffalo proper, and were covered with mud and grass when they arrived. That treacherous leap from the train found soft ground that, due to that night's storms, was soaked through. Sam had landed on his back, but Victoria was not as fortunate. Her face planted square in the mud and her whole front got covered with filth. She found a clean shirt, but had not been so lucky with her pants. Her bag got caught on a stump and ripped, flinging her back-up jeans into its own puddle. She was forced to make do with pajama bottoms that had stayed relatively mud free. Sam was thankful the briefcase and its

271

precious contents remained intact, but the two of them had no way to appear like they belonged outside that bar.

The bar was fairly small with two large windows facing the parking lot. Their theft could have been seen by anyone inside. Sam figured that Victoria was banking on the hope that anyone still in that crappy bar that late on a weeknight would be too blitzed to notice. She could have been right. She was in the car in no time and they were driving away in less than three minutes. Still, there was no way of knowing who might have seen them or if those Vatican agents were still out there somewhere. Sam couldn't see how they could have escaped the Madrid airport, but he knew better than to underestimate their tenacity.

Together, all of this led Sam to the one place he least wanted to be in the world at that time: awake. The rattling engine didn't inspire confidence, yet the Buick continued south. Sam figured talking was probably his best bet to avoid nodding off. He turned to Victoria and asked, "So, what happened between you and this, what was his name, Hector – if you don't mind me asking?"

She smiled a weary, exasperated smile. "Well, about eight years ago, now, I was already in Europe working on my own. My list of contacts had grown with my reputation. If you want the big payouts, you build your reputation through experience and contacts. Anyway, Hector reached out, and I was flattered to get a job from him. He was a big player in Rome and wanted me to make a delivery. It was a huge break, and would likely mean much bigger fish down the road. The package had to go to London. I didn't expect chunnel security to be so exhaustive that day, but my package got tagged by a security sweep and I bailed. Hector reached out to me big time afterwards.

"Things were really rocky at first, but eventually I got accustomed to his style. That was eight years ago, and since then, I've whittled the debt down to something like $40,000 US. I never suspected that he would sabotage a job like he did with your passport. It actually makes me suspicious of the chunnel security back then. Regardless, just need to keep my head clean and get you home safely."

Sam, while relieved Victoria was truly opening up to him, was unsettled that something as precious as his life or the truth he carried could be jeopardized by a single thug's whimsical ploys half a world away. *These documents are the light in the darkness, but that light is so fragile. The slightest breeze could snuff it out in an instant.* He felt his hand reaching down,

272

as if on sheer impulse, making sure his briefcase was still resting beside his mud-covered feet. It was.

The lights and buildings of Buffalo gave way to the timid landscape of suburbia, which in turn, gave way to forested wilderness as they continued southward. Dark outlines of hills and trees framed the blackness overhead. Heavy clouds still lingered above, serving as a grim reminder that the rains could resume at any moment. Sam peered into the blackness and resumed talking without invitation, "I can't believe everything that's happened to me on this trip. I take my first vacation in years and wind up around the world discovering what represents hope for humanity's salvation. I've been trapped and dehydrated, stowed inside a beer truck, almost drowned, beat up by Canadians, and leaped blindly from a moving train. Certainly not what I expected when I left home two weeks ago. Still, I guess nothing good comes without some degree of sacrifice.

One of my toughest cases back home involved a trio of young girls from a really bad home. Their father was nowhere and unknown. When their mother abandoned them, they moved in with their aunt. She was mixed up with all the wrong characters. Those poor girls were exposed to drugs, violence, terrible neglect and malnourishment. You could see the despair on their faces screaming at you through their silent mouths. Sometimes, our system doesn't work the way it should, and that malfunction was happening to them. There was little evidence, and no one was talking. They teach us during training to distance ourselves – to not approach cases with emotion. 'You can't save the world' is one of their mantras they repeat over and over.

"None of that mattered when I saw those girls, that house; when I interviewed the aunt and her boyfriend. I did something in that case that I'd not done before nor since: I doctored the file – made up evidence where none existed. I pushed a button and made something happen. They were rescued from their aunt and placed into foster care. Four years ago now, and I still check on them periodically. They don't even know me, and I never speak to them. Everything I need to know, I get from the way they walk home from school with their friends or how they play with each other outside. I made a difference, but it cost me. Several months later, the case file was tagged for review. When they discovered the discrepancy, there was no way to prove who doctored the file, but everyone knew. I didn't get in trouble, but I've been passed over for promotion three times since then, and will probably never move ahead. My boss won't say more than five words to me at a time, and I

273

still sometimes hear whispers fall silent when I enter a room. Do I regret my choice? Not for a second. It was a price that needed to . . ."

Victoria cut Sam off without uttering a sound. Her face changed abruptly, as though she were straining, grasping for something with her thoughts she had only just now realized was missing. Sam stopped abruptly when he caught the change in her expression. Victoria, after all, had far better instincts for sensing danger. He turned the car radio off and waited silently for her response. Booming silence filled the car; only the rattling of their engine disturbed the night. Seconds became minutes before she rolled down her window and tilted her head slightly outward.

"Here. Take the wheel for a moment, would you?"

Without a word, Sam reached over and began steering. The road was fairly straight just then, so it wasn't challenging. He looked over at Victoria. *Her eyes are closed! What is she doing? If she's praying, so help me . . .*

Victoria opened her eyes. "Sam, we're being followed. Our Catholic friends are far more clever than we thought – clever *and* dedicated. Not sure why they are so hell-bent on getting their hands on you, but this devotion is beyond anything I've ever seen!"

"Wait a minute. I can't hear anything. I don't see anything either – just darkness. What do you think you heard?"

Sam felt the car speed up as the engine rattled harder and more frequently, melding into a loud hum. "Sam, I can train my senses to dim. It's a gift I've had for a long time. When I turn off my sight, my smell and touch, my hearing improves. I can do the same for sight and smell. Beyond this beastly engine and the whine of our bald tires against the asphalt, I heard something – something unnatural. I focused, and am pretty sure it's a helicopter. Helicopters have no business flying this late with such terrible visibility. They're most likely stalking our headlights. In this darkness, it would be easy . . ."

Victoria stopped mid-sentence to stick her head out for a second and look to the night sky behind them. "There!" She screamed through the air slamming against her before ducking back inside. "I saw them – two pairs of red lights over our left shoulder. Too many trees out here for a chopper to land. They've got someone on the ground. Our Vatican friends are probably following some distance behind in a car. We can lose the chopper easily enough. Just need to run dark."

Victoria relieved Sam of the steering wheel. "Run *dark*? Is that what you just said? In this blackness? Are you crazy?!"

"Sam, hold on," was her response. Victoria flicked the headlights off and the silhouette of trees framing the night sky vanished instantly. There was nothing but black. Victoria sped up for five, ten, twenty seconds, and Sam felt his fingers digging into the leather seat. They were clearly in new territory – a sudden curve and they would simply veer off plowing into the forest. Anything in the road, stalled car, stray cow or debris, could be a death sentence. Sam closed his eyes in terror. Moments later, he felt it: they were slowing. *Thank God!* Sam opened his eyes as the car came to rest. They were safe and resting comfortably on the shoulder.

*　　　*　　　*

Thursday, May 26, 1999 – Early Morning, Northern Pennsylvania

"Gentlemen, I think we've got them. They just turned left onto a Mt. Alton road heading east toward the prison, assuming I'm reading this infernal atlas right!" Haygoode's exasperated voice cracked over the radio. They were all wiped out for that matter. Lukas had last awakened from real sleep over thirty hours ago and time continued stretching. After reaching the U.S. checkpoint well ahead of the train, Haygoode, rather than simply refueling and returning home, helped check out the train. In fact, Haygoode noticed that open freight car four cars ahead of their inspection detail. Two scissor jacks wedged against the frame, clearly confiscated from the Ford's inside, revealed how Sam had pried the massive door. That open door also evidenced that Sam and his helper had escaped.

Just as Alfons had finished thanking the American inspection team, the call came in: auto theft from a local bar in Buffalo echoed from a nearby police radio. Lukas thought little of it until overhearing Alfons' thick German accent ask where that bar was located. When they discovered how close the bar was to the rail bridge, they knew they had their quarry. It took time arranging a car. Fortunately, Haygoode leaped into action to find and tail them as far as he could from above. He could guide them later.

Alfons plead with the rail inspectors and local police for a car, but none of them were interested despite his urgency. Haygoode, yet again, came to their aid. While in flight, he woke up a cousin living nearby and convinced him to drive over. That cousin wasn't nearly devout a Catholic as Haygoode, and demanded a considerable cash payment before handing over the keys.

275

Eventually, it had worked out and they drove that cousin's blue GMC pick-up from the freight yard and into the desolate streets of Buffalo.

Ammorette had apparently been spot on as it seemed they were, in fact, heading straight for Mt. Jewett, Pennsylvania, after all. She had called earlier while they waited on Haygoode's cousin. Though Lukas couldn't hear Ammorette's end of the conversation, he knew something good had happened by the extremely rare smile forming along the edges of Alfons' tight lips. Once he hung up, Alfons explained Ammorette's brilliance. Using Sam's companion's passport photo, Ammorette ran a photo recognition search against recent female passport photos in Europe and North America. It was a terrible long shot. The field of potential photos was immense, and photos made for a slow, arduous search. Even worse, their target was an expert at disguise: skin complexion, hair and other features could vary wildly. Ammorette, however, spotted something on the rental car paperwork: a smudged signature. It reminded her of those made by left handed people with messy pens, smudging the text to the right while dragging their left hand across. Using some exotic filters and databases that tracked that sort of thing she narrowed her search drastically. She soon found a second photo recently used in Poland and a third from Ireland before that, each with different names. Afterwards, it had taken only simple deduction using Interpol databases. As it turns out, criminals tend to make mistakes early on before they master their craft. In Victoria Sawyer's case, a handful of early arrest records betrayed her true name. That name appeared in the Pennsylvania real estate records as a joint owner of an old farmhouse on a few acres outside Mt. Jewett.

Though Lukas was still shocked that databases existed tracking whether we are right or left-hand, Alfons seemed practically jubilant as he headed south. His jubilation stretched only a few moments, however, as quiet solitude again draped over them and the weight of exhaustion resumed exacting its toll. Haygoode, once given a destination, spotted the pale Buick sailing down the highway like a white whale thrashing across a dark ocean. Outside the city, it had become far simpler to merely track their headlamps than the car itself.

Alfons and Lukas made good time, remaining only thirty to forty minutes behind. Lukas struggled to stay awake in the passenger seat. Victoria would not likely let Sam or those papers go without a fight, and he needed to remain vigilant. Suddenly, the radio crackled alive with alarm. It was Haygoode in the night sky far ahead of them. "I've lost them, buddies! They

276

just went dark for no reason! It's awfully dark down there already, and with them keeping to small roads between the trees, I can't track them without their headlights. Pretty reckless for them. They were going sixty-five on that road when they went dark. They couldn't see anything that way either, so they may have run into the woods by now. Want me to hover a bit and see what happens?"

Alfons picked up the handset, "No. You have done a remarkable service for your Church and God. You cannot be thanked enough for everything already. I gave you our office number earlier. Use it. Ask for Ammorette – you probably spoke with her earlier. Find a safe place to land and find an open hotel. Ammorette will make arrangements for you to be reimbursed for everything. Might I add, you are one of the best helicopter pilots I have ever seen, and as a former officer of the Swiss military, I assure you, that *is* a compliment. Good night to you, sir."

"Got it. You pals drive safe and mind yourself. It's been an honor." With that, the radio went silent. *Why turn out the headlights? Did she hear Haygoode's bird overhead? No. He would not get that close. Something tipped them off, though. Pity, they will be waiting for us, now.* Lukas had taken considerable comfort knowing their mission lay in secrecy and might be resolved peacefully by taking them unaware. Sam and Victoria now knew they were coming, leaving them only two choices – keep running or hide and fight, if necessary – neither inspired Lukas.

He turned to Alfons who was speeding up a bit, likely hoping to close the distance between them. "Begging all pardon, Mein Herr. Are we being smart here? She knows we're following her, and we are beyond tired. Chasing this elusive prey for so long is taking its toll."

"Mr. Dietrich, I know you are tired. I, too, am exhausted. We have not yet been this close to our goal. I smell victory in the night air. These manuscripts were stolen under dark of night from the Church forty years ago, and though we kept them from going public, we failed to recover them. Seldom do we have a chance to remove a past stain, but such an opportunity is at hand."

"It is not victory or stain removal that worries me, with all respect. It is safety. If we corner this rat, will it fight or cower in fear? If there is to be a fight, I fear that, at least as to myself, I would be prone to error. Errors with guns drawn create far worse stains."

277

Lukas noticed Alfons' grip on the wheel tighten. He responded slowly and almost in a whisper. "We have been dragged and beaten by this 'Victoria' person too often. She is an expert, Mr. Dietrich. Do you realize what that means? If we pause; if we rest; if we succumb to that all too comfortable human desire to sleep, Sam will vanish. Sure, in a few days he will be back working in California, but by then those documents will be somewhere far beyond our reach."

"Mein Herr, I do not disagree. My suggestion, however, is that perhaps our safety should take priority over the recovery of old manuscripts. You mentioned faith earlier. Where is your faith, now? Have you no confidence that God will make plans to thwart these documents in His own time?"

Alfons raised his voice considerably as he fired back with uncharacteristic emotion. "Mr. Dietrich, you ignorant neophyte, God *has* made plans! *His* plan is for US to recover those documents! It is not His will for us to pursue our prey around the world only to surrender once we draw close simply because we are tired! If you desire sleep so much, by all means, take your leave!" Alfons pointed to the door as he concluded, "We are the dividing line. We are the safety net. It is OUR job to ensure God's will on Earth gets executed. It is for OTHERS to have FAITH that WE will succeed. You question *my* faith? My faith is not based on God making an *alternate* plan, but, rather, for Him to give me the strength and alertness to complete *this* one."

Lukas knew to remain silent. Alfons' eyes mirrored his soul and Lukas had seen that reflection before. He knew monomaniacal behavior would suffer no challengers. Alfons, for all his efforts remaining calm and emotionless and all his brilliant observations and deductions, had exposed a vital flaw: delusions of grandeur. Lukas remembered Alfons' referring to himself as the Hand of God on Earth when he was recruited. Back then it had seemed so noble, but now, seeing its true, ugly meaning unleashed, it had become something else entirely. This mad, illogical devotion made Lukas sick. *I only hope his tenacity compensates for his exhaustion in the end.*

The road stretched onward and they followed, until eventually Alfons made the same left Haygoode had mentioned before the enemy's lights went dark. They were now headed toward Lafayette, Pennsylvania – a small town, barely worth being labeled on the map. The road was curvy enough to cause concern. *If they flew through here without headlights, they could be wrapped around a tree. We need to keep a good watch for any signs of wreckage.*

278

Alfons must have been thinking the same thing as he spent more time looking out the side window than minding the road. At best, they were now merely twenty minutes behind and any wreckage only twenty minutes old would leave fresh signs everywhere. However, no signs of wreckage appeared. Soon enough, they drove into Lafayette and out of it just as quickly. No white Buicks were in sight. They were forced to press on. This road eventually intersected with another that supposedly led to Victoria's farm house.

With each passing mile, Alfons grew more and more uncharacteristically agitated. Lukas understood. Each mile devoid signs of that white Buick narrowed their options. Once reaching the farmhouse, if there was no sign of them, this pursuit was over. This was their last lead and Victoria had proven far too resourceful to continue embarrassing themselves with further requests. This was their final breath, and Alfons allowed his frustration to show as he struggled against exhaustion, fatigue and the relentless darkness.

Without any warning whatsoever, Alfons suddenly slammed on the brakes and they screeched to a grinding halt. Lukas, half asleep himself, was jerked into the seatbelt across his chest and feared for his life momentarily. "What happened?" Lukas exclaimed.

"A whitetail deer. Just there grazing alongside the road. You saw it, yes?"

"I saw something, but was preoccupied searching for Buicks. Are we to hunt deer now as well?"

Aflons, ignoring Lukas' obvious sarcasm, explained "Those deer have been hunted relentlessly for centuries. Evolution has bred them to be extremely skittish and nervous. That one spirited away as fast as she could once she caught our scent." Lukas' expression must have betrayed his confusion. "We have missed something, you see. That deer would not be casually grazing here if any Buick had come through here in the last half hour. Humans, especially while driving our fume emitting cars, emanate a unique, distinct scent. Animals, particularly those as keen as a deer, know not to mindlessly idle anywhere our scent lingers. Our missing Buick turned from this road at some point earlier."

Lukas was astounded. *How can he still be so observant? I did not even see the deer, but he noticed not only its species, but also that it was a doe. Wonder if his hunch will pan out or if he has resorted to jumping at shadows.*

279

"Interesting, Mein Herr," was all Lukas could offer, as Alfons spun around and slowly drove back the way they'd come.

Alfons drove slowly, at least slower than before. In the end it was Alfons that saw them: tracks of wet, flattened grass heading into the brush alongside the edge of the road – the side Lukas should have been watching on the way up. A quick inspection found neither wreck nor passengers. Something certainly happened to them or the car, but they had no time for an audit. It was vindication enough for Alfons to have found the poorly hidden car under some brush. Lukas read the smug satisfaction on his face. Regardless, both of them knew what was to follow. Lukas grabbed their flashlights from the truck – relics from the one pit stop Alfons had afforded them.

*   *   *

Thursday, May 26, 1999 – Early Morning, Northern Pennsylvania

Out of gas. Out of gas. Out of damn gas! Sam couldn't believe his horrible luck. They survived Victoria's death race through the dark without a scratch, but now with Victoria's grandparent's old farmhouse only minutes away, the old Buick sputtered before dying completely. Sam was so tired. It took nearly everything in him to help push the white hulk off of the road and into the underbrush. It wasn't hidden well, but ultimately there wasn't time to do more. At least in the brush, there was a chance their pursuers would pass it by entirely.

He had thought pushing the heavy Buick through wet grass was difficult, but what followed was far more onerous. It wasn't too terribly bad at the outset. He toted his briefcase while following Victoria. She had insisted they walk single file to mask their trail, but Sam, from a quick glance behind, could see their trail easily. Soggy grass they trampled underfoot as they went betrayed them to any caring to look. *We might as well be wearing orange road crew jackets and waving our arms.* There were few alternatives, however. Had they stayed with the car, they would have been easily captured. Along the road, their trek would take infinitely longer than cutting across country. Hiding, hoping for danger to pass only guaranteed those Vatican goons would close to within a few feet and their chances of staying awake sitting still like that were slim.

Walking cross country wasn't particularly difficult. Difficult began a couple of miles later when they reached some railroad tracks atop a small embankment. Victoria explained that the tracks were their road now and would lead them within a mile of the farmhouse. She then made a petty attempt to throw off their pursuers by tramping forward through the grass a few hundred feet before backtracking. Sam didn't see how that bought them any time.

Victoria had explained the premise to him afterwards, "They won't know which direction on the tracks we've taken because they don't know our destination. A trail leading away from the tracks altogether gives those two agents three choices. With luck, the confusion will force a discussion of their plans– buying us more time. When one of them hikes out there only to have his trail go cold, that might cause more confusion. By the time they piece it together, they will have to circle back and try again. Our five minute delay could cost them half an hour of confusion. Also, don't forget. You know how tired you are?"

Sam nodded in silent agreement.

"Well, they are just as tired – maybe even more. We know where we're going, but they are stuck following our bread crumbs. Trailing someone, even someone driving a monstrous white Buick takes energy."

Almost immediately, the train tracks proved challenging. It was pitch dark and their only light was a tiny flashlight that Victoria carried. *I guess it took so long to grab a pistol, she only had enough time for one flashlight.* Sam stopped before souring his mood too much. Victoria was still wearing pajama bottoms soaked through with sweat and moisture from the tall grass. Also, to be fair, she had not planned on hiking cross-country. Had she not picked up their tail earlier, they would have likely stopped for gas. Regardless, he struggled on the tracks. Slight changes in elevation between rails, ties and gravel were difficult to predict in the black and he found himself stumbling often. Worse still, there were two sets of rails here, side by side. A second set of rails had been laid at some point, though no one had removed the first. His toes were sore and he needed sleep desperately. But all of that melted away immediately being replaced by sheer terror of a kind he'd never encountered before.

The gravel between the rail ties gave way to nothingness as the earth opened up ahead of them. The ground alongside the track descended, but the track itself stayed level. *A trestle!* From the feel of things it wasn't a mild one either. Sam gripped his briefcase tighter and tried keeping close to Victoria. His heartbeat raced as he felt himself climb. Though drained from exhaustion, he was no longer sleepy. He took a breath. Victoria called out, "Keep in the middle, between the rails! This is the Kinzua Rail Bridge and it's for real! You

281

wouldn't see anything anyway, but DO NOT look down!" Sam let a nervous chuckle escape as he promptly looked down. *Who is more foolish, the person that looks down after being warned, or the idiot warning them, knowing it's the first thing someone does when told not to.* The wooden ties were still wet from earlier rain and keeping atop them was a delicate matter. There were no handrails spanning the chasm. He would have to manage this on his own. Step by treacherous step, he pecked his way forward, clutching the briefcase to his chest as he went. Shortly, the ground disappeared altogether. A hint of moonlight struggled to peek around a few dark billows overhead, and Victoria's tiny flashlight beam bounced about several feet ahead. She tried staying close, but he was going far slower than she was. Sam wasn't generally afraid of heights, but this – this was an altogether different matter.

Further and further out he climbed, one daring step at a time. The air was still, and the emptiness overwhelming. Even without seeing the ground, he sensed the vastness of the chasm below. The moist air around him was cool to his shaved head, but afforded him no comfort. They were extremely high above the ground, and Sam was thankful Victoria hadn't told him exactly how high. He was now a circus performer with no audience – walking a tightrope between skyscrapers while wearing a blindfold, without a net. He tried breathing slowly. It didn't help. With each exhale, the emptiness around him pierced his conscious, reminding him of his impossible predicament.

The minutes stretched as he continued slowly working his way across. Victoria would periodically wait for him to catch her up or turn around and shine the tiny light on his path for a few moments. It helped when she did that – not only with finding his footing on the cross ties, but as the slightest reminder that he wasn't utterly alone. But those interludes were sparse – brief moments of trivial comfort, like eating a decadent, scrumptious cookie while attending a loved one's wake. He made as few sounds as possible. Even a cough or a yawn would echo in its own way, forcing the gravity of his situation back upon him. There was no way of knowing how much further remained or exactly how high up he was, but none of that mattered ultimately. The trestle would end when it ended, and he would again find solid ground. For now though, only his briefcase and silent breaths of still night air kept him company.

Sam made it about two thirds of the way across, though he had no way of knowing that, when the unthinkable happened. Wind. A light gust swept across their path breaking his focus and he staggered. "Aaaaggh!" He cried out trying to regain his footing.

282

Victoria spun around shining the light on him. "Hold on! I'm coming." She hurriedly tried getting back to him, but she wasn't fast enough. He was off balance and couldn't regain stability. He extended his right foot to the tie in front of him, in hopes that spreading his legs apart might afford him more balance. That should have worked, but his foot slipped and instead of flat atop the crosstie, landed at an angle. He faltered, and crumpled down hard on the tracks. He couldn't hear Victoria coming as he screamed out in intense pain. Though still atop the trestle, a miracle in its own right, his right ankle had gotten caught and twisted between the two sets of rails. The searing pain was immense, but he dared not move for fear of toppling over into the bottomless pitch below.

Sam was facing down, looking between ties, into the blackness. There was no hint of the valley floor beneath him, nor even the tops of the tall pines littering the countryside. His eyes watered with pain as he lay there helplessly clutching the briefcase with one hand and the metal rail with the other. Victoria was soon upon him. "Don't move! Don't move!" She screamed into the night air.

Sam had no intention of moving nor even knew if he could move had he wanted to. "Am I on the edge?"

Victoria leaned down, "Not completely. Is something hurt?"

While he dared not look into her face, he could tell from her abnormally calm tone how dangerously close to the edge of the trestle he must have truly been. "My right ankle. I twisted it up bad."

"OK. Hang on to what you've got. Give me the briefcase."

Sam handed it over with some reticence. She knelt down on one knee, cradling the flashlight between her neck and shoulders. She then sat the briefcase down gingerly with her backpack on top, probably to keep it from blowing off. "Sam. The hand you were holding the briefcase with – use it to grab the rail closest to your butt. Feel for it without rocking the rest of your body at all."

He complied and, sure enough, found the track she mentioned.

"Good, hold on tight. I'm going to move you closer to the center now. Let me know the second this hurts, OK?" She placed her hands on his chest and rocked him toward the center of the trestle, between the rails. His body moved some until he tried adjusting. The pain hit then – once the range of motion reached that right ankle.

"Christ! Stop!" Sam shouted.

"Alright, I see the ankle now. We've got to free it from between those rails. I need you to close your eyes and trust me. It will hurt. Ready?"

Sam nodded, mentally preparing himself for the worst. He felt her hands gently reach around and grab his ankle. Slowly and steadily she began sliding it free. Her simple touch and light pressure on his ankle seared and burned, sending fresh waves of pain through him. He winced, poorly masking the hurt in front of Victoria.

Victoria must have sensed his agony, however, as she whispered, "OK. You're free." She rolled him over onto his back and guided him away from the edge and back to the center of the trestle. She rolled up his wet pant leg before offering. "Good news. It doesn't look broken, but don't put any pressure on it. This changes things a bit. There's no way we walk all the way to the farmhouse now. Way too far with me helping you hobble along. We'll have to hole up in the old warehouse. We can't stay out here. Bad things could come down the tracks any minute. We've been moving pretty slowly, and they could be right on top of us. So, I've got the briefcase and the backpack. I'll hold the flashlight between my teeth and help you along, but we're going to have to do this together. Lean on me for support. Remember, keep weight off of that ankle. Let's go."

With that, she hoisted him up. Sam kept trying to mask the pain stabbing through him with each step while focusing on stepping safely. It was easier with the light and Victoria carrying the briefcase, but slower. She was right, they had likely lost considerable time pecking their way across this thing. Eventually, he felt the emptiness around him shrinking. Later, he could make out the outline of tree tops contrasting against the night sky. Those dark silhouettes continued growing until he saw it – ground ahead. "How far to the warehouse, now?" Sam tried focusing on anything but the intense ache of his ankle.

"If it were daylight, you could see it. It's just ahead. Come on. Keep going."

The two of them limped along following the train tracks through the night until at last they reached the ruin. The building had fallen into decay and abandon. Vines and shrubbery had covered its bulk and had to be cut back until finding a door she could pry open. They stepped inside, Sam still hugging Victoria's shoulder, like foxes mindlessly clawing their way from the madness of a painful and unforgiving forest into the warm embrace of a hunter's snare.

"The life-giving earth crashed around in burning, and the vast wood crackled loud with fire all about. All the land seethed, and Ocean's streams and the unfruitful sea. The hot vapour lapped round the earthborn Titans: flame unspeakable rose to the bright upper air: the flashing glare of the thunder-stone and lightning blinded their eyes for all that, they were strong." – The Theogony by Hesiod

Thursday, May 26, 1999 – Pre-Dawn

Mildew's stink filled the air. Old machine parts, decayed and ruined, littered the warehouse floor. The warehouse was large though, Alfons noticed, apparently once a distribution center for farming equipment. Time had helped rain and the elements wriggle their way inside through the broken, dilapidated roof. Sam and Victoria were inside awaiting them; there was no doubt of that. A heavy, rust coated mowing blade, propped against the warehouse door, echoed a booming crash into the pavement when Lukas swung the door open, alerting the entire countryside of their arrival. *Clever*, Alfons had thought as his eyes strained to refocus in this new, even darker abyss.

That pitch darkness was a tremendous liability. Using flashlights would paint targets on their backs, while remaining in the dark invited injury – potentially life-threatening ones. With their ears still ringing from the makeshift alarm, he had scanned the interior with his flashlight. *Right now, it matters little if someone sees our light.* Once inside, however, Alfons sternly warned Lukas of the flashlight's danger and to only use it in the direst of need. He also shared with him how to aim the light downward retaining as much stealth as possible. *If we leave here without those documents, they are lost to us*, he had thought to himself as he stepped through the door.

He had immediately dispatched Lukas to the far other end of the warehouse. The strategy was to pincer Sam and Victoria between them and methodically tighten the noose until there could be no escape. He had noticed, however, a potential weakness in his plan: the warehouse mid-section was composed of freestanding racks – metal shelves over twelve feet high chocked full of boxes, parts and old odds and ends. Should Sam and Victoria cower amongst those racks, they could merely wait for him and Lukas to head down the wrong aisle and simply slip through the snare. *If they*

285

managed it quietly, we would not know of their escape until we had scoured the entire place clean.

The warehouse roof was in such ruin that entire sections of its membrane had rotted away over time, exposing the dark canopy of night. Alfons had just began his slow march to meet Lukas in the center when the heavy billows in the night sky began breaking up, revealing the bright moon they had masked all night long. Moonlight reflected through holes in the roof, barely illuminating the warehouse. It was enough light to reveal something that had escaped him earlier: a wrought-iron catwalk ringing the perimeter like a halo around the warehouse core. He had no way of knowing if it had retained its integrity over the years, but from up there Alfons could oversee huge sections of the warehouse floor at once, creating an opportune vantage point from which to strike.

He heard faint noises in the distance. *Could be anything. Our presence here is bound to send wildlife scurrying. Must be careful not to jump at every simple flutter.* Alfons made for the closest catwalk ladder; always slowly and methodically, ensuring no one was hiding nearby. This entire search reeked of the improbable. Both he and Lukas were beyond tired and the precious scant rays of moonlight were of limited help. Though Alfons needed to stay positive and focused, as he stepped over a collection of rancid and decaying boxes, his memories betrayed him.

Memories of Copenhagen suddenly rushed to his mind. *This will not be a repeat of Copenhagen.* That warehouse in Copenhagen so long ago was quite different to be sure. It was active – with electricity and a solid roof. Exhaustion had not been an issue then either. He and his younger partner, Frederich, had gotten a solid night's sleep the night before. Still, far too many things echoed back to Copenhagen for his comfort. This same layout and strategy – splitting up trying to corner foes in the middle – had failed miserably then. No one anticipated a third gang member. The subtle 'pop' when that knife pierced young Frederich's lungs still haunted him. He had seen it coming, though he had tried desperately over the years to convince himself that nothing could have been done. That is what he wrote in the file after all, but it was a lie. He could have made a sound, any noise to alert Freidrich of the looming shadow behind him. His own cover would have been blown, and the mission would be scrapped – something he could not allow.

His angry words to Lukas earlier stood as his defense. *Why can not this younger group understand? We are the thin line. If we fail, abandon a*

286

mission, or go nighty-night just because we get sleepy, God's work remains unfinished. Where was their dedication – their commitment? Commitment had never been Alfons' weakness. He could chase the devil back to the gates of hell if necessary, without ever stopping for a drink. His commitment triggered the Copenhagen job's fall into ruin. He had succeeded – recovered the stolen artwork, but when he emerged from that warehouse, he did so alone. Guilt still tugged at the corners of his mind. He told himself, *it is just emotion.* Alfons could deal with emotion. Shove it away. Beat it down. Focus on the mission. There would always be time for emotion afterward. Hopefully, if that time ever came, some quality rum would be on hand to drench them before their smoldering embers ignited.

He was still shoving Copenhagen from his exhausted mind when he reached the catwalk's iron ladder and grabbed ahold. He had heard no more sounds – nothing from Lukas or their prey. *This is not Copenhagen.* The ladder felt old; its weathered metal cold against his palms, but also solid. It was from a time when things were built for longevity and not necessarily by the cheapest bidder. Alfons began climbing; slowly, stopping on each rung to listen, hoping his ascent would go unnoticed. Rung after rung, he eventually reached the landing. With sweaty palms, he rubbed swollen eyes, ignoring his body's pleas for rest.

A bulky air compressor shielded him from anyone hiding amongst those racks but also blocked his line of sight. To be of much use, he had to circle around. Alfons crept forward. While sturdy, the walk was old and creaked. Only painstakingly slow steps would mask his movement. Anything faster would announce his presence as subtly as screaming through a bull horn. *Where is Lukas? He should have reached those metal racks by now. I should have heard something, unless . . .*

She is lying in wait! Lukas is walking into a trap, and I am helpless without knowing where they are hiding! Just as he cleared the air compressor, he saw it! A quick flickering of light from between two racks – mere rows ahead. *I have you!* He turned to see Lukas cautiously walking alongside the racks below, checking each row as he went. Fear strangled Alfons' indifferent and driven heart. Lukas would reach Victoria before Alfons could corner her from behind. *This cannot be!* He studied the impossible situation with the same cold, calculating exactness he approached most everything. Alfons had to react, and he had to react now. If he stayed true, he would have her, but not before likely losing Lukas. If he rushed her from behind, he would betray his position.

This is not Copenhagen! Blood rushed recklessly through his veins. One true path remained. He stormed forward in a blind rage. Mentally and physically exhausted, anger and hostility pulsed through him like flood waters through a ruptured dike. His steps pounded against the metal walk, shattering the stillness. He raced forward and turned to take the shot. It was too late. She was ready. He saw the flash from her gun barrel before he raised his weapon.

The single gunshot boomed – a solitary clap of thunder flooding the building! Dark blood splashed as the bullet pierced his chest. Alfons reeled backward against the handrails, but they buckled under the pressure, and he toppled twenty feet into the concrete slab below. He gazed up at the sky overhead. He was so cold, but not for long. It was over. He felt no pain. He was no longer tired. Then, there was no moonlight and no darkness. A brilliant white light filled the corners of his vision, closing toward the center. Though he had failed the mission, he had not failed his partner.

*   *   *

Thursday, May 26, 1999 – Pre-Dawn

Run! Just run! Victoria desperately needed to understand what just happened, but knew better than to stand idly by. She had to remain utterly focused. *Keep running!* Her hiding spot behind that stack of rusted tractor wheels had been perfect – for someone approaching the front. She had been crouching, gun drawn, waiting for a clear shot. She had no intention of killing anyone – a simple leg shot would have sufficed. She had hidden amongst rows of shelving in the warehouse center, fashioned in aisles like an abandoned grocery store. She had even heard the first agent; walking, looking down each aisle before moving on. Her plan was perfect. But everything changed when hushed silence was drowned by the sudden heavy pounding of feet thundering on approach from behind. She couldn't cover both front and rear simultaneously, and she could have been in both their sights at the same instant.

Victoria had chosen and faced the excessively loud threat from behind. He came into view, and she fired without hesitation. Later she could ponder her choice's morality. If his partner arrived just then, she would make an easy target. *Run!* She sprinted in a dead heat, making a hard left toward the outer wall, hoping she didn't trip on some random part or debris littering the floor. So far, she had been fortunate. The warehouse was cavernous, and she had a

288

treacherous several hundred feet to the outer wall and temporary safety. She heard noises behind her between breaths. *No time for noises – run!* The dark outer wall loomed high in front of her as she finally reached its edge.

Victoria's legs were jelly from exhaustion and anxious tension. She wasn't a killer, though she had killed before. Killing is to admit failure. A smuggler smuggles. They don't wade in with guns blazing. These tenacious Vatican goons had cornered her. She paused, listening for footsteps. *Nothing – at least nothing close. That second agent is seeing to his partner. That's probably not going to go well.* Victoria's mind echoed the splattering of fresh blood when her shot pierced that agent dead in the chest. It was a clean shot, especially for a moving target, and threw his center of gravity – toppling him from the catwalk. The shot, coupled with that fall, meant certain death. *Keep running!*

She hugged the curved outer wall as it bent back toward the far end of the building, not stopping until she had reached the end. She panted, trying to regain her breath. She crawled underneath the hulk of a decrepit tractor and turned to face whatever might emerge from the darkness. Despite the descending mottled moonlight, she saw nothing, though her doom could be out there, just beyond the edge of sight.

Her gun was drawn, but nothing appeared. As she waited with nervous anticipation, her mind wandered to places she didn't care to visit. *The agent I shot. Why make so much noise? He had managed to sneak up on that catwalk and circle around without me hearing a thing. I should have heard him. He was clearly an expert. Why then tromp around like a horse, unless . . . Ohh . . . He wanted me to hear him. He knew where I was? It's possible – from up there, he could have seen my shadow or something. Ahh . . . he sacrificed himself to save his partner! By drawing my fire, his partner lives.* That terrible truth struck home inside her in a new way. She was merely the blunt instrument striking a man down for daring to spare his partner. Guilt could never hold sway over her for long, though. *Had I not shot, he certainly would have. The blood is on their hands – not mine!*

Minutes ticked away with Victoria sensing nothing. So, she slid from underneath the tractor to plan her next move. The dilemma was simple in her mind. The agent who had just lost his partner will be emotional. *Emotional and tired: a deadly combination. He'll seek vengeance. There's no way that agent doesn't seek some sort of retribution for his dead partner. He's coming for me. He heard me sprinting away and knows I'm back here. Problem is:*

289

"back here" is a death trap – a wide, open area with no decent cover. That tractor was the only object of any size around. She could either retreat to the back corner or stay out here in the open with no way to cover her blind spots. The impenetrable darkness of the warehouse was bitter-sweet, making her harder to find while simultaneously making it impossible to strike back.

Victoria fumbled about, not daring to use her tiny flashlight. The random debris scattered about the warehouse floor might help if she kept quiet. She could possibly arrange a couple of traps, nothing powerful or sophisticated enough to stop a pursuer, but perhaps she could force him to reveal his location. "Stopping" him would be up to her. She got to work. For starters, she noticed several old wooden pallets. She arranged them to form a makeshift pill box for herself. It had gaps, but it minimized any lines of attack. They were rotted through and had to be moved gently or risk falling rotted planks echoing on the concrete floor. It was slow going, but eventually she had a hiding place. Now, there were three potential danger zones. She could focus straight ahead, but would need help guarding her flanks.

Sound would be her first champion. If the enemy made noise, she would be ready for him, but it had to be subtle. Too loud, and he'd know what happened and retreat. It needed to be loud enough to hear but not so loud as to spook the poor chap. *Something small – something small,* she thought to herself as she fumbled about the warehouse floor. The floor's scattered remains stood as a tragic memorial to a more prosperous past. Loose parts and pieces could be found littered about, but nothing easily moveable – until she noticed a box bathed in moonlight. It was, as luck would have it, full of bolts of varying sizes, riddled with rust and aged filth. This was not the time to be dainty, however. She quietly littered the area far to the left with bolts, in hopes that anyone coming would shuffle them around just enough.

Shadow would be her other champion. Her tiny flashlight was just barely strong enough to be useful. An overhead metal beam and a length of bailing wire were all she needed to rig the light up high on her right flank. From that angle, anyone approaching would cast a subtle, but detectable shadow. She drew her pistol and nestled in.

Waiting was stressful. Soon, though not soon enough, conflict would visit her again, and only she or that agent would walk away. She heard her heart pulsing, felt the cold grip of the pistol against her palms. Victoria kept a level head in most situations, but squatting alone in the darkness, knowing

290

someone was coming to kill her, wore on her nerves. She could curse and grumble, but when all her cursing and grumbling were done, she would still be right there in soggy pajama pants, sandwiched between pieces of rotten wood, her revolver trained into the cold, empty blackness.

Time stretched, testing her patience. Having heard nothing, her mind began playing games. *Is he still back there, mourning? Is he setting his own traps for me? Would be awkward – both of us waiting for an attacker that is not coming. Did he abandon or call for help?* She could shut down and strain for distant sounds, but that meant closing her eyes, rendering her defenseless. *Maybe – just a quick listen.*

Victoria shut her eyes, and the world around her shrunk. She was no longer in a warehouse, but a tomb. All was still: no movement; no rats scurrying by, no birds overhead, and no cautious footsteps approaching from the shadows. She reached out, trying harder – still nothing. But, then again, it wasn't the typical sound of nothing, but a peculiar artificial nothingness, like radio static playing softly in the distance. It was not close by, but felt nearer to . . . *the offices! Sam's hiding in those offices!* Her confidence melted as she opened her eyes, peering toward the front. Her heart pounded harder and faster. *This, this trap – this whole damn contraption I've built, was for nothing. He's not coming for me at all – he's headed straight for Sam and those damn documents!*

*   *   *

Thursday, May 26, 1999 – Pre-Dawn

So much blood! The image of Alfons' broken body shattered on the floor, soaked through with blood, flooded his thoughts despite Lukas' best efforts to shove it aside. He had seen blood before, though never quite so much at once, but something else haunted him. Bathed in pale moonlight and the greenish hue from Lukas' flashlight, Alfons' blood was not crimson as expected; rather, it appeared a desolate, milky gray. Seeing his partner saturated in horrific, gray blood filled him with surprising horror. Though beyond exhausted, fresh adrenaline raced through him as he checked Alfons' pulse.

That was over fifteen minutes ago, but each time that image slammed into place, he suffered the tragedy once again. He was alone now in this desolation, and one of these two had taken his partner. Though less than three weeks had passed since being recruited, life before seemed blurry. His military service and all his Vatican training were fading echoes of yesterday;

291

like memories of events from a movie, instead of his own life. The one thing that truly felt comfortable was his new found isolation. Though constantly surrounded by people, Lukas had been alone his whole life – never truly fitting in: in school, the military, not even in the Swiss Guard.

At first impression, the Swiss Guard program had seemed a perfect match: long hours at attention, never worrying about what to say or avoid saying. He had forfeited such blasé comfort for this rare chance to do something magnificent, to somehow make a difference. Rather than quaintly inserting a square peg into a square hole where it would be subdued and of no further consequence, Lukas opted for more. That dismal blood pouring from his partner might have shattered all those aspirations, however. If he returned to Vatican City, he might well discover he was no longer wanted. He would not make a difference; he would not matter; he would likely no longer even qualify as a square peg.

He tried pushing those fears aside and focusing – to work out his next move in this deadly chess game. His first impulse had been to run after those footsteps sprinting away into the darkness; find out who they belonged to and steal from them what they had stolen. But those heated words from Alfons in the truck rushed back as he towered over his broken body, *"We are God's plan."* Alfons would never condone mindless vengeance. Had Lukas taken that bullet, Alfons would not blindly pursue his shooter into the dark unknown. He would stay on mission, retrieve those documents, and fulfill God's will.

When they first entered the warehouse, Alfons had directed Lukas to the far end. That section was flat and open with little cover – mostly just loose debris. Alfons' shooter was down there now, alone. Only one pair of footsteps sprinted into the void. *His* target was no killer. *His* target would not be there. *His* target was tucked away somewhere secure. *If not here, and not exposed on the far end, Sam was either cowering amongst the center racks or nestled away in the office area along the eastern side.* The offices were the most logical. They would keep Sam from any unnecessary chance of accident, allowing Victoria the freedom to shoot anything moving.

Lukas had drawn his sidearm and was ready. He remembered his military training – how to clear a room, check for blind spots and keep moving. The smallish office section was far from a labyrinth, but completely in ruins. The first chamber off of the main floor was an open space likely used as a reception area in the past. Pieces of broken office furniture were strewn about, though nothing big enough for Sam to hide behind. The scent of intense mildew hung in the air and the whole section was terribly dark. Unlike the warehouse floor, the offices were deprived of any ambient moonlight. The few flickers of his flashlight revealed no traces of anything hopeful.

From there Lukas could choose either a side door, likely opening into a pair of restrooms, or the back door, presumably opening to the remaining offices. Lukas chose the restrooms first. They were likely dead-ends and would bring a far quicker end if Sam was inside one. Lukas took his time, carefully scouring both restrooms. Though he found nothing significant, he did succeed in accidentally startling a family of raccoons in their den of rotted trash behind a cracked toilet. A mother and her four babies scurried frantically past him through a hole in the wall and into the darkness beyond, catching Lukas by surprise. He didn't fire his pistol, but he did jump aside – betraying his only remaining companion: silence. It was little more than a subtle thud on old tile, too quiet be heard from the warehouse floor. *It could've been heard by someone up here, though. If Sam got spooked and ran back out to that warehouse floor . . .*

Lukas hustled from the restrooms back to the other door. As expected, it led to a small collection of offices. He was now standing in the middle of a dark hallway, his light revealing nothing important in either direction. Lukas' gun felt heavy and his heart thrummed inside his chest. Just as he reached up to wipe a bead of sweat threatening to drop into his eyes, he heard something. Not loud or startling, but definitely a sound – akin to a dull, droning tone. He turned, trying to face the noise; training his gun into the empty void. Lukas flicked his light. No one was there. The sound was now behind him! He turned once more. Again the light. Again nothing. The mysterious noise reverberated all around him. He admitted that exhaustion might be concocting these strange sounds – feeding his panic. There was nothing for it. He had to stay on mission.

While one end of the hallway ended in an office door, the far end made an 'L' turn before opening onto to the warehouse floor. If Sam slipped past, he could easily escape. *At least one end of this damned hallway needs to be secure before opening doors down the row.* The other end was open with no doorway or barrier, so Lukas focused on this end. He turned, facing the door he had just come through. Its rusted lock was worthless. He ran his hand along the edge of the door's wood. It felt surprisingly sturdy. Lukas made an exasperated grin as a distant memory stepped forward – one from his days in the military academy. The trick had been on him then, but he could easily reproduce it. A few coins jammed tightly together between the door and its frame triggered immense tension keeping the door from opening. Some less than friendly comrades had made him late for roll call that cold morning. *Today is my turn.*

Lukas rigged the door in short order and took off, circling around to the halls' open end. While running, he noticed the vibration growing softer, more distant. *Whatever it is, it is coming from those offices. Gut. It is soft enough; no one on the warehouse floor would hear it.* There were no signs of movement. He was drained and growing weary of this ultra-quiet game of hide and go seek, but it was now two against one, and he had a mission to complete.

As Lukas approached the hallway's rear opening, the vibrations returned. Of the hall's six doors, the lone door on the left was most likely a . . . *utility closet! I have heard this sound before! Pipes. There is no power, but, perhaps sewer or gas . . .* He shook his head. It was irrelevant. It mattered little which pipe rattled about in this giant's belly.

He began checking doorways – one at a time. Each old office space was as ruined and dilapidated as the one before it – rotted through, devoid of anything useful. The overwhelming scent of dank must soaked his nostrils as he progressed, but at least it helped keep him awake. Though his hunch had been right regarding the utility closet, it yielded no more secrets than anywhere else. Frustration swelled with each barren office. The tiny light at the end of this arduous, tragic tunnel dimmed to almost nothing, until at last only one door remained. He slowly turned the knob, exposing the office's interior. As he quickly scanned the traditional blind spots, a distinct shuffling from the other end of the hallway interrupted him. *Dammit. Someone's coming. I might be trapped between the two of them.* Lukas backed up into the office beside a rusty shelf stacked with ancient boxes and knelt down on one knee, training his gun into the darkness at the hallway's end. From here he would get the drop on anyone coming down that hallway. *At a minimum, I take one of them with me when I answer to God.*

*　　*　　*

Thursday, May 26, 1999 – Pre-Dawn

White hairs, like fine, miniature spires of the most fragile starlight, danced along the window sill – gnarled claws lightly clicking against cracked tile as the rat waddled forward. The glass barrier separating the bathroom

294

from the woods outside had long since shattered and what sparse light this night offered, trickled inside. The rats making this tiny washroom their home strutted from side to side, likely skeptical of their gargantuan intruder. Sam huddled on the washroom floor gazing up at them as pale moonlight ignited the silhouette of tiny white hairs mottling their backs. *Stay calm. Stay calm. The window's edge was narrow and ran high atop the washroom wall. There is nowhere left. I'll just sit waiting for that door to open and see who turns the handle.*

Sam had scuttled into the washroom several minutes ago when something close by rustled – likely some critter bigger than rats getting spooked. It had been the first sound since that thundering gunshot followed by the crash. *Did someone get shot? Was it Victoria or did Victoria do the shooting?* His mind had played as many angles as he knew how to play. *There was one shot, but no return fire? Everyone here has a gun – well, except me. Only someone shot wouldn't return fire. What about the other noises? That crashing metal clanging, what was that? With only one shot, what are the odds of someone being hit in this blackness? That was twenty minutes ago and no one came for me. Is one agent down while the other was still out there; or was Victoria down and they just haven't made it over here yet?* Each possibility only invited more questions. Just as in Seville and fumbling about on that trestle, he was once again isolated, bathed in both a literal and figurative darkness.

Just after breaking into this warehouse, Victoria had made straight for this section. She had told him, "They're coming, undoubtedly, and I have to be in place before they barge in. You're the wild card here, Sam. If we stay together, I can try keeping you safe, but we'll be rats trapped in a maze. If I leave you, I'll have a shot at doing what needs to be done, but I'm nervous about them stumbling across you first."

Sam plead for an alternative, "Go. Leave me here. These guys are relentless. With my ankle twisted up, there's no way through this without someone getting hurt. Take these with you. Here! Get them to Gerard in California, and tell him everything I've told you. *This* is what really matters!" He had shoved the briefcase forward while pleading as earnestly as he knew how. His face confirmed his passion as well as intensely piercing agony.

Victoria rejected him out of hand, as though perhaps she hadn't even heard his offer. "Listen to me. We're not debating. You have to get off that ankle, so get in there." She pointed to the office at the end of the hallway as she finished. "Find a dark corner, hunker down and stay quiet. Things are gonna get really quiet." Afterwards, she turned and ran, and Sam had heard nothing from her since. He simply hobbled inside, toting his briefcase, sitting, as Victoria suggested, on the damp, filthy carpet, waiting.

The minutes following Victoria's departure had proven agonizing. The sanctum within which Sam was meant to remain safe began feeling more a cage than a haven. That musty office was devoid of light, and Sam was the only one about with no flashlight. His enemy, his single biggest enemy during that terrifying blackened silence, had been exhaustion. The agony from his ankle was the only force keeping him awake. Although night was slowly fading, morning's first light lingered far out of reach. If he succumbed to sleep, danger would have no harbinger. Relentless eyelids continued their pilgrimage, descending across his pupils, but with fear of the unknown and persistent agony as allies, he resisted.

Time was not his friend, and Sam knew it. The more time that passed, the greater chance an agent barged in before Victoria. His fears materialized when those animals scurried away followed shortly by footsteps in the outside hallway. His heartbeat thundered, and he quietly crawled across the floor, dragging his hurt ankle behind him, scrambling for anything to crouch behind. Finding nothing but filth and desolation, he was ready to surrender as he felt the crack along the bottom of the washroom door.

Sam reached up, gently turned the door knob, and swung it inwards, but encountered a problem hoisting himself inside. The jeans covering his hurt leg had snagged something, not allowing him to pull free. He dared not condemn himself with sound, but knew he was an easy target lying helplessly prostrate on the carpet. He was eventually forced to pull himself free through brute force. As soon as his leg broke free vibrations began in the walls – old pipes rattling as they equalized pressure. Sam assumed he must have snagged a gas valve on the floor, likely serving an old Dearborn heater at one time. There would be no gas leak, not from an old abandoned place like this, but those vibrating pipes were the true foe.

So Sam silently waited, cowering on the floor of that washroom, watching two rats parade along the window sill gradually losing interest in him. The washroom's past had been far brighter than its present. Tile chipped and splintered, paint peeled away and rusted pipes jutted from walls and the floor. One large circular section in the wall no longer even existed – a gaping hole between the washroom and the office interior. Only a section of rusted shelving piled with boxes shoved against the hole concealed the opening from the other side. He had no compulsion to investigate further as any contents would be either useless or dangerous. Sam could afford neither.

When the outer office door at last opened slowly and the flashlight flickered, Sam immediately knew it wasn't good. He unconsciously gnawed the hem of his shirt harder as his mind raced through dwindling options. The light ignited for but a split second before recklessly sweeping back to the hallway. It flicked off as suddenly as it had turned on, but the office door stayed open. *Something's happening out there!* Sam's spirit lifted. *This guy senses something in the hallway. Victoria must be coming.* Sam hugged the floor and slowly scooted closer, against the opening in the wall. As he squinted, searching for any hint of anything, silence smothered all movement. Even the rats on the window sill stopped their shuffle. He saw nothing. He heard nothing. But it was exactly this sort of nothing that mortified him. Whoever was crouching just beyond that wall, just past those boxes, was lying in wait.

His flashlight was turned off! That's Victoria out there soon to be in this guy's crosshairs! He's not using his light because he doesn't care who's coming. His partner has already fallen! Sam's mind raced. *What can I possibly do from in here – reach through and push a box over on him? That would likely only get me killed with no real assurances that Victoria gets away. So much bloodshed – all on my account; it has to stop, now!* He thought of any and all possibilities. At last, he eyed the metal shelving on the wall's other side. His first impulse was on target: just not quite large enough.

Sam had to act right now before anyone else got killed. He fought through the hurt and pulled himself to his knees and up to what was left of the wall. His ankle pulsed with a fresh piercing pain, but there was no longer anything for it. With both arms in unison, he pushed up and out against the shelving itself. Those boxes were heavy as were the metal shelving they rested upon. His arms still ached from that jammed railcar door, but they took a distant back seat to the pain searing through his ankle. He bit down hard on his shirt's hem and pushed with everything inside him. The shelf was heavy, but it moved. Sam kept going, tilting it higher, until the boxes on the top began sliding. He had it now. He used it all, keeping nothing in reserve; his hatred for all the needless violence caused by his whimsy; all his exasperation and frustration; it would end now – and he would end it. This was his final push. He was no longer tired. His arms stopped hurting. Even

297

his ankle numbed as he rose from that washroom floor, stepped through the large maw in the wall and toppled the metal shelving along with several heavy boxes of rotted papers and files atop an unsuspecting agent. The unmistakable crash of a gunshot fired just as the shelves crashed down.

Light instantly shot in from the hallway – another flashlight. Sam was done. He crumpled to the floor as a beleaguered Victoria rushed in. Pain returned – quickly. So much pain. Victoria kicked the gun from the agent's hand and turned to Sam. Tears were falling from his eyes as Victoria checked him over, likely worried that he had been hit. Though not shot, he made no response. Once satisfied, she turned to the agent and began clearing debris. He was hurt, though not terribly. His knee was twisted and perhaps his wrist broken, but he was alive. Sam looked over at him. The agent lay there, apparently expecting one of them to finish him off. Sam glared into his eyes through pale light, gathered his voice and yelled, "Why? . . . Why? You work . . . work *for* the Church! THE CHURCH! Why fight so hard *defending* the darkness?"

The young agent looked at Sam's weeping face and meekly replied, "My brother. It is not the darkness I defend, but the integrity of the light."

"Jesus said to him, Thomas, because you have seen me, you have believed: blessed are they that have not seen, and yet have believed." – John 20:29

Friday, May 27, 1999 – Late Afternoon

Aside from the incessant "tick-tock" of the small cuckoo clock Sam had felt compelled to wind, the farmhouse was quiet and still. The afternoon sun cast its hypnotic hue of orange and crimson across the dark blue sky as it gently descended once again. Victoria listened to crickets outside the thin walls orchestrating their evening serenade from her perch, lazily stretched across the old blue sofa she'd grown up with. She had not been here in over a decade now. The farm belonged to her and her cousins and was supposedly available when any of them wanted. They each knew where keys were hidden and how to turn on the electric. Still, it was hard being back in that house again. Though comfortable, it was an uneasy comfort she couldn't truly embrace. Her mind caught glimpses of her grandfather occasionally; he'd be looking out a window, rustling logs in the fireplace, or sitting contently on the porch. Those blurred images simultaneously generated both comfort and melancholy.

She and Sam were now merely waiting. After they had, as promised, anonymously dropped the young agent at a nearby emergency room, they drove to the farmhouse, hiding their borrowed truck in the barn. They had agreed to not call in the shooting. The agent had requested it be cleaned up by the Vatican directly, rather than through local, and likely far more public, means. In exchange for not abandoning him to that desolate warehouse to likely starve or bleed out, they agreed to leave matters in "God's hands," as he had put it – assuring them no further pursuits would be made. Victoria had promised a number of horrific consequences if he went back on his word, though in truth she and Sam had few realistic options. Sam needed to stay off of his ankle, but they couldn't chance a hospital. He also was in no condition to travel. So they waited.

She had braved one quick trip into town for a few essentials: a crutch, ankle brace, pain meds, and a bit of food to hold them while waiting on Gerard. Victoria, though she had grown to respect Sam's dedication and kind heart, was relieved not being burdened escorting him all the way back to California. She had made arrangements with Gerard for him to retrieve Sam here in Pennsylvania, allowing Sam a couple days of recovery. Gerard should arrive around mid-day tomorrow, finally putting this madness to rest. She figured Sam would likely be more comfortable riding back with his friends anyway, including some woman named Sarah.

Throughout this whole affair, Sam had been a human pincushion – suffering the sting of every turn of bad luck. Heartfelt respect had, at long last, replaced the pity she felt first seeing him sprawled lifelessly on the concrete in Seville. At that moment, she had mentally labeled him as dead weight – pathetic, damaged human cargo needing a ride. Sam had ultimately become so much more. He had confronted her directly on the plane. Exhausted, with his ankle twisted and swollen, throbbing with severe pain, he had risked his life saving hers in that old warehouse. Of course, there was this – this other matter. Her eyes darted to the jumble of papers and the notebook spread across the old coffee table. *What to make of this? After everything, Sam still believes these documents contain more than stories of misery soaked in blood and tears, but also reveal the invisible hand of God. Could it be? Am I as closed-minded regarding God as those Bible thumping Christians – just in reverse? Doubtful. But I should probably read a little for myself.*

She snuck off the couch and peeked down the hallway. Dull light continued seeping under the bathroom door. *He's been in there a while. That's not good – that chili was probably a bad idea.* She walked to the binder and removed two shorter accounts tabbed together. Sam wouldn't likely even notice they were gone before she could put them back tomorrow. She quickly tucked them away under her bedroom pillow for later, safe from Sam's judgmental eye. *Was it he that was judgmental or me? My need to stay strong and in control, never harboring doubt, might be keeping me from dealing with some of this honestly with someone watching.* On her way back, she heard the "flush" from down the hall and turned to see Sam hobbling up behind her, crutch tucked under his shoulder.

"Sorry. Damn chili," he chuckled, struggling back into the living room. Victoria, not ready for toilet humor just now, kept quiet; merely offering him a quick smile. As she settled back in, Sam asked, "How old is this place, if you don't mind?" He found his groove in the oversized leather chair opposite her.

She didn't know exactly. Her grandparents had lived here as far back as she could remember. She shared what little she knew as they discussed routine things like old houses, farming, and even the weather for some time – nothing deep or emotional, which suited Victoria. During their talk, her

300

thoughts meandered, though she did notice one thing: Sam's spirit. *He is always so good-natured. That man has been through hell and continues to thrive. I would be pissed at me if things were reversed. After all, I was too far ahead of him on those tracks. Poor guy – fumbling along in almost total darkness. If he had leaned further to either side...*

I've been treading these hypothetical paths too often lately. I can blame myself for so much, but here we both sit. Safe. On that coffee table sits Sam's infernal document collection. Safe. Tomorrow, he'll return with his friends to his simple life. Actually, his safe life may not be that simple anymore. He's likely been over-exposed to my world, a world of deceit and corruption. But Sam, not me, chose to fly to Spain, and Sam leapt into that river. His baptism by pain and fatigue had been the ultimate price for that tenacious curiosity. None of that was my doing. Had he left these documents behind in that utility room, this situation would likely have never escalated. Even worse, there's a remote chance he's right and the world embraces his "proof" for what he claims it is. If that happens, I don't want to be around that bizarre explosion of fame and notoriety. Something like that changes anyone.

Still, Sam's fate was no longer in her hands. He seemed relatively content with how things ultimately sorted themselves out. Their conversation had continued for another hour or so as the last bit of sunlight quietly dissolved along the edge of the world. Victoria decided to turn in early. Not that she was particularly sleepy or tired; it was far too early for that sort of thing. She had, however, grown tired of obligatory conversation. Having grown up with few friends, she tired of being 'social' quickly. She had done her best lately helping Sam feel comfortable and at ease, but the exercise had worn thin. She made her excuses and dismissed herself.

Once in her room, she laid her head on the pillow and heard the light crinkling of paper. *That's right. I swiped some of those cursed stories, didn't I?* Victoria pulled the few pages and looked them over: dark typewritten letters, pounded into yellowish paper decades ago. She didn't bring herself to start reading straight away as her more pressing need was quiet and solitude. Eventually, however, curiosity came to collect its due, and she picked up the pages and began reading.

The first entry seemed straightforward: an exorcism of a slave in Georgia prior to the Civil War. While the other slaves believed Ezra's symptoms were the work of black magic or voodoo, the plantation owner was less convinced. After much cajoling from his wife, however, he had summoned

301

a Priest. That Priest was immediately convinced a demonic spirit was at work and called for an exorcist. The exorcist's letter said Ezra had been possessed by a demon, calling itself Vefar, and had been inflicted with terrible sores, akin to infected boils. They appeared all over his body, the soles of his feet, his tongue, his genitals and anus, his palms, and even atop one of his eyelids. They were hideous to behold, hemorrhaging putrid puss and blood – some even with maggots breeding inside. The exorcism had proven successful, though stretching over a week. The tale was interesting, but contained nothing particularly unique from those Sam had read throughout this ordeal: different demon inflicting its own unique set of malformations and injuries – nothing more.

The second account, however, was special. Though written by a Priest, it was not penned by an exorcist. This account was being related by a Priest who had allegedly been the demon's host. This piqued Victoria's interest. None of the accounts she had heard related anything from the victim's perspective. *How could they? Possessions are pretty rare themselves, so what are the chances of unearthing an instance of a Priest being possessed?* She continued reading . . .

Father Hawthorn – Edinburgh: 1905 AD

"Bishop Gentry, please accept this letter as both my formal recounting of the bizarre events several months ago and, for reasons soon to become obvious, my formal resignation of my post. Please also extend my most heartfelt gratitude to Father Felix and the undoubtedly heart-breaking and demanding task he performed so dutifully and professionally. I have served here in Scotland for over twenty years and have endured many hardships and trials. However, nothing holds a candle to recent events. Things began with a fever, of which I thought little, though when the fever grew dramatically, I took to bed and began seeing a local physician. I would find myself shivering uncontrollably one moment and sweltering the next. It was terrible and persistent. Not long afterwards, the dreams began. These dreams were unique creatures. They came on suddenly and without warning, and it mattered not whether it be daylight or night. I suppose, thinking back, that they were more flashes than dreams – flashes of places I had been, voices I had heard and people I had known. My nurse Rebecca started making terrible accusations of things I would say and do while

302

dreaming. Such curses and spiteful, hate-filled venom, though I remembered nothing. When I would awaken, I could see terror reflecting on her face. Soon she stopped speaking with me altogether - aside from curt pleasantries in passing. Whatever was happening while I dreamt had driven between us an insurmountable wedge.

The first sore appeared in my armpit, a boil triggering great pain merely resting my arm. The smell was unbearable, and despite efforts to cleanse it, it festered. I remember the voices starting around that time as well. I could hear them in my mind, indiscernible chatter in the distance. They were, at first, merely noise - persistent enough to deny me sleep, but they grew louder in time. What at first seemed a cacophony of voices conversing at once, like listening to a nearby cocktail party, became unified - singular. It was masculine, and it called me by name. I ignored it at first, assuming my mind was buckling under the fever and pain. It persisted, wearing me down until at last I answered its call. I can still hear its dark, guttural laughter when I finally answered its beckon: the gnarled and twisted laugh of a deranged lunatic.

It knew far more than my name. It knew my past: things I have never shared, outside of a confessional. Lies I had told, secrets I had kept, it even remembered Allyn - sweet, wee young Allyn. I had struggled for so long to purge those memories, but the voice remembered the atrocities I inflicted on that poor lass - the nights I slithered into her room and took her childhood. Though long before taking my vows, those abominations stained my soul with a blot that would not be cleansed no matter how many tears tried scrubbing it away. She was my niece, only a wee thirteen years of age when I moved in with my older brother. Hard times had brought me low and my brother allowed me to stay with him for a time. My soul must bear the horrible things I did in the darkness while the rest of the house slept until I pass from this earth.

Though I've confessed these sins often - pleading for Jesus' grace, I can only hope that through Him, my deeds later in life have somehow glorified the Church. To my knowledge, Allyn has never spoken of those things, but the voice knew. It remembered. I heard it mimic her perfectly - pleading with me to stop amid her sobs. Dark memories from my mind's darkest recesses rushed forward reducing me to a shriveled version of my former self: a babe, sobbing

303

alone in the woods. The voice knew, and it pounded me under, destroying my will.

Whilst my mind was beset with horrors of my woeful past, my body became pocked with those damnable sores: disgusting, puss filled sores, some ruptured, one even festering with maggots. I would plead with the voice in the end - pleading for mercy, hoping it would take me and spare those in my wake. But it seemed to delight in their agony. Eventually dreaming hours - hours spent wallowing in my filth as the voice plagued my spirit - were more common than hours of lucidity. I knew what I had done. It convinced me that I deserved nothing better. Soon I would be dead from the infection from the pustules and boils. I was nothing. My life was nothing; my service for God - a mockery. My legacy was naught but pain and loathing. The voice knew, and so did I.

The exorcism itself was equally painful. As Father Felix performed the rites, I felt the weight of that dark spirit tugging on me as if to tear me in half. Though my body had not moved, I felt though I was being drawn and quartered - as if my soul was being ripped from my body, into the void along with the demon. The battle waged for days, and the searing pain and tormenting persisted. The voice had grown strong. In desperation, it flooded my mind with visions of those dark nights. I saw the horror in Allyn's eyes, felt the pain of her tears, and it crippled me. I wanted to die. I was wholly unworthy of life. How could I live with the knowledge of everything I had done? At one point, I even tried piercing my eyelids - to claw my eyes from their sockets. My arms had been restrained by then, and I only succeeded in rupturing an oozing sore in my left palm. The anguish heaped upon me by the voice will echo the rest of my life.

There is no longer room in my heart amid the darkness for God's mercy. The dark spirit and its voice are gone now. The sores have healed, though hideous scars serve as dark reminders. I will go on, though not as a Priest. Death would be but an escape from my guilt. I should not be so fortunate. At a minimum, I deserve to live as many days as God elects, toting shame and horror as my sole companions. Every night I wonder if my dreams will be of Allyn or if the voice will return. God may have it in Him to forgive me. I leave that to Him, but I can never forgive myself.

```
Sincerely,
Karl Hawthorn"
```

In that last account, there had been something new masked behind those words — something more real than anything Victoria had encountered before. She doubled over reeling from all the anger, guilt and helplessness washing through her. She had never faced simultaneous saturation of both frozen remorse and scorching hatred. There it was, however, hiding amongst the Priest's words, in the spaces between the lines and under the heavy type pounded into the page. Behind our dark, horrific masks, behind the awful and destructive pain, beyond all our greed and apathy, lay something frail and utterly beautiful. This Priest was no monster. He was but a man. He was not strong. He was fragile as fresh spun silk. He held no hatred for his niece. He hated himself; hated his frailty and weakness. Victoria, for the first time, saw beyond the disgusting vile abuse — *inside* the man. His soul was pocked with holes, huge gaping holes that he desperately yearned to fill. All efforts failed, leaving him with the only companions he would ever know: guilt and self-loathing.

Victoria didn't want any of this. People that do things like this were supposed to be aberrations — mere results of random chance being dealt a shitty hand. Yet, the veil had been pulled back and could not again be drawn shut. A life of pain coursed through her: pain for the things she had done; pain for the people she pushed away; pain for all the hatred she had borne on her shoulders.

As Victoria replayed the Priest's cold words, she felt the heat of tears welling behind her eyes — old tears. These tears she had denied passage for years upon years. Though she struggled resisting them once more, the well had crested and it overflowed. Pain and anger from losing her mother, hatred for her father, and even hatred for God — all rushed forward. It had been far simpler to deny God's existence. If there was no God, no one could be blamed for life's afflictions and scars. It was pointless denying it further. These writings forged something utterly impossible: proof that there was, in fact, a God. Though such a revelation, at first blush, would seem a moment of overwhelming joy and bliss, Victoria's present experience was far from joyous. Her entire worldview crashed around her in large thundering chunks, and there was no halting the cascade. There is a God, one supposedly all-knowing and all-powerful, who had elected to sit idly by watching as her father beat her and stole her childhood; watched her being attacked repeatedly by her foster dad, a priest no less; and saw her starving on the brink of death on the cold Pittsburgh streets. She felt no jubilation. She was crushed under insurmountable misery and defeat. There was nothing left. On her grandfather's old bed, she lay utterly still – sobbing into the pillowcase. After some time, she glared upward through tear-soaked eyes not knowing, for the first time in forever, what was meant to come next.

*   *   *

Friday, May 27, 1999 – Evening

Sam sat in thoughtful silence for quite some time in the disheveled living room, his mind spinning. So much had happened, and tomorrow this journey would finally draw to a close. Gerard was on his way and was even bringing Sarah along. He smiled thinking of her stubby legs bounding across the lawn, her oversized purple tongue flailing as she ran. Sarah wouldn't know what he had been through. She wasn't there when he twisted his ankle on the trestle, when he almost drowned in the Guadalquivir, when he toppled that shelving on that unsuspecting agent, or even when his face got slammed by the Canadian inspector. Gerard had originally urged him on this voyage by demanding he enjoy a taste of life. He'd certainly gotten far more than a mere taste.

While he had experienced so much, the biggest, most awe-inspiring element had been Manuel's collection of manuscripts. Each page detailed horrific episodes of demons and fallen angels wreaking agony on their hosts and families. Physical wounds, skin ulcers, defecation, mutilations, torture, and unmentionable dark obscenities poured from those texts like water through a sieve. In the most fascinating twist of serendipity, those dark tales, when woven together, produced something wonderful. Demonic hordes inhabiting hosts, striving to undermine spirituality and inflict unrelenting despair, had inadvertently given humanity a most precious gift – dispositive proof, not only of their existence, but the existence of the God they trembled before.

As he sat in stillness, barely noticing the distant radio's humming of antiquated country music, his eyes, for no particular reason, landed upon a hutch nestled in the corner quietly minding its own business as it likely had for decades. Though time had taken a toll, its wood remained strong. It was Dutch, most likely Amish, and quite old – assembled long before Amish

306

furniture became trendy. It was exquisite. The unadorned style and simple beauty reflected early nineteenth century craftsmanship. Sam took a closer look, and as he glided his palm deftly across its dusty surface, a thousand memories returned from a life that seemed so distant. He grinned, remembering the buffet from the Halpert estate so many months ago that had almost single-handedly paid for his trip to Seville.

As his curiosity swelled, he strolled through the old farmhouse with fresh eyes and couldn't believe what he discovered: a turn of the century bookcase in spectacular condition and the dining room table and chairs whose Victorian design could easily grace the cover of an antiques magazine. In all, he found about eight or nine impeccable pieces. Sam recalled their conversation about Hector. With a little help from him, this furniture could snatch her neck out from under Hector's iron boot, if she could manage it without telling her cousins. *That dinette set alone is not just old – it's rare! Its maker turned out less than a handful of those!*

He wanted to share his news with Victoria straight away. She had retired early, but dim lamplight reflected under her bedroom door. She was still awake. Sam poured two glasses of their boxed wine and walked down the hall. As he approached, he heard her voice, though he couldn't yet make out the words. Her voice was soft – barely a whisper. He slowed his steps and crept forward, doing his best not to be heard. The task was tricky, managing two wine glasses and a crutch, but he gave it his best. He drew closer and her muffled voice cleared. He pressed his ear to the wall and was astonished to hear something he would never have anticipated: sobs. She was crying, though not the cries of an infant or of someone in pain, these were sobs of surrender. It was the sound of someone finally reaching the point of forfeiting all control and releasing that tremendous pressure – the pressure struggling to maintain confidence, command, and free will. Sam had made those sobs before, most recently lying on the pavement of that electrical closet in Seville. He made them when he lost his mom so long ago. *Victoria might have never felt this before. She is always so hard, so in command of everything. Surrendering is completely alien to her.*

What he heard next was even more shocking. Sam heard the honest infant-like beginnings of . . . *a prayer? Surely not! Did she suddenly succumb to the truth and take it to heart so strongly?* Yet, amidst her sobs, she was speaking aloud to a God that, according to her, didn't exist. *She is beginning to believe! The evidence was too strong in the end. If someone as determined as*

307

Victoria could see the light through this dismal kaleidoscope, only the willfully blind could remain in darkness. Emboldened by this remarkable twist of fate, he turned, carefully creeping back to the kitchen. *Prayers should never be eavesdropped upon.* Sam's spirit soared as he hobbled forward. His discovery, of Manuel's sacrifice and brilliance of course, could shine light upon the darkest hearts! He had just witnessed its power.

It would start with his father. That infernal bastard had denounced God's existence as long as he could remember while Sam stood across the chasm on his own pedestal preaching the opposite. Both of them had argued the point until little of their relationship remained – torn apart by the gulf between them, as each had closed their mind and hardened their heart. Aside from occasional obligatory gestures – a birthday or father's day card or an hour together wolfing down a bit of turkey at a local diner on Christmas – there was no longer any real connection. These documents would change all of that. *He can't refuse what will be staring him in the face. He'll have no choice but to acknowledge that I've been right all along! We can finally start rebuilding. All the arguments, the screaming and hours of enraged silence will be forgiven and our hearts can start mending!*

As Sam walked forward, his steps, at first robust and swift, slowed. His head was spinning. *Why does he have to admit that I'm right for us to rebuild? Have things actually gotten that distant between us?* They had, and he knew it. It wasn't solely his father's fault, either. Thomas Johnston was a stubborn academic asshole and an avid atheist, but this chasm between father and son had been carved through hatred, not love. *My love for God is not what drove me from him. It was something else. My incessant desire to be right has pushed things so very far. If we disagreed about UFO's or Vampires, perhaps things wouldn't have become so awful. But, God? That's different. When dad rejects my God, he rejected my refuge, my shelter. When mom died, God's embrace warmed me – not his. When dealing with impossibly tough cases at work, watching families being torn apart, I turn to God for support and understanding, not Thomas. When my father, this hard, distant figure, rebukes and ignores the one thing so true and essential to me, how can I accommodate that?*

By the time Sam reached the kitchen, he was moving so slowly his pace would barely qualify as a shuffle: his feet hardly escaping the carpet with each step. His mind raced in varied and conflicting directions. This business with his father was unsettling, and something darker lurked beyond, though he couldn't yet understand what. His anticipated victory was akin to winning a baseball game because the other team forfeited. Much of his adult life had been wasted in vain pursuits to convince a stubborn atheist that something wonderful and magical existed out there despite its lack of concrete evidence. The notion of beating his father into submission with this new concrete evidence didn't fit somehow.

He finally reached the countertop in the rustic kitchen and stopped walking entirely, setting the wine glasses down and resting the crutch against outdated wood paneling. The wind outside rattled the glass panes in the eastern window. Amidst all the sundry thoughts swirling inside, a distant conversation with his grandmother rushed forward. She had lived in a house much like this one, though in a suburb. She would dig out some old electric blankets when the wind whipped up too much. One night, in particular, they had been talking of Sam's most recent failed relationship. He remembered sitting huddled under his blanket, the wind beating against the outside glass, while they talked plainly together. While Sam couldn't recall all the details of that discussion, its essence stampeded across his thoughts.

Though the hard truth of it is unsettling, she had mentioned, life is a perpetual war on multiple fronts. Starvation, loneliness, insecurity, poverty, doubt, vulnerability, and a host of others comprise the enemy ranks. There are brief respites and temporary truces, but the war is ever-vigilant. Our wall keeps us, saves us – the emotional, financial, and spiritual wall we construct around our perimeter separates us from harm. Out of desperation, we defend the wall at all costs. Sanity, peace, warmth, hope, and comfort only exist so long as the wall holds true. There are times, however, when, despite every effort to hold them at bay, our enemies breach. Falling in love, helplessly watching as a loved one suffers, finding spiritual salvation, and protecting a child from danger are just a few of these moments of complete despair when the enemy hordes storm the gates. At those moments, we surrender control and stand atop the precipice exposed, naked and shivering against the violent storm. Sam felt the lump in his throat tighten as he recalled his grandmother's central point. In those moments, it is not for us to condemn our fate, or curse the heavens, or collapse under the weight of fear, for in that same despair, those same agonizing moments in the blinding dark, in our time of greatest weakness – single shining moments of the purest, most exquisite clarity and beauty are bred.

309

A Roman soldier working the Coliseum, trained to follow orders without hesitation, reaches for the lions' next victim. Their eyes meet, and in that moment, instead of the usual gaze of fear, dread or anger, he feels love and compassion – forgiveness. The soldier's heart melts as he crumples to his knees in despair. He is fighting for evil, and his soul can't bear the burden. A plantation owner grips the lash, unleashing retribution upon a runaway slave. This is not the first time he's used a whip. His daddy showed him how when he was only fourteen. The slave makes no sound – only the whip's crack and the tearing of rendered flesh echo across the night. That stillness shatters his wall, and a lifetime of guilt washes over him, tearing his soul asunder in but an instant. His eyes swell, and new tears fertilize seeds of salvation and liberation as his lash drops to the ground. A woman, jaded from a previous marriage to an abusive husband, finds comfort, years later, in the heart of another. His heart is pure, and, despite all efforts to keep it at bay, new love disintegrates her wall of resentment and solitude. She is, in a single moment, vulnerable once more to the same hurt, pain, and loneliness, but her heart reflects perfect clarity as a new relationship blooms.

The unabashed intimacy of Victoria's prayer and the shadow of his father pierced Sam's soul, pummeling the commanding wall encircling his heart – the same wall forged through a lifetime of seeking God's face. His lower lip quivered as years of arguments assailed him. Exhilaration from his unwitting discovery of this wondrous, inconceivably precious thing melted in a heartbeat. He held his head in his hands and leaned against the counter. Warm, bitter tears fell from his eyes as he succumbed to this new revelation. He was on the wrong side. Sam grit his teeth as his mind struggled to conceive what his heart had accepted. Reality is separated from all things supernatural by only a thin sheet – a cheesecloth veil keeping things like Angels and Demons outside our experience. That veil is so fragile – a delicate porcelain figurine poised atop the tip of a dagger. Sam had uncovered, on the bottom of that river, a solitary loose thread in the fabric. His initial jubilation at the prospect of yanking that thread and unraveling the veil had blinded him from the truth, now shredding his soul in a mesmerizing and awful clarity of thought.

With this veil down, mankind would see plainly. There would be no more doubt. While doubt remained, humanity would cling to it as a babe suckles its mother. Victoria's transformation, though initially wondrous, was vivid proof that once the warm embrace of doubt is jerked away, teeming masses would have no choice but to accept the truth: there is in fact, a God, a

Heaven, a Devil, and a Hell. Once those concepts left the esoteric and became truths, no logical recourse would remain but following God seeking an eternity in his presence. Doing otherwise would only ensure damnation and a future wallowing in darkness and pain. Without that thin veil, without at least the tiniest shreds of doubt, the choice to believe in God becomes cheapened, stained. While doubt remained, humanity had a real choice, a choice based on faith and not reason; a choice based on belief, not knowledge. The veil between us and the supernatural protects the very essence of faith itself. Those words from the warehouse echoed as tears streamed down his cheeks, "It is not the darkness I fight for, but the integrity of the light." *That agent knew something I'm only just now glimpsing. The uncertainty surrounding God's existence, while providing a comforting place for the masses to hide, preserves the wonder and majesty of someone choosing to believe in Him on their own terms.*

Sam clenched his fists, his fingernails digging into his palms. His stomach churned, and he barely had strength enough to breathe. Gazing toward Heaven, he offered a silent scream amidst his tears. His heart pounded inside his chest, a caged beast yearning to be free. Sam tried praying for guidance, some hint of inspiration to light his path. God's only answer was fresh tears. So much anguish and darkness in the world, and he alone possessed the light that could penetrate every dismal crevice. His heart ached for the billions lost to damnation throughout history that could have been spared if only some real proof had been there to roll away their fear and doubt. His heart broke thinking of those, like Victoria and his father, who would only leave doubt's comforting embrace by being yanked away through brute force. Was there glory in a decision that was no longer truly a decision at all?

Time passed without sound or disturbance other than his own breath escaping his quivering lips. He eventually rose and wiped his face with the tail of his shirt. He had decided long ago to accept God based on faith, and faith alone. At that time, he had no concrete evidence supporting his choice. There was doubt and disbelief to vanquish. He had deprived Victoria of her own conquest. She was a believer now, and those documents, echoing unspeakable horrors from yesterday, had dragged her, kicking and screaming, from her darkness into a bright future. She would reach the destination God yearns for all of us, but Sam had denied her the experience of the journey. Sam couldn't deny that same journey to all of humanity.

311

He rifled around in the kitchen, searching through old cobwebs and decades of neglect. Buttons, ink pens, old envelopes, and other sundry junk and loose items littered its rustic drawers and cabinets. Eventually, he found what he wanted and closed his hand around the matchbook. He hobbled over and gathered up the binder and papers along with the briefcase. Fresh tears swelled behind bloodshot eyes as he quietly opened the door and stepped outside. It was dark now, and nature was announcing the change. Crickets chirped. Frogs croaked. The wind, though no longer as strong, rustled metal chimes under the porch eaves. He forced himself forward, one deliberate step at a time, off the porch steps. He grabbed an empty wooden crate nearby. He hobbled toward an old windmill some distance from the house – clinging to the crutch with one hand and his discovery in the other. The windmill had withstood the depression, two world wars, and the moon landing, and would now witness first-hand humanity's eternal damnation.

Sam sat the crate down and gently placed the briefcase and all the sundry documents and papers inside. He opened the matchbook and paused, staring down at the weathered matches with tear-soaked eyes. *No matter the course, all of us are cheated – either we are damned to continue stumbling clumsily in the darkness as we have for thousands of years, or we are left with no alternative but blindly following in the wake of a light so bright it would drown the authenticity of our faith.* He wiped another tear from his now blistered cheek and struck the match. It lit immediately, showing no struggle against the Pennsylvania breeze. He sat it atop the bundle and closed his eyes. He couldn't bear to watch as flames licked and blackened everything he had fought so hard to preserve. Although he never saw the inferno, its heat bathed his soul in an apprehensive yet clear and precious glow that would stay with him, in secret, forever.

Epilogue

Three Weeks Later - Dorotea, Sweden

Another straw fell listlessly from the broom to the stone slab below. He knelt, noticing the broom's few remaining straws. Soon, it would be time for another. He had been through several, but this last one had endured the longest, until recently. Leaves, scattered by northern winds, found their way upon the patio slab, and it was his duty to sweep them away. Though only one of many tasks at the abbey, sweeping was his favorite. It got him outside – out of the dank interior and under the sun where he could feel the warm breeze upon his face, gaze at pinkish clouds nestling into the horizon, and hear occasional birds squawking their summer's call.

He rose and resumed sweeping. The patio was rather large and took some time to clear all the dirt and leaves. He knew exactly how long it took, and so did they. They always watched, marking the time. They knew how long he slept and when he ate. No words were uttered – never any words. He had tried, long ago, to speak with them – merely making acquaintance. He was locked away for two days for that indiscretion. He soon learned the few, though strictly enforced, rules. No speaking. Never find yourself idle. Cleanse yourself and your garment regularly. However, avoiding the foyer was the greatest commandment. He broke that rule once – once. He was deprived of food, water, and sunlight for five days. He was far younger then, of course: forty years younger. Days stretched becoming years, and those stretched into decades. Manuel had resigned himself to his fate. It was, in the end, a small price to keep his sister safe. They had assured him of that when he accepted their offer. He would never see her again, but she would remain safe. This abbey would be his home, his life, the remainder of his years. He had sinned against God, and sin's wages must be paid.

The abbey was immense, and, apart from the foyer and private cells, he had the relative run of the place. It was three stories in places, adorned with a large walled garden at its rear. Though forbidden to step onto the grass, his time sweeping the patio got him close enough. Once each month, though not this day, he scrubbed the windows. While a menial task, he liked cleaning the third-floor windows. From up there, he could see beyond the garden, beyond the tall trees surrounding the abbey, and into the villages just at the

313

edge of sight. There were three of them, and they had remained unchanged for four decades – the same church steeples, the same stores, the same houses. He was sure the world had changed much in forty years, but the world from those abbey windows reflected none of that. Still, the sprawling countryside would fill his spirits, reminding him of the world beyond these walls.

He finished sweeping and went to clean himself and make ready for dinner. On his way to his cell, however, one of the brothers was unexpectedly standing in the hallway near the foyer. The brother stood motionless, a grim, imposing figure catching Manuel quite off guard. Nothing random or unexpected happened at the abbey – ever. Manuel knew better than to brush past him, so he paused at the open doorway. The brother, without a word, smile, or any expression whatsoever, stretched out his left arm, motioning into the foyer. Manuel took a lone step forward, peeking into the forbidden room. Emotion swelled inside as he realized that today would be something the thousands before it had not: different.

The foyer was a circular room with three doors: the one Manuel was peering through, another connecting to the kitchens, and the final one leading outside to the drive. Near the outside door stood another figure. Wearing not the robes with which he had become so accustomed, but a gray suit. His right arm was bandaged, and he was supported by a crutch under his left shoulder. The man looked up as Manuel peered in. The sun outside reflected behind him, making it difficult to be sure, but Manuel thought the man was smiling. He motioned with his good hand for Manuel to approach.

Manuel looked back to the hall, but the robed brother remained stoically motionless. He lightly placed one foot on the foyer's tiled floor. Nothing happened. Then, a second. Still, nothing happened. He stood still, dreading the impending doom, but no doom descended. He sighed deeply before taking another step, then another. By the time he reached the center, he had gathered the courage to look back over his shoulder. He trembled as he turned, but it was for naught. The doorway remained empty. He faced forward and walked toward the stranger. When finally in front of him, he simply stared blankly, knowing better than to speak inside the abbey.

The stranger met Manuel's eyes and smiled. He stretched his left hand outward toward the open door – *outside* the abbey. Manuel smiled back sheepishly and leaned forward, peering outside, wondering what horror or new trick this could be. Instead, he saw only a plain brown sedan with a dark

314

figure in the back seat. Manuel peered back quizzically. The stranger smiled again and stepped outside.

Manuel followed this stranger with a blind faith he had forgotten. His bare foot landed upon the grass. The soft earth below was moist and gave somewhat under his weight, cradling his foot so softly – so simple a thing, but he had not touched natural ground for four decades. Ancient memories rushed to his mind – feelings from so long ago he feared they had been lost. A puddle of yesterday's rain sat placid nearby. He leaned over, gazing into its glassy surface. An unfamiliar old man stared back at him. Mirrors were forbidden in the abbey, and he had not seen his reflection. Though he could see from his hands and body how much he had changed, to see his face was something altogether different. Sad eyes, sunk deep into their sockets, and aged skin with dark spots sagging from his neck and face stood in stark contrast to the memories he harbored of himself. He looked at the stranger as he pressed his second foot into the soft earth, his legs trembling.

The stranger was still smiling, but his smile had assumed a melancholic hue. He pointed to the car and made but one command, "Go to your sister, Manuel. Both of you have been waiting long enough.